Mandy Robotham saw herself as an aspiring author since the age of nine, but was waylaid by journalism and later enticed by birth. She's now a practising midwife, who writes about birth, death, love and anything else in between. She graduated with an MA in Creative Writing from Oxford Brookes University. This is her second novel – her first, published as *A Woman of War* in the UK and *The German Midwife* in the US and Canada, was a number one *Globe and Mail* bestseller.

By the same author:

The German Midwife

The Secret Messenger

Mandy Robotham

Published by AVON
A division of HarperCollins*Publishers* Ltd
1 London Bridge Street
London SE1 9GF

www.harpercollins.co.uk

This paperback edition 2020

First published in Great Britain by HarperCollins*Publishers* 2019

Copyright © Mandy Robotham 2019

Mandy Robotham asserts the moral right
to be identified as the author of this work.

A catalogue copy of this book is available from the British Library.

ISBN: 978-0-00-838462-3

20 21 22 LSC 10 9 8 7 6 5 4 3 2 1

Typeset in Bembo by
Palimpsest Book Production Limited, Falkirk, Stirlingshire
Printed and bound in the United States of America by
LSC Communications.

For more information visit: www.harpercollins.co.uk/green

To my mum, Stella –
a woman of stamina and enduring style

Author's note

War is ugly. Wherever it strikes, it destroys people, families and places, decimates lives and precious objects. Yet being so widespread, conflict also happens in beautiful places, and it was that contrast of light and dark which prompted *The Secret Messenger*. For me, there is no more stunning or fantastical place on earth than Venice; since my first trip in 1990, I've been beguiled on countless visits by the idea of a city effectively floating. I'm still in awe of its very existence and its beauty.

When I began to research how World War Two affected Venice, it became clear that historians were less captivated by its story of Resistance as perhaps in France or the Netherlands; that Venice, by comparison, had experienced a 'soft' war. What research I found seemed brief and factual, but those details of Venetian life – of how Venetians existed day by day – were scant. On a research trip (yes, of course, I needed to go back again!) I walked miles through Venetian *calles*, itching to know which areas of the city played their part in the fight against the Nazis and fascists combined.

It wasn't until my return home that I struck gold; a chance email launched into cyberspace sparked a reply from the wonderfully named Signor Giulio Bobbo, a historian at IVESER, the Venetian Institute for the History of Resistance and Contemporary Society. His own area of expertise? The Resistance in wartime Venice. It was like manna from heaven.

Thanks to Giulio, his grounding in factual research and the nuggets of priceless detail about real life in wartime Venice, the book began to take shape. At last, I could *see* a Venice under the cloak of war. The more Giulio and I traded emails, the more my search seemed to run parallel to the quest within the story – it seemed only fitting Giulio's character should make an appearance, along with Melodie the cat who, by the way, is very real and does indeed love a warm photocopier!

I knew also that I wanted to highlight the role of women in the eventual victory over the Nazis; not only the bravery of undercover agents, but the army of female messengers across Italy – *Staffettas* – who helped the Allies to victory. It's hard for us in this day of social media and instant messaging to understand the value of transporting a simple slip of information on foot or by boat, but in those times it was crucial. Life-saving, in fact. Without the thousands of mothers and grandmothers across Europe who risked their own lives by carrying contraband in prams and shopping bags, we might never have seen peace at all. I hope Stella is an embodiment of those women – selfless for those around them.

Once Stella and her city became my backdrop, the next element was easy. Where else is better suited for romance to blossom than a place that hovers amid the constant ripple of water and sits under the most stunning of sunsets? And, of course, my Venice is in there too: the Accademia *is* my favourite bridge, Campo Santo Stefano among my preferred piazzas to people watch, and there is a small café in the corner opposite the church doorway where I have sat many a time with a good coffee and my notebook, imagining myself as a writer. Oh, and to the side is a very good gelato parlour. You can't escape it – Venice gets under your skin.

I hope I have paid homage to those who braved the conflict in Venice; there is no such thing as a 'soft' war when one person loses a life, one mother a son. Venice lost too. But as with the previous centuries of invasion and plague, it recovered. It remains a jewel. Glittering. And I'll be back there soon.

THE SECRET MESSENGER

Prologue: Clowns

Venice, June 1934

A sudden eruption of noise guided us – one burst after another, pushing up into the air like fireworks on a dark night. We zigzagged through the crowds, my grandfather slicing through the swarm with his broad muscular shoulders – still with a boat-builder's strength despite his sixty-five years. Reaching the edge of the vast piazza he pulled me by the hand, threading his way to the front of the audience, which was fenced off with a line of black-shirted militia, their backs to the expanse of the square and their stern, fixed faces towards the crowd. Inside the square, lines of Italian troops paraded up and down like ants to a continual brass band pomp of military music.

At seventeen, I was of average height and had to crane my neck to see the object of our attention, along with the rest of the crowd. The imposing, rounded girth of Benito Mussolini was easily spotted – a common figure on the front pages of the fascist-run newspapers. Even from behind, he had the appearance of being smug and overbearing, strutting next to the slightly smaller man walking beside him, distinctive only because of his dark suit rather than a gilded uniform dripping with medals. There was nothing physically remarkable about Mussolini's revered guest from the distance we were at. I knew who he was, what he represented, but to my young eyes his presence didn't warrant the thousands of fascist militia flooding Venice over recent days, let alone the crowds mustered to welcome him – some of whom we suspected had been strong-armed into their flag-waving support.

'Popsa, why have we come here?'

I was perplexed. My grandfather was a confirmed anti-fascist and, though he kept his hatred of Mussolini largely within the family, he had nonetheless been a fierce opponent in the twelve years since 'Il Duce' had ruled Italy with his brigade of militarised bully boys. Quietly, at home or in the cafés with his most trusted friends, he raged over the way good Italians were being trodden on, their freedom curtailed, both morally and physically.

He bent to whisper into my ear. 'Because, my darling Stella, I want you to see with your own eyes the enemy we will face.'

'An enemy? But isn't Hitler proposing to be a friend to Italy? An ally?'

'Not to Italians, my love,' he whispered again. 'To good, ordinary people – Venetians like us – he is no friend. Look at him, watch his stealth – know your enemy when the time comes.' His heavy, lined face set into a frown, and then he painted on a false smile as the militia neared, hoisting their guns to elicit a timely cheer from the crowd.

I peered at the object of their fraudulent praise, dwarfed by Mussolini's pompous stature. I couldn't see the distinctive face or the sharp lines of his frankly mocked hairstyle, which had dominated the newspapers in recent days. Yet the way Adolf Hitler moved among the Italian troops in the Piazza San Marco seemed almost reticent, guarded. Was this what we were supposed to be afraid of? Next to Mussolini and his army of bullies, he looked smaller in every way. Why did my big, burly and strong grandfather seem almost fearful?

Looking back on that day, Popsa's whole demeanour was my first experience of the mask we Venetians – Italians, in fact – needed to adopt over the coming years. Behind the beautiful and glittering facade of Italy's jewelled city, the veneer of Venice would take on Popsa's frown, hiding its determination to maintain the real fabric of its people against Hitler and fascism.

But, back then, in my late teens, I wasn't politicised – I was a young woman enjoying my last days at high school, relishing a summer on the beautiful beaches of the Lido, the late, low sun of endless Venetian days and perhaps the prospect of a fleeting summer romance. It was several years before I appreciated the significance of Hitler's visit on that warm June day more than five years before war broke out, or the impact of Mussolini's public fawning to a man who would become the devil to a good part of the world. At the dawn of war, when Italy pledged its military might alongside Hitler, I recall telling my grandfather what I later learned about that day in 1934.

'You know what Mussolini said about Hitler on that visit?' I asked him, pulling up the blanket over his whispery chest hair, watching his beleaguered lungs fighting the pneumonia which only days later would defeat him. 'He called him "a mad little clown".'

Popsa only smiled, suppressing a laugh he knew would force his lungs into a lengthy coughing fit.

He scooped in a breath. 'Ah, but Mussolini is simply a big clown. And you know what clowns do, Stella?'

'No, Popsa.'

'They create havoc, my darling. And they get away with it.'

1

Grief

The tears come in a torrent – great fat orbs that well up from inside her, catching momentarily on her eyelids. For a second, she feels as if she is looking through a piece of the thick, warped Murano glass dotted around her mother's living room, until she blinks and they roll down her dried-out cheeks. Ten days into her grief, Luisa has learned not to fight it, allowing the deluge to cascade in rivers towards her now sodden chin. Jamie has helpfully placed boxes of tissues around her mother's house; much like city dwellers are supposed to be never more than six feet from some kind of vermin, now she is never without a man-size hankie to hand.

Emotional fallout over, Luisa faces a more frustrating issue. The keyboard of her laptop has fared badly from the human cloudburst, and a glass tipped over in her temporary blindness – several of the keys are swimming in salt tears and tap water. It's too late to mop up the flood – even a consistent jabbing of various keys tells her the screen is frozen and the machine displaying its dissatisfaction. Electronics and fluids do not mix.

'Oh Jesus, not now,' Luisa moans into the air. 'Not now! Come on, Dais – work, come on girl!' She jabs at the keyboard again, following it up with a few choice expletives, and more tears – this time of frustration.

It's the first time she's been able to face opening Daisy, her beloved laptop, since the day before her mum . . . died. Luisa wants to say the word 'died', needs to keep on saying it, because it's a fact. Her mum didn't pass away, because that somehow alludes to a serene exit, floating from one dimension to another without rancour, where there is time to put things to right amid crisp white sheets and soft blankets, to say things you want to say – *need* to say. Even with her limited experience of death, Luisa knows it was short, blunt and brutal. Her mum died. End of. Two weeks from first diagnosis, one week of that in a drug-induced coma to combat the unbearable pain. And now Luisa is the one enduring the inevitable ache of grief. Throw anger and frustration into the mix and you might touch on the myriad of emotions pitching and rolling around her head, heart and assorted organs, twenty-four/seven.

So, Luisa attempts what she always does when she cannot settle, eat, speak or socialise. She writes. Battle-scarred and sporting dog-eared stickers of love and identity, Daisy has been a reliable friend to Luisa in her need to bleed emotions onto a screen page. Often, it's nothing more than crazy ramblings, but occasionally there is something of worth amid the jumble of words – a sentence or string of thought she might squirrel away for future use or that might well make it into the book one day. The book she will write when she is free of the inane meanderings she currently commits to the features pages of various magazines about the very latest thing in cosmetics, or whether women really *do* want to steer their own destiny (of course they do, she thinks as she writes – do I really need to spell it out in no more than a thousand words?). But it's work. It keeps the wolf from the door while Jamie establishes himself as a jobbing actor. But one day the book will happen.

Daisy is party to this dream, a workmate and a keeper of secrets too, deep down in her hard drive.

'Christ Daisy, what happened to loyalty, eh?' Luisa mutters, and then feels immediately disloyal to her hi-tech friend. Half drowned in human tears, she may well have reacted in the same way and refused to go on. Daisy needs TLC and time to dry out on top of the boiler. In the meantime, there are pent-up emotions to spill – and for some inexplicable reason a pen and paper is not up to the job. Luisa feels the need to hit something, to bash and clatter at the keys and watch the words appear on screen as if they have magically appeared from somewhere deep inside her, separate to her conscious thinking. Being a child of the computer age, and with her grief threatening to spew, a pen will simply not allow those words to explode from her with venom or unbounded love, or the anger that she cannot contain.

A thought strikes her: Jamie had been up in her mother's attic the day before to assess just how much clearing out lay ahead of them. As Luisa was tackling the cancelling of direct debits and council tax, he mentioned seeing a typewriter case tucked in the eaves, one that looked fairly old but 'in good nick'. Would it be worth anything? Or was it sentimental value, he'd asked. At the time, she dismissed it as non-urgent but now her need is greater.

The loft space is like a million others across the globe: a curious odour of old lives dampened and dust that flies up with irritation as you disturb its years of slumber. A single light bulb hangs from the timbers, and Luisa needs to adjust her eyes before objects come into focus. She recognises a few Christmas presents she took pains to choose for her mother – a thermostatic wrap for her aching back and a pair of sheepskin slippers – both of which look to have been barely out of their wrappers before being abandoned to the 'Not Wanted' pile. Another reminder of the distance between mother and daughter, now never to be bridged. She pushes the memory away – it's too deep inside her for now, though it constantly threatens to push through into her grief. It's therapy for another day. Luisa ferrets around for a few minutes, feeling her frustration rise and wondering if this is the best pastime at this moment, when things still feel so raw. She both relishes and dreads finding a family album where she knows she won't be able to stop herself from turning the dog-eared pages of so-called happy memories. All three of them on the beach – her, Mum and Dad – fixed Kodachrome smiles all round. In better days.

Mercifully, an object that is not a fat bound book of memories pushes its way out of the gloom. Instead, it's a grey, moulded case whose shape – square and sloping towards a brown leather handle – means it can only be one thing. It has the look of a life well worn, the scuffs and scratches immediately reminding her of the history Daisy sports on her own casing. There is a distinctive twang as both clasps spring upwards under Luisa's fingers, and what almost sounds like the escape of a human breath as she lifts the lid. Even under the dim light, she can see it is beautiful – a monochrome mix of black and grey, white keys ringed with a dull metal and glowing bright against the dimness. Luisa puts a tentative finger on one of the keys, pressing it gently, and the mechanism reacts under her touch, sending a thin metal shaft leaping towards the roller. It hasn't seized up. She notes, too, that there is a ribbon still attached and, even better, a spare, sealed reel tucked alongside the keyboard. The aged cellophane is intact but almost disintegrates under her finger. If fate is on her side, however, the ribbon won't have dried up.

Luisa fixes the lid back down and pulls the case away from a pile of boxes – it's surprisingly light for an old machine. As she pulls, the lid on one of the boxes slides off, sending a puff of dust in its wake. She turns to replace it, but her eye catches a single photograph, black and white yet sepia-toned with age. It features a man and a woman – their joyful expressions suggest a couple – standing in St Mark's Square in Venice, the distinctive grandiose basilica behind them, surrounded by a groundswell of pigeons. She recognises her mother in the features of the woman, but not the man. Luisa searches her memory – did her mother and father even mention going to Venice, perhaps for their honeymoon? It looks that kind of photo – the couple seem happy. It's not how she remembers her parents, but she thinks even they must have been in love once. And yet the photo looks older than that, from a bygone age.

Luisa is aware of her Italian roots, the spelling of her name being an obvious indication. Both of her mother's parents were Italian, but they died some years ago; her grandfather when she was just a baby, and grandmother in her early teens. She knows very little about their history – her mother would never talk about it – except that they were both writers. She likes to think she has inherited at least that family trait from them.

She flips over the photograph; scrawled in pencil are the words 'S and C, San Marco June 1950'. Her mother was Sofia, but she was born in 1953, so maybe it's her grandmother's face beaming contentment? S for Stella? Perhaps that's Luisa's grandpa standing alongside her – Luisa barely remembers him, only a fleeting image of a kindly face. But his name was Giovanni. So who is C? It's entirely possible he was a suitor before Grandpa Gio, as she knows they called him. Luisa's curiosity gives way to a smile, her first in days, and the movement of the muscles feels odd. She thinks they look so stylish, he in his high-waisted suit trousers, and she in a neat Chanel-like suit and elegant court shoes, her hair swept in a chic, black wave.

Luisa bends to replace the photograph in the box, but sees that underneath a decaying layer of tissue paper there is more – photographs and paper scraps, some hand-scribed and others typed in an old font, perhaps on the newly discovered machine? To any other curio browser it would warrant a look at the very least, but to a journalist it spikes the senses. There is something about the smell too – the pungency of old dust – which sticks in Luisa's nostrils and makes her heart beat faster. It reeks of lives lived and history unmasked.

The whole box is heavy and awkward to manoeuvre down the attic stairs and into the living room. In the daylight however, she sees the real treasure come to light. Under a layer of loose type and several browned, brittle newspapers bearing the name *Venezia Liberare*, Luisa can sense it: a mystery. It's in the fine sandy texture under her fingers as she gingerly lifts the paper cache – men and women grinning in fuzzy tones of black and white, some she notes casually using rifles as props, or proudly holding them across their chests, women included. Momentarily, she is shocked; in a distant memory, her grandma never appeared as anything other than that – a sweet old lady who dished out cuddles and chocolates, grinning mischievously when she was inevitably rebuked by Luisa's mother for spoiling her with sweets. Sometimes, Luisa remembers her slipping little wrapped bars when no one was looking, whispering 'Shh, it's just our secret', and she felt like they were part of a little gang.

The typewriter is momentarily forgotten as Luisa picks up each piece, peering at its faded detail, squinting to fill in the gaps of pencil scratchings lost to the years. It hits her squarely then – how many people's histories are contained in this cardboard box with its sunken edges and corners gnawed at by the resident mice? What might she discover in its depths amid the deceased spiders and smell of mould? What will she learn about her family? She wonders, too, if there is an element of fate in her discovery, if today of all days she was meant to find it – to piece it all together in some order, and in turn glue her recently shattered self back together. For the first time in weeks, she feels not defeated or leaden with grief, but lifted a little. Excited.

2

The Lion's Den

Venice, early December 1943

I think of that pre-war exchange with Popsa often; the word 'havoc' resonates a lot these days, more so after last night's atrocities in the Jewish ghetto: hundreds rounded up like cattle by Nazi troops and their fascist handmaidens, men and women pulled out of their homes – stoical in the face of their screaming, tear-stained children abandoned behind them – and herded into boats destined first for the prison of Santa Maria Maggiore. To be separated from their families was bad enough, but all of Venice knew their eventual destination, and they did too – east into Germany, to Auschwitz. To an almost certain death.

I rub the obvious lines around my eyes, hoping to smear away any smut from the fires that continue to smoulder in the ghetto. Having spent the early hours running from house to house across Venice, breathlessly passing messages and false identification papers to those in need of them, the smell of

13

cordite and desperation is still there in my nostrils. If there was any chance to save even a few families from the cull, we – the Resistance – had to try; huddling women and children in the smallest of hiding places, in cupboards and attics. I saw mothers trying desperately to keep their babies quiet, hands cupped over little mouths, the fear of just one cry or murmur etched on their faces. Our partisan leaders were taken by surprise by the Nazis' sudden strike on the Jewish enclave; as I weaved breathlessly through the warren of alleyways and tiny passages, avoiding the Nazi scrum, staying out of sight of any patrol and their inevitable questions as to why I was out during curfew and where exactly I was going, it felt like we were fighting a losing battle. We worked all night but, in the clear light of day, it's evident we only succeeded in damage limitation.

My whole body feels limp and defeated, though I've had the luxury at least of returning briefly to my own apartment for an hour's sleep, a change of clothes and a smear with a wet flannel. Those Jews taken simply for their birthright, born into a religion despised by the Nazis, are now on a cold, inhospitable floor with little respite to look forward to. I am a lucky woman.

'Another espresso?' Paolo pulls away my empty cup from the counter and pushes a second, full cup in its place, without waiting for an answer. He only has to look at my face, hastily touched with some of the precious make-up I've been rationing and a smear of red lipstick. The coffee is welcome, though it isn't, of course, the sharp but silken blend of pre-war days. Paolo and his father, owners of the café in the square below my apartment since time began, are masters at making the fake coffee – *ersatzkaffee* – *seem* Italian at least;

the hiss of the gleaming machine, the way Paolo pours it lovingly into the tiny cup with a true flourish. If nothing else, it helps wake me up.

'Good luck, Stella,' Paolo chimes as I swallow down the coffee and wave goodbye. His parting wink tells me he knows exactly where I'm going.

I walk the twenty minutes from streets around the Fondamenta Nuove to the Nazi headquarters on the grand central piazza of San Marco, trying to nurture a spring in my step the closer I get to the Platzkommandantur. The bright winter sun rising over the Arsenale helps lift my mood, lending a distinct pinky hue through the smaller canals, from one bridge crossing to another, the milky jade of the water lapping at the red and orange brickwork. Usually, this is the best time of the day for me, when Venice is waking up, stout old women in black optimistically on their way to buy whatever they can in the relatively sparse markets. Today, though, the morning buzz feels dampened as news of the ghetto's cull winds its way through the city. Soon, each and every café and bar will have talk and opinion, someone will know of another who has been taken – be it relative or colleague. In a city like Venice, the people connect and weave like the canals that are its vital arteries.

There are few troops – either Nazi or fascist – around at this time of the morning, but we Venetians have been schooled into believing that eyes are everywhere. Despite my true feelings, those of a proud anti-fascist, like my beloved grand-father, I have to look eager as I'm about to enter the enemy's nerve centre – and not as a prisoner or suspect, but an enthusiastic new member of staff. Automatically, I adjust my mask and take on the look of a grateful collaborator, a

Venetian glad to have the protection of our better, bigger German cousins. We Italians have learned to play the part of the poor relation very well. We've had years of practice.

We know what people in the outside world say – that Venetians have had a 'soft' war, protected as a kind of oasis because of our city's beauty and grandeur, its precious art, targeted by the Allied bombers as a place to avoid rather than effect ruin. To some extent it's true: the classical music still plays in Piazza San Marco, although these days it's more likely to be the Hermann Goering Regimental Band with its stylistic pomp, replacing any true elegance. The annual celebration of art at the Biennale continues, attracting the rich and beautiful, as well as the Nazi propaganda king in Joseph Goebbels. But tell that to the mothers whose teenage boys were swiftly marched away to Lord knows where as slave labour for the Nazi machine, like a warped playing out of the Pied Piper fable. That early September day only a few months ago is still fresh with me, when the coloured leaflets fluttered from the sky, informing us that the Nazis were coming to conquer our city. To most Venetians – after years of fascist dictatorship under Mussolini – it was simply another coup, another plague. It was followed only days later by the resounding stomp of jackboots on our ancient flagstones, and the Nazis quickly made themselves very comfortable in our requisitioned palaces on the Grand Canal, easing themselves into the bars and outdoor eating places like it was some sort of vacation.

Venice appears on the surface to be compliant, relenting. But I know different. For all its outward splendour, Venice hides itself well; in deep, dark alleyways, behind the painted green shutters, I know for certain there are hives of activity, thousands working to skew the intricate planning of our unwelcome squatters and claim back our city. For now, we do it quietly. But we aim to be ready.

It was a heart-stopping moment when I received a message to attend the offices of the German High Command, on one end of the Piazza San Marco. Since the full occupation in September, when the city swarmed with the grey-green troops of the Wehrmacht and the ashen colours of the SS, it's a place I've taken pains to sidestep, going out of my way to avoid walking across the piazza in full view of the young German sentries, bored and eyeing up pretty young Venetian women. On being summoned, I imagined my membership of the anti-fascist Action Party had been discovered or revealed, but, if it had, there would have been no request to attend – more likely a sudden raid by Italian fascist Blackshirts, and a stay in their none too salubrious headquarters at Ca' Littoria, becoming painfully familiar with their torture methods. We have learned quickly that the Germans are not here to get their hands dirty if at all possible. Only to oversee the annihilation of freedom.

I have been careful in recent years to publicly align myself with no one in particular, keeping a low profile as a typist in the Venetian works department, the government division responsible for making our fairy-tale city function day to day, even through war. I'd been 'recommended' for the job by Sergio Lombardi, a seemingly fine upstanding citizen who, in his other life, is Captain Lombardi, the commander of Venice's Resistance brigade. The information I gleaned while in the works department proved useful to the partisan groups fighting the Nazis and fascists across the entire Veneto region, though I never imagined it saved lives. When I doubted it, when I itched to do something more useful – more visible – Sergio took pains to reassure me that the detailed knowledge of the city's workings was vital in helping their troops move undiscovered in and out of Venice. The comprehensive plans I had access to were perfect tools for ghosting Allied soldiers away to safety now the Nazi occupation of Northern Italy made it impossible to move freely.

And now, thanks to maintaining that low profile, I am here, about to enter the lion's den; my transfer to Nazi High Command – the Reich headquarters – has been requested because of my fluent German, although the move couldn't be more timely or fortuitous. Or intimidating.

Beyond the grand exterior near the Correr Museum in San Marco, I present my pass from the works department and a young German soldier runs down a list for my name. He seems pleased to find it.

'Up the stairs, first door on your right,' he says in faltering Italian.

'Thank you, I'll find it,' I say in German and he smiles his embarrassment. Poor boy, he's no more than a child, perhaps the same age as my brother, Vito. Too young for this, both of them.

The office at the top of the sweeping marble stairway is behind a large, ornately carved door. It's filled with desks in a strict formation, the opulent walls of the vast room deadened by the austere dark wooden furniture and the Nazi icons dotted around. A fierce clattering of typewriters hits me like a wave and I'm briefly startled. I must have shown it because a man approaches – I can tell from his face and his civilian clothes that he's Italian, and I'm surprised again, though pleased too. Even now, a stark Nazi uniform makes me pull in a short breath and I feel a guilt rising in me, although I've become adept at hiding it.

'Morning. Can I help you?' the man, in his well-cut grey suit, says in Italian. He's not Venetian; his accent says he's from the south. Tall and with a short, dark beard – in his early thirties I guess – he looks immediately out of place amid the military surroundings, reminding me of an academic or librarian. His whole demeanour is Italian; it's only the tiny metal pin on his jacket lapel – the jawless death's head insignia – that tells me he is a fascist too. A paid-up member of Mussolini's gang. In any other scenario, I might have thought him attractive, but here, he is marred by his allegiance.

'I've been sent here by the works department – as a typist and translator,' I venture, holding out my references. 'Am I in the right office?'

He scans the papers, holding them closer to his face, and I notice his large brown eyes scanning the script.

'Welcome Signorina Jilani,' he says. 'Yes, you've found the right place. I'll show you to your desk.'

He turns and leads me towards the back of the room, passing a vacant desk with a silent typewriter upon it. Backing onto a wall entirely shelved with books and files, he gestures to an empty desk with a large machine to the side.

'There, that's for you,' he says.

'Oh, I thought I would be over there with the other typists,' I say, casting a backwards glance. The desire to blend in is well grounded in me.

'Well, as you'll be translating for General Breugal, I thought it would be better if you were nearer his office' – he nods his head slightly towards a closed door, even larger and more

19

ornately carved than the last – 'since he has a tendency to be a little brief when it comes to instructions. I can't see him striding across the office ten times a day – he would get a bit annoyed about that. It will hopefully spare you some of his . . .' he falters over the next word carefully . . . 'irritation.'

He smiles as he says it, an embarrassed offering, perhaps because he's betrayed a little of his opinion of the general, in painting him as some blustering despot. Except the general's reputation is anything but – a despot, yes, but his cruelty is already well known within the Resistance.

'Well, thank you for that in advance,' I say. I'm genuinely grateful, since the last thing I want to do is attract any unwanted attention. I'm here to type, to translate and to absorb what will help the partisan Resistance wage war with effective sabotage against our German trespassers. But I'm also here to be utterly compliant, in office hours at least.

'Marta will show you the bathroom and the canteen, and I will arrange a meeting with General Breugal when he arrives shortly.'

I nod, and he turns to go. 'Oh, and by the way, my name is Cristian – Cristian De Luca – under-secretary to the general, admin mostly. Civilian.' He adds the last part most definitely, as if he doesn't want me to guess he's a card-carrying fascist. As if by not wearing a black shirt and donning a dark ski cap, he's not part of the bully brigade. But I know plenty of innocents who have been condemned by a type-writer, by being on a list. I have to remind myself that what I'm doing is not collaborating – my Resistance commander assures me the information I can absorb will save many more lives than I could ever condemn.

'Please come to me if you need anything, or you have a problem.' Cristian De Luca smiles weakly, but even his friendly eyes don't convince me. I nod again and return his expression, because that's what I'm supposed to do.

I have time enough to meet some of the other typists over tea before I'm called in through the foreboding door. I grab the pen and notebook on my desk, not knowing whether it's simply an interview or if I'm expected to begin work immediately. Beyond the door, the walk towards the desk is a long one as the office is vast, with high ceilings and walls crawling with carved plaster figures. My eye is drawn to the overly large picture of the Führer placed over the grand fireplace. His expression in such portraits never ceases to make me laugh inside, as though he's swallowed too much of my mother's chilli pasta and is feeling the effects on his digestion. There's an unmistakable stench of cigar smoke, and the winter sun streaming through the tall windows creates a swirl of dirty white clouds.

'Fräulein – I beg your pardon – *Signorina.*' A voice comes from behind the smoke, and I see his face at last. It's fat. That's my first impression. He's vast. His red, oily skin is stretched tight over wide cheeks, pumped up no doubt by good living and too much grappa, and he sports a meagre moustache, not even worthy of being fashioned into anything like Hitler's silly little brush. His black eyes sit like minuscule cherries in the pudgy dough of his face; his body a larger version of the same, squeezed with effort into his green Wehrmacht tunic. At first I think he has the face of a fool, but know at the same time it's never good to underestimate the hatred he and his kind might harbour; hatred for Jews, alongside a disdain for weak Italians who need hand-holding

21

in this war. He hasn't earned his place behind that desk by not showing strength. Already General Breugal has made a distinct – and deadly – impression on Venice's opposition to Nazi penetration of our city; last night's ghetto cull was just one example of his zeal to carry out Hitler's cleansing of Jews from our city.

Breugal doesn't get up, but merely extends a hand across the desk and I have to make contact with his moist fingers before I sit down in one of two chairs placed in front of the desk. He looks up from his furious scribble and digs the stub of his cigar in a nearby ashtray.

'So, I will need a minimum of two typed reports daily, translated from German to Italian,' he says in clipped German. 'I take it you are fluent?'

'Yes, Herr Breugal.'

'General,' he corrects briskly.

'Sorry – General,' I say. I worry that I've marked myself out already but he barely looks at me, so I feel safe his arrogance will lead to a general ignorance about me. And that's the way I want to keep it.

Once I'm dismissed with a grunt and a wave of the general's hand, I head back to my desk, clutching the first report I need to translate. Outside the door, I meet the general's long and lean – and much younger – deputy, Captain Klaus. He introduces himself, but there's no emotion in his voice – it's merely duty. There is, however, a steely glint to his blue eyes. I do the best I can to remain businesslike even though I can almost feel the heat of this first report on my chest.

Finally, Captain Klaus feels we have exhausted the formalities and I sit down and open the pages. This is pure gold for the Resistance, information straight from the horse's mouth which they will use to plan sabotage of German movements, initiate rescues of targeted families, and generally be a thorn in the side of the Nazi regime. Tempting though it is, we can't use all of the intelligence consistently – my Resistance colleagues have made it clear my position is to be protected, so that I can remain in post without arousing suspicion. To General Breugal, and the slightly odd Cristian De Luca, I am a good Italian girl, a patriot and lover of order, a true believer that fascism will win out over the current chaos. I am to be trusted.

At first glance, the report I am to translate looks to be merely an engineering update on precious water supplies in Venice, pumped in from the mainland. But as I consult my German-Italian dictionary for more specific words, I discover it's also about rerouting food supplies through new shipping lines, although the word 'supplies' doesn't always appear to refer to scarce flour, sugar or wheat. The report's complexity means I can't possibly remember it word for word, despite having a talent for ingesting and harbouring facts. Luckily, the Resistance has prepared for this. They know I can't risk making a carbon copy of my translation, or writing notes in my own hand, so it's been agreed with my unit that I'll type up brief notes I can immediately recall in the office. Operating in plain sight is sometimes the best form of camouflage and I'm suddenly grateful that having a desk backing onto a bookcase is useful for not being overlooked. Or else I will scribble any facts the minute I can make excuses for a toilet break. A sympathetic cobbler has already made adjustments to several pairs of shoes, allowing me to hide folded notes in my heels. I'll return to my desk, with an expression of indifference and a willingness to carry on the Reich's work. That's the plan.

'Fräulein Jilani, have you settled in?' The voice is raised above the office noise and takes me by surprise, not least because Cristian De Luca's German is cut-glass perfect. He sees my surprise.

'Yes, we speak German in the office – the general prefers it,' he explains. 'Do you have everything you need?'

'Yes, thank you,' I say, my eyes glancing back to my keyboard. I need to work quickly to complete both the official and unofficial notes, though not so noisily that I attract attention. Sergio, Captain of the Venetian Resistance Central Brigade and my commander, has stressed that I'm to lie low for several days, or even weeks, not be intent on passing information, but this to me looks too important. I feel sure it could really make a difference. I need to get on and this man is loitering.

Still, Cristian De Luca hovers beside my desk. I look up, inquisitive.

'Erm, I'm just hoping everything was all right with you and the general?' he ventures. 'Nothing too . . . brusque?'

'No . . . no,' I lie, purposely upbeat. 'He was . . . direct, but perfectly charming.'

'Good, well, don't hesitate to, you know . . .' His last words are lost as the general's voice comes booming from behind me, prompting one of the secretaries to scurry towards the door, almost turning a heel as she goes.

Cristian De Luca walks towards a desk by the window, annoyingly only two away from my own. He puts on a pair of tortoiseshell-rimmed glasses and opens up a file to read. Now I think he looks even more like a librarian.

★   ★   ★

The efforts of the previous night are beginning to take their toll – my eyes are smarting with tiredness as I pull the cover over my machine at the end of the day, while the office begins to empty. One of the office girls asks if I'd like to join them for a drink but I make an excuse that I'm expected at my parents' for dinner. The thought of a bowl of Mama's pasta – exquisite even with increasingly scant ingredients – makes my mouth water, but instead I grab a bread roll from a nearby bakery and head briskly in the opposite direction, wrapping my coat around me as I head towards the canal's edge. Despite my fatigue, it's time for the third part of my full and sometimes complicated life.

Waiting at the stop for the *vaporetto* that will transport me across the expanse of water to the island of Giudecca, I stare at the soaring tower of the church of San Giorgio Maggiore, perched on the adjacent island's edge. The Palladian monolith looks particularly magnificent tonight, caught in the occasional beam of boat traffic toing and froing across the lagoon. I'm not particularly religious – not as much as Mama would wish anyway – but the tower's continued existence through centuries of war and strife warms my heart. That warmth is particularly welcome now since the bitter wind is apt to whip through this wide stretch between Venice proper and what's considered the less ornate, more industrial Giudecca. But that's what's so attractive about it tonight, for me at least. The sometimes choppy waters are a divide which helps more than hinders.

The crossing is unhindered by German patrol boats and takes just ten or so minutes; I'm one of only a dozen or so passengers stepping onto the pontoon at Giudecca. The streets are mostly dark with minimal lighting – a consequence of burned-out bulbs not replaced – but I have a mind map of where I'm going. I think I could find it in my sleep, which is a bonus since my eyes are struggling to stay open after so little rest. But I must. This is business and not pleasure. However tired I am, there is more typing to do, though rather than reports to uphold the Nazi occupation, these are my words. Each time I come to Giudecca, I become a different type of translator, one whose fiercely loyal passion for the Resistance is laid on a page for all of Venice to see. It's one part of my contribution to the partisan cause, defenders of our city. Popsa always said that one day my love of words would mark me out and, each time I step onto Giudecca, I like to think he's right.

As I round the corner into the tiny, darkened square, a glow pushes out from the ground-floor windows of the café-bar, blinds only half drawn, while the low hum of conversation from behind a heavy wooden door is the sole noise in the empty plaza.

'Evening Stella,' says Matteo, the bar's owner, as I walk in to a general wave of welcome from the ten or so customers. I'm among friends here.

'Hello everyone,' I say as chirpily as I can manage. I walk to the back of the bar and into a tiny room, little more than a cupboard, where I replace my coat with a white waitress's apron around my waist. Instead of heading back out to the bar, though, I knock three times on a door tucked in one corner of the room and turn the handle.

'It's Stella,' I sing in warning as I descend a short set of wooden stairs, towards the dim light below. Arlo looks up from his desk, squinting at me and then back at the paper he's working on. Poor Arlo – his eyesight is bad enough as it is, without the strain of the faint light and the tiny print he peers at for hours on end. His thick glasses lie discarded on the table as he pulls the page close to his face – his eyesight is a family trait that saved him from an enforced draft into the Italian army, and more than likely prevents the Resistance from allowing him anywhere near a gun, but he's the best of typesetters. Twice a week, our little band of aspiring paper-producers meets under a cloak on Giudecca to create and construct the weekly *Venezia Liberare* newspaper. As its name suggests, it's about spreading the word of liberty and freedom for all Venetians, reclaiming something of our own. And amid the typeset lines of news and local chatter, there is – we think – a manifesto of hope.

Yet *Venezia Liberare* does not lie side by side on the news-stands with *Il Gazzettino* and other mainstream papers, those largely controlled by fascist sympathisers. It's created, printed and collated in this tiniest of spaces, packed and transported under cover of darkness to all corners of Venice, where shopkeepers loyal to the cause will keep a pile of 'something special' under their counters, passing over the goods on the quiet, and, with it, the word that we are all still here. Ready and waiting.

'Hey, Stella, we've got eight pages to fill tonight. I hope you're raring to go,' Arlo says enthusiastically. My heart sinks for a second and my fatigue rises like a wave but, as I pull up my chair and lift the lid on my typewriter, there's a rush of energy within me. Just the sight of this machine has that effect on me. It's much smaller and neater than my industrial-size typewriter in the Reich office, the one with a high slope of keys and tall roller, the shiny metal of grey and black, emulating the SS livery. The shine that my own machine once sported on its black frame is now dimmed and scratched, and some of the bright white keys are grey and smudged with ink, tattooed with my own fingerprints, but it cheers me like a good friend. For years now, since Popsa brought it home on my eighteenth birthday, this small machine has been my workmate, my comrade even. My voice.

We've been through quite a lot. In what now seems like an entirely different life as a journalist, I shunned the heavy, brooding office typewriters in favour of my neater, more portable tool. We went on story assignments together, allowing me to type up my notes quickly, settle my thoughts on paper, sometimes sitting on the steps of a nearby church or outside a quiet café, basking in the spring sunshine. I was a junior reporter only, but it was my dream job after high school: slightly frowned on by Mama, secretly tolerated by Papa, and overwhelmingly encouraged by Popsa.

'This could be your future,' he'd beamed as I'd opened the carefully wrapped birthday present. 'You can win battles and change minds with this, Stella – better than any weapon.' He had insisted on buying an Olivetti machine, the good Italian family firm having solid anti-fascist affiliations, later proven in their wartime actions of creative sabotage which saved many lives.

Of course, being Popsa, he was right. I typed until I drove the entire household to distraction; I created stories, I tapped out memories and wrote fairly terrible poetry. And all those words, channelled from inside me onto the page, via the conduit of my beautiful, clattery Olivetti, helped me towards securing my dream post on *Il Gazzettino*, the influential daily covering the entire mainland Veneto region surrounding Venice. I was blissfully happy for a time, until its increasingly fascist politics became as dark as the storm clouds of war over Europe.

However, I haven't got time to dwell on that as I sit in the much less salubrious – but no less important – underground office of our clandestine newspaper. In my hand is a sheaf of hand-scrawled notes on crumpled scraps of paper, some typewritten reports and shorthand transcripts of radio transmissions. Each has made its way from Resistance members in Venice or captains in charge of the mountain fighting groups, via several messengers, to our unassuming basement office. Mothers and grandmothers have sat for hours in their dimly lit kitchens listening to transmissions via Radio Londra – the aptly named BBC service which brings us news of the outside world – scratching down details of the fight beyond Venice. Somehow, in the next three hours, I have to understand and shape these snapshots of defiance into news stories, in time for Arlo and his one regular helper, Tommaso, to typeset and print our weekly edition of *Venezia Liberare*. It's our own, tangible way of telling ordinary Italians that they are not alone in the fight against fascism.

Matteo brings me another welcome cup of coffee and I set to work. Not for the first time, I thank providence that my first year on *Il Gazzettino* was spent converting press statements into readable stories. Back then, I thought it a form of punishment for the new girl, intensely frustrated at not being allowed beyond the office doors to carry out any real reporting. Now I know it was a valuable skill to perfect. As each story is finished, I tear it from the machine, lean backwards in the chair and hand it to Arlo and Tommaso, a young boy not yet out of school whose father is a partisan lieutenant, as they set to work mapping out the pages.

Tommaso is fairly new to our little workroom and, we've recently discovered, is something of an artist with a gift for adult cartoons; his dry, sarcastic take on fascist leaders – our pompous beloved Benito Mussolini especially – has worked its way into the pages. In among the serious reports of partisan victories in the mountains, ground captured and trains derailed, we're able to provide a lighter tone to our readers. After all, it's our sense of humour as Italians that's enabled us to survive through twenty years of fascist oppression, and a war to top it off. In the cafés and canteens and *campos*, you can still hear Venice laugh.

When he first joined us, I could sense Tommaso's wonder at the barmaid in her apron typing out the stories – the whispered question to his fellow setter – until Arlo explained that my name is on the bar's list of employees and as such I have to be ready to play my part at a second's notice, albeit quite badly. Fascist soldiers occasionally make it over to Giudecca in the late hours, looking for trouble, alcohol, or both. Only a month ago. two officers – already half-drunk – demanded drinks along with the employee rota; I just managed to make it up from the basement in time to grab a discarded apron, steering them away from the 'beer cellar' with a winning smile and several more drinks. Since then, I've donned an apron as a habit.

As the evening wears on I feel myself flagging, and several times Arlo prods me playfully.

'Come on, girl, anyone would think you've done a day's work!' he teases.

I see him peering at my copy intently, rubbing his ink-marked fingers on his forehead, and I wonder how many typing mistakes I've made out of sheer tiredness. Ones that he will have to correct in the final print.

'Everything all right, Arlo?' I say.

'I'm just wondering when you're going to replace that old crock of a machine, Stella? This wayward *e* is driving me crazy.'

Automatically, I put a hand to my beloved machine in defence, taking comfort from its familiar, rough surface. It's true that being a little too portable has caused one of the metals shafts to shift slightly, making my typed sentences easily recognised with a sagging *e*. It's only Arlo's expertise in re-setting the print that makes sure my machine's quirk doesn't transfer to the finished newspaper.

'At least you can tell it's written by a master,' I come back swiftly. And that's how we combat our fatigue: with innocent banter, to shield against the bad news that occasionally filters through the ranks – having to write of fellow partisans captured or tortured, at times executed. In those moments we force ourselves to think of the bigger picture, of what we can realistically achieve in a tiny basement with almost no resources; we do what we can to inform, to spread the word and help fuel solidarity among fellow Venetians.

I stretch and yawn as I finish the last piece for Arlo to edit and set.

'Have you enough to fill the pages?' I say, hoping he does. My eyes can't seem to focus beyond my nose at this point. Usually, I stay until the setting is complete, but I need to catch the last *vaporetto* from Giudecca back to the main island and I'll have to walk home quickly to beat the curfew. More than once I've been stopped by a fascist or Nazi patrol, and

I've all but used up my smiles and excuses of a sickly relative needing medicine.

'More than enough,' Arlo says. 'Your copy gets more lyrical by the day.'

'Too much? Too flowery?' I counter anxiously. 'Should I tone it down?'

'No, no. I happen to think our readers are inspired by the way you describe even the harshest of events. My mother says she looks forward to your storytelling!'

'My grandma reads it cover to cover,' Tommaso cuts in, shyly. 'She pesters me until I deliver one personally.'

'I only hope it comes across as fact and not fiction – these things are real,' I reply. 'Horribly real.'

'Don't worry, you're not soft-soaping it,' Arlo reassures. 'If anything, your descriptions make us feel we're all living it. Which we are.'

He's right – everyone knows someone with a family member taken or killed. Even so, I make a note to keep an eye on my language, perhaps to stick to the facts and not embroider the copy too much. It was always the criticism of my news editor on *Il Gazzettino* – 'Stella, your idea of a "short" is five hundred words!' he would bellow from his desk, striking through my words with his red pen. It was clear from the beginning I was much more suited to the lengthier feature stories, where I could happily tinker with words, rather than strip back to the bald facts. And I would have made it as a feature writer, I'm sure, had that career path not been abruptly cut short.

Finally, I untie my apron and head on up the stairs. Soon, several other members of the brigade will join Arlo and Tommaso in the tiny cellar, moving to crank up the small press shrouded in a nearby outbuilding, working through the night to produce and assemble the paper. Before she turns in, Matteo's wife will haul down a large pot of soup she has managed to conjure up, from whatever ingredients she can find, to help them push through into the small hours. It's a team effort, always. We know our only hope of surviving this war is with a combination of loyalty and friendship.

For now, though, my work is done. I pull the cover over my typewriter until its services are needed in a few days' time. I climb the stairs wearily, hang up my apron and pull on my coat, saying goodbye to Matteo, who is washing glasses in a bar where a lone figure lingers over his beer.

The icy wind whipping through the open-sided *vaporetto* is the only thing keeping me awake, and I have to consciously propel my legs through the almost empty streets, making a mental search of what I have in my cupboard to cook up a soup or a bowl of pasta. It's too late to divert to Mama's for a hug and a welcome hearth – she and Papa know little of what I do outside of work, and I don't need to worry them.

I see only a few bodies moving under the ghostly blue streetlights in the larger *campos* – after last night, and away from the Jewish ghetto, everything seems to have calmed for now. The narrow alleyway leading to my door is pitch black, rendering me almost blind as I approach my apartment, but I know every cobble and paving stone, the way my footsteps echo, and I can tell instantly if there's another body in my midst. My tiny second-floor apartment is freezing, and I don't need to check the scuttle to know I have scant coal for the burner. The food cupboard, too, is almost bare – one solitary onion stares back at me, alongside a handful of polenta in a paper bag. I weigh up what I need the most – to dive under the blankets piled on my bed and shiver myself into a vague warmth, or to satisfy my hunger. I decide I'm almost past hunger now, so I boil the kettle and take a hot cup of tea to bed, having wrapped my nightdress around the kettle for a few minutes before swiftly undressing and pulling it over my head, relishing the patches where it has made direct contact with the hot metal. The thick woollen socks Mama knitted for me last Christmas are already under the covers, giving my feet the impression of warmth.

In the few minutes before I fall asleep, I reflect on the past twenty hours – as different as day and night for me. For eight hours I could be accused of helping the German Third Reich to consolidate control of our beautiful city and country – yes, *our* country – and for the last four or five of aiming to knock holes in their plans to ride roughshod over Italian heritage and pride. I feel like a female Jekyll and Hyde. Yet what helps me sink into a satisfying sleep is the knowledge of what we – me, Arlo and everyone else in our secret cellar – are doing. It may only be eight pages of print, and yet I firmly believe in Popsa's principle: that they represent immense power. In my mind's eye, communication is like the fine lines of a spider's web; one tenuous strand makes little difference, but put them together – weave them well – and you have something of inordinate strength. A web that can withstand the mightiest of tanks.

3

Bedding In

Venice, December 1943

'Jilani! Here!'

Over the next few weeks I get used to General Breugal's gruff call, largely when he can't raise his increasing girth from his chair and travel the short distance from his own desk to mine to hand me a report. Which is most of the time. Venetian living clearly suits him well. I note that in the outer office, his manners are charming towards all the female workers: German and very proper. Behind his own, closed door, however, he tries to engage me in conversation on the pretext of practising his appalling Italian. It's a shame that he feels the need to attempt his impression of Casanova too, the leer on his broad face becoming frankly laughable. More than once I've had to skip out from the reach of his grasping, pudgy paw, affecting a tinkling laugh that I know is a necessary part of the facade, but that still makes me feel grubby from head to toe.

The work is challenging, mostly due to the technical nature of the translations. But it's their complexity, I'm told, which is helping the Resistance understand German movements, and, more importantly, their thinking too. My reports and the scraps from my shoes are passed promptly via a chain of Staffettas – a whole army of largely female Resistance workers, like me, used to move vital messages across Italian cities and towns. They are passed to the underground offices of the Resistance, vital information that helps to thwart Nazi efficiency in occupying our city. In office hours, I am responsible for gleaning that critical information directly from Breugal's reports and passing it on to my fellow Staffettas, organised in a network between each of the partisan battalions in Venice. Once I step out of the office, though, I become one of that army – those who slip nonchalantly into bars with girlfriends, chatting in groups, who might slide a message under the table or pass notes via a waiter in the know. A whole other band of mothers and older women are employed in the same task, secreting written missives in baby carriages, nappies and shopping bags, innocently sailing through the checkpoints set up around the city. It's merely a piece of paper, but the consequences of discovery by Nazi or fascist patrols are grave – at times, deadly. It's war work and we are all soldiers in some way.

Some evenings, I will stop for a coffee in Paolo's café, other times at a string of bars in the Castello or San Polo districts, sharing a drink and deep conversation with women I barely know as though we are best friends, looking as if there isn't a war on. As we embrace goodbye, each of us slips the other a piece of paperweight contraband, and we say '*Ciao*' with smiles and waves. I move on to my delivery destination, and she to hers, while the Nazi officers who are sometimes in our midst carry on, none the wiser. It makes my stomach flip with fear as I move away, then do somersaults of triumph when I round the corner with no patrol on my tail. I realise sometimes I actually enjoy the excitement, and it makes me think of Popsa and his defiant streak.

The pretence, however, is exhausting. I seesaw between the persona of a flighty office girl, with the daily demands on my memory for such detail, and the physical role of a Staffetta – the time and energy spent zigzagging across Venice on foot to pass messages and parcels along. What with visits to the partisan newspaper cellar at least twice a week, it means I barely see my own friends. Trips home to Mama and Papa's house, the home where I grew up in the streets around the Via Garibaldi, are once a week at best. It's not enough, but it's all I can manage with my double – no, triple – life.

'You're getting thin,' is Mama's familiar refrain as I arrive unexpectedly at her door one evening. She would be within her rights to make a flippant remark about my gracing them with my presence, but her mother's love stops her. I don't tell her I've made a message drop just two streets away, and that familiar guilt gnaws at my stomach. It's only manageable when I think of the greater good – bringing back the Venice that belongs to hard workers, honest people like my parents.

'How's work?' she asks, as she serves polenta on my plate, along with the lion's share of a thin mixed-fish stew, which needs to be stretched after my arrival.

'It's fine,' I lie. 'Lots of activity in keeping the water supplies coming in from the mainland.' I haven't told them of my move to Nazi headquarters, and I don't plan to yet – Mama worries enough. While both are confirmed partisans, sharing anti-fascist beliefs and willing to help the cause, they are not active in the way I am. Out of the corner of my eye, though, I note a twitch to Papa's normally calm face. He swipes his eyes away as I flick mine towards him.

'Stella, you should move back home again,' Mama goes on, in her unending plea. 'We could manage the household much better, and we would know you are safe. I worry about you so much. It seems as though Vito is never here either. You shouldn't be on your own.'

As with every visit, I say, 'But Mama . . .' trying to justify my need for independence. She doesn't need to know how much she would worry at my trips across Venice, sometimes on a boat to the Lido or the mainland under cover of darkness, wherever the message takes me. Her ignorance is bliss, although she doesn't know it.

Papa walks out into the yard as I'm taking out the rubbish. I know enough of undercover work now to sense the cigarette he is lighting is simply a ploy, but I don't stop what I'm doing. He draws hard and the scent catches in my nostrils, his plume of smoke a sheet of white in the cold December air. Finally he speaks.

'So how is it working in the wolf's lair?' He looks directly at me as I spin round. I say nothing, but my own stare doesn't deny it.

'What did you expect, Stella? I work in the docks – there are ears and eyes everywhere. I hear things. And people know you, care about you, enough to tell me.'

Even so, I'm shocked that the news has travelled, like a baton in a relay race, to my father. But then this war is all about information and gossip. And isn't that what I trade in, every day? 'Just don't tell Mama – please,' I entreat. 'She'll only worry. You know she's already suspicious about Vito.'

I, and perhaps Papa, know about my younger brother's place in the Resistance brigade. Coupled with his sometimes reckless pursuit for adventure, it would send Mama into a spin if she knew for sure that both her children were courting danger. On the grapevine, I hear of Vito's hunger for 'doing his duty' as a partisan and it makes me nervous; I've heard his name mentioned more than once in plans to derail troop-carrying trains into Venice, or scupper German supply boats – plans that involved explosives. Sometimes I wish my hearing wasn't so acute.

'Do you know anything about Vito?' Papa asks anxiously. Seeing my strained look, he adds: 'Please, Stella – look, I know he's in the brigade. I can't stop him doing it, but I just want to know he's safe. He disappears for days at a time.'

'Papa, I'm in a different battalion,' I sigh, and he knows what I'm saying. Either I won't or I can't talk about it. It's a mixture of both. He slumps back against the brick wall, draws on his cigarette again. The pause is leaden.

'So, how did you get the job in the Reich office?' Papa asks at last, if only to break the impasse. 'Was it Sergio who managed to place you?' His natural protectiveness towards his only daughter brings an edge to his voice, an unspoken suspicion that my own commander would willingly put me in harm's way.

'No,' I say truthfully. 'It wasn't really a choice. I was simply seconded by the Reich department, because I speak decent German.'

'Ah, the benefits of a good high school education.' He half laughs, but without humour.

'It's just a job, Papa,' I say, looking at the night sky so I don't have to meet his accusing eye.

'And I'm an Italian who hates pasta,' he says, a smirk beginning to curl his lip. Now he stubs out his cigarette and faces me, grasping my arms with both hands. 'Just be careful, my love. I know you're far smarter than you probably let them believe, but I also know you have too much of my father in you. And that's the bit that worries me. These are dangerous people.'

'The Nazis or the fascists?'

'Both,' he says resolutely.

I shrug, trying to make light of it, to protect him as much as Mama. 'I will be careful, Papa, I promise. Listen, I want to be around to see the Venice of old return. I want to preserve us as much as anyone else. That's why I need to work there.' I kiss his cheek, and make to go back inside. 'Didn't you know, I'm a good Italian girl, who adores our beloved Benito?'

'Like I say, I'm an Italian who loathes pasta,' he quips back, and follows me inside.

Christmas comes and goes – our first under the awning of occupation – and a cloak of snow covers the city, marking out the waterways and canals of the city as the lifelines that they are. Venice exists under a muffler of white powder, cut by a distinctive chipping of the icy water as the boatmen free their craft each morning. In black and white, the city somehow seems starker, better defined. And yet still so beautiful. As I lie every night under my heap of blankets, a new

40

pair of Mama's knitted socks over the old, I think of the young partisan men and women up in the mountains near Turin, fighting the elements as much as the Nazi patrols, and my heart goes out to them.

The snow, however, helps the Resistance cause in our city. To an outsider, Venice is a labyrinth at the best of times, with one *campo* looking much like another, tiny streets and alleyways virtually indistinguishable to those with an untrained eye. Under a carpet of white, it becomes a complex maze – except to those who know its cobbles and pavements off by heart. The Nazi patrols are less visible in the cold; they remain holed up in their barracks or keep warm in several bars that have become their hangouts. For a few weeks at least, I and my fellow Staffettas feel a sense of freedom as we weave our way almost unchallenged.

I have to be careful not to feel a sense of overconfidence at work. Breugal becomes less of a prowler in the office – word has it that his wife has come to soak up the Venetian sights, as if we are still some cosmopolitan centre for the rich and bored. No doubt she will fill her time drinking real and expensive coffee in Florian's on Piazza San Marco, and later have cocktails in Harry's Bar, perhaps beside the sign that clearly states: 'No Jews here'. She might parade alongside the Venetian women of a certain age who try to maintain the city's grandiose reputation, even though these days the collars of their coats are more likely to be fashioned from rabbit or cat fur than anything exotic.

In the office, then, the atmosphere feels slightly less frenetic, although Signor De Luca continues to ensure that it runs with industrial efficiency. I note he never indulges in idle gossip or lunchtime chatter, and disappears each day at 12.30

41

precisely, returning exactly thirty-five minutes later. I tend to take my own lunch as he arrives back, since those precious minutes when he's absent give me time to type frenetically while not under his watchful gaze. My position to the right of him means I can see his face as he leans over whatever document he is reading or correcting. It's always intense, eyes tracking back and forth, nostrils twitching occasionally – which strangely reminds me of Popsa reading his daily paper. Sometimes, Cristian takes off his glasses, pinches his nose with his long fingers and draws the paper nearer to his face. If he's suddenly distracted, he peers upwards without replacing his glasses and squints into the distance, adding to the look of a bibliophile. He's something of an enigma to the other office girls, who find it hard to ally his appearance with the strict work rate he demands, occasionally raising his voice to quell any chatter if it threatens to slow the steady production of reports.

'Bloody fascist,' Marta, one of the other typists, mutters if Cristian takes her to task, although it's under her breath and masked by the thunder of typewriter keys. Breugal appears to rely on him entirely – not least because his own Italian is so poor and Cristian's German crisp and fluent – and calls him into the inner office a dozen times a day with a smart 'De Luca!' though I note it's rarely with an irritated bark. For all their innate cruelty, their bulldozing of nations and countries, we in the Resistance realise the secret of Nazi success is that they know how to use people – via a combination of flattery, stealth or the simple and stark threat of death. With Cristian, Breugal is definitely on the charm offensive.

I have perhaps more to do with Cristian than some of

the other typists, because of my role as a translator. He sometimes walks over to query a word or a phrase, and if it's especially puzzling we both stand over the huge dictionary and work out the phrasing. He always smells nice, of soap and what I seem to recall is Italian cologne. Who can afford, or even access, cologne in wartime? Those that have good Nazi connections, I suppose. But still, he perplexes me. He doesn't fit – a square peg in a round hole – and yet he appears snug within the Nazi hierarchy. I resolve to be wary; Cristian De Luça is meticulous and observant. He could easily be equally as dangerous as the general controlling our occupied city.

4

Discovery

Back home in Bristol, Luisa flicks through more scraps of aged paper, the fibrous edges disintegrating a little more each time she unfolds the fragile notes. Some of the ink has begun to fade and she needs to hold the paper up to the lamp to make out the scrawl. Some are just letters, numbers or nonsensical phrases – and they are largely in Italian, with the occasional message in phonetical English. 'My beard is blond,' one says, with what is presumably the Italian equivalent below. The sometimes bizarre nature of the messages only makes her delve deeper and wonder more. She buys a cheap Italian-English dictionary and pores over the words to try to make some kind of sense of them. In the month since Luisa discovered the attic box, its content has become like the richest compost for her imagination. She finds herself racing through real, paid work, forcing herself to concentrate on its suddenly inane message, when all she wants to do is get back to her large box of intrigue.

'Lu? Lu, it's supper . . .' Jamie calls from downstairs, in a tone of early despair. He already knows he'll need to remind her several times to descend from her office in the smaller bedroom. In what seems like every spare moment, Luisa is engrossed in that box attempting to unravel the mysteries amid the dust within. Daisy sits alongside, humming with an impatient flickering of the screen, waiting for Luisa to continue the article she should be working on. Jamie sees that the collection of old paper and photographs has more than captured her imagination – it's become a purpose, perhaps morphing into an obsession of late. She's become withdrawn but not in a morbid sense, and that can only be a good thing, he thinks, given she's just lost her mum. Except he seems to have lost Luisa too. Hopefully, it's temporary. He has to be patient and wait for her to re-emerge, take her nose out of those dusty scraps and be the Luisa he knows and loves. Right now, it appears that might take some time.

Luisa runs a hand over the keys of the monochrome typewriter she brought from her mum's house, which takes pride of place in her office now. On that day of discovery in the attic, she bashed out her frustrations – though was careful to be kind to the keys, in deference to its age – and it felt good: the rhythmic tackety-tack of the mechanism winding up speed as her fingers became accustomed to the keyboard. It produced a rambling array of thoughts, now stuck in a notebook entitled 'Head space'. She's certain the machine is the origin of some of the typed pages – the dropped letter *e* bears that out – but the mystery is that some look like fact and others a kind of story, with a fictional, descriptive air. What are they doing amid the pictures of suave Italians with guns and camouflaged faces?

The office wall is now papered with a mosaic of scraps and photographs, topped off with coloured Post-it notes in Luisa's scribble, as she tries to understand the timeline and characters in this war tableau. As she reads and deciphers over her Italian dictionary, she is becoming convinced that her grandmother was more than simply a bystander to war; that she had some part to play in its direction and the eventual liberation of her city. But what part? The mystery gnaws at her, night after night as Jamie snores lightly beside her. Who was her grandmother? Certainly, someone with more to her past than Luisa could have ever imagined. And why didn't her own mother ever talk about this potentially colourful life? With her storyteller's head, it's not that much of a stretch for Luisa to imagine her grandmother as some sort of underground spy; she's sure that if it were her own mother, she would have wanted to shout it from the rooftops, been prodigiously proud.

She scrolls back in her memory of her grandmother; Luisa's own mother always seemed short with her, impatient, as if there was a long-standing feud between them. Something in her past had seemed to colour her mother's personality, making her bitter and bad-tempered towards almost everyone. Certainly, Luisa's father had retreated inside himself before his death. Yet no one ever spoke of it.

This new search, however, is a welcome distraction to those memories of home life as often cold and humourless. Luisa has researched enough articles about the grief process to know that it is undoubtedly helping with her own; to imagine something of her family within the paper bundles means she feels closer to her long-dead grandmother, whereas she struggled to find a connection with her own mother in life. Luisa has always known that her grandma Stella was a writer of novels – three or four family dramas written under the name Stella Hawthorn, but long since out of print. Just one had been on her mother's bookshelves, and Luisa had read it with pride in her early teens. It was good, a definite page-turner, filled with sumptuous descriptions of both places and emotions and a hint of her Italian past as her nineteenth-century characters travelled to and from her native country. Luisa could almost taste the gelato of Milan, imagine the gossamer pink drench of a Naples sunset, the lilt of an Italian lover against the hard vowels of an English accent. Strangely, though, there was nothing of Venice in that volume, and she's been hard at work since her mother's death in trying to trace the other three texts, trawling websites specialising in old books or second-hand texts. The publisher, sadly, has long since closed up shop and, aside from visiting every antique shop she can find, Luisa has been reduced to sending feelers out into cyberspace and eagerly checking her email every day. So far, nothing.

With the codes, warped messages and strange initials, threads begin to weave in Luisa's mind. Had her soft, demure grandmother been part of the Venetian Resistance, donned the rough uniform of a partisan soldier, or even sported a gun? Or acted as some glamorous spy working in plain sight of the Nazis, a Mata Hari character? She laughs then; her imagination is running riot. Still, it's possible in the shapeshifting of a world war. But where did her Grandpa Gio fit into all this, if at all? It makes for a puzzle of layers, and one that both frustrates and fuels her curiosity.

'Lu? Luisa! It's getting cold,' Jamie shouts, clearly irritated now, and Luisa is forced to leave her past behind and move into the present. But not for long.

5

A New Task

The early months of the year crawl by, with Venice holed up in its own weather enclave, wet and miserable. Due to the transport, the flow of Resistance reports from outside Venice slows to a trickle and it's harder to fill the newspaper with positive news. Arlo and I flesh out the gaps with Tommaso's illustrations, housewife recipes designed to eke out the week's rations, and tips on the best places to shop. As I type, it hardly feels like fighting talk, and I have to remind myself that the paper is as much about helping ordinary people as waging a military campaign. Occupation is a fight against the enemy every day, and even the foe you might tentatively smile at across the market stall could make the difference between liberty or capture. While we all live alongside our Nazi occupiers and under the shadow of their politics, people still have to eat — small trade crafts come and go across the water, gondoliers who once conveyed tourists now scrape a living as supply carriers, avoiding the wash of ominous German gunboats, their weapons cocked and ready. Venetian life, though, functions in spite of our unwelcome visitors and the drone of aircraft passing like small swarms of bees overhead. Like people throughout Italy and Europe, we carry on.

There's a welcome gap in the clouds in mid-February. At Nazi command, I take the cover off my works typewriter early one morning and see a tiny folded square of paper under one footing. I scout around the office – only Marta is humming to herself as she lays out some of the day's work. I'd never had her down as a Staffetta, but equally I'm not supposed to be one either, so her innocent enough looks could be her best ally. Looking around me, I slide out the note and pocket it quickly. Cristian strides into the office, looking strangely upbeat and sporting something like a smile.

'Good morning, all,' he says, in Italian this time, since it's only Marta and myself, and then, 'Good morning Signorina. Are you well?'

I stammer something positive and quickly make my excuses to go to the toilet. The note has all the hallmarks of Resistance, using language and a code known only to my local battalion. It says to meet a contact in the corner of Campo San Polo and await further instructions. I deposit the piece of paper in my heel and head back to the office, barely suppressing my happiness. The tone of the note doesn't sound like a routine message drop; perhaps there's something I'm needed for, a task that will make me feel of even more value to the cause.

Cristian looks up as I return to the office, with a smile to accompany.

'Ah Signorina Jilani, you're back—'

'Sorry. I'm needing to visit the—'

'Yes, yes, no mind at all,' he says, moving towards my desk, a large book in his hand. 'I simply wanted to give you this.' And he lays the volume down. It's a thick, dictionary-like tome of technical translations. 'I thought it might make life easier,' he says. 'For all those tricky words you – we – ponder over.' Despite tiny flecks of grey in his beard, he looks like a boy who's just given his teacher the shiniest, plumpest apple. There's a proud half-smile under the bristles of his neatly clipped beard.

For a few seconds, I'm stumped for a reaction – part of me thinks I've already been found out, and it's his warped sense of humour presenting me with a fait accompli. Any minute now a line of fascist police will come thundering through the door to escort me to a dungeon somewhere and an unthinkable future. But the expression on Cristian's face says he's genuinely pleased at the giving. And there is no rumble of footsteps up the marble staircase. I really wish in that moment that he didn't sport a death's head badge, so I could like him more.

'Well, thank you,' I manage. 'It will undoubtedly be very useful.' Part of me wants to laugh at the ridiculous nature of it – the fact that a fascist overseer is helping a member of the Resistance better translate valuable documents. And yet, I don't want to laugh at him. I hate to admit it, but it's a very human act of consideration.

'Thank you, Signor De Luca,' I say again. 'I do appreciate it.'

He looks about the office, making sure that Marta is out of earshot. 'Cristian, please.' He turns and sits back at his desk.

The clock hands crank slowly towards 5.30, and I am packing up as the hand strikes half past, a jangle of emotions inside but careful to appear outwardly relaxed, as if it's just another end of a normal day. Cristian is still hard at work on his document and looks up only briefly to say goodbye. I have to walk fast to weave my way through the network of streets towards Campo San Polo, taking time to double back, stopping to window-shop as a way of ensuring that no one is following. No matter the hurry, it's been drummed into us that checking is vital. It saves lives – ours and many others possibly. I feel sure the way is clear as I enter the vast *campo*, and head towards the church entrance – it's a good place to loiter at this time of day, as I could easily be one of the worshippers making their way in for evening service, the resounding clanging of the bells calling them to prayer. Ever since I was a small girl, the deep chime of church bells across the city has felt like a security blanket; present each and every day, enduring through war and famine. I feel sure that if they carry on, so can we.

Several older women pass by, bundled in their winter coats, rosaries in hand, looking at me quizzically. They are followed by a few men, some with the hint of a leer. I ignore each, stamping my feet against the cold, and they move on. Ten minutes go by and I'm wondering if my contact will arrive at all – the meet will be cancelled if any fascist patrols are nearby. Any longer and I will start to look suspicious, meaning I'll have to simply walk away, affecting the irritated look of a woman being stood up by her date, swallowing the pitying looks of those around me. That's the role of a Staffetta.

In the next minute he comes from behind me, swings

around in front and makes to kiss me on both cheeks. In the split second before, I see the subtlest of nods and a raise of eyebrows that signal: it's fine, play along.

'Gisella! So sorry to be late. Can you forgive me?' he cries, at just the right pitch to be heard, but short of a bad actor overprojecting on stage. As he moves to kiss my cheek, he whispers: 'Lino.' Gisella and Lino, young lovers. He's used my Resistance code name so I'm happy to slip into the lie.

'I forgive you, Lino – just this once,' and I tease out a smile.

'Shall we go?' He proffers a hand and I take it, skipping alongside him like a woman excited to be with her lover.

He leads me through several streets towards the Croce district and we work hard at playing the convincing couple as we pass by others in the street. 'How was your day?' he questions. 'What did you have for lunch?'

Eventually, we reach a darkened alleyway, pass under a low, stone *sotto* archway, opening out into a courtyard of houses. It's empty aside from a traditional stone well to one side, and 'Lino' leads me to a darkened door. He raps three times on the door, pauses and knocks three more times. The door opens and we climb a set of granite stairs, not dirty but dank, as though someone has brought in canal water to wash them. My heart is pumping, although my breathing is under control for now. In these situations, I always question: *Does this feel right?* In a strange place, where no one knows where I am. It has to be.

Once we go through a door on the second floor I relax. There's a welcome orange glow of light in several rooms of the apartment, and an older woman emerges from the kitchen, a vegetable knife in hand, but sporting a big smile.

'*Ciao* Mama,' Lino says, 'this is a friend.' He leads me to the living room as she retreats to the kitchen.

'Please sit,' he says.

It's now his demeanour changes. Not brusque or unfriendly, just more businesslike. Now we can drop the facade. I don't ask his real name, since it's best not to know, and I'm not likely to see him again.

'The brigade commander has asked if you can be part of one more task,' he says, his brown eyes wide and intent. My own eyes flick up with surprise and pleasure – there's not much I won't do for Sergio Lombardi, a loyal Venetian and a good friend of my grandfather's since the fascists took control of Italy back in the 1920s.

Months before, when the Allies stormed Southern Italy and it was effectively sliced in two – the Nazis to the north and Allies occupying below Rome – Italians were forced to make a choice between fascism and the fight. Mussolini took up comfortable residence in Salò with his puppet govern-ment, its strings pulled by Berlin, and the Italian army was effectively dismissed, but thousands of ordinary Italians raised arms of protest and guns in a different vein. There was a buzzing in the *campos* and cafés as Resistance fighters emerged from the woodwork, small bands of partisans willing to give their lives for Italy's freedom. Those who couldn't actively fight pledged their support in any way they could; patriot shopkeepers stored covert messages, and elderly couples gave up their homes as safe houses for pursued partisans, risking life and liberty. In its underbelly, Venice was fizzing with sedition.

I still remember that intense feeling when Armando Gavagnin activated the partisan cause in Piazza San Marco, raising his fist and standing tall on a table outside Florian's, the oldest of Venetian cafés and a hot spot for age-old rebellion. My throat was dry as I listened to his calling on Venetians to fight, so fired up that I was ready to give up my job, ditch my skirt suits and don trousers and neckerchief, rifle in my arms. For Venice and Italy. For Popsa to be proud.

It was Sergio, the new leader of the Venetian brigade, who persuaded me otherwise back then, toning down my revolutionary fervour and persuading me I'd be more use on the inside, waging war with information. 'You can be the mouse to outwit the large, predatory cat,' he had phrased it, with his bushy eyebrows dancing a lifetime of mischief. 'Bide your time,' he advised me. 'Without the likes of you we are an army fighting blind. We need your eyes and ears in the works department.'

His weathered, open face made me think of my grandfather in his younger days – so sure that we would triumph. Even then, Sergio made me feel like a soldier, albeit with heels and a handbag. Yet that romantic image of fighting for the cause has never left me. I want – I need – to make a difference. Perhaps now I can.

'Lino' speaks again, bringing me back to the moment. 'Sergio also insists that you can say no if you want – we're all aware how much you are doing right now.'

'I'm fine,' I say. 'I can manage. What is it?'

'You'll be contacted on your next trip to the newspaper office on Giudecca in two days. There's a job we need doing there, and, as you're already back and forward frequently, it will raise less suspicion if it's you.'

I leave soon after, despite the kitchen mama generously

offering to share their evening meal. I'm hungry, but this is business, and 'Lino' deserves his privacy.

I walk home thinking how exhausted I am day to day. This new task is one more thing to draw on my senses, forcing me to be on constant alert. Yet I'm also excited as I walk the long stretch towards home at a pace. I know my contribution can never compare to some of the suffering or sacrifice in this war, and I want to do what I can, when I can.

The two days before my next visit to the newspaper cellar drag by. At times, my day job and the German translations appear turgid and unimportant, although I still have to feed the details via my regular contacts so the Resistance are able to further sift through the information. Cristian De Luca is largely absent and General Breugal is in a foul mood, barking orders and stomping about the office in frustration, upending trays of typewritten notes in a childlike temper.

I feel a sense of relief as I hit the cold, fresh air and cross the wide canal towards Giudecca, enjoying the roll of the boat and the slapping of the water against its sides. It's tempered when a small German patrol boat cuts across us, sailors shouting over the engine's throaty roar, making my insides swell along with the water. But what words I catch are nothing sinister, general chit-chat only, and I breathe again.

When I arrive, Matteo is at his usual place behind the bar, a few customers in front of him, but as I move to take off my coat he passes me a tied linen package.

'My wife asks if you can take this to one of the nuns at Santa Eufemia,' he says. 'She's laid up with a bad back.' His tone is relaxed, as if it's the most natural of favours to ask.

'Of course,' I say. 'I won't be long.' Since Matteo has never before used me as a general messenger, I guess it's something to do with my new Resistance task.

The wind whips up a spray as I walk along the waterfront towards the church and I pull the frayed wool of my coat closer. Santa Eufemia is an ancient building with a long history but, compared to some of the more notable churches in Venice, it's rundown and slightly scruffy. The vast, vaulted space is empty of bodies as I enter through the scratched doorway, but warm compared to outside. I make the sign of the cross, take a seat in a front pew, and wait. When there are no other instructions, you simply wait. There's lots of meandering and staring into space when you're a Staffetta.

I consider taking this opportunity to pray – it would please Mama certainly. But I have never been especially religious and the war, with its stories of families being torn apart, severe beatings for no apparent reason than thought crime against fascism, has taken what faith I had left. I wonder if it will ever come back to me.

I barely hear the soft footsteps of someone approaching, only sensing the gentle waft of her habit as a nun approaches. She comes and sits next to me.

'Evening Sister,' I say. 'I have something for you.' I offer up the parcel, and she smiles and rises.

'Come,' she says.

We move behind the altar, through the vestry and beyond into a corridor, the air colder as we step into an open walkway behind the church. On the opposite side of the small garden is an old brick building that looks like a store-room, with just two blacked-out windows above head height.

The nun gets out an old key from under her habit, so big it looks almost theatrical. She unlocks the door, glances left and right, and ushers me in. There's a glow from a candle in one corner, and from the gloom nearby I hear a single cough. A shifting movement seems to disturb the combination of soap and disinfectant, plus the musty, aged smell all such buildings have.

'Sister Cara – is that you?' a voice croaks.

'I've brought you a visitor,' the nun says, and there's some more shuffling, although no one approaches.

'You'll have to go to him,' she says to me. 'He can't get up.'

She brings another candle and sets it down on an upturned wooden box acting as a table. The cast of light outlines a man, his well-worn, dark clothes peeking out from under a rough woollen blanket. His face is grimy, and in his hairline are crusts of dried blood he hasn't managed to wash away. Out of the bottom of the blanket sticks a limb, braced with wooden struts and heavily bandaged, a loose old sock unceremoniously stuck over his toes.

'Welcome to my humble abode,' the man says in Italian, and there's a grimace as he tries to haul himself into a sitting position on the old metal bed.

'No, no don't move!' I say in alarm. I pull up a wooden box that looks hardy enough and sit on it. He extends a hand from his half-sitting, half-lying position. Less grimy but not clean.

'Pleased to meet you,' he says, breathing heavily with the effort. 'It's nice to have a visitor. Thank you for coming.'

His Italian is faultless but his accent is strange – foreign perhaps? There's a small pause during which we simply size each other up. He is handsome under the fresh scratches around his high cheekbones and forehead, dark and with full lips. He looks Italian, but that accent . . .

A boat horn honks outside and breaks the spell.

'So, I've been told you need some help,' I say.

He laughs good-naturedly, despite his obvious discomfort. 'Yes, clearly wasn't as good a parachutist as I thought.' And he looks down at his prostrate leg. 'Well and truly broken.'

He was part of an Allied parachute mission, he explains, designed to drop in radio sets for dispersal across the north of the country, allowing the partisans vital links with the outside world. There are unknown numbers of Allied soldiers still stranded after the Nazi invasion without any contact, as the Germans cleverly suspended all Italian radio communications when they occupied the country in September '43. Since then, we in Venice have relied heavily on Radio Londra, the BBC's daily broadcast to Italians, to bring us coded messages about partisan and enemy movements. But Radio Londra is reliant on a good radio signal and we know the fascists have spent millions of lira on jamming equipment to prevent such dispatches reaching us. Even a small network of radios would improve communications between the Allies and the Italian Resistance, but they are of little use lying dormant in this church.

'Thankfully my radio equipment fared better than me and it's intact,' he adds. 'Would you be willing to transport it across to the main island?'

I think of how big the equipment might be, how I will hide it and look in no way suspicious. A larger bag would almost certainly be searched by a fascist patrol. Even in the gloom, this man sees the working of my mind.

61

'Don't worry, it comes apart in multiple pieces,' he says. I see the white of his teeth in his smile. It's nice. He looks friendly, genuine.

'How small?' I wonder.

'I can make each package small enough for your handbag, at worst a small shopping bag. But it will mean several trips.'

'I'm here on Giudecca twice a week, but I can easily manage another trip,' I say, not daring to think how I will fit it into my life.

'Well, I'm not going anywhere, not for a while,' he quips, and taps the brace on his useless leg. I feel sorry for him, trapped in this dank hole. He's undoubtedly well looked after by the sisters, but he must be bored stiff.

'Is there anything I can bring you? Books, or a newspaper?' I offer.

His face lights up. 'A book would be wonderful, even a cheap thriller would lift my head out of here for a while.'

I get up to go, and hold out my hand to shake his. 'I can be back in two days. Is that enough time to get the first parcel ready?'

'Plenty,' he replies. 'I look forward to it . . .' and he's clearly hanging out for my name.

I look at him intently – the expression that says no names are safer.

'Please,' he says. 'Listen, I'm a sitting duck here. I don't think names between us will make much difference. It's just nice to have contact with the outside world.'

'Stella,' I say after a pause, for no other reason than I think I can trust him.

'Jack,' he offers back, still holding onto my fingers.

'Jack? Surely that's English?'

'Which I am – sort of. It's Giovanni, really. But everyone at home calls me Jack. Except my mother, of course.'

The perfect Italian with a foreign accent suddenly fits into place, and the fact that he's part of an Allied operation.

'Seemingly, they thought I would be better equipped to blend in, with having Italian parents,' he adds. 'Only they didn't reckon my coming down on some very hard Italian stone. Just my luck.'

I find it difficult to concentrate as I return to the bar and descend into the cellar. Arlo is already starting to lay some pages – I have to work fast to catch up. At the back of my mind, projecting a very distinct image, is this evening's earlier meeting – both Jack, and the job ahead of me. Every time I make the journey over to Giudecca I'm breaking fascist law, since even owning a wireless tuned into Radio Londra can earn you jail time. Being caught creating anti-fascist propaganda will undoubtedly result in far worse than that. Each paper message I transport is heavily weighted contraband, and yet it has never felt dangerous, or potentially fatal. It's just what I do. I wonder if adding one more task is pushing my luck? And whether I will live – or die – regretting it?

6

Two Sides of the Coin

Venice, late February 1944

It seems like a lengthy wait until my next visit to Giudecca – to Jack and the task ahead of me in transporting his hand-made receivers. Luckily, Mimi is there to distract me.

'So, come on, tell me all,' my oldest and best friend says as we nestle into the corner space of a crowded bar in the Santa Croce district. It's tucked down a side street and not widely known by Nazi or fascist soldiers. Still, we're careful to keep our voices low, hunkering under a fog of cigarette smoke for cover. Mimi's big eyes are even wider than normal, her painted red lips pursed in anticipation. With her near-black curls, she often reminds me of the American cartoon character, Betty Boop, though Mimi is infinitely more beautiful.

'I've made contact with an Allied soldier, and I'm to transport some vital packages,' I tell her. Saying it aloud still makes me fizzle with both nerves and excitement, and I can see Mimi – a seasoned Staffetta herself – is impressed. I tell her why the soldier can't deliver the radios himself and she's aghast at the story. Since Mimi also has a reputation as a shameless matchmaker, I brush her off when she asks whether Jack is good-looking, saying simply, 'He's very grubby.'

For all her flightiness, Mimi understands the risk I'm taking. 'Be careful,' she says, although she knows I will be, as we all are — have been trained to be. We are all too aware of the consequences of being caught; man, woman or child, the Nazi and fascist regimes are uncompromising when it comes to betrayal.

Being with Mimi, full of fun and smiles, and talking about her latest flirtations, is the release I need when I'm holding myself in for days at a time, strapping myself into a straitjacket of a different persona, whether it's at the Reich office or slipping into another guise as a Resistance messenger. It's good to feel like the real Stella, even for just a few hours, and we dip into what I've come to think of as 'normal conversation', events untouched by war — the handsome operator at the telephone exchange where she works by day, and her plans to secure his affections. 'You're incorrigible,' I say to her, although I'm full of admiration for Mimi's ability to rise above the dense cloud of conflict. She's not unaffected, but she refuses to let it crush her natural optimism.

'You never know, my current fancy could well have a nice friend,' she says with mischief.

'Stop that, Mimi!' I chide her. While I'm not averse to having someone in my life, I just can't fit them into it right now.

The next day passes slowly, and I find myself willing the clock to go faster and release me from the endless tapping and chatter. At lunch, I simply have to escape the stifling Reich office and take a walk along the water towards the Arsenale, drinking in my share of the sun's glittery reflection on the lagoon. Reluctantly, I cut into the side streets behind, where the sun is spliced with shadows and there's an instant chill, knowing there are some second-hand bookshops I can trawl through to pick up a few cheap volumes for Jack. My own shelves are full of mostly Italian classics, and I'm not sure he would be in the mood for the classically Italian Boccaccio, amusing though he is. I pick out something light, and then an English copy of Agatha Christie's *Murder in Mesopotamia*, thinking it really will take his mind far from Venice. I treat myself to a cheap, dog-eared Italian translation of Jane Austen's *Persuasion*, having left my old copy at my parents' house.

I'm walking back towards the office when I spy someone familiar standing on a small bridge gazing intently into the still canal water, his elbows leant on the brickwork. I make to turn sharply, away from the waterside. Too late – he pulls up his stare and clearly recognises me. His expression means I have no choice but to approach Cristian De Luca like the friendly colleague that I am, the pleasing office girl and follower of our great leader, Il Duce.

'Have you spotted the answer to the universe in there, or simply some poor unfortunate after a night with too much grappa?' I say lightly.

He looks up, smiles instead of grimaces, catching my humour. 'No, I'm just admiring the shapes, the sunlight. It's beautiful.'

He's right. The reflection of the houses onto the green channel creates warped lines and colours, like some enticing, modernist painting. Every second, each subtle swirl morphs the scene into something more beautiful.

'See, even the water is art in Venice,' he says.

'Really? Even under the cloak of war?' I turn my eyes away from the water and upwards, to the drone of aircraft overhead – perhaps Allied bombers determined to lay waste to some poor unsuspecting Italian city, either Turin or Pisa. No one around us scrambles for cover; in among the revered beauty of Venice, we're generally safe, as it's those vessels out on the lagoon – fishermen or ferries – that run the risk of being strafed with bullets.

He smiles some understanding, showing white teeth and full lips under his neat moustache. I watch his brown eyes track across my face, trying to read me. I've seen that deep, enquiring look before – in Nazi and fascist officers, trying to scan inside you for the dirty truths hidden behind the inno-cent facade. I'm still unsure what Cristian's motives are though.

Finally, he lets out a laugh. 'You Venetians! You're far more practical than the city itself, clearly.'

'Perhaps it's a good thing we don't wear our rose-tinted glasses all the time, or we wouldn't have a city to wallow in,' I shoot back, though with an element of humour. 'Plus, we would fall in the canal far too often – and that's never good for anyone's health.'

He pauses to ponder again, eyes on the water, as if he can't steal them away. I'm just about to walk on when he raises himself up to his full height alongside me. Now I'm genuinely curious.

'So tell me, what were you really thinking? Not about to toss yourself in, I hope?' I add.

'If you must know, I was wondering how many people – classes, creeds and colours – have travelled under this bridge over the centuries. What they would have worn, talked about, were eating, drinking or reading.' He looks at me directly, like it's not a musing or a rhetorical question. It's the longest conversation we've ever had. And the most revealing. 'Do you ever wonder that, Signorina Jilani?' he adds.

I have, many times. Despite its familiarity, and the practicalities of living in a place that hovers between reality and fantasy, I spent endless hours of my childhood pondering over the colours and past opulence of my own city, the love stories buried in the mud, alongside the wooden piles on which Venice is suspended. Some of those stories were created in my head, to be crudely drawn on the paper while sitting in the kitchen next to my grandfather, as he smoked and dozed. It's the war that has halted my imaginings on the past or the future, stone dead. Much like my lack of religious faith, I hope it's temporary. These days, I dream only in grey – a slate war hue. The Venice of now is all that matters; day by day, it must survive and bring with it some sort of future, so we can bring back the colour and vitality to our city.

Cristian's brow furrows at my silence, and I bring myself back from a sugary nostalgia. 'So, do you wonder what it might have been like?' he presses.

'A darn sight smellier, I would imagine,' I reply, and turn abruptly off the bridge, in the direction of the Platzkommandantur. I'm purposely glib because I don't want him tapping into what's in my head, either past or present. I hear his footsteps as he follows, several steps behind me. Perhaps he imagines – rightly so – that I wouldn't want to be seen walking with a badge-toting collaborator. And yet I don't feel any hatred towards him, only slight pity. There is a heart inside him, clearly – one capable of deep feeling. It's only a shame about the shell he covers it with.

He catches up with me, the clip of his smart shoes resounding through the alleyways. We pass wordlessly under a covered walkway leading to an open street. There's an old man under the oncoming archway lighting a cigarette and he looks up as we approach.

'Good day,' he says and smiles at us both. 'Come to express your devotion?' He's clearly amused at his own humour.

I know exactly what he's referring to – the small, reddish heart-shaped stone standing proud above the arch brickwork, a natural relic apparently, and a popular pilgrimage for tourists and lovers alike. I try to satisfy him with a weak smile, but the old man is having none of it.

'You need to touch it,' he insists, 'the both of you.'

Cristian is looking perplexed, and I go to explain swiftly so that we can move on, but the old man is in full flow.

'It's an old tale from centuries ago,' he rambles. 'If you both touch the stone your love will be sealed forever,' and he coughs from too many cigarettes, chuckling to himself as he shuffles off.

Cristian looks at me for clarity. 'It's true,' I say. 'Or at least it's true that's what the myth says.' I duck under the stone *sotto* before he can ask any more.

He catches up again. 'What is it, Signorina Jilani – don't you believe in fairy stories?'

He's smiling once more and I see he's looking directly at the volume of Jane Austen clutched in my hand.

'Oh, this? This isn't a fairy story,' I come back, striding ahead to avoid any awkward conversation. 'It's literature.'

'I agree,' he says. 'It's very good literature. But equally, it's not real life, is it?'

'All the better in this day and age,' I snipe, though not

meaning to do so quite so sharply. 'Everyone deserves a place of fantasy and safety.'

'I couldn't agree more,' he says. But he's no longer smiling or making light, and we walk the rest of the way in silence.

It gets me thinking, though. Cristian De Luca, as much as I hate to admit it, has touched a nerve. I indulge in past centuries and places away from this war by devouring what books I can, on the occasions I'm able to stay awake after the day's activities. But I miss the creation; as a journalist, I indulged my free time in writing short stories, one or two of which were published in sister publications of *Il Gazzettino*. It was a total release to open up my beloved machine and simply lay down sentences and words, fabricate people and conversations, without once glancing at notes or quotes. I felt free.

I realise war has stifled me since then. Unsurprising, given the simple desire and effort to stay alive. All the same, I find myself resenting it. Typing up the news stories for the partisan paper comes easily, almost automatically. But it's not me – yes, there's a passion in the aim for freedom, but nothing of my heart in the words, despite Arlo's teasing about my lyrical language. I resolve to try and write. As me, for me. Just for pleasure. Is that so wrong in the times we live in?

If only I could stay awake at the day's end and find the time.

7

New Interest

Venice, March 1944

Jack is a little more mobile on my next visit. He's out of bed when I arrive, although limping with obvious difficulty. The sisters have rigged up a table with an oil lamp for him to work at, and there's an array of metal pieces strewn across it. His welcome is warm; he's clearly glad to have anyone visit, and is even more delighted with the books I've brought.

'Amazing!' he says. 'I do love a good Agatha Christie. Listen, can I offer you some tea? I had some in my pack as I dropped in, and the lovely sisters have given me a small stove.'

I look at my watch, wondering how much time I have.

'We Brits are very good at tea,' he urges. 'Put it this way, you wouldn't want my coffee!'

I've rushed from work, barely having had time to eat or drink, so I say yes, but I can't stay too long. Arlo will be thinking I've abandoned him.

Jack hobbles to and fro on a makeshift crutch, clearly in pain, but doing his best not to show it. I'm not normally much of a tea drinker, but this is good, stronger than I usually take it. I ask him about his home, and he adopts a sanguine look for a moment, telling me his parents run a delicatessen in central London. 'We're surrounded by Italian families – sometimes I'm not really sure which part of the world I really do belong to. But' – he holds up his mug – 'I am a bit of a tea lover, so I must have some English in me!'

'Were you born there?' I ask.

'Turin,' he says. 'My parents emigrated when I was a baby. Both families are still in Turin, so obviously that's a worry. Not much news gets out. Which is partly why I volunteered. I know I'm unlikely to find any trace of them in this chaos, but at least I feel I'm doing my bit for the family, for Italy.'

I understand his need, and I warm to him all the more. He asks about my family, and I tell him about Mama and Papa, and a little of my past life. He has a copy of *Venezia Liberare* on the side and it's clear he knows who writes the words, telling me: 'It's good. Engaging, fighting talk.' I feel it's not flattery, but rather his open manner, causing me to trust him almost from the outset. So much so that when he tells me about his brother still missing in action in France, I feel I can open up my concern over Vito's role in the Resistance, of which I still know little detail, but even the scant gossip in the battalion makes my heart crease at the danger he could be in. I stop short, however, of telling Jack about my day job in the Nazi headquarters. *I* know my own motivations, my reasons and the work I do, but even so, it feels hard to defend.

We part with my nestling a small parcel in my handbag,

little more than the size of an orange and wrapped in an old rag. Its destination is a house not far from my own apartment, and I'm to deliver it early the following morning, before work. The next section will be ready in three days.

'I'll see you then,' I say as I head towards the door.

'I look forward to it,' he says, his broad smile apparent in the gloom. And I can't help feeling I will too.

What odd surprises this war springs upon us.

The journey back to the mainland, with the small but seditious package in my handbag, causes ripples of uncertainty inside me, even though the tide under the boat is oddly calm. As I step onto the cobbles of the main island, each stride heightens my anxiety and I have to stop myself hugging the stone walls of the alleyways to stay out of sight. I've made hundreds of journeys across the city with covert messages, but none so risky as this. I can feel my breathing deepen as I try to sidestep one checkpoint, but walk too late into another barrier, only recently set up.

'Evening, Signorina,' the fascist patrolman greets me, and I smile widely, affecting a half wink in his direction, while trying my utmost to make it seem genuine. Am I trying too hard? *Be natural, Stella, be calm*, I chant inside my head. *You have nothing to hide.* I go to open my handbag as a matter of routine, but as the top flips up, he waves me on, his eyes dressing me down as I go. He doesn't see my knees almost fail me when I round the corner. I have to stop and take several conscious breaths on the pretence of blowing my nose, then there comes a swift rush of adrenalin which causes me to smile and puts a spring in my step. Still, I'm exhausted by the time I reach my apartment, as well as elated. I realise part of what drives me is the unknown, that cat and mouse with the Nazi regime that Sergio alluded to. I wonder if it's a good or bad trait for an underground soldier to have.

The package drop to my target destination the next morning is uneventful, thankfully, and strangely I'm relishing some of the dull routine of Breugal's office. It's Cristian's behaviour, however, which proves out of the ordinary. Breugal is away from Venice on war business, and the office is naturally more relaxed. The tall and sombre Captain Klaus takes the opportunity to strut around, attempting to issue orders, but he barely seems more than a boy in a man's cloak and doesn't share the bear-like stature of Breugal. I see some of the girls simply titter behind his back and I feel almost sorry for him. In these times, it's Cristian whom the typists defer to, and some of the German officers too.

I'm struggling with a particularly complex engineering report when he approaches me nearing lunch.

'Signorina Jilani,' he begins – in Italian, which makes my head snap up with curiosity. 'I wonder if I might have a word with you. In private. Perhaps you can join me for lunch?'

I can almost feel the blood drain from my head. I'm not prone to fainting, but for a brief second, I think I might. I take a deep breath and realign my head. He smiles – it seems quite genuine. But then Nazis and fascists alike are good at smiling as they deliver the death knell.

'Um, yes, of course,' I stumble. What else can I say?

At 12.15, he puts down his report and tidies his pens, a signal that he's ready. He approaches the desk.

'I'll follow you out in a second,' I say, before he has the chance for anything else. Nonetheless, I feel several pairs of female eyes dressing me down as I get up and leave – their smirks especially boring into my back. How much more like a collaborator can I feel?

Cristian is waiting in the lobby, and leads me not to the building's canteen – which I'd hoped for – but out into the bright spring sunshine; he lifts his head automatically to catch the warmth, a look of satisfaction spreading across his face, as if he's refuelling. For what, I can only imagine. We walk a few minutes to a café in a side street off San Marco, and I'm both thankful and wary that it's quiet. The waiter knows him well, so it's obviously a favourite place. We order coffee and sandwiches with whatever bread and filling they have. It's when the waiter leaves that there's a void.

'So, have you had more grand philosophical thoughts on Venice?' I begin in a tone that says I'm teasing, but only a little. My training has taught me the art of small talk, rather than risk leaving a hole where doubts can breed.

He laughs as he sips at his coffee. 'No, no it's all right, the population of Venice is safe from my musings.' He looks at me fixedly, as if about to reveal something profound, of himself perhaps. Here it is, I think, the interrogation, under the cloak of an innocent lunch date. He's cornered me out in the open.

'I was really wondering if you might do me the honour of coming to an evening function with me?' he says, suddenly taking a deep interest in his near-empty cup. Then, no doubt sensing the look of shock on my face, he adds, 'I mean it's fine if you can't. I just thought I'd ask. General Breugal is away and it's one of those pompous, military parties and it would be . . .'

Now he's not the assured, calm and controlled Cristian

De Luca of the Reich office. He's flushed under his beard and I wonder how many women he has ever asked out, in this life or before.

'Um, I would be delighted,' I say, only just remembering that my loyal fascist self would see it as a real honour – ever the compliant typist happy to fraternise with German officers and saviours of the Italian nation. Inside, the dread is already rising at the prospect of being in such close proximity to the grey and black characters of war. But what a gift to the Resistance, what tittle-tattle I might be able to pick up and pass on to my unit command. Even if it saves one life, one uprooted family, it will be worth the indignity. I smile sweetly, my face doing its best to express radiance.

'I'm so pleased,' he says, equally unseated. He leans in, as if in some form of schoolboy collusion. 'If it's a real bore, at least we can stand in the corner and talk literature.'

Which is a cue for us to do just that now, swapping favourites and stories. The hour passes – I'm ashamed to admit later – quite pleasantly.

'Oh,' he says, as we get up to head back to the office. 'In all this talk I almost forgot this.' He pulls out a small package from his jacket, wrapped loosely in brown paper. As I peel off the covering, I see it's a small, beautifully bound Italian edition of Austen's *Pride and Prejudice* – second-hand but in good condition.

'Thank you,' I say. And I mean it. It's a book I love, and will read again and again. And I'm genuinely taken aback at his thoughtfulness.

'You probably already have it,' he adds awkwardly. 'I mean, it's her best work. Or at least I think so.'

I look at him directly. 'Are you referring to the writing

or all the hidden meanings?' I aim to diffuse with a little humour, and I'm smiling as I say it, but it comes out in a different vein. As a challenge almost.

But Cristian De Luca is back to his controlled, assured self. 'Both,' he says, as we begin walking. 'Elizabeth Bennet, she's one of my favourite characters – smart and knowing. I thought you might like her too.'

And much as we did on our previous encounter, we head back to the dark austerity of the office in silence, drinking in the bright white light of Venice.

I'm forced to relay my frustrations to Mimi as we queue for bread in the market just days later.

'I mean, what am I to think of a fascist who gives me sensitive literature, after inviting me to a party destined to be full of Nazis?' I whisper, careful to contain my voice, with ears all about us.

Mimi's chestnut eyes stare back at me, trying to hide her mirth. As my best friend since school, I want her opinion more than anyone's; for years now, we've laid every secret bare, unaware at the time that discretions about schoolboys and wishes were child's play compared to what's at stake now. Still, she says nothing, knowing I'm not quite finished yet.

'I suppose he could simply need a girl on his arm, just to make a good impression at the party,' I ponder.

'And he could have asked almost any girl in the office,' Mimi pitches in at last. 'There's a reason he chose you.'

'No! I've never given him any encouragement, Mimi. Not in that way.'

'Maybe not, and maybe you don't need to. Just face it,

Stella – those dark, mysterious looks of yours are attractive to men, despite you imagining yourself in some grubby old shirt up in the mountains, with your wild hair flying on a partisan raid.'

'But a fascist? Really?' I sigh. 'He's deep in Breugal's pocket.'

'All the better for the cause,' Mimi says defiantly. As a fellow Staffetta, she knows the benefits of talk loosened by an excess of good cheer and alcohol. And a pretty girl on a man's arm, I think to myself with dread.

'Anyway, tell me about the other one – the soldier on Giudecca,' Mimi urges as we find a quiet corner table in Paolo's café. 'He sounds nice.'

'Jack. He is – I like talking to him.'

'And is this one into literature and the arts?'

'Not sure – I don't get that feeling. We talk mainly about family, or the war. Sometimes about the cinema.'

'So, you don't fancy a trip to London after this is all over then?' Mimi is being deliberately flighty, bent on teasing me.

'No I don't,' I say flatly. 'Besides, he'll be long gone soon, as soon as his leg is halfway mended. I won't see him again.'

Mimi won't let up. 'Strange things happen in wartime,' she grins. 'It's a time of change, all right.'

But I'm not concentrating. I'm thinking about how I will survive the next few days, in being a clandestine carrier for the Resistance, and then donning my best dress and mingling among the Nazi High Command. That's as much of a seesaw as I can manage for now.

The first step, however, is to transport Jack's second parcel across the canal from Giudecca. This time, I finish the news-paper work a good half hour early, largely due to an absence of real reports from the Veneto's partisan groups – it seems there can be pockets of quiet, even in a war. Luckily, Tommaso is on hand with his pen – sharp in more ways than one – to whip up an apt cartoon. I hear both him and Arlo giggling behind me at Tommaso's latest caricature of 'Il Duce', painting him as the clown that my own Popsa predicted he would be.

'You should make him even fatter than that!' Arlo teases.

'He's already busting out of his uniform,' Tommaso argues. 'Besides, there's not enough space to fit in all of his girth!' The two pitch back and forth, a background noise that makes me smile, and I half wish it was Vito sharing the work with Arlo and Tommaso, instead of being out there risking himself.

The other pages of the paper we fill with news of the war in Europe, gleaned from Radio Londra. Once again, I'm grateful to the army of grandmothers listening slavishly to the broadcasts next to their stoves, scratching their reports in the dim kitchen light.

I leave the team about to print, as I change roles once again and head to the vast, empty space of Santa Eufemia. I duck behind the altar and catch myself pulling at several stray strands of hair and tucking them away.

'Silly woman,' I mutter to myself.

Jack is at his desk, peering into the spotlight and fiddling with a screwdriver.

'Ah,' he says. 'I was just about to put on some water for tea. I'm assuming you've come early for the best seat at Café Giovanni?'

'Nothing less than your best table, Signore,' I say, sitting on the wooden box.

He's still packaging the latest parcel, but I'm not late. I'll easily make the curfew, I tell myself. I'm happy to stay. Eager even.

We talk about our different lives again – him quizzing me about growing up on the fantasy island of Venice, hopping on a boat to go anywhere, the isolation of living out on a limb in the lagoon.

'I'm sure Venetians never think of it as isolation,' I say. 'It's more like our cocoon of water makes us special. That it's the rest of the world which has it wrong, in living on swathes of solid land.'

'Some people might call that elitist – grandiose,' Jack says, offering me a cup of his special brew.

'They might,' I concede. 'But you know, we've been taken over – borne plagues and invasions – that many times, I don't think we care any more. We only worry about the survival of Venice.'

'I'll drink to that,' he agrees, his expression becoming pensive. 'When I see the holes made by Hitler's bombs in London, I fear for its future. But then I remember she's a great old dame and she'll survive, even if it means losing a bit of her sheen. The heart will keep beating.'

In the candlelight, I can see his eyes glaze over with memories – of his family and the street where he lives – and I love the fact that he loves his hometown. Even if it's not in Italy.

The parcel tucked deep in my handbag, I catch the last *vaporetto* over to the main island. It's full, passengers grumbling that the previous one has been cancelled.

'You're lucky this one's running,' the boatman says to the muttering crowd. 'We've nearly run out of coal.'

I make a mental note to talk to Sergio's deputy in my battalion – if the *vaporettos* stop travelling to Giudecca, we'll have to arrange an alternative boatman to reach the newspaper office in the evenings. Even so, I don't relish the journey in a rowing vessel across the sometimes-choppy expanse, caught in the rough wash of German patrol boats.

Venice is quiet and eerie in its blue sulphur light as I walk quickly home, wishing my shoes didn't clop and echo on the pebble walkways. I'm cutting it fine on the curfew and quicken my pace, hoping it doesn't sound like I'm walking too fast for some sinister purpose. Which, of course, I am. After the first transport of radio parts I feel confident of being able to smile my way through any checkpoints.

I realise too late that complacency is a dangerous thing – I emerge from a walkway just two streets away from home and run straight into a German patrol. I feel my face constrict, but pull on my muscles to produce the right smile. Hoping my eyes don't betray me.

'Good evening,' I say in German. There are just two of them but, as we are well aware in the Resistance, it takes only one weapon to make a fatal difference. They each have a small machine gun hanging casually across one shoulder, plus a holstered handgun.

Fortunately, one returns the smile at my decent German. 'Evening Fräulein,' the taller one says. 'You're out late.'

'I know, I know,' I say, affecting the fluffy tone of just one glass too many, 'too much talking and not enough clock-watching, I'm afraid. But I'm almost home now.'

I can sense the shorter one isn't so beguiled, looking at my handbag with real interest. 'Can we?' he gestures. When given a sharp look by his colleague, he adds, 'It's just policy, you understand.'

'Of course, of course,' I trill, and go to open the bag. My heart is a piston on full pelt; alongside my eternal notebook, which thankfully contains only my personal ramblings, Jack's package is nestled in the bottom, wrapped in a piece of cloth which – fortunately – has only recently been cloaking a block of some particularly strong parmesan. The odour rising from my bag almost makes the short one recoil as he peers in.

'What's this?' he points, his finger hovering just half an inch from the package. If he touches the sharp metal edge he'll know instantly that no parmesan is ever that hard.

'Cheese for my grandmother,' I say innocently. 'The family have come together to buy a little for her birthday. Silly, isn't it? But she adores it. I can't wait to get rid of it, stinking out my handbag.' I giggle, my anxiety an unwitting help in sending my voice higher and more ridiculous.

The short one continues peering, but still doesn't touch. The seconds crawl by as time ceases, only cut by his friend shifting beside him. 'Come on Hans, nothing here,' he says. 'We're off duty soon.'

I close the bag, feeling my heart plummet back to earth. As I round the corner after politely declining the offer of an escort back home, a sour retch rises inside me and I have to force myself not to bring up what little is in my stomach as I walk on. I'm still sweating as I reach the sanctuary of my apartment, although I don't switch on the light for several minutes, peering out of my second-floor window, making sure the twosome haven't followed. Paranoia comes easily when there is leaden contraband nearby.

84

And then, the adrenalin rush again – the satisfaction of having gotten away with it. I'm almost laughing to myself as I crawl into bed. Two trips down, although this last one brought me closer to discovery. Am I pushing my luck too far, and will it run out?

8

Finding and Frustration

London, September 2017

Jamie looks up into the dark hole of the attic entrance, and sighs.

'Lu? You still up there?' he calls. 'Come on down, I've brought some lunch back.'

There's a grunt and a shuffling in the space above his head, which he takes as something like an 'OK'.

She emerges in the kitchen, several cobwebs nestling in her hair. He pulls one away and kisses her cheek, but she barely notices. She hardly notices much these days, beyond what's in that ruddy box. She's matching his frustration now, although for different reasons; as Luisa moves about her mother's kitchen making tea and not saying anything, he knows she is muttering to herself inside. Fretting.

'So, anything interesting up there?' Jamie asks as they unwrap the deli sandwiches he bought on his way back from the third tip run of the day. Luisa's mum had her fair share of life's baggage buried deep in dust-lined drawers and cupboards, old gifts from Christmas crackers and 'handy' battery-powered kitchen gadgets never used. Having crawled over the house already, Luisa is going through the attic one more time for personal items before the house clearance company moves in to scavenge for their spoils.

'No, nothing else,' she says, her gaze on the wild growth in the back garden. 'I felt sure there would have been more, aside from that one box. I still don't know why Mum didn't talk about it, never showed me. I would have been prodigiously proud if I'd had a mother like hers.'

Jamie says nothing, pretending to be occupied by his sandwich. He doesn't dare suggest it may be the type of person Luisa's mother was – at times cold, petulant and self-obsessed. He's never told Luisa of his shock when he was first introduced, at the difference in character between mother and daughter, at how distant the mother was both with him and her only child. He never found out the reason why and, it seems, neither has Luisa. They were just never that close, and Luisa has never seemed to miss what she didn't possess in the first place – until now at least. He feels sorry for her when he thinks of his own mother, always ready with a hug, a kiss and a bowl of soup, and that comforting smell only mums possess. He never detected so much of a whiff on Luisa's mother.

Clearly, though, the wife that he loves is desperate to find some kind of connection with her family, and he should support her, whatever he really thinks. Since she found that ramshackle box of history, almost everything else has become secondary to her piecing together the jigsaw of Stella and Gio, the random photographs that might become a pathway towards Luisa's desperately needed past. It's as if it's becoming a search for her identity, except he loves the person she already is. How can he convince her of that, with this new 'mission' of hers? With Luisa, he knows she won't let it alone; she is tenacious and determined. A dog with a bone. That's what makes her a good journalist.

'I was actually wondering if you'd spotted anything valuable, something that could go to auction,' Jamie pitches. 'We might find some priceless old painting like they do on the TV – make our fortune.' And he tries prodding at her with a smile, something that will at least make them connect in the same room. Have the same goal.

'Oh, no,' she says, shuffling absently through a pile of post. 'I mean, you can go up and have a look – you watch more of those antique programmes than I do. Maybe you've got a better eye.'

Jamie tries not to take it as a slight on his none too professional life as a 'resting actor', but with Lu he knows it's not a criticism. She's just distracted, he tells himself – less by grief these days than the prospect of opening up her own life by pinning down her past.

'OK,' he says. 'Lead the way to the cobweb cavern. Let's get this job done.'

Later, they sit in the half-empty living room over take-away Chinese, and Jamie watches as Luisa chews on her meal and casts around at the walls now stripped of pictures and family photographs. There's a despondency about her, though not – he guesses – about leaving it behind, but at being here at all. Her expression tells him she won't be sad to close the door on her childhood for good. She might even relish throwing away the key.

'So what do you think the house will sell for?' he says chirpily. 'Enough for a deposit on our dream home?'

Luisa looks at Jamie quizzically, then narrows her eyes. He's clearly said the wrong thing again. Walked on those eggshells and cracked every single one.

'Christ Jamie, what is it with you and money today? My mother's not yet cold in her grave and you're already thinking about the cash!' she snaps, throwing aside her carton of noodles and storming into the kitchen.

'Luisa, come back – that wasn't what I mea—' he stammers, but she's already trying to muffle the sound of her sobbing with the grotty old tea towels her mother insisted on keeping. He doesn't get up. He's become used to not being able to comfort his wife. There's only one thing she will turn to this evening. And these days, he can't compete with a dusty old pile of photographs for comfort.

9

Drinks with the Enemy

Venice, March 1944

I hate the fact that I'm fretting over what to wear. It's never bothered me before, and in reality there are few choices; a couple of decent dresses from before the war, certainly nothing new since. I'm hot and bothered, by my own vanity mostly. In the week since our lunch date, Cristian has kept a professional distance, and I was almost wishing he'd forgotten his invitation to the military function, until he sidled up at five the previous afternoon and reminded me of the date and time, and that it is to be formal wear.

'Shall I pick you up at your apartment?' he'd said, prompting a swift but, I hoped, gracious 'No thank you' in reply – I would meet him in the Piazza San Marco, from where we could either walk or take a Motoscafi taxi boat.

The reception is set for a Saturday evening, which fortunately doesn't interfere with a trip to the newspaper office on Giudecca, and a chance to see Jack. I try to convince myself it's missing the former which would upset me the most, though that in itself is a hard enough task. Irritated at myself, I'm glad to finally make a dress selection and be done.

'Back to something that's actually important!' I grumble into the empty air, though it's not until later, when I meet with Sergio, that I am truly convinced – again – that this type of intelligence work is vital for Resistance planning.

Without revealing too many details – it's often safer not to know – he tells me my flow of information is building a picture of the Nazis' way of thinking: their patterns, but also their expertise in laying false trails to divert men and supplies. Assembling the radio parts I'm transporting will allow the Resistance to spread information even further, Sergio assures me. I imagine he's simply being kind, in the same way he encourages all those under his command, with a real twinkle in his eye, rather than the frown that any Resistance leader might be expected to wear, given the task we have ahead of us. But it does make me feel better, as though I'm truly useful.

I don't tell him I'm nervous about the reception, but he guesses, of course.

'If you hear only snippets of conversation then it will still be valuable,' Sergio adds, hunched over a glass of grappa in the corner of a quiet bar. 'But I stress you should not compromise yourself by appearing to linger or listen. It's the personalities and who they are talking to that truly interests us. I know your visual memory is good, so we'll meet soon after the event while it's fresh, perhaps with any recent photographs we have.'

I leave the bar with Sergio's reassurances and a strange sensation in my stomach – a mixture of anxiety and excitement grappling at its walls. But that feeling is quickly side-lined when I bump into my brother, Vito, just outside.

'Stella!' he says, with what seems like genuine delight – though not surprise – kissing me on both cheeks. 'Fancy seeing you here.'

I note he doesn't ask what I'm doing at this particular bar or who I'm meeting. And nor do I. The fact that it's well known among Resistance members is reason enough for both of us. We're part of the same brigade within Venice, but in separate battalions – and I'm guessing that's the way we both prefer it.

Wearing my big sister expression, I relay that his presence at home is sorely missed, and he rolls those big, boyish eyes at me.

'All right,' he says, with a typical, uncompromising grin. 'I'll try and be a better son. Having been truly ticked off by my bigger and better sibling.' And he uses that wide smile again on me – his tool for winning over almost everyone. It works on Mama, and it normally would on me, but not this time. He's not taking the situation seriously and my face shows it.

'Vito,' I half plead. 'Please don't give them more cause to worry. They're suffering enough. Show your face more, eat with them – that will be enough.'

This time, his face assumes an oddly serious look. 'OK, I will try harder,' he says. 'Promise. Now, Stella, I must go. Be careful yourself.' He squeezes my arm, harder than if it was a casual remark – I know then that even if we don't speak of it, we understand each other and what we do.

Back home in front of my ancient, cracked mirror, I do make an effort in how I look, though for whom it's hard to say. I don't want to make a spectacle of myself, but also I don't want to embarrass Cristian – as Sergio says, it could be a lucrative relationship for the campaign to free Venice. I style my hair in a wave, with the help of the mother-of-pearl combs given to me by Papa one birthday, and put on matching earrings. I scrape out the dregs of my compact and paint on a touch of lipstick – this party isn't important enough to lavish it upon my lips, but the end result is sufficiently different to my appearance on a work day.

The evening is cool but dry, and the light is dropping rapidly as I wait in one corner of San Marco near the Palazzo Ducale – otherwise known to pre-war tourists as the Palace of the Doge. Its ancient pink brickwork – the colour of the most tantalising ice cream – is in competition with a shellfish sky overhead and I can't help staring intently at the beauty of my city. Not even the buzzing of aircraft, returning no doubt from their spoiling of war, can overcome the sight of a burning sun squatting above the vast stretch of water. As I scan the sky above and then gaze over at the shallow waves, there is little hint of the past few days, when we came under the heaviest bombardment by Allied air forces yet. They targeted German shipping in the docks until one side of the city glowed with a different hue entirely; a stark contrast of thick, black smoke and a destructive flame red. Over the years, through endless invasions, Venice has proved to be a master at recouping her beauty, and she seems to have bounced back yet again. I wonder that we could ever think seriously of losing this gem to raiders, aliens or incumbents for good, and then I know exactly why I'm standing awkwardly in my best dress, nervously about to enter the devil's dancehall. It's for Venice, plain and simple.

'Good evening Signorina. You look wonderful, if I may say.' Cristian's voice startles me as he approaches from behind. He's smiling, his face brighter and more relaxed than I've ever seen. He is well groomed, his beard trimmed and hair slicked back, wearing an ebony double-breasted jacket, bright white shirt and emerald green tie. It's not an evening suit, but near enough. He's without his glasses, which makes him naturally squint a little. I wonder why he doesn't just simply wear them, since they distinguish his features, mark him out as different.

'You look well yourself,' I say, and he offers me an arm as we head towards the water's edge.

'So will I know anyone there?' I ask while we wait for the transport he's arranged, the lagoon lapping noisily at our feet.

'General Breugal is away, but Captain Klaus will be there, of course,' Cristian says. 'We're the only others from our department. It's a reception for some visiting dignitary from Berlin, so they like to put on a good show – different sections from across the city.'

He looks at me and smiles. 'I've no doubt I'm there to simply make up the numbers,' then adds quickly, 'Not that you are, Signorina – I'm delighted you could make the time.'

'Well I'm sure you're there for a reason – as far as I can tell, you are vital to the running of General Breugal's office. He certainly couldn't do without you.'

I'm fishing for his reaction, but he doesn't answer. Our Motoscafi arrives and he helps me step down into the vessel bobbing on the waves.

'Miss Bennet,' he says mischievously as he takes my hand, following up with a very boyish grin.

'Why thank you, Sir,' I say, joining his charade, though I can't quite bring myself to think of him as Mr Darcy. More and more, I feel I'm indulging in some kind of elaborate game, yet unsure whether there will be any winner.

The reception is being held in one of the lesser known palazzos on the Grand Canal, and it's strange to see all of its floors lit up, glittering in the near darkness as we approach. By contrast, even the wealthiest of families have retreated to the top floors of their grand houses on the canal, the upper rooms being easier to heat with limited fuel. Tonight, though, the entire Ca' Foscari palazzo sparkles like the proverbial Christmas tree.

Inside is no different. There is no war on tonight, judging by the tables spilling over with food and wine, brandy and champagne. I feel a deep sense of injustice and shudder in my stiff dress. And is that a wrinkle of distaste I see flash across Cristian's face? If so, he recovers quickly.

'General, hello, good to see you here . . .' He's straight in with a hand and the diplomacy, introducing me either as his 'companion' or 'colleague', and we do the rounds of the clumps of people milling about like groups of country dancers. The chatter rises towards the high ceiling, along with a fug of cigar smoke clouding the expensive chandelier, while a small string quartet does its best to compete. There's an abundance of green and grey uniforms, more than a few medals pinned to puffed-up chests, and few women to break up both the muted colour scheme and the overwhelming stench of machismo.

Everyone is speaking German and, though I'm fluent, it's exhausting keeping up with the varying accents and switch in topics. The subject of everyone's conversation is, of course, the war, but there are no detailed plans being discussed here – the alcohol hasn't loosened tongues to that extent. So I concentrate on what Sergio has suggested and marry images with words to help the retrieval of personalities from my memory: that one with the moustache, or the lieutenant with a limp and a helpful lisp. That's in between smiling and laughing where appropriate and swallowing the sick taint of collaboration and subterfuge.

Several times I make my excuses and head to the ladies' room; my small heels are not fitted with a convenient hiding place, but I've sewn a separate pouch into my clutch bag and I stow my notes in there, fervently hoping the bulk of the notes and the clumsy stitching won't be too obvious if I'm called to open my bag. Sergio has shown me pictures of prominent members of the German hierarchy, and from memory I write down who is talking to who, those that laugh together and others who struggle to feign civility. Despite the military order, it's personal relationships that heavily dictate the smooth running of occupation. Or not, so Sergio says. Scribbling over, and my mask of compliance reapplied, I take a deep breath and head back out in the fray.

Cristian is hovering near a side table as I emerge, sweeping me not into another gathering but up a shallow flight of stairs and onto a little balcony, with several tables overlooking the main floor.

'You're doing very well with all the small talk, but I thought you might welcome a break,' he says, offering me a chair. Instantly, a waiter appears and sets down two more glasses of champagne. I've already had a couple and my head is starting to feel the effects, but it's the best wine to coat my taste buds in an age and I find my fingers gripping the stem.

'I'm sorry if it's been a real bore,' Cristian goes on. 'Perhaps just a little while longer, and then we'll make our excuses.'

'No, it's absolutely fine,' I lie. 'It's certainly an eye-opener to see how the other half lives.'

He frowns, perhaps assuming it's a criticism. 'I just meant . . .' I try to qualify.

'No, I agree,' he says. 'It wouldn't be my idea to flaunt such opulence when there are troops and families out there struggling. But this is fascism meets the Reich. It's what we do.'

He says 'we' but I can't help noticing it doesn't sit easily on his tongue, or in his expression, for that matter. He might be a fascist, but I am beginning to think he is different in some way. And that's what confuses me.

Cristian's face brightens, and he casts a look over the floor below and then back at me – his features full of mischief again. 'I'd say this is a perfect opportunity for us as Austen lovers to transport ourselves to the ball at Netherfield? Darcy and Miss Bennet doing their sparring perhaps?'

'Oh?'

'Well, it might not have been too different,' he argues. 'Swap the grey uniforms for scarlet and imagine a few more women in their finery. The pomp and the bluster would – I imagine – be very much the same.'

In such surroundings, I'm amused by his playful imagination, and we lean over the balustrade, neatly camouflaged by a large flower display hung from the balcony, each picking out individuals we would place in our ballroom scene. Cristian helpfully puts names to faces that I haven't yet committed to memory. It might be the champagne, or the fact that I am – guiltily – enjoying myself a little, but we giggle like schoolchildren as we paint Austen-esque portraits, some of them none too complimentary.

The game exhausted, he leans back in the chair and lets out a large, cathartic sigh. I watch his shoulders sink down under his suit. It lasts all of three seconds before he's back to being Cristian De Luca, reliable servant of the fascist state.

'I suppose we had better return to the floor and do our bit,' he says, a touch of weariness to his voice. 'Can you bear another round of hand-shaking before it's acceptable to leave?'

'Of course,' I say, re-dressing in my own virtual cloak once more. I surprise myself at how easy it's becoming.

Our duties over, the fresh air of the canal is a welcome change from the smog of good living inside, and we both take a large breath. It's well after curfew, and the canal is virtually motionless. Only the gentle push and pull of the wider ocean on the lagoon creates silver flecks under a half moon, uncut by returning aircraft. I breathe the stillness into my lungs.

'I'll call for the boat,' he says.

'Couldn't we just walk? It's not that far.' I figure if a man with the Reich on his side can't get us through the checkpoints easily, then who can?

'If you wish,' he says. His tone says it's not an unwelcome surprise. Like any man escorting a young woman, he offers his arm and I take it. The fresh air has brought me round a little, but the effects of the champagne are still lurking.

'I don't think I've ever heard such silence,' I say at last, as I curse my heels for spoiling the hush.

He turns his head with a quizzical look. 'Poetry, Signorina Jilani, at this time of night and after such an evening?' The smile says he is teasing.

'Well, you have to try,' I retort. 'And please, call me Stella. I think when we've shared the delights of the Netherfield ball, formalities can be pushed aside – Mr Darcy.'

Was that me or my persona uttering it – the Resistance flirt that I am tonight? In that moment, I question my own motives; I want to cultivate this relationship for the cause. It's necessary. Yet, at the same time, I don't harbour the same creeping dread of contact with Cristian as I would for, say, General Breugal, or the wheedling Captain Klaus. It feels wrong – it is wrong – to enjoy the company of an active fascist. I think of Jack in his dank hole on Giudecca, in pain and unable to enjoy the beauty of even this muted Venice, and suddenly there's more than champagne swirling around my insides. I feel I've let my guard down, allowed Cristian De Luca to look a little beyond my guise. While it feels uncomfortable, I can't seem to stop it.

The walk back is uneventful and we encounter only one patrol, who are easily satisfied when Cristian pulls out his identity card. We're a few streets away from my apartment when I slip my arm from his.

'I'll be fine to walk the last few streets from here,' I say.

'It's no bother to see you all the way,' he says. 'I'm not in the least tired.'

I hesitate, considering whether insisting on walking alone will incite suspicion on Cristian's part. Very few people know my home address – I'm still officially registered at Mama's house – and I want to keep it that way. It's my bolthole, where I'm Stella, not of the Resistance or the Reich's office.

Just me. It's where I shed my clothes and my various personas and I'm free within my own walls. But I reason that even a coy refusal might breed some mistrust in me as an employee.

'All right,' I say. 'Although don't be surprised if there's a few curtains twitching even at this time of night.'

True to form, a sliver of light from Signora Menzio's ground-floor window cuts through as we enter the darkness of my own little *campo*, our steps echoing off the uneven flagstones. For me, though, my elderly neighbour is not being nosy, merely giving me her usual signal that all is safe, a certain ornament on display in her window. She rarely leaves her apartment these days, but the widow's keen eyes and ears are part of a valuable armoury for the stealth of the Resistance.

As we stop outside my door, Cristian casts around the tiny square, adjusting his gaze to the gloom – its ancient well at one end is just visible, with a tiny, these days unused, chapel alongside.

'It's beautiful,' he says.

'In its own way,' I concede. 'It's not Santa Margherita or Santo Stefano, but I like it. We're a friendly community.'

'Perfect,' he whispers, and I know then that it's Cristian the art lover and the bookworm who is appreciating Venice, and not his other, politicised self.

'I'll say goodnight then,' he adds. There's no awkwardness, no suggestion that he's hanging out for an invitation upstairs, or even to offer a peck on my cheek. 'Thank you for coming and making my evening much more bearable, Miss Bennet.'

'It was a pleasure, Mr Darcy,' I say as I turn to go. And I wonder how much I mean it.

10

A New Role

Jack is not his chirpy self on my next visit two days later, after my newspaper shift. He's back in bed, with a sheen of sweat on his brow. Still, he makes the effort to smile as Sister Cara shows me in.

'Stella, so lovely to see you.' He tries to make more of an effort to appreciate the new books I've brought – a mixture of English and Italian novels – but it's clear he's not well. The wound on his leg has become infected, Sister Cara whispers to me; they are cleaning and dressing it as best they can, but it's clearly spreading. Jack tries not to show it, but he is worried. Mostly alone, and without proper treatment, he is clearly aware this may be the battlefield that he succumbs to.

'Surely, they can get a doctor out to you?' I say. 'Someone sympathetic.'

'Apparently, no one can be spared at the moment – too

many men being shipped in from outside the Veneto. A couple more days in bed, and I'll be fine.'

His face, though, and his pallor suggest rest isn't enough. I'm no medic, but I can see he needs a doctor – and soon. I make a decision, potentially a foolish one, but it's born of true concern rather than any rational thought.

All next day I can't shift the image of Jack's pale and sweat-stained face from my mind, and I have to concentrate at work just to appear focused. I leave the Reich office a little early, feigning a headache, but with a firm purpose. Instead of walking towards home, I divert the few streets from my apartment towards the main hospital that sits behind the choppy water's edge of the Fondamenta Nuove. I know my brother Vito has a partisan friend whose own brother is a doctor – I can only hope and guess this doctor shares the family's politics, but it's a chance I have to take.

It's strangely quiet as I enter through the large doors, flashing a smile and my Reich department ID at the guard and pretending I'm there to visit the sick. I find Doctor Livia on the medical ward, slumped in a chair against the wall of the sluice room, eyes closed and his head almost lolling with exhaustion. He seems unaware of the low-level stench of bedpans hovering around his nostrils.

He opens his eyes smartly when I say his name – 'What? Oh, sorry!' – but calms when it's clear I'm not one of the senior staff or a Nazi commander on an impromptu visit. Despite his clear fatigue – his eyes sit in deep, grey circles of skin – he listens carefully when I explain about Jack.

'And he can't be moved to a house on the main island?' he quizzes. 'I could go to him there.'

'I don't think so. He seems to have a low fever, and his leg – if anything – is more immobile with the pain.'

'Hold on a minute, wait here,' Doctor Livia says, and exits the sluice. He comes back a minute later with a small bag, and ushers me out.

'If we go now, I can be back before I'm missed,' he says. But it's already six o'clock, and I'm concerned about beating the curfew if the boats are delayed.

'Don't worry – we have a boat set aside for emergencies,' the doctor reassures me. 'We won't advertise it, but if we get stopped, the driver has papers.'

'And is he trustworthy, the boatman?'

'He's one of us. I would trust him with my life – I have done.'

It's good enough for me. It has to be – I've asked for help and Doctor Livia has responded without hesitation. I have to return the trust. My one concession is that I swiftly don a nurse's spare uniform in the event of spot checks on the boat, pulling the cape tight against me to disguise the poor fit. I've given up guessing at how many guises I will have adopted by the time this war of theatrics and deceit finally ends.

The journey on the water from the Fondamenta Nuove and around the curve of the Arsenale – the navy barracks under total Nazi control – is strangely uneventful, which makes me more nervous. The boatman, however, is experienced, slowing the engine if any craft nears us, and only pushing its raspy growl to a certain noise level so that our trip appears routine and not urgent. Doctor Livia dozes in his seat, not even the wind spray interrupting the precious minutes of sleep he grabs, a world away from the anguish I'm feeling and the vision of Jack's face draining of life. I have to gently nudge the doctor awake as we moor up in the small canal beside Santa Eufemia.

Doctor Livia – Ignazio, as he tells me to call him – needs almost no light to make a diagnosis. Sister Cara is with Jack, sponging water around his flushed face, and he's clearly deteriorated in the twenty-four hours since I left. Ignazio gets to work with the equipment he's brought, pushing a needle line into Jack's arm and hoisting a rubber tube attached to a bottle containing precious antibiotics, which I work to prop up on whatever wooden shafts I can find. Finally, he unwinds the bandages; even the good doctor almost recoils at the putrid odour that floods the room. I think it's almost better that Jack is now slipping in and out of consciousness, as the sister fetches more boiled water, and the doctor does what he can to scrape away the decay of Jack's leg. It's safe to say that if he makes it out of Venice, Jack's war is over, or his active part at least.

The smell I can tolerate, but the obvious cries of pain that break through Jack's semi-conscious state are harder to bear. The antibiotics are rare enough, but the little anaesthetic they possess at the hospital is needed for more serious wounds. I want to push my fingers in my ears at his agony, but I'm needed to fetch and carry, and even hold some of the dressing as Ignazio works his medical magic.

Finally, the doctor refixes Jack's leg in the brace, avoiding contact with the wound and leaving it accessible to the sisters for further dressing. Jack is asleep, and I'm grateful to see his chest rise and fall noticeably. He is alive at least.

Ignazio gives instructions to Sister Cara and packs up his equipment. The treatment has taken longer than expected and he may not make curfew.

'We'd better go. The late-night water patrols will start soon, especially around the Arsenale,' he says.

'I'll stay,' I say. 'At least tonight. I'm sure the sisters are busy, and he shouldn't be left.' Although it's a work night, I feel sure I can use my earlier headache again as an excuse to turn up to the Reich office later in the morning.

Ignazio looks at me quizzically, but he's either too tired or too busy to query my motives, or my relationship with Jack. 'All right, just make sure you wake him every two or three hours to drink. Sister Cara will take down the drip tomorrow. If he improves slightly overnight, we'll know we caught the infection in time, but if he deteriorates . . .' He doesn't elaborate, but there's little need. Jack will either improve, or we'll require a different service, one which the church can perform very well.

I clutch at his hands. 'Thank you,' I say. 'For coming. For doing something.' He looks at me, as if to say: why wouldn't I help a human being? And then he's gone.

Sister Cara returns with a blanket and a cushion for me to make up a bed of sorts. But I'm too wired for sleep. I want to hear Jack snuffle and snore occasionally. I want to be here when he wakes and feed him the water he needs. Despite the fakery of my dress, I am no nurse, but I feel strongly he should not die in this dank, lonely room, thousands of miles from his family. Not when he's given so much of himself to the Allied cause, to Italy and Venice.

I sit at Jack's desk, underneath his lamplight, and I do what I do each time I feel unsure, scared, overwhelmed or just not myself. I write. I write what comes into my head, scribbling in the notebook I keep constantly in my handbag, pages to scratch partisan codes or messages, but which are firmly torn and then passed on or burned. Only what's in my imagination is fixed on the remaining pages, nothing to incriminate me if I'm caught except my own silly ramblings.

For the first time in an age, my thoughts turn to love. How it's been thwarted by this war, destroyed in some cases, but also how it can survive, like the timeworn bricks of Venice, or the ancient wooden piles on which we're all suspended in this city. Love can endure.

It's a love story pulled from my head in the stillness and the rhythms of Jack's deep sleep. Where it springs from I don't know, and I try not to connect it with the company I'm keeping, either here in this room, or across the water in my 'other life'. The characters simply form, and I've learned not to shun the gift of words when they come. Much like the tide of the ocean, you roll with the words and not against them. And this is how the tale of Gaia and Raffiano is born – he from a good Italian family, she from a long line of Jewish Venetians. Such a union of cultures has been frowned upon throughout history, but in this cruel war it could also prove to be a death sentence – handed down by those who recognise only the stark lines between religions. Gaia and Raffiano, they see beyond those boundaries; they are simply people. In love.

Once the first paragraph is set, I am lost in the narrative, conversations and images flooding my mind, tic-tacking back and forth – it's the task of my granite pencil to translate the colour I see onto the page. I write for so long that I almost forget to wake Jack. He is drunk with exhaustion, and it's hard work pulling up his head and cajoling him to drink. But he does, opening his eyes only briefly and muttering something in English, then sinking into sleep again. As my watch inches towards three a.m., I surprise myself with how awake I feel; I'm forced to use Jack's penknife to whittle more of my pencil, and it's only as it becomes a stub that I wake Jack one more time and then give in to eventual tiredness myself, covered with Sister Cara's blankets in the chair.

It's her gentle fingers that wake me – though I come to with a start – a few hours later. Only when I see Jack's eyes open does my heart pull itself back to earth. The early morning light pushes in through the top windows and rouses me further.

'He seems to be through the worst,' the sister reassures, and Jack's weak smile tells me she's right.

'I thought I was imagining things when I saw a nurse's uniform hovering above me,' he says, as we help him sit up a little. I'd all but forgotten I'm still in the badly fitting uniform lent by Doctor Livia.

The tea the sister brews stirs me just enough to make it home, and I send a hasty message to the Reich office that I'm still sick. With the reassurance that Jack is improving, I sink into a deep and satisfying slumber – oblivious to the drone of heavy aircraft pulsing overhead, like queen bees in a grand formation, homeward bound to their hives.

I'm disorientated when I wake at midday. With little food in the house, I make the few steps to Paolo's café, where he rustles up some soup and works his magic with the coffee beans again.

'I'm not going to ask if you were up for business or something else,' he says. 'But you, Stella Jilani, are burning the candle at both ends. Your fingers are in danger of being singed.'

'Yes, Papa,' I say, with a wrinkle to my nose. I know the

gentle jibe is because he cares — where Vito is my younger brother, Paolo acts like an older sibling — but I also know he's right.

It doesn't stop me making the trip back over to Giudecca in the early afternoon, careful to skirt around San Marco and the Reich office so I'm not seen out of my sickbed. The spring sun follows me over the canal's expanse and a wind ripples across the water, helping to clear the cobwebs filling my head.

I'm soon satisfied Jack really is improving, without any sign of a relapse. He's eating a little and, with help, he can put a half weight on his leg. His face doesn't have that deathly pallor and, although he's weak, he seems back to being the Jack that I've come to know, if only for a short time.

'You saved my life — does that mean I am beholden to you to the end of my days?' He says it with a grin, but his eyes are red and intent.

'Don't be silly,' I reply. 'I'm not about to make you the genie of my lamp. Anyway, it was Doctor Livia who saved you.'

'But you called him. Without you, I would be fish fodder for your lovely lagoon.'

'Well, that's a nice image, I must say!' We're both aware of trying to keep it light, but I can tell there's genuine gratitude in what he says. 'Perhaps you will parachute in one day and save a damsel like me from certain death, like in all the best films.'

'Hmm . . .' He gestures at his leg again. 'Can I hobble instead? I'll do it very gallantly, I promise.'

'Well, OK, but only if you are *very* swarthy.'

★　　★　　★

110

I depart from the church, promising to visit in two days when I'm next due at the newspaper office. Unusually, I'm at a loose end as I've had no instructions that my services as a Staffetta are needed; Mimi is at work and I can't face the third degree from Mama, telling myself guiltily that I will do my duty and visit at the weekend. She'll only wonder why I'm not at work and I haven't the energy to fabricate another story amid the layers that seem to make up my life. On Sunday, I'll go with her to church and make her smile.

Still, there's an unsettled air inside me. It's not Jack, since I know he's no longer at risk, and I'm so used to the general feeling of life on a knife edge in this war that danger barely registers as anything unusual nowadays. No, this is something different. Tiny bubbles of unease are captive inside me.

Walking along the blustery waterfront at Giudecca to the *vaporetto* stop, I finally realise what it is. I need my typewriter. I ache to feel the keys under my fingers, clatter and trip-trap my thoughts onto a blank page, see the type laid down. I imagine my notebook bristling in my handbag, crackling with a desire to work its way out. It might never be read but it's a rush I need now in my veins – adrenalin of a different sort from the previous night. Still potent but more stable.

Matteo is surprised to see me on a day when the paper isn't in production, but I make the excuse of wanting to catch up on some work, and I don my apron out of habit, disappearing into the basement. I must appear needy or grey or both, because – bless her – Matteo's wife, Elena, follows me down with a steaming bowl of pasta, which I eat while I stare at the blank page and stroke the smoothed keys of my beloved machine. I like to muse that Popsa had it specially

111

made for me, as my fingers fit perfectly into the well of each letter, although I know that's my own fantasy.

As with every story I've ever written – fact or fiction – it's the whiteness of the page causing a ripple in my stomach, now that Elena's offering has seen to my hunger. It's my turn to fill the white, yawning space. Every writer's nightmare, I imagine; excitement and dread in equal measure. Luckily, my notebook lights the spark. I edit as I type, the noise muffled by our makeshift sound-proofing and the window closed on my world. I don't notice, though; soon I'm within Gaia and Raffiano's lives; their innocent meeting on the Lido before the rolls of Nazi barbed wire force people away from the beauty of its beaches. Swiftly, it develops into the hot, urgent love born of war, when there are so many boundaries that a forbidden passion is only one of many restrictions. Every day of their lives, it seems, carries a threat of some sort, so why not? Why not live instead of just lingering?

I'm unaware that it's becoming dusky outside until Matteo comes down, peering into the gloom of my one desk light. He says business is slow and he's shutting the bar early. The chilly evening air and the dense inner feeling that's been purged make me forget my lingering fatigue; I feel lighter, less encumbered. I take the *vaporetto* back to the Zattere waterfront stop, neatly sidestepping the hotel on the front that's become the base for the Military Police. It's around eight but I don't want to go home yet, feeling somehow restless and exhausted in unison, and so I walk towards the Accademia Bridge and over into the large Campo Santo Stefano. There I linger at a table outside one of my favourite cafés over an aperitif, reading my copy of *Pride and Prejudice*. For the second time in one day, I'm transported out of reality, to a different time and place, to somewhere hearts can be lifted and mended. I know I'm not the first to appreciate the way love transcends time, space and the ugliness of war, but it warms me all the same. Looking at the beauty of the square, however, with the yellowy café lights framing its ancient order, it is almost hard to believe there is so much conflict, with such suffering as we hear on Radio Londra.

On the page, Mr Darcy is making awkward entreaties to Miss Bennet when a voice cuts into the exchange.

'Good evening, Signorina. You look engrossed.'

It's Cristian, and I look up, clearly with an expression of real surprise – so much so that he almost seems to recoil. I worry that I've been caught out, having called in sick, though to judge by his expression he doesn't seem irritated.

'Oh! Evening, Signore,' I say, bringing my tone up several notches. 'Yes, just escaping for a few moments. To clear my head.' I know that he of all people appreciates my meaning, and he nods in response when I hold up the book's cover.

He's wearing what I would describe as a non-work suit – something in a deep blue – and although he's sporting a tie it seems slightly more casual. There is an extra adornment: a woman hanging onto his arm. She is anything but casual, dressed to impress in high heels and a fur stole, her pout marked in a deep crimson. She tries to smile weakly, but fails. I wonder where she thinks they are going dressed like that, with him so understated. I berate myself then for judging a book by its cover so harshly, then swiftly wonder why I am bothering at all. What do I care where Cristian goes outside of work, or with whom? And I push down a tiny, indistinct niggle inside that says otherwise. Once again, I hate myself for it.

'I'm very glad your headache appears to be better,' Cristian says, as the woman pulls, though tries not to tug too noticeably, on his arm. In this, she fails again. 'We'll leave you to your book. Goodnight, Signorina.'

And they are gone, and I'm left staring at the words on a page and musing over the strangeness of my day.

11

Casting Out

Bristol, September 2017

'I need to go to Venice,' Luisa says suddenly, while they are
— somewhat ironically — halfway through a bowl of pasta.

'What?' Jamie almost splutters. He feels sure it's not the
quality of his cooking, or lack of, which prompts Luisa's
outburst. 'What do you mean? When? What for?'

He's not entirely sure why he bothers to ask for reasons,
since it's obvious. They've skirted around the subject of The
Box since Luisa's outburst in London, and he has tolerated
— or tried to ignore — the time she spends on it. But why
else would she want to go to Venice? To find some answers,
to quell his wife's insatiable curiosity. To give her some peace.
Of course.

'Um, just for a few days,' Luisa says hurriedly into her
plate. 'I was thinking fairly soon. Work's quiet at the moment
— I thought I should take the opportunity.'

In contrast, Jamie chews his pasta slowly. For what seems like an age, it's the only sound in their orbit.

'Jamie? What do you think?'

He looks up. 'Lu, you know I can't go right now, let alone afford it. I've got those two auditions lined up in the next few weeks, and then what if I'm called back—'

'I don't mind going on my own,' she says abruptly. Jamie is a seasoned enough actor to know she's been preparing the line, word for word. He thinks back to when they both went to Venice for an indulgent, romantic weekend. When was that? Three, four years ago? Then, Luisa didn't think about her family heritage, even though she knew her roots were there. They went as tourists, fed the pigeons in San Marco, rode the waterbus the entire length of the Grand Canal and paid exorbitant prices for coffee outside elegant cafés. It was fun. They walked for miles, talked intensely and made love often. They were in love. These days their relationship feels more like work, which this trip promises to be. He wonders, does he really want to go? And besides, it's abundantly clear she's not asking him to.

'Can't you persuade one of your mates to go with you? It's not much fun travelling on your own,' he says, then remembers when he first met Luisa. She'd just returned from six weeks' backpacking in Africa on her own – sticking to a well-worn trail of travellers, but solo nonetheless. It doesn't faze her.

'I'll be fine,' she says, almost as if she's booked her ticket already. Clearly, she was never asking for his approval.

'And what are you going to do once you're there, Sherlock?' He's trying to make light of it and mask the hurt inside.

'Find her,' she says defiantly. 'What else? I'm going to find my grandmother, her history – discover what she was really like.'

Jamie wants to ask: *To what end, for what eventual purpose? She's dead and you can't even ask her.* But that seems petty and futile. It's plain that Luisa is still grieving, for her mother possibly, but also for what her mother didn't allow her to have – connection and intimacy. As an only child and with a father largely absent, and then dead by the time she was a teenager, Luisa is grasping at any link with her past. Her relationship with her mother was strained, but it was still a string on which to hang. Now she has nothing.

Jamie tries to imagine how he would feel if his two brothers and both parents were gone – suddenly not there on the end of a text or the phone. But he can't. Luisa is an adult, yes, but effectively an orphan at thirty-three. How could he possibly know how she feels? Especially since she won't confide in him, preferring to invest her thoughts within those scraps of paper. Her fervour and her grief as she sinks into that box and the promises within are obvious, and Jamie has little choice but to pray that the attic hasn't been hiding a painful Pandora's Box.

12

Opening Up

Venice, late March 1944

Cristian isn't at his desk when I arrive for work the morning after our short encounter in Santo Stefano. For some inexplicable reason I'm put out, but then I see that his desk looks occupied, with his pen and notebook laid out. I feel slightly calmer at the sight, and I tell myself it's simply because the office runs noticeably more smoothly when he's present.

He comes in as I'm translating a report on shipping supplies in and out of Venice. I'm tucking details into corners of my brain for later use; the ports have become vital to Nazi movements of weapons and troops since many of the railways in Northern Italy have been blown up by my fellow partisans. This is essential information for our fight, although we are mindful that translations of German messages intended to inform the Nazis' fascist counterparts are not always the complete truth. On paper they are bedfellows – Hitler and Mussolini holding the same beliefs

– but Italian fascists are still treated with some disdain by the Germans, considered unreliable.

I don't pay much attention to Cristian for a good half an hour, only seeing him out of the corner of my eye casting the odd glance in my direction. It never fails to make me nervous – I feel of all the people in this office he has the measure of me. Maybe I let my guard down too much at the reception? Perhaps he's simply biding his time before he exposes me in some grand – and deadly – fashion? The fact that I can't gauge him at all both irritates and drives me to discover more about him. What, aside from his love for Mussolini, motivates him in this chaos of a world?

'Signorina Jilani, might I enquire when this report is likely to be ready?' He ghosts up beside me – something of a habit he has – and I have to dampen my surprise.

'Not too long, Signore, I'm on the last section,' I say brightly. Clearly, there will be no chance to make a typewritten copy of this dispatch, and I'll need to cram my brain to capacity before I can get to the toilet and scribble any memorised details. Cristian is not helping, as he's hovering beside my desk – another habit he's developing. I look up briefly.

'Is there something else you need, Signore?'

'No, I was just wondering if you enjoyed your reading last night? I always think you're never alone with a book when you're waiting for someone.'

'Oh, I wasn't waiting for anyone,' I say casually. Easy enough since it's true. Inside though, my mind is reeling – he's clearly fishing, but for what? Does he suspect that I'm a Staffetta and spend half my life waiting for other message-bearers in cafés and bars?

He looks at me, this time squarely through the lenses of

his glasses, his eyes made slightly smaller by his short-sightedness but still large and enquiring. 'And do you prefer that, Signorina – your own company?'

'At times,' I say. 'Sometimes it's much easier to be with a book – there's no two-way exchange to have to worry about.'

It's too late – it's out of my mouth before I have time to think and I check myself for opening up another part of me to him. I'm still in disguise: Stella the loyalist. Nothing of my own self should come through. But he only nods, as if he understands, and turns back towards his desk.

'And did you enjoy your evening, Signore?' I say as a parting comment. 'With your company?' Again, my mouth is moving faster than my brain, although the noise of the office masks our exchange.

He stops, wheels back round. 'It was a pleasant enough evening,' he says without enthusiasm. 'A work engagement – I was escorting the niece of an army officer.' He smiles weakly, and I'm left wondering why Cristian De Luca feels the need to explain himself so fully to me, a mere typist. And, unbeknown to him, a traitor to his world. And more so, why I care at all.

Jack has improved again by the time I see him on Giudecca later that week after work. I call in before I go to the newspaper office, and he's out of bed, dressed. Even in the gloom of his glorified cell, I can make out that he has some colour in his cheeks. Without asking, he brews us some tea and we talk while he prepares the penultimate package. Part of me wants to suggest he split the last two into three, as I'll have no real excuse to visit once the task is done. Do I need an excuse, I wonder, other than friendship?

121

I leave with a neat package in my handbag, although I know the next one will be the size of a shopping bag – the equipment can't be broken down into smaller pieces – and will demand the most nerve.

Back in the newspaper office below the bar, I feel energised and finish the week's articles quickly, just as Arlo and Tommaso arrive, reporting that they've been held up by Nazi patrols searching all young men on the streets of the main island. It's fortunate all the material for the paper stays on Giudecca until its publication.

They begin by sifting through my written copy and the other notices that need to be included in the week's paper.

'Hey, switch on Benito,' Arlo says as they get to work, and I reach over to our well-worn radio set, brazenly named after Italy's beloved leader. Instead of Radio Londra, though, we tune into some music and the atmosphere is almost party-like. I've noticed in recent weeks that Tommaso has grown out of his shell, bantering back and forth with Arlo and it's good to hear. He tells us of the classroom talk at the Liceo and how the students are planning minor acts of sabotage, as if they are in training to be Resistance through and through for the rest of this seemingly endless war.

'We're arranging a leaflet drop around all the schools and some of the streets,' he says, and his face glows with pride. Like him, some of the students have parents who are noted partisans and want to follow proudly in their footsteps.

'Just be careful they can't link you to it in any way,' Arlo warns him, like an older brother. As he squints at the copy, I know he's thinking of his own brothers courting danger in the war arena.

Then, in the next minute, Tommaso produces the cartoon

strip he's been working on and they are both giggling like schoolboys again at the subversive sarcasm.

I stay on a while to help fold and bind the sheets as the first pages of the weekly edition roll off the press like Mama's pasta, fresh with news. It's the best part of the week for me, to see something tangible in our fight in this war of bullies. The pages are not filled with award-winning journalism, I know, but I am a firm believer in the old cliché that the pen is mightier than the sword. It's a shame that we have to engage the sword as well.

As I wait to see if there are any loose ends to pick up with the paper, I tinker with my own story of Gaia and Raffiano, weeding out some of the passages that suddenly appear too 'flowery' and paring down the words to speak of emotion instead of bleeding it. I'm happier when it's more succinct – no matter that it's just for me. Doesn't every writer create for themselves, first and foremost?

To ensure that I catch the last *vaporetto*, I leave before the others, just as Matteo closes the bar and joins them in the basement to help string up the bundles. As with every Monday, his brother-in-law is waiting in the canal off the main expanse with his small, flat-bottomed motorboat. He is a fisherman by trade and knows the best routes to avoid the water patrols and the shallows of the lagoon; he and his cargo will skirt the deeper channels with the piles of papers, zigzagging towards the main island, where groups of distributors are ready to receive and begin handing out the link to the outside world – under the counter of shops and cafés, sometimes in churches, left in recognised places in the *campos*.

It's on my own journey home each Monday evening that I feel the most . . . is it satisfaction? On the other days, when we're simply preparing the pages, I do have a sense of achievement, but it's when I feel the newsprint under my fingers that I'm truly aglow. It's my own form of fulfilment, and one that I'm sure Popsa would have been proud of too. Certainly, it's the nearest I feel to being a partisan soldier.

Tonight, my journey back to my apartment is uneventful – I weave a route to sidestep all the checkpoints and I slump into bed exhausted. Three journeys done and still nine lives intact. Or is that a dangerous way to think? The radio parts I deliver safely the next morning; the patrols are focusing mainly on younger men and wave me on in my work suit. My heart still races as I walk through the barrier, and I try not to feel smug in my duplicity. But, inside, I'm smiling.

It's not until a few days later, when the paper has been out a full twenty-four hours, that I notice anything at all. I'm on Staffetta duty, outside a bar on Castello waiting to pass on a message to an unknown contact and sipping at a very poor excuse for coffee. My eyes are peeled for any suggestion of a fellow messenger, but my ears can't help but tune into the table alongside, where two middle-aged women are gossiping over drinks.

'Good luck to them, I say,' the one in a striking blue hat says. 'Everyone loves a bit of romance.'

'It's nice to indulge in a bit of fantasy, especially in these times,' the one opposite in a bright green scarf agrees.

'At our age, it is fantasy,' number one laughs, and then drops her tone to serious. 'I just hope there's a happy ending, with Jews and non-Jews daring to . . . you know.'

'Surely, it's just a story?' number two says, and their conversation tails off into the background as a woman approaches; I recognise the tic-tac of her eyes in pinpointing her contact while retaining an air of nonchalance that might mean she is simply looking for a free table. Fortunately, there are none and, as we lock pupils for less than a second, she asks casually if the chair beside me is free. I nod. There's no guarantee she is on the same mission as me, and for now we regard each other with a healthy suspicion. There's a process to follow and nothing can be assumed, other than that, if we make the wrong move, it might result in a group of fascist soldiers emerging out of the brickwork to haul us off to somewhere much less amenable. We have to assume that even the simplest of drops are a trap until proved otherwise.

'Is the coffee decent here?' she says, and takes out a pack of cigarettes from her handbag, leaving it on the table between us.

'Passable, but nothing like before the war,' I reply. It's a lie because the weak brown liquid is quite foul, but it's the answer she needs. She is my link, and I am hers. She smiles behind a plume of smoke and we begin the fake dance, idle chatter about the war and our boredom of rationing, food and make-up especially. One more coffee is brought over, and I'm forced to sip at it, gesturing towards her pack of cigarettes.

'May I take one for later?' I don't smoke – never have done – but when she nods casually I pull the pack towards my lap and with a sleight of hand that Sergio Lombardi himself taught me, I rapidly pull a small piece of paper from the pack and slip it into my sleeve.

'Thanks,' I say, holding up the cigarette, and I bid this stranger a good evening, as if we've just had the most pleasant of impromptu chats.

As I do after every exchange, I wind a lengthy route

towards home, to identify any possible tail. Once I'm certain of not being tracked, I call in to my nearest grocery store, hoping to pick up whatever I can to replenish my almost bare cupboards: pasta or polenta, or even a precious tin of meat. I'm usually so busy that I'm last in the queue for anything remotely appetising and end up with a mixture of random ingredients that even the paper's frugal recipes can't improve. I peer over the counter and note with pride the corner of a copy of *Venezia Liberare*.

'I'll have something extra,' I say to the patriot shopkeeper in the accepted code and nod towards the counter. I may have typed almost every word, but I still like to roam over the details at home, not having eyed the final edition. Call it vanity, but it's my own private indulgence.

Once home, I shut and bolt my door to the world, make tea, cut the precious seed bread and thinly slice the tiny block of cheese I've managed to secure. It's my own portion of heaven, and I pull open the pages to peruse the week's edition. As I leaf through, a loose sheet of paper falls out and floats to the floor. Bending to pick it up, I see immediately it's not set with Arlo's skill, double-sided and unfolded. I recognise it instead as my own typeface, not least because running through both sides of the paper is the familiar dropped *e* of my own machine.

I'd hastily titled my story *The Barb of Love* and almost laughed at my own syrupy nostalgia in referring to the rows of ugly wire lining the beaches of the Lido, coils of it set up by the Nazis to prevent enemy boats landing. It's where Gaia and Raffiano first set eyes on each other, in those relatively carefree months before the invasion and the wire, and so it seemed the obvious title. But how on earth did my ramblings make their way into this week's paper? I can only imagine it's a mistake on Arlo's part, as the sheet in my hand is not the one copy I typed. Perhaps it's been left in the pages by mistake; it has the slightly blurred lines of the mimeograph machine we use to hastily copy whole pages of text, rolling out leaflets for immediate dispersal without having to set them on the larger press. The process is quick but the quality is poorer. It's clearly been replicated. But why? It's an error, surely? I'm shot through with embarrassment at the thought of wasting so much precious paper on my flippant endeavours. It will be tomorrow before I can ask Arlo about it, as we make little contact between our time at the newspaper office, for safety.

13

Story Time

I'm itching for time to pass quickly the next day in the Reich office, although Breugal has returned to Venice with either new fervour or pressure from his High Command and the pace is necessarily faster – everyone's machines are jumping at speed to satisfy his rantings. Breugal's burden conveys itself to Cristian, who is like a lion on the prowl in making sure everything runs smoothly. The girls tut at his increased zeal as a taskmaster, and I find myself irritated by their own lack of loyalty, then wonder at my own feelings getting in the way. And indeed, what they mean. I keep my head down and type like the wind, and he neither addresses nor rebukes me.

I'm kept back half an hour to finish a report and I miss the *vaporetto* for Giudecca, leaving me an hour to wait until the next. Once again, I find myself hovering in a café on the Zattere waterfront, this time with a beer and a book for company. It feels odd to have a little free time,

129

and not be on the lookout for a stranger cum friend, feeling the weight of forbidden messages in my bag.

A young woman next to me is scanning the Veneto edition of *Il Gazzettino* with interest – I look at her and wonder how she can believe the pages of propaganda and headlines that are clearly inflammatory. An Italian guard saunters by and smiles at her choice of reading, and she obliges with a friendly nod. As she shifts, though, I see the woman is not actually engrossed in the newspaper at all; nestled inside is the story of a lovestruck couple, their passion equally illicit and forbidden, told in type with a dropped *e*. Is it my imagination, or do I see the corners of her mouth lift in a smile as she reads intently? And is that my heart skipping a beat too?

When I finally reach the newspaper office, Arlo is apologetic, though somewhat mystified.

'I thought it something you wanted to include,' he protests. 'It was in the folds of the typed copy that you left.'

'But why would you think a story is in any way related to what we do?' I'm slightly frustrated and trying not to show it.

'Stella, I barely take in the content of what's actually in the copy until I read it the next day,' he says defensively. 'I trust you to sift and choose the meaning – which you always do. I only have time to ensure that it's set right, and the sentences are in order. If it's there, I produce it. That's my job.'

I apologise, appreciating the sacrifice Arlo makes each week; he's the only one of three sons left to care for his widowed mother, while two of his brothers fight in the mountains. By day, he works long hours in the flour factory and gives his precious time by night.

'I'm just wondering what Sergio will say,' I ponder. 'It's a bit of an embarrassment.' As our brigade commander, Sergio is responsible not only for the direct action of our two battalions and the flow of information, but the paper's production too. Although the page content is generally decided by whatever we have available week to week, Arlo meets with Sergio to discuss any shift in its political stance, and he relays it to me. The final product also depends on how much we can afford to produce and distribute and what paper supplies are being donated and ghosted in.

As expected, Sergio Lombardi makes contact the next day requesting a meeting, and once again, my time in Breugal's fiefdom crawls by. I am distracted, almost certain my indulgence will be dimly viewed by Resistance leaders. We meet in our usual small bar in San Polo, and I'm surprised when he greets me with a smile and not a grimace.

'I'm so sorry, Signor Lombardi,' I babble. 'I don't quite know what happened – it was simply a mistake and I don't know what to—'

He puts up a hand to stop me. 'Maybe so, Stella, but sometimes good things are born out of a misunderstanding.'

And to my utter amazement, he tells me that the Venetian partisan groups are delighted to have a story of love over oppression – albeit a fictional one – in their dispatches. The response from across Venice has been positive, visibly engaging partisans and patriots.

'The winter has been long and hard, with little good news – you know that better than anyone,' he says. 'So it's good to be able to lift everyone's spirits. I take it there will be a happy ending?'

In all honesty, I haven't thought of a middle, let alone an

end, but yes, I've always seen in my mind that Gaia and Raffiano's love will survive the turmoil. If I didn't think that, then how could I write it? Or even live my own life and push on, day by day, and have hope we will all come through it?

Readers want more, Sergio tells me – a chapter with each week's paper. Is that possible, on top of everything else? The truth is, the first episode felt so little like work and so much like an opening of my heart that I can only agree to it. I'll simply take four trips to Giudecca each week instead of the three of recent months, especially as Sergio says they will hold back on my work as a messenger a little. And in one corner of my mind, I can't help thinking it's one more opportunity to see Jack.

The man himself is pleased to see me and delighted with the news when I shyly tell him on my next trip to Santa Eufemia.

'Something else for a poor convalescent to read,' he says. He's ploughed through the books I've bought already and is eager for more. 'I read the first instalment, and it's very . . .' Jack's hesitation is agony as he holds up the single sheet of paper.

Oh Lord, I knew it – it's a total embarrassment, I tell myself.

'Good,' he says at last. 'I'm honoured to have an authoress in my midst. Can I have your autograph?'

'Stop it!' I cry. 'Now you're just teasing.'

'I'm not actually,' he says, this time without amusement. 'Even in that short chapter, I can already sense the love and need of this couple, almost taste it.' His dark eyes are directly on me, bright and vibrant now he's well. They hold mine

132

for a few, brief seconds, only Sister Cara's noisy arrival breaking what feels fleetingly like a spell. Then he's back to being jokey Jack.

'So, what delicious offerings have we today?' he says as she brings in some soup and bread – a meagre amount for a recovering man of his stature, but it's all they can spare. Being Jack, he is gushing with gratitude: 'What a feast!'

I leave with my shopping bag stuffed with the largest part of the transmitter in the bottom, well-padded with cloth, books and topped off with an ageing smoked herring, donated by the sisters. We can only hope any prying eyes will be put off by the pungent smell and not want to poke too far.

At the newspaper office, I race through the week's news, and use the spare time to start on the second chapter of *The Barb of Love*, which seems to flow out of me with ease. There are elements of so many people in Gaia and Raffiano and their family and friends – Mama, Papa and Vito and Mimi included. I tell myself I am not embodying too much of Jack, and I know I will have to be careful later not to paint a parody of Breugal that could be easily recognised.

Sure of their growing love, the couple seek to hide it from both their families and, more crucially, the outside world, finding ways to meet in secret. They have to be satisfied with snatched moments in abandoned buildings or casting out onto the water, out of sight, where they can be themselves. They live for the here and now, trying not to predict the world which might play out before them. If Hitler wins this war, both know they will have an even tougher battle ahead.

Tapping away at my typewriter, the keys feel well-oiled

133

and the words transfer themselves easily onto the page, almost as if I am merely the conduit and not a creator of any sort. Such a sense of freedom makes me think of family days out on the lagoon before the war, the wind ripping through our hair as the boat gained speed, skin taut with the spray. Totally free. Even Arlo smiles at my industry, he and Tommaso humming as they work.

'Hey, listen to our very own Shakespeare over there,' Arlo nudges at Tommaso. 'She'll be an award-winning writer soon and she'll leave us poor sops to our rough-print paper.'

'Well, since I'm pretty sure Shakespeare didn't have a typewriter, it's not likely,' I quip back at him.

'If he did, I'm damn sure he'd have had one without a broken *e*,' Arlo laughs, and I shoot him a playful scowl.

I'm forced to stop only by the curfew and the increasingly unreliable *vaporetto* from Giudecca.

My head is so wrapped in the story, it's only as the boat nears the mainland that I become more conscious of the shopping bag I'm carrying and the contraband tucked inside. Suddenly, I'm acutely aware of my pace and my manner as I walk off the boat, holding my head high, but allowing no hint of a swagger. I'm making good headway towards home, spying the odd patrol and diverting under *sottos* and into alleyways, when I note there are footsteps behind me. They are constant and not urgent, but something doesn't feel right. They are too measured. As casually as I can, I pause in a shop doorway and pretend to search in my pockets for a handkerchief, hoping the steps will overtake me. Instead, they slow and stop. I peek tentatively out of the doorway. Nothing. Only city noises in the distance, breaking into the silence of the street. The bag is heavy with metal and guilt and I wonder if I'm simply losing my nerve slightly, my imagination running riot. I start off again, willing my ears to screen out the deafening throb in my head. Only it's my heart. Beating in double time.

I'm so intent on what's going on behind me that I take my eye off the scene in front. Literally. I see jackboots standing in front of me too late to mask my obvious shock – and possible guilt – and I snap my head up to meet their granite expressions.

'Evening Signorina,' one says in poor Italian. My heart sinks as I recognise him as one of the soldiers who's stopped me before, the one who viewed me with deep suspicion and was intent on poking into my bag. But does he recognise me now?

'Evening,' I reply in German. It's flattered other patrols before, so why not try?

There's the inevitable barrage of questions: *Where are you going? Where have you been? Where do you live? Where are your papers?*

Strangely, my updated documents which list my employer do nothing to soften the hard, cold stares. They are either bored or under pressure to produce results from their stop and search routines.

One crawls over the script of my papers, while the other's eyes bore into my face, flicking suddenly to the bag in my hand. My fingers are burning from the weight, the handle cutting into my skin, but I'm trying not to move my hand an inch.

I see little point in trying to flirt my way out of this – they are clearly in no mood for it – so I focus on maintaining a veneer of indifference, as though it's a mild irritation to be delayed.

The papers are finally folded and handed back. For a half second I think I will be waved on, but it's wishful thinking.

'What's in the bag?' the one I recognise says. A single dewdrop of sweat snakes its way down my back.

'Oh, just some groceries I'm taking to my mother,' I say. 'Turnips, potatoes.' *Don't overdo it, Stella. Not too much detail.*

Two pairs of eyes narrow in suspicion. 'Open it.'

I'm praying the kipper has aged towards putrid through the evening, so that we'll be greeted with an unholy stink as I pull the handles apart. It's certainly strong, enough to make one of them jerk backwards.

'Holy cow!' he cries. 'What the hell is that?'

I affect a laugh. 'Oh that – it's a kipper. For my mother. Sometimes it's the only fish we can get. Strangely good if you rub some polenta against it.'

'Disgusting,' one mutters, making it difficult to tell if he means the fish, me, or Italians in general. But he's not satisfied. His eyes constrict further and he reaches towards his belt for a thin, wooden cosh. This he pokes into the bag, reaching towards the bottom, inches from the hard shell of the wireless casing.

The sweat is now a continual trickle from the nape of my neck, which could be easily seen from behind as my hair is scooped up in a beret. I'm beginning to feel it prickle at my hairline. One more second and it will break free onto my forehead, signalling my guilt.

'Empty it out,' the one bearing the stick says.

I've no choice but to obey, moving slowly to put down my handbag, playing for a few extra seconds as my brain spins. Is there anything I can do? *Anything?*

'FUCKING NAZIS!' There's a roar to the side of us and,

seconds later, a crack of what could be fireworks or gunfire, followed by another, and another. The corner of my eye catches the remnants of orange flashes lighting up the street ahead.

'LONG LIVE ITALIA, DOWN WITH FASCISM!' the voice echoes again in retreat. Both Aryan heads snap up, eyes hungry. Their bodies swivel and they give chase, leaving me in the street with my haul about to be revealed. In the next second, I've ducked under a *sotto* and, keeping to the dark shadows of the covered alleyway, I move as nimbly as I can. In any direction, just away.

Coming out into a small *campo*, I see that I'm a small bridge away from a Resistance safe house I've visited previously. Keeping my breath under control, I creep towards it, knocking quietly until I get an answer. The muttered password is recognised and I'm admitted. I quickly explain and ask to lodge the bag until it can be picked up. They are elderly patriots and agree. They kindly invite me to stay the night, but I don't want to jeopardise their safety or generosity any more than I have to. I have twenty minutes before curfew and I can make it if I hurry, with no load, and nothing but my near-empty handbag to search.

My heart doesn't slip from inside my throat until I'm behind my own door, and I lie on my bed, scooping in air and placing my hand above my breastbone, plugging the hole where my heart is trying to leap from my chest. One of my nine lives well and truly gone. I think of Mama and Papa, opening the door to Sergio Lombardi, or one of his brigade, and Mama breaking down in utter despair at the news of her daughter's execution for treason against the fascist state. And then I'm sick with remorse – not for what

I did, but for nearly being caught. The consequences for me . . . well, I wouldn't feel them, after the torture or the bullet. But this war pushes its ugly tendrils into every family, every heart, squeezing the life out of kindness and humanity. I weep into my pillow for those I would have left behind and the misery I might have caused; for the partisans we have lost, and those we stand to lose yet.

Lying in bed, my face still wet with sorrow but my pulse calmed, I begin to think about it rationally. I try to imagine how I would have reacted if they had discovered Jack's package. Been stone-faced in guilt, or tried to babble it away as a plant? That would have been stupid and unbelievable, but it might have played for some time. And then I wonder at the commotion which saved me. It was either supremely convenient, or a well-timed diversion. I can't help pondering if it was anything to do with the footsteps trailing me and who it could have been.

I struggle to piece it all back together in sequence, yet it remains a blur. Whatever the reason, I feel grateful for fate, and I endeavour to be more careful. To be smarter, more alert. Keep safe, Stella. No sudden moves. Isn't that the one rule of survival?

14

A Voice from the Lagoon

Bristol, October 2017

Soon doesn't come soon enough for Luisa. Her plans for an impromptu trip to Venice are scuppered by the legalities of being the sole heir to her mother's small estate – words like 'probate' and 'inheritance tax' pepper her post and emails. She's needed to sign documents or witness statements. Annoyingly, a major commission arrives at the same time – one she can't turn down, but it will at least go some way to financing the Venice trip until the proceeds from sale of her mother's house finally come through.

Instead, Luisa spends the time preparing by reading as much literature as she can about the wartime Resistance in Venice, of which there is surprisingly little. The books by her bedside soon resemble a major study project; she wouldn't want any government prying into her cyber search history, with its preoccupation with the keywords of 'fascism' and 'Nazi occupation'.

Her Italian is progressing nicely, though, thanks to a friend of Jamie's who is in need of some PR work, causing them to broker a convenient exchange of skills once a week. It's bound to be wishful thinking on her part, but there are some phrases that resonate – the way the tutor pronounces '*Prego*' like Grandma Stella did when forgetting herself sometimes. It nags at her brain like a type of dimmed déjà vu, and she likes to imagine there are shades of her grandmother being meticulously uncovered. Luisa has no memory of her own mother speaking Italian at all, though she would surely have known how, with two Italian parents? The faint shadow she hears must have been Stella, or even Grandpa Gio. Surely?

In between the commission and the exchange with solicitors, Luisa begins a wider search. She pays for a probe into her family tree – though omits to tell Jamie of the cost – and sends out feelers via email, hopeful of befriending English speakers in Venice with family to help forge any links. And then she waits, eagerly prising open Daisy's cover each morning and checking her emails. For weeks she goes around in circles, it seems, being sent from virtual pillar to post, those who 'may' have had an elderly relative, but whose memories subsequently prove to have shrivelled with time or desire.

And then Luisa hits the jackpot. A reply in English from a certain Giulio Volpe, research fellow at the Institute for the History of Resistance and Contemporary Society, or IVESER for short, situated on Giudecca island. There they have not only the most comprehensive history of the Resistance in Venice, but proof – photographs, letters, newspapers. It's like Christmas and birthdays all in one for Luisa. Signor Volpe goes on to say that he has checked and cannot find any record of a Stella Hawthorn, though this comes as no real surprise to Luisa, as it's so obviously not her grandmother's original name. There's nothing in her mother's correspondence that stretches back to her maiden name – only Grandpa Gio's surname of Benetto – but equally, she feels sure her grandmother was unlikely to have been already married in the war. The photograph from San Marco – with the man clearly marked as 'C' – shows she wasn't yet with Grandpa in 1950.

The promise of a cache of photographs is far more valuable to Luisa. Alongside those in her precious box, it's a potential key to the puzzle, and in the marriage of the two she might well have her answer.

For the first time since her mother's death – perhaps even before that – Luisa feels a sense of exhilaration mixed with calm. That there might be some resolve. Something on which to fix herself.

Now she can go and discover Venice, and perhaps herself in unison.

15

Love and Fury

Venice, April–May 1944

The days roll swiftly into weeks – work at the Nazi head-quarters, newspaper production and the flow of Gaia and Raffiano, which pours out of me like a fountain that's finally been unblocked. The only hole in my life is Jack; his leg has improved enough for him to be moved from the church on Giudecca to the smaller island of Pellestrina, which runs alongside the Lido and is well out of the way of patrols. Once he's strong enough, he'll attempt the long journey home over the mountain passes, hopefully before winter sets in. Meanwhile, he's to be employed in relaying messages on his homemade transmitters and helping to repair holes in the nets of the local fishermen.

'I'm just glad to repay the debt and be good for something,' he'd joked at our last meeting on Giudecca. 'My mother taught me to sew at a very early age. I felt sure it would come in handy one day.'

His humour is to cover up the sadness. I'm certain we both feel it, having formed a firm friendship. Is it something more? It's hard to tell as we embrace what we suspect will be a final goodbye. I simply know it will leave a gap in me somewhere. His face tells me he will have regrets too.

Over the next week I do miss my visits, but I'm so busy I barely have time to think about anything aside from work or surviving; the shortages mean food is scarce, especially with the city's population swelled to almost double with refugees. The water supplies are also low as a result of the bombings in nearby Mestre and Marghere and damage to the precious pipes. Waiting in the endless queues for the pumps has a silver lining, though, since it's the perfect time to gauge the effect of my blossoming story, which is now slipped into the paper in weekly instalments. I can't help smiling a little when I'm party to the gossip surrounding Gaia and Raffiano, almost as if they are a living, breathing couple and the readers prophesying on their love and fate are their friends.

'He's just like my nephew, Alfredo,' I overhear one woman say. 'He sounds so handsome, and my nephew is so giving, just like Raffiano. I'm *sure* the writer knows Alfredo.'

I'm never tempted to break out of my anonymity though – it could cost me my life, for one, but I also find I like that cloak of mystery it creates. I'm having fun with it.

Hearing the reaction first-hand reassures me I have the right tone, and at times I absorb people's aspirations for the couple into my writing, as if Venice itself is determining the direction of their love.

Sergio, too, relays messages that the story is having a positive effect on morale as the love-struck pair use their guile to dodge and dupe the Nazi machine. It's timely, since in reality the Allied and partisan fight in Italy is making slow progress, with the Allies focusing elsewhere in Europe for their victories; Radio Londra tells us of the Allied destruction of Gestapo headquarters in Hungary and Yugoslavia, and the British RAF's attack on Gestapo HQ in The Hague. Less welcome are the stories of German reprisals that we hear of via underground messages, and which I like to imagine are something to do with Jack and his magic with the transmitters: the Nazi murder of eighty-six French civilians as pure revenge for partisan aggression. It's painful to hear, but we have to know – we in Venice need to use it as fuel for our fight against our own occupiers.

I begin to hear the effects of my story from other quarters too – loud and clear bellows of fury pushing out of General Breugal's office one morning in late April. The rant is muted by the heavy wooden door, but I catch snippets of his diatribe from my desk.

'Fucking partisans!' he's virtually screaming, and I can picture the purple veins in his fat neck at bursting point. 'As if I haven't got enough to deal . . . without . . . bloody writer . . . wasting my time . . .'

Cristian is sitting at his desk, pretending to check through a report, although I sense he's not focused. It must be Captain Klaus who is bearing the full force of Breugal's tirade. For a brief moment, I almost feel sorry for the second-in-command, his thin body bending against this windstorm of anger. Almost.

It's swiftly replaced by a sense of satisfaction at being the engineer of Breugal's – and the Nazis' – frustrations. If I've caught the words correctly, it's Gaia and Raffiano they are

145

talking of – their effect on morale in the city and the partisans' sheer audacity in producing it under their noses. Popsa was right – the gentle needling of words can become a thorn and then a sword in the flesh of our enemies. I'm anxious and pleased at the same time. What happens if they find an enemy in their midst? What lengths would they go to silence someone like me? My cheeks are suddenly hot, despite the cool breeze running through the office.

The ranting stops eventually and Captain Klaus emerges, his brow creased like he's faced the bloodiest of battles and half wishing he had succumbed. Breugal's voice follows him out of the door. 'De Luca!'

Cristian gets up from his chair, though not as swiftly as I would expect, given the previous exchange. Calmly, he picks up his pad and pencil and enters the emperor's lair. There are voices, but annoyingly low and I can't make out any of the conversation, even though the rest of the office has slackened the pace of work noticeably, typewriters almost holding their breath. It's a full ten minutes until Cristian emerges, stopping to cast an eye around the office, noting the pace. One stern look and the clatter begins again.

He works at his desk for half an hour, scratching on sheets of paper. My curiosity burns and finally overwhelms me; I sidle up to him with the excuse of needing assistance over a technical phrase but with my eyes scanning his papers. Spread across his desk are several instalments of *The Barb of Love*, and my heart skips to see them here in this office, his hands upon them. Cristian is clearly sketching out what looks to be a handbill, effectively a 'wanted' poster – there's a reward, a substantial one, for the whereabouts of the typewriter and, more importantly, for the scribe responsible.

Whatever I'd expected from their reaction, I hadn't been prepared for this. I can barely get my words out as a hot sweat overtakes me at the reality of myself as a wanted criminal, and I mumble an excuse to leave his side.

In the bathroom, I have to control the noise of my breathing, silently gulping back the air which threatens to overwhelm me. Stupidly, I had thought it a bit of fun at first, was overly flattered by Sergio's enthusiasm. I should have known that a regime that values propaganda and the sheen of power above real substance would be angered at the influence of such challenge, even one rendered as fiction. Of course they would never tolerate such brazen defiance. And now I am a target, plain and simple. My only hope is that the bedrock of the Venetian Resistance – Resistance everywhere in fact – will save me. We need solidarity – to close ranks and stand firm, like the wood and mud on which we all exist in this suspended paradise. Any breaches, any gaps amid the piles, and we will all sink. Plain and simple.

I desperately want to prod at Cristian for more information, as he's clearly party to Breugal's overall plan, but I stop myself. I remember that, despite the friendship he's shown me, his unobtrusive nature likely makes him more dangerous than even the generals. Cristian is clever, and very possibly powerful in his own way, but doesn't take pains to advertise it. He is, first and foremost, a loyal fascist.

He's unusually quiet through the afternoon, moving in and out of Breugal's sanctum, and I see what is clearly the finished poster return from the printers posthaste. There, larger than on any of the sheets typed so far, is the distinctive droop of my letter *e*. It challenges in hard, bold script:

Cristian sits back and peruses his creation with what appears to be satisfaction.

I leave the building that night feeling as though I have a target on my back, that when the handbills are dotted around Venice, tied to lamp posts and tacked onto doors, it will be my face up there; Stella Jilani – it's her, *she* did it. Betray her, catch her. Kill her.

I can only take some comfort in the realisation that my beloved machine is across the water on Giudecca, buried in a basement, and that it will stay there, hidden from danger.

I wander for a time around the streets. I'm due at my parents' house for dinner, and my stomach growls with the anticipation of Mama's cooking, but I need to order my thoughts beforehand, especially with the added turmoil of today. I can't let my face betray any worry, enough for Papa to suspect and pull me aside. Equally, I don't want to sit in a bar, hearing the clink of glasses and everyday chatter; no one in this city is devoid of worry, but I feel there's a load on my shoulders that I need to disperse by myself, quietly.

I head towards the normally tranquil set of streets around the Zattere, which have little passing traffic aside from the odd chug of a small boat. I'm deep in thought, doubtless looking at my own feet, when I'm yanked into the present. Again.

'Signorina Jilani?' It's his voice again – unmistakable. I'm disorientated by shock. Is the voice behind me, or in front?

Eventually I spot him: Cristian is to my right-hand side,

at the water's edge, opposite an old building yard for gondolas, and he's turned to face me. How many times can you come across one person by accident? My Staffetta's paranoia rises; I suspect that it's anything but. Has he been following me, and I've dropped my guard entirely? The events of the afternoon churn within me.

'Oh! Evening, Signore,' I stammer.

'It's a beautiful one, isn't it?' he says, and casts his eyes across the water again. His voice is calm and in no way sinister. He appears to have left the turmoil of work back in the office.

'Are you looking at something in particular?' I'm genuinely curious, but I also want to try and flush out his reason for being here. If he's not tailing me, then what?

'The gondolas,' he says, almost wistfully. 'I always said to my mother that if I came to Venice, I would take a ride for her, take lots of photographs. But those seem only to transport supplies nowadays.'

'I daresay you could find a willing gondolier in some bar or other, for the right kind of money,' I reply still mystified. The age-old impression of Venice's canals teeming with lyrical gondoliers has been largely interrupted by war, the only 'tourists' now being Nazi soldiers on leave. The skilled pilots are employed elsewhere or off to war, but they still exist in the fabric of the city if you know where to look.

'Hmm, it wouldn't feel quite the same,' he says, and affects a weak smile. 'And besides, I'd like to take that ride with someone special. It seems only right, being such a seminal event.'

Is he hinting, or teasing? Or just playing with me? It's said with good grace, and even some humour. Is this the same man who drafted a warrant for my arrest only this afternoon, who can and will enforce my capture if necessary? My mind is an eddy of thoughts.

He whips his head out of a fantasy and towards me. 'Are you heading anywhere in particular, Signorina?' he says, seeing that I'm rooted to the spot in my confusion.

'What? N ... well yes, actually. I'm going to see my parents,' I say. 'My mother's cooking.' I speak the truth so as not to tie myself in more knots.

'Can I escort you anywhere?' he offers.

'No need to trouble yourself, thank you. I need to stop off somewhere on the way, buy some bread if I can.'

'Well, have a good evening.' And he turns back to musing over the dry dock gondolas, barren of their precious water and needing more than a lick of paint to restore them to glory. I step towards the Accademia Bridge, peering over my shoulder every few steps, sure that he will have disappeared from the waterside and be following only a few steps behind, hidden in the walls. But he remains on the same spot, stock-still, hands in his pockets.

I wonder how, after this exchange, I will ever get my own thoughts in order?

16

A Lull

Venice, May 1944

As with most imaginings, the reality is not always as bad as the grey forecasts your mind is capable of. I spy the first poster the very next morning only a few streets from my square, fluttering in the morning breeze, nailed to a post. I would have turned and walked the other way rather than look at it, had it not been for the group crowding around and peering at its message. I eavesdrop on the edges of the gathering.

'Well, who'd have thought a little story could get the Nazis all fired up,' mocks one woman.

'Scared of their own shadow, are they?' says another, and they join in with a group cackle, although mindful of any lingering patrols.

'Good on whoever is writing it, I say,' an old man pipes up. 'I read it to my wife every week. She can't see too well now, and it always cheers her up. She'll be upset if it stops now, without knowing how it ends.'

151

At their words, I feel the strength of my own two halves fighting against each other: proud and scared, wary and overwhelmed, terrified and defiant. Having always been a fairly decisive person, I now feel completely in sync with the ebb and flow of our beloved Venetian *laguna* – labile and uncertain, a continual shift. I know where my heart lies, but on which side of the equation does common sense sit?

I have to endure another day under Cristian's gaze before I can speak to Arlo, Matteo and Tommaso, find out what Sergio and the commanders have said and discuss how we keep ourselves safe.

The indecision gnaws at me in the Reich office, and I try to immerse myself in the work. The atmosphere is lighter as Breugal is away for the day, which Marta informs me with noticeable relief as I arrive. Cristian, too, seems a little less beleaguered, and I see him again studying the fiction that has sprouted from inside my mind, his glasses on top of his head and the paper close to his eyes. Yet his face doesn't sport any anger as he reads one sheet after another – occasionally his brow knits, but he seems genuinely engrossed. Apart from interest, his expression is devoid of anything else, however, and I realise I'm slightly disappointed; after all our conversations over literature, I'd perhaps been relying on Cristian to appreciate a good story, to see some reaction in his mouth or his eyes as Raffiano contemplates risking all for his love – he won't bow to his family's demands and give up Gaia, pledges to stand by her, wherever she goes. I want my words to incite some emotion, at least. And then I cut short my own inflated conceit. It's a story, Stella – written simply to amuse and perhaps prompt a passing comment, a fleeting

152

warm glow. Nothing more. There's no room for overblown egos in this war.

On Giudecca, Arlo is at first buoyed by the Germans' reaction – that we have poked at the wasps' nest – though he is sensitive to my anxiety. It's not his fingerprints that are recognisable in the text. Tentatively, he voices what I have already been thinking – that I should get rid of the typewriter, bestow it to the care of the sea bed forever. But as I stare at the familiar keys, feel its idiosyncrasies under my fingers, and hear the sound that has been part of my life's melody for so long, I know I can't do it. And that's before I even begin to think about Popsa. It has to stay – hidden, but here.

In the next few days, Sergio is quick to reassure me of anonymity, and although he suggests we suspend the instalments, he doesn't propose stopping forever. I wonder if he's simply placating me, but I'm secretly a little relieved. No one enjoys being a target.

'If we stop now, the Reich office will simply think we're scared off,' Sergio convinces me. 'It'll give them a sense of superiority, and that's always good to nurture. It's then that they are more likely to make mistakes.'

He squeezes my arm. 'You'll be back,' he says, 'and with more imagination, more ways to illustrate our strength, than before. I'm sure of it.'

For a time, I'm a little relieved at the extra space in my life – I'm told my work within the inner sanctum of the Reich is continuing to be crucial to understanding their plans across the region. Reading between the lines of each report I type and convey, there's a wealth of information on troop numbers in and out of the Veneto; Breugal's office is responsible for tracking their movements. We're learning rapidly which rail lines are vital arteries for supply chains and – in turn – which ones the partisan brigades can sabotage. Sergio tells me it's all helping the Resistance to construct a map, one key to keeping our Nazi invaders constantly on the back foot. When Sergio grasps my hand and tells me I am a vital cog in the machine, I'm flooded with a sense of worth. And always, always, I think of my beloved Popsa and how he would have smiled like a mischievous little boy to see the enemy scuppered.

I do miss Gaia and Raffiano, though – the incentive to lay their lives on the page has been because of the people out there wanting to hear. I never write well into a void. So, for the present, they hover in my head, ready to reignite when the call comes.

My duties as a Staffetta increase and fill the gap a little, meaning I'm never idle, although I do have more time to devote to Mama and Papa. I'd always thought them strong and unbending – isn't that how most children view their parents, as enduring heroes? Increasingly, though, I see the worry etched on their faces. Papa's normally sturdy shoulders are becoming thin from the food shortages, bowed under the strain of war's daily angst, while his muscles recede under his skin. It's only as I see my parents more frequently – twice a week if I can manage it between my day job, evenings at the paper and occasional night work as a messenger – that I notice the anxiety take its toll on them physically. Each time I visit Mama tells me that I look tired, but there are much deeper grey patches under her own, normally bright, eyes. Papa pushes me for information in the minutes when we're alone, but I tell him very little. How can I, when they already worry so much about me and Vito?

While I know for sure that my younger brother by three years is a partisan, I think that they have long suspected, even though Mama tries to shield herself from the knowledge as a type of maternal self-protection.

In Vito's childhood, she spent years worrying over the deformity that he was born with in his foot – a bone or ligament twisted and set in the womb, cruelly labelled a club foot. Like any mother, she blamed herself. It was operated on when he was a baby, and he grew up to become nothing more than an irritating younger brother who scaled walls with his friends and chased me mercilessly, albeit with a limp.

Mama crossed herself and thanked the saints when Vito's so-called disability saved him from the Italian army, or being used as labour fodder for the Nazis – he could emphasise his limp superbly when needed. Perhaps naïvely, she thought he would be safer here in Venice. But, clearly, Vito sees his role as something other than that of a silent observer in this war.

'He's barely here, Stella,' Mama bemoans again. 'He comes in at all hours. Sometimes, he's filthy, and I know it's not just from work. How can he get that dirty day to day?'

I'm certain he can't – not from his job as a machine operator at the docks. But in other activities, certainly – scrabbling down railway sidings and crawling through the underbelly of Venice. Papa beckons me with his eyes out in the yard as Mama clears away the dishes.

'Have you any clue as to what Vito is doing?' he says. Papa is fishing, but even he can't ask outright – whether, as a fellow partisan, I know what my own brother is up to in the small hours. Even within families, loose talk can have fatal consequences, and it's often better not to know the details. You can't betray what you don't know.

Papa shoots a plume of smoke into the air – these days I note he smokes out of need, not pleasure as he did before the war. 'Stella? Your mother is worried sick.'

'I don't know, Papa,' I say, but only half in truth. I have heard, on a well-stretched grapevine, that Vito may be part of a group activating raids on the Arsenale, the heavily fortified base for Nazi weaponry. So far, they amount to small acts of sabotage, which are irritating to the Reich rather than disabling. Mimi once alluded to there being a young man I might know involved in Resistance missions, and I've sometimes seen Arlo looking at me sideways as we're compiling the paper. His expression is often strained then, as if he doesn't want me to put two and two together while I'm typing the reports. I have, but not enough to be certain. It concerns me, though, as it does Papa now – irritation in the Reich will soon turn to anger, and the consequences will be harsh if Vito is caught.

'I'll talk to him, Papa,' I promise, if only to appease my parents' worry – just as they've comforted me so many times in my life.

'Thank you, Stella. Thank you, *cuore mio*.' His gentle touch on my arm is like the thousand hugs he's given me over my entire life.

I leave a note with Mama for Vito, a chirpy, 'Hello brother, haven't seen you in a long time, let's have a drink' type of message, asking him to meet me in a café next Saturday, when I know he won't have any excuses about being at work. I'll leave the same note at Paolo's, where I know he

156

drinks once or twice a week. That's all I can do; I hope that his sense outweighs his zest for glory.

In the Reich office, there's much to occupy me, but little to get excited about. Copies of *Venezia Liberare* are stacked in the corner of Cristian's desk, and it feels odd knowing that something of me is sitting there in front of him. One of his tasks now seems to be to scan the paper as it comes out and he does it diligently, his glasses hovering on his brow, the paper pulled closely to his face. My skin itches each time I see him do it, as if he might be able to smell my collusion, some odour lingering on the pages. This is what paranoia feels like.

However, as the weeks go by without the inserted sheet of Gaia and Raffiano's growing love, the fervour surrounding the typewriter subsides. There seem to be no further directives to go out on specific searches, and I detect neither mutterings nor tantrums coming from Breugal's office, rather that he's immersing himself further in Venetian good living. Cristian, though, seems to have adopted a more formal air around me, and we've lost that brief flash of friendly intimacy. I can't help feeling some disappointment, though I'm not sure why. I am, however, glad not to be in his sights for any other purpose.

I finally meet Vito in Paolo's bar, judging it to be the safest place. Even so, we sit in the corner, away from too many ears. He has a day's dark growth around his chin, and his eyes betray a tiredness around the edges, but at the same time his pupils are sparkling with mischief. I recognise the look – he is alive with the satisfaction of duplicity.

'So, what have you been up to?' I begin casually.

'Oh, this and that,' he says, hiding his expression by sipping at his beer.

'Is it a girl keeping you up and out at night? You look exhausted.'

'Do I? Maybe,' he beams.

I lean in closer, this time with an expression that's much less relaxed. 'Vito, be careful,' I half whisper.

'What? I'm not getting married, if that's what you mean!' He pushes back, laughing, still trying to keep up the light pretence but I'm already bored with it.

'Vito, this is me you're talking to. You are dangerously close to getting your fingers burned. Badly. Perhaps the rest of you too.' I raise my eyebrows in a determined look that says: let's drop the charade, we need to talk about this.

He puffs out his cheeks, attempts a half-smile and then abandons both. I can see his brain ticking – there's no point in this facade with Stella, he's thinking. I always knew when he was lying as a boy. His eyebrows ripple just slightly. Now, they twitch automatically; no, he won't tell me of the recent incident in which a weapons store was set on fire, or his part in laying explosives in the docks he knows so well, but his signature is all over them.

He leans in. 'But what we are doing is making a difference,' he urges. 'I have to help, Stella. I need it.' And his eyes flick beyond the table top and towards his foot underneath. Still apologising for what wasn't his fault, was no one's doing. Proving himself. 'Anyway, you're one to talk.' His black eyes are steely now, full lips pursed.

For a minute, I'm taken aback. It hadn't occurred to me he would know the depth of my activity – the battalions are co-ordinated, but we operate under different lieutenants, overseen by Sergio. I see my own facade instantly fall away.

'I don't know how much closer you can get to the devil's cauldron than being right next to the fire,' Vito goes on. His expression invites an answer, but I have little defence.

'Sometimes, it's actually safer working in plain sight,' I try. 'I'm careful. I'm safe – I don't take chances.'

With anyone else, Vito might have tried to convince them that he doesn't either. But he knows our shared history all too well – the times he and his school friends dared to goad the local police into adrenalin-filled chases, hopping over and under bridges, hiding in derelict buildings. It was child's play, irritating more than illegal, but Vito always did push the boundaries to prove himself.

'Promise me that whatever you take on, you'll think of Mama and Papa. Think of them *not* attending your funeral.'

'I will – I do,' he says earnestly. 'But if they did have to, they would be proud. Of what I will have done for us, for Venice.'

'They might be proud, Vito, but even more, they will be sad. Very, very sad.'

We part outside Paolo's with a hug, much like the ones I've shared with my so-called suitors when passing messages. Yet this one lingers: we squeeze tightly and he kisses my cheek.

'Be safe, Vito,' I whisper.

'Venezia Liberare,' he whispers back. He's grinning as he backs away with a wave and an audible '*Ciao*'.

17

On Hold

Bristol, November 2017

'Jesus!' Luisa feels exasperation again as she checks her emails. More legal hoops to jump through, more papers to sign. It's the one tether – aside from not wanting to leave Jamie, of course – that's keeping her from jumping on a plane to Venice, in her search for the key. Thanks to the wonders of the internet and budget airlines, she could be on a plane tomorrow, book a hotel with a click of the finger. Were it not for the endless meanderings of the legal property world. And yet that is also a passport of sorts; property prices are sky high in Bristol and her mother's inheritance is the only way she and Jamie will ever afford a real home of their own, to put down roots, to perhaps expand their family, as Jamie keeps hinting. Luisa, though, isn't sure she's ready to be a mother yet, worries that she won't have the necessary skills or patience it clearly takes. Genetics can account for a lot, can't it? Nurturing was never her mother's strong point, even she knows that.

Not that she has a plan for Venice, but that doesn't stop Luisa wanting to just get there, step on the mud flats turned to land and feel she's closer to . . . well, to something. The tendrils of enquiry she put out into the internet world have ground to a trickle of 'No, sorry', and so far all she can pinpoint within the box are some random addresses and key areas within the city. There's the Jewish Museum to visit, but really she's pinning her hopes on Giulio Volpe and his archive to set her on some kind of detective trail. But to what end?

She suspects this is what occupies Jamie's mind, but he has too much love for her to voice it. If she looks inside herself – something she's been almost afraid to do in recent months – even she isn't sure. Inevitably, Luisa has spent an age, usually in the early hours of the morning when Jamie is blissfully asleep beside her, wondering why her mother felt unable to give much of herself to her only child, or her husband when he was alive. Luisa remembers her father as so loving, days out when they would walk and sing, always laughing. In the background was her mother, tight-lipped with a shadow of grey cast across her features, reminding them not to jump in the puddles, or that it might rain very soon and then where would the two of them be without a coat?

What made her like that, Luisa thinks, when her grand-mother always seemed to be laughing, or getting herself into minor scrapes and giggling at being told off by her own daughter? Luisa feels she may never know what caused her mother to be born without a sense of adventure or fun. The nearest she can aspire to is discovering what made her grandmother into the adventurer she is now proving to be.

It has become her sole purpose, a driving force that has become all-consuming, but it makes her feel something other than empty and adrift. And for that reason, she has no choice but to go forward.

Luisa just needs to step onto Venetian soil and float among its islands, to feel she is halfway there.

18

Small Talk

Venice, June 1944

The first days of June bring a cause for celebration that gradually filters through the airwaves to our Venetian enclave; Rome is liberated by the Allies on 5th June, and just a day later the Allies breach the French coastline with widespread landings on the Normandy beaches. In our basements and with heads bent tightly together in cafés we rejoice at the tide turning in Europe, and the thought of Romans taking to the streets in sheer relief at reclaiming their city. Breugal is, of course, fuming. He struts and stomps his childish fury over the entire building while we put our heads down and type at speed to avoid his backlash, which – given his reputation – could have more serious repercussions.

Strangely, though, the news sees a renewed civility towards me from Cristian. He is suddenly more open and approachable, and I wonder if perhaps he senses which side of the coin holds most value. It may be that he's realised being a fascist as the Allied line crawls northwards is becoming increasingly uncomfortable. Except that his manner seems genuine and I'm once again blindsided by the contrast between his general demeanour and my suspicions about his motives.

In this new mood, he asks me to accompany him for a drink one day after work, on the premise of discussing a particular translation. I'm tempted to say I have a prior engagement, but then I'm torn not only by my loyalties as a collector of information for the Resistance, but also because I feel slightly glad at his asking. Once again, it doesn't feel right to hold those emotions. In the end, I find myself saying yes, convincing myself I'm simply a loyal partisan.

I dally awhile so that we leave separately again, me following several minutes behind and meeting under the clock in the corner of San Marco, though I can't decide whether the location purposely makes it appear like some kind of secret rendezvous. I have enough of those in my life already. My natural suspicion leads me to imagine he has a photographer lurking in the shadows, gathering evidence to use as blackmail at a later date.

Immediately, though, he seems different. Outside of Breugal's sphere, away from the confines of our high-ceilinged but oppressive office, he smiles a good deal. A weight is clearly lifted. At our table inside a small trattoria, he pulls out a file, but I quickly sense that he has no intention of opening it. I'm itching to know if it contains the sheets of *The Barb of Love*, or his promised translation.

Instead, it becomes clear he wants to talk literature and stories. Part of me suspects he's simply hungry for conversation – and his eyes light up as we talk of books we've both read, those that have influenced us. We steer clear of political tomes, sticking to the historical, romantic or those that shaped our lives as Italian people rather than its complex array of politics. Eventually the time causes him to offer up dinner, and the prospect of a plate of squid-ink pasta is far more appetising than my near-empty cupboard at home.

When our talk steers towards Dickens's instalments of *Pickwick Papers*, I finally pluck up the courage to casually touch on the weekly contributions of our home-grown illicit scribe, my bravado fortified by the good Chianti we're working our way through.

'You've seen it, then?' he says.

'I think most Venetians have.' I'm exaggerating the reach of the newspaper, but it never does any harm to bluff a little in the face of the enemy.

'And?'

'And what?'

'Do you think it's good? Do you like it?' he says. Again, the way he holds his mouth, lips slightly parted, makes me wonder if there aren't several troopers outside, waiting on his word to arrest me. Or if he's genuinely asking for my opinion. The light on his glasses masks any sincere look in his russet pupils.

'I think it's touched a nerve, possibly speaks for some Venetians.' I'm eggshell-hopping with my words.

'No, I mean, regardless of the message, do you like the writing? The style?'

Again, I can't tell if he's attempting to trip me up. I decide to brazen it out.

'I do,' I say. 'Perhaps a little flowery in places, but it makes me read on. Isn't that half the battle for a writer?' I'm being decidedly non-committal, but I reason that being too vague will only fuel his suspicions if he has any.

'I agree,' he says, sipping on his wine.

'So do *you* like it?' My curiosity, and perhaps my vanity, override any common sense now that I'm almost three glasses down the bottle.

'I do,' he replies. 'I think it's very good. I was immersed.' He pulls up his head. 'And that means I'm glad it's gone. It wouldn't be a popular opinion with Breugal or Klaus, and I've enough to do in keeping them satisfied.'

I note it's the first time he's referred to them by their surnames only, or alluded to his own irritation – the wine chipping a little at his own hard shell perhaps. He seems softer, helped by the fact that he's taken off his jacket and I can no longer see the glint of his fascist loyalty pin. His colours removed from the mast.

Again, I seize the alcohol-fuelled moment, my abandon teasing out an intense curiosity. 'What did you do, Cristian? Before all this?'

He glances up, his brow knitted, perhaps unseated that I even want to know. 'I was a part-time teacher at the university in Rome,' he says. 'While I was doing my doctorate.'

'In what?'

'European Romantic Literature.'

Suddenly, it all begins to fall into place for me: his intelligence, but also his love of history and literature, his need to talk and discuss, to cast backwards into many other, older lives – in short, his desperation to keep the words alive inside himself. This is why he seeks me out as a fellow book lover – to remind himself of the world he lived in before the war. Isn't that exactly what I do with Gaia and Raffiano – keep my former life and love of writing alight within me? The leap for Cristian to Breugal's office and what he represents now is harder to fathom, but I've almost given up on that for now. Instead, in the here and now, the wine and the pasta give me almost a sense of enjoyment. And that provokes another stab of guilt within me.

My silent musings prompt another searching look.

'You seem surprised?' he says.

Yes and no. I've never questioned his commitment to a career, but his efficiency and drive in the Reich office have always led me to assume he was in politics or working his way up in some government department. The love of books I'd put down simply to an escape.

'Um, not surprised exactly,' I lie. He raises an eyebrow. 'All right, perhaps a little,' I concede.

'That I'm human?' But he doesn't wait for my answer, instead sweeping a hand across the table, perhaps alluding to all of this – outside the cosy restaurant, in Venice, Europe, the world. War. Killing. Domination. All of it.

'Well, it's all academic now,' he says, scratching awkwardly at the table cloth. 'This war has put paid to that.'

'You won't go back to it?' I ask. There's never any need to say *if you survive* – it's the proviso that no one needs to clarify in these times. Every plan and every thought for the future depends on surviving the turmoil.

'Hmm, maybe.' There's a faraway look in his eye and we're saved any more introspection by the waiter bringing the bill.

As we leave amid the darkness, he offers to walk me home. For a second, I think about declining with a valid excuse of needing to stop off and buy provisions, using the lone walk to help sober me up and collect my increasingly scrambled thoughts. But I don't. For reasons even I don't understand, I find myself saying 'Yes, thank you' to Cristian De Luca. In the warmth of the evening, he doesn't put his jacket back on, but drapes it casually over his shoulder, hooking it with one finger. He doesn't offer the other arm to me, and I'm relieved – with everything that's passed since the military function it would feel too intimate.

Ever the diplomat, he steers the conversation to a time way back, when we might have had something in common as young Italians growing up in the early days of Mussolini's fascism, when we were too innocent to make distinctions; life surrounded by copious relatives and grandparents, family dinners and the food of childhood – mouth-watering sweet cannoli and tiramisu that we can still taste in our memories if we try hard enough (and hope to again in reality when war rations allow).

'I was always considered a slightly odd child because even on the sunniest of days I was holed in the town library with my nose in a book,' Cristian tells me, laughing at his own strangeness.

'Me too!' I say. 'Poor Mama was forever trying to drag me out to play with hordes of girls – they just thought I was boring. Only my grandfather understood the wordsmith in me . . .' and I'm cut short not only by the memory of Popsa but by the realisation that I am straying into my former life as a journalist. That part of me needs to stay hidden for sure.

'Seems like we both have ended up in places that aren't quite right,' he muses into the night air. 'What is it the English say? "A square peg in a round hole"?'

Inside, I laugh at the self-same label I'd already applied to him in those early weeks in the Reich office. What else is it that the English say – 'Great minds think alike'?

And then it feels as if he's the one cutting himself short, for fear of peeling back too much personal identity. I decide then that I hate this war, for all the death and destruction it brings, but also for changing us as people, for making us afraid to *give* to each other.

In no time at all we reach the small *campo* of my apartment. I note my elderly neighbour's curtain twitch, but I'm grateful that Signora Menzio is simply checking my safety. I'm even more glad that Cristian's jacket is still slung across his shoulder and she can't see his badge, firm anti-fascist that she is.

Cristian walks me to the door, hovers for a second and seems unwilling to say goodbye, smiling that 'well, here we are' expression. It's utterly stupid, but I honestly don't know how it happens. We sort of drift towards one another. The space between us narrows, and in a moment that lasts forever our lips are touching. Willingly. His are soft and warm and I hope mine aren't chalky and ungiving. It goes on for a second maybe, long enough that it's not a friendly peck, or colleagues simply saying '*Ciao*'. I think I even close my eyes, but it's hard to be sure.

He pulls away, not roughly, but to stop it moving into anything else, I imagine.

'Signorina, I'm so sorry,' he blusters, eyes down to the ground. 'I didn't mean to . . . I didn't think . . .'

'No, no. It's fine, honestly fine,' I stutter back, because it's all I can think of to say. I'm more embarrassed than horrified. We're like teenagers on an awkward first date. I drop my door key and we almost bang heads as we both try to recover it. 'Sorry, sorry,' we both blather and I see he's desperate for an escape.

'Well, good evening.' He smiles meekly and almost runs towards the nearest alleyway leading out of the *campo*. I push myself inside and up to the apartment, hovering motionless in my kitchen for an age. What did I just do? I kissed a known fascist. Or did he kiss me? Does it matter, since I didn't object?

I'm filled with a dense guilt, first that it happened and, secondly, that not every part of me regrets it. *Oh, Stella, pull yourself together. Feelings like this could lead to your heart breaking and a noose around your neck.* Yet efforts to order my mind fail miserably.

I climb into bed with a canopy of confusion sitting above me, a thin, impermeable veil. What is Cristian De Luca about? And why can I not fully dislike him?

The next day, I seek out Mimi, who – as only a best friend would – points out the grey bags under my eyes. She half guesses at my sleeplessness and I come clean about the kiss, thwarted though it was. I wonder, though, thwarted by what and by whom? Guilt, mostly, on my part at least.

Mimi isn't as shocked as I'd expected – she's always been a true romantic and, for her, love overrides all. I see in her so many elements of the imaginary Gaia and resolve to try and disguise it better.

'But there's no getting away from the fact he is a fascist,' I confess to her.

'And what on earth makes you think that fascists don't have feelings or desires?' Mimi pitches. 'We might not like their politics, but it doesn't make them monsters in every

172

sense. Well, not all of them, I'm sure.' She carries so much sense in her tiny frame, and yet my shame rides up to nip at me when I least expect it.

'But I have to work with him!' I bemoan.

'And very likely he will be feeling the same way, and so you will both be very embarrassed and that will be the end of it,' she adds. 'It's not a hanging offence, Stella.'

She leans in further, eyes wide and full of conspiracy. 'Your secret is safe with me.' She throws her head back and squeals with laughter and I can't help but smile and feel my guilt has amplified the significance of one brief kiss. It was simply a mistake on his part. Mine too, in receiving it.

I note Mimi's complexion is looking quite the opposite of mine – she's blooming – and I steer the questioning to her. 'Speaking of secrets, how's the romance in your life?' Her perky demeanour usually means she has a new love interest.

She colours more deeply than ever before and I can guess this is one she likes very much.

'So, who is he?' I probe. I assume it's the operator at the telephone exchange where they both work.

'All in good time, Stella,' she replies, and I think she's being unusually coy, but I let it go. She adds, 'It's not been very long, and I want to make sure before I say anything.'

Mimi adores the drama of the chase and the reveal, and I love her for it – the fact that she can maintain such energy and enthusiasm amid the demands of war keeps me hoping.

'Fine,' I say. 'But I want to know soon.' Good news might distract me from the mess of my own feelings.

19

A Detour

Venice, late June 1944

Seemingly, Cristian either wants to forget our doorstep assignation or he regrets it entirely, because it's never spoken of. He doesn't so much ignore me in the Reich office, rather he returns to treating me exactly as he does the other typists – with a certain, businesslike detachment. He makes pains never to lock eyes with me, or approach me with a question unless there are other workers around, and I find myself more hurt by that than anything – that he daren't trust my discretion in something personal. I resolve to push it out of my head and get on with helping to bring down Breugal's kingdom. In the back of my mind, though, I always question if I'm including Cristian De Luca in that equation.

Elsewhere, though, the war is gaining pace and I have little time to dwell on the matter. The good weather prompts more intelligence from the outlying partisan brigades, meaning we have more to sift through for the weekly paper, and there's renewed sense of activity in acts of sabotage perpetrated across Venice, some of which I suspect Vito is involved in; warnings from his older sister have clearly fallen on deaf ears. Almost all my time outside of work is spent on partisan tasks, and every evening seems to be taken up either bar-hopping with virtual strangers or on boat trips across the Lido, tolerating the stares of Nazi troops toing and froing on the Motonavi ferry. As I return their smiles like I'm supposed to, I can't help laughing internally at the message tucked inside my beret or my shoe, and even sometimes in my underwear. It sends a shiver of satisfaction through me and, despite the enduring fear of capture, I realise I am suited to this task. As I cross the water, I can't help thinking of Jack, not exactly a stone's throw away on Pellestrina, but close enough to be accessible. And then I have to forcibly bring myself back to the task in hand.

With the whirlwind of emotions inside me, I'm relieved to be busy, buoyed that beyond the Veneto both the Resistance and Allies are making headway; after Rome they have forged northwards to Assisi and then Perugia, slowly but surely towards us. In the wider world, the Russians have gained ground in Finland and are marching towards Berlin. Gradually, it feels as if one day we might be free of this turmoil, though no one supposes Hitler will give up gracefully. It will be ugly, fraught with danger, and there will be casualties. We just have to be prepared for it.

Doubtless in response to the general tide of the conflict, a combination of Nazis and fascist squads have resumed their merciless raids on the Jewish ghetto. Several times I'm plucked from my bed to help with movements of families to safe houses across the city, but all too often the Resistance is taken by surprise and cannot react fast enough to skirmishes in side streets, or houses targeted because the fascist guard, fed by information from Gestapo spies, suspects they are hiding Jews. The night-time curfew from eleven p.m. is more strictly enforced than previously, which means we can't operate the same surveillance. I hear on the highly charged grapevine that Vito has been almost caught several times by the patrol dogs, and a shudder runs through me at his refusal to admit the limitations of his running speed. I'm only glad that Mama and Papa remain blissfully ignorant, although Mama is looking increasingly tired and she's lost much of her normal zeal.

Despite my position, I am not party to advance warning of the increased raids via the Reich office – it seems the Gestapo and Breugal operate in different spheres, fuelling the general's fury once again. The daily talk in cafés and shops breeds a fog of unease and fear spreading from the ghetto side across the city; morale is low in the Resistance and it seems that with every family taken, every prisoner hauled to Santa Maggiore jail, it sinks even lower. Sergio does his best to boost the mood with an anonymous rallying in the paper, but day after day I have to remind myself that what we are doing is better than nothing at all, that Popsa would be proud. Ironically, the weather is glorious, the water glittering under the fierce rays, but war has the effect of staining even the most stunning of sunsets. Mere beauty – even the Venetian type – cannot override all.

Amid all this unrest, I'm charged with relaying a package to a contact on the Lido, the plan being that a boat will await me one evening after my newspaper shift, take me to the Lido and back to the mainland. It will be under cover of darkness, and I'm relieved to see my transport is a small flat-bottomed *sandalo* boat with a tiny outboard motor. As much as I don't relish being out on the open lagoon in such a minute craft, potentially dwarfed by the patrol boats which sweep across the water and send wash and spray in their wake, I also know a good pilot can skim over the shallow sandbanks and dodge the sweep of their searchlights. The boatman is old and grizzled, born out of the lagoon, it half appears, with pimples that look like barnacles and a thick beard hanging limp like seaweed. He speaks little, which is a blessing, since I'm tired and in no mood for chit-chat. But I smile broadly as we meet – I need his favour to make a detour. That and the lira notes in my pocket should persuade him.

The journey to the Lido is uneventful, with only small waves plashing at the boat sides. The boatman motors past the Lido dock and around to a small inlet. There's no one about, thankfully, and he leaves me in a small cove on the beach, weaving the boat neatly between the coils of barbed wire to land me on wet sand instead of letting my feet get sodden in the surf. The sight of the wire coils reminds me again of Gaia and Raffiano's first encounter and their presence warms me in the relative chill of the evening, even though it's only inside my head.

My contact, a middle-aged man in casual clothes, emerges from the shadows as I walk onto the sand. As always, there's a 'stand-off', which lasts a second or so as we look each other up and down, trying to assess whether we can trust each other with our lives. I've often mused after a drop that, despite the hardware of guns and machinery, this is an intensely human war – heavily reliant on faith in the good nature of people, whatever their origins. Kindness and softness, and not the cold metal edge of artillery, are what will win this war.

Clearly, this man and I decide we share that crucial belief and exchange the code words. It's the only time we speak – I hand over the package, he retreats to the shadows and I return to the boat. I'm always tempted to scurry the last few steps, but force myself to maintain a steady, calm gait; there could be a lookout with binoculars trained on the beach. I'm relieved as the boatman pushes off and the water deepens under us.

'Can we make a stop in Pellestrina?' I say, my sweetest smile on show. It's more than a little detour, I know, but since we're so far out in the lagoon I feel it's worth pushing for. The boatman shakes his head at first, until he spies me pulling out the notes. His eyes are noticeably wider.

'How long?' he asks.

In truth, I've no idea. It depends if I find what I'm looking for, but another few notes and he's persuaded to stay and take a drink while waiting. There's been little planning on my part; I hadn't considered anything beyond getting there. He consents, and we putter along, hugging the edge of the Lido, and then the long string of land that is Pellestrina island.

The tiny dock is deserted, aside from a mangy but friendly cat who greets us, mewing over the rhythmic clanking of a few masted boats, and the tackle of the smaller craft like our own.

'Is there a bar?' I ask. The boatman points a grimy finger past the dock and towards some houses, although there's little light to head towards. I know the houses to be brightly painted, a patchwork of colours in daylight, but in the darkness they are simply light and shade.

As I get nearer to a small clump of buildings, I hear a general hum of voices and background music, though nothing is recognisable as a bar until I follow my nose and duck under an archway. Then, the glow is apparent, the hum cheerful, and I gather the courage to push through the door. All I can do is to enquire after Jack, although I may need to describe him and brook their suspicious denials, then prove I am no threat to his capture, before they will point me in his direction. Besides this, it's an impulsive endeavour – unplanned in that I'd simply said to myself any trip to the Lido seemed a good opportunity to make it to Pellestrina. To say what to Jack? Even as I near the bar I still don't know, confused even further by the disastrous encounter with Cristian's lips. I'm not even sure where the need comes from. I'll only admit to myself that I miss him and his cheerful company.

As the door creaks open and a roomful of people swivel to land their stares upon me, I'm already regretting it. Mr Barnacle's company seems preferable to this stern suspicion. One face, though, is immediately open and welcoming, turning his body on the bar stool, the injured leg outstretched.

'Hello stranger!' he says. And Jack's reaction causes a thaw in the icy glares of his loyal new friends. We are soon snug in a corner table, Jack having introduced me to the room as Gisella – an instruction whispered in his ear as we embrace. He looks different; the grey, faded pallor is gone and, although he hasn't gained a lot of weight, what flesh he has is pink and sits well on his face.

'You seem to have landed on your feet,' I say, before realising my unintentional pun.

'Ha ha, ever the joker,' he grins. 'They're a good bunch here. I owe them a lot. They're taking really good care of me – I've been adopted by at least four mothers.'

I don't doubt it. Jack has that easy charm which makes older women want to feed and couch him in their arms. The younger ones . . . well, I'm here, aren't I?

As if to prove a point, a rounded Mama-shaped woman comes across and lays down two bowls of steaming fish stew in front us. The smell is intoxicating and I realise, once again, that I've missed another meal.

'Are you keeping busy?' I ask, in between spoons of heavenly broth.

At this he sighs, looking around lest he offend the ears of those he's come to love. 'In all honesty, I really could do with more to do,' he says in a hushed tone. 'I'm sent transmitter parts when the transport lines are safe and I've managed to make up several wireless sets, but it doesn't feel enough. I could be doing more.

'On the other hand,' he adds, 'my sewing skills on the nets are coming along nicely. Though I'm not sure of the demand on the banks of the Thames once I get home!'

I'm relieved he's thinking of surviving long enough to make it home, even if the prospect of such a permanent parting causes a twist deep inside me. I haven't been able to see him much as of late, but it's been reassuring at least to know he is just across the water.

Jack is hungry for information and I tell him what I know – the Allied advances he's already aware of, but the local partisan triumphs in the north are news to him. We agree the tide is turning against Hitler and fascism, although we both realise the war is far from over. And he's still stuck on

181

a tiny island in the Adriatic Sea without the means to get home.

The stew consumed – we have no embarrassment in scooping out the last of the delicious liquid with our bread – Jack suggests some fresh air outside. His walking is definitely improved, although he's been left with a marked limp, and I feel a pinch of pity that he will always bear the scars of war. I'm certain he doesn't feel in the least bit sorry for himself, merely grateful he's alive, but we're both aware it could hinder his escape, especially if he needs to make part of the journey on foot.

Jack's conversation, however, is nothing but upbeat. 'So just passing tonight, were you?' he teases.

'Oh, well, you know us island-hoppers,' I beat back. 'We're apparently born with webbed feet.'

He leans into me and chafes at my shoulder with his. We reach the edge of the dock and I'm glad to see my boat pilot is not hovering nearby. It's deserted, and the water is quiet too, licking rather than slapping irritably at the lines of boats. Jack guides me to a pile of wooden boxes and we sit, he rubbing instinctively at the top half of his leg.

'It's beautiful out here,' I say, drawing in the night air. 'So quiet.' As if on cue, a droning moves across the sky, faint tail-lights just visible in the navy expanse, and we both laugh at the irony.

'Do you miss home?' I ask, though the question is partly rhetorical. Of course he does.

His response, however, is surprising. 'I do and don't,' he sighs. 'Obviously, I worry about my family but if it wasn't for this war, my pathetic parachuting and this leg' – he slaps at his flesh good-naturedly – 'I wouldn't have had this time here, with these lovely people.' He skips a beat. 'And with you.'

He turns, smiles and moves his lips towards mine. Once again, I'm blindsided by a man and a situation, and by the last kiss I shared. With someone else. But isn't this what I want, deep down? What I'd hoped for – with Jack? I lean into him and his soft flesh. He smells and tastes faintly of fish stew – we both do – but the overriding tang is of pleasure and delight. Our tenderness is only interrupted by a gruff cough nearby. Jack and I pull apart, with smiles instead of embarrassment, and I see it's Barnacle Man.

'We need to go, Signorina,' he grunts. 'Any later and we'll run into trouble.'

He doesn't seem irritated – perhaps the grunt is how he normally speaks. I wonder if the lira bought him a good plate of something tasty and more than one beer. Do I want to be piloted by an inebriated sailor across the vast harbour with Nazi scouts chasing at its rudder? But then I reason that, even drunk, Signor Barnacle knows every inch of this water better than most. Anyhow, I'm in no position to stay and make it back for work in the morning; a brief, split image of having to stammer explanations of why I didn't make it back to my two, very cross superiors – Sergio Lombardi and Cristian De Luca – flashes across my eyes, and I know I must leave.

Jack parts with a lingering kiss on my cheek, his distinct stubble tickling at my skin. He stands waving from the dock until he disappears into the blackness. 'Drop by again soon,' I hear him call, still teasing.

The boatman is true to his word, and more. The journey back is necessarily slow and seems to take forever. Because curfew is long gone, he skirts expertly around the Arsenale and deposits me on the Fondamenta Nuove, just streets away from my apartment. I take off my shoes and silently track through the *campos* and streets, keeping to the shadows, reaching my own apartment without sighting a soul. In bed, I hug my thoughts like a pillow, considering, yet again, the strangeness of war and this life. I relive the piquancy of the moment, taste Jack on me, the tartness of the food and the lagoon's lingering salt spray. For the first time in an age, I am satiated.

20

Arrival

Venice, early December 2017

The sunlight is blinding almost as soon as Luisa emerges from the airport and makes her way to the dock, her small suitcase rattling on the concrete. Queuing for the waterbus into Venice on the edge of the water, she's already struggling to take in the fantastical nature of leaping out in the expanse, albeit on a sturdy boat, to a city that hovers mid-lagoon.

The journey doesn't disabuse her either, the sudden sight of islands appearing in the green carpet of water, as if they've just risen from the depths like the lost city of Atlantis, their concrete edges definite and not sloping into the waters like a beach oasis. All around small boats are buzzing to and fro, weaving between the poles that seem to determine the confusion of the shipping lanes. Some are taxis, others clearly supply boats moving boxes of everyday items, their drivers casually sporting sunglasses against the fierce winter sun.

Clearly, normal life goes on in this modern-day paradise and that, too, is mind-bending.

Luisa steps off the boat and into the throng of tourists moving towards Piazza San Marco, the well-known hub of Venice, its iconic stone lions keeping watch from the top of their imposing columns, alongside the subtle, scalloped pink hue of the Doge's Palace; against the brightness, it's an edifice made of ice cream. She could easily take a *vaporetto* along the Grand Canal to the tiny studio apartment she's rented for the four days of her trip, but Luisa would rather walk, begin to absorb Venice in the limited time she has.

The map she has is vast and detailed, and she tucks herself into the corner of the imposing piazza, under the ornate walkway and away from the pigeons' flightpath, folding the paper to the portion she needs. Once her suitcase is safely in the apartment, she will do her best to look less like a tourist. Is she one? She doesn't feel it. More like an explorer on a mission. If she was simply a sightseer, she might head to the ornate and ancient Florian's café on the opposite side of the piazza, drink coffee at vastly inflated prices and post pictures on social media to prove her presence. On their trip together in 2013 she and Jamie didn't 'do' Florian's itself, preferring more out-of-the-way cafés. Now that time seems to her like another life, her delightful but slightly blinkered view of Venice as a holidaymaker in love. This time, she has business. She has been made into a different person by age and grief, and by this passion to find a little part of herself in this amazing, fantastical city. Let Venice display a different sheen now.

As Luisa walks away from the square and into the warren of streets – or *calles* – weaving across the tiny bridges towards the renowned Rialto, she is struck again by a magical, un-worldly quality. If you attempted to explain this city to anyone who had never set eyes on even a picture of Venice, they might imagine a vast flotilla of bobbing pontoons simply strung together, with visitors hopping from one to the other, needing to steady themselves as the water ebbs and flows underneath. Yet the opposite is true – Venice is solid. Nothing under Luisa's feet is tenuous or yielding, with countless towers and square, concrete buildings squatting atop the jade waters. So it's easy to forget that while Venice and its people may not be floating, they remain guests on the water – that the canals which seem to snake around the heavy stone *campos* are not secondary. They are the lifeblood on which Venice rests, and the lagoon remains its bedrock.

To Luisa, in what she feels is her first real snapshot, this is what makes Venice appear like a floating fantasy – a figment of a writer's imagination perhaps, where the atrocities of something ugly like war seem too stark to be a reality. How can there be death and destruction in something that resem-bles a fictional utopia? But the history books and her research tell the opposite – Venice has been the object of countless wars and invasions over the centuries, not to mention a deadly plague. She suspects that the next four days will only cloud that lustre even more; that there was, and is, all too real life in this paradise. But isn't that what she wants? To find the stark truth?

It takes an hour or so to find the apartment after several wrong turns into tiny *campos*, banked by ancient apartments, which make Luisa draw in her breath at the beauty and the longing for such a Venetian bolthole of her own. Eventually, though, she tracks down the street and number in the Ca d'Oro district and meets with the studio's owner. His English is good and she grills him for information on the best nearby coffee shop, the tastiest pizza and a supermarket where she can pick and choose in silence and not embarrass herself with fledgling Italian.

It's still only three o'clock when the owner leaves, so Luisa hooks up to the Wi-Fi and hurriedly taps out a short text to Jamie: *Here safely, flat great, just going to explore. Miss you, love you. Lx.*

The last sentiments rankle slightly with a loud echo of the cross words they had parted with on the previous evening. Jamie had earned a second callback for a crucial theatre part and was clearly delighted, but Luisa's immersion in her own project meant her reactions were dulled, too slow. Jamie was hurt – that much he had made clear. She'd apologised, kicking herself inside, but the damage was done. He'd kissed her goodnight as she headed to bed early and wished her a good trip, but pretended not to stir as she got up and left in the early hours, even though she saw his eyes twitch noticeably. Despite her way with the written word, texting never relayed feelings in the way she intended. Luisa pledges to ring Jamie later and attempt to cement the rift. Then she packs her notebook, organises the map for discreet viewing, and walks out to explore.

There is no real plan. As much as the attic box has set her on this trail, and the internet vital in covering some cracks, there are still gaping holes in her grandmother's story that the scraps of notes, faded scribblings and coded messages have not filled. She knows it's unwise, but she is relying entirely on Signor Volpe to at least give her a direction. His work commitments mean he cannot meet with her until the next day, which leaves her only two full days in which to piece it all together. Is it possible, she wonders. Now that she's here, it seems ever more urgent.

Today, though, Luisa decides she cannot do anything other than soak up this unique, enigmatic place. Her first aim is for a coffee, and she's practised asking politely in Italian over and over. She finds a small square, reasoning it to be far enough away from San Marco to have normal prices. Despite being December, the sun is still coating one half of the *campo* and it's warm enough to sit outside. There's just one modest café-bar, and Luisa pulls up a chair next to a table of undoubtedly Venetian women. Their fur coats, tiny toy dogs and painted lips murmuring Italian are a real giveaway. She smiles as they glance over but their mouths remain puckered. The waitress is, thankfully, a little friendlier and smiles at Luisa's valiant attempts to order coffee in her native language. If she is laughing inside at Luisa's pitifully poor accent, she doesn't show it.

The coffee is good, stronger and slightly more bitter than the one served at her own café haunt at home, and it does the job of lifting her after the early start for the airport. Part of her wishes Jamie were here to see it, share it, and yet she doesn't feel lonely. She noted several pitiful glances at the airport at the sight of her travelling alone, which she ignored by pulling out her electronic notebook and pretending to be businesslike, although her casual clothes were anything but. The man sitting next to her had attempted a polite enquiry.

'I'm travelling for work,' she'd said, with an attempted air of confidence. She'd wanted to say 'I'm visiting family', because, to her, that was the truth, but she didn't. Doubtless, she didn't fool him, either way. Now, though, Luisa feels calmer. She is here, in the place where half of her family – a good portion of her – stems from. Does she feel the connection, her roots submerged deep in the mud? Not yet. There's still time though, even if it's limited.

Refreshed by caffeine, Luisa determines to use what light is left to familiarise herself with the route back to the apartment, seek out some pasta or pizza and take advantage of what she remembers is the most spectacular but reasonable sightseeing trip there is in Venice – a waterbus running the entire length of the Canal Grande, a slow meander to marvel at both the beauty of the palazzos and life on the water. It's her one concession to being a true tourist, she tells herself.

In the meantime, she sets out to visit some of the places jotted in her notebook, random locations listed on the scraps from the box. Some she has found easily on her map, others she's had to fill in the gaps with her imagination – there are scores of 'Santos' and 'Margaritas' and it's almost impossible to pinpoint them all exactly.

She wanders for well over an hour before finding her first objective, Campo Santo Stefano, mentioned several times in the same ornate writing amid her precious scraps. Luisa marvels at its vast rectangular space, weighted at one end with a huge ecclesiastical edifice, which appears to be a functional church and not simply a relic. There's a welcoming café opposite the church door, and she's suddenly weary. She positions herself at a table outside and orders a balloon glass of Aperol aperitif; around her, each table is dotted with glasses of the bright orange liquid and she vaguely remembers that she and Jamie sampled it on their trip. 'When in Rome . . .'

he'd joked then. The thought of him pinches at her conscience, and she guiltily pushes it away.

As she sips her drink, Luisa watches and observes, fascinated by the streams of people coming in and out of the church in the early evening sun, mainly women and older men. Luisa thinks of the photographs in her box: the elderly women seem not to have changed in more than seventy years – many are short in height and box-shaped, clad in black wool, collars lined with dark fur. Their tight curls sit on stooped shoulders, their bodies balanced on robust, stockinged legs. If she closes her eyes and pictures the black and white aged pictures she has safely tucked in her suitcase, these elderly Italians don't look out of place.

Time here is not at a standstill, she thinks, but it does move slowly.

Luisa underestimates the orange cocktail – the alcohol marries with the fatigue from her early morning flight and she finds herself stumbling a little on getting up, head woozy rather than spinning, a heavy feeling in her limbs. She needs to eat, clearly. She's too tired to search for long and settles herself in a small restaurant at the smaller end of the *campo*, noting there are Italian speakers in its midst as well as tourists, and orders a bowl of pasta. Whether it's the holiday feeling or not, it tastes amazing – the flavour is '*pomodoro*' and the pesto almost certainly fresh. It wakes her taste buds and feeds into her limbs a little. No wonder Italians rarely eat anything other than their own cuisine, she thinks.

The food is restorative but not magical. It's only eight o'clock, but Luisa is beyond even the twinkle of the Grand Canal – it's been there a long time, she says to herself, and

191

it's not going anywhere. While she is loath to waste even a minute in the city she's already smitten with, common sense wins out and she heads back to her apartment. She needs to be fresh for the real fact-finding in the morning.

21

The City Cauldron

Venice, July 1944

Early July beats down its consistent summer heat on Venice and the swell in population, sporadic water shortages and increase in squadrons of aircraft over the lagoon create a cauldron in the city, pressed and heated from all sides. Unrest is inevitable. And it comes.

I wake to a hum of noise through my open window, along with a slight breeze. It's nothing specific, just general unease, but it's certainly not the light clipping of feet I'm used to hearing below my window as people make their way to work or the market. A slight increase in pace, maybe, and the sound of murmurings designed not to be heard. From my window, the little square looks the same, cut by a shaft of bright sunlight that signals we're in for another day when the city's buildings will be baked and the water warmed to ooze its sulphurous smell. But the feeling carried on the air makes me get up and dress earlier than normal. I walk the few steps to Paolo's for coffee – and gossip.

Paolo knows what's happening, of course he does, but waits until my coffee is poured and I'm sitting at one of the back tables before he dips his voice to a whisper. There's been a fascist raid in the Cannaregio, the ghetto district, and five locals have been killed – butchered – as a reprisal for the shooting of an officer and one, maybe two, fascist guards.

My heart stops a second for Vito, but Paolo would know already if he were involved. Instead, my head and heart starts to pound for those sacrificed innocents, possibly someone I've had contact with in these past months. It's likely they had nothing to do with the shootings, merely happened to be in the wrong place at the wrong time, in the eyeline of angry fascists with a score to settle. How will their families feel, knowing the victims were not even true casualties of war, but unfortunate bystanders? Your aunt, or brother or mother – real people with love and laughter and a history – classed as collateral damage?

I make my way to work feeling utterly winded and depressed. I wonder how many episodes like this one there will be before we in the Resistance finally make real ground against the evil. True victory. When I arrive, Cristian only glances at me, wearing a slight frown as he rushes by.

It's a week or so later when the heat of war and summer combines to create a real furnace of the city. I wake that morning to a definite scent in my nose – the acrid smell of burning. I see the plume of smoke above the orange roofs before I reach Paolo and his font of knowledge. The fire is in the Luce Institute, a branch of the fascists' revered propaganda machine, which churns out endless films of smiling generals strutting alongside bronzed and proud Italians. Visiting dignitaries to Venice are a particular focus for their cameras. The building, it seems, has been razed to the ground, a vast spiral of black smoke rising into the clear sky near San Marco.

As I make my way to work, the Military Police are out in force, audible several streets away as their boots clomp in rhythm on the flagstones. Aware of the recent reprisals, Venetians will be holding a collective breath: if this is a partisan act of arson, will it ignite another dangerous game of tit-for-tat? Fascist and Nazi guards will be ferreting for the partisan culprits, raiding any suspected homes hiding them. And again, only one word comes to my mind: Vito. After our last conversation, and the rumours I've been hearing since, this type of attack is something Vito would relish.

As with every major upset, Cristian is in and out of Breugal's office all morning, his face etched with concern. He barely acknowledges me, and I'm glad, because I feel my face is betraying my angst. I'm thinking constantly of my younger brother: I need to find out where he is, what he's done. I'm only relieved there are no reports of any casualties, and so no immediate spark to the anger that would lead to more innocent deaths.

I make excuses at lunch that I need to take medicine to my mother – Cristian waves away my request in his need to calm Breugal's fresh fury about incompetent troops. I walk hurriedly, feeling the heat beat down and trying to ally it with the winter smell of cinders in the air. Our glorious lagoon sparkles as if untouched by the events and, once again, I love its ever-changing and yet enduring nature more than ever. Its solidity revives my spirits for a while.

Mama is home, as she always is at lunchtime.

'Stella! What are you doing here?' she greets me with real cheer. 'How lovely. Sit yourself down – I have a little cheese put by.'

I feel the cool echo of the air inside the house; I can hear no one else within its walls.

'I had an errand nearby,' I lie guiltily. 'Thought I'd say hello.'

I sit at the kitchen table while Mama lays out what she has. 'How's Papa, and Vito?' I ask lightly.

'Papa? He's fine. Working too hard – taken on some boat-building work in his spare time, but he's not really fit enough if you ask me—'

'And Vito?'

She looks up sharply. I'd thought the way I cut in was innocent enough, but maybe I don't enquire after my brother as often as I think I do. Or with that much fervour.

'We haven't seen him the past week,' Mama says gravely. 'He sent a message that he's staying with a friend, but honestly, Stella, we don't know what he's doing. I've been worried sick.'

What she says almost convinces me Vito is involved – heavily embroiled – in this latest act of Resistance sabotage. One half of me applauds it: fighting for the Venice we love is admirable and it's what I myself am doing, albeit more subtly. But I know Vito's impetuous nature and his attraction to the thrill of danger. Add that to the danger of a raid, and he could get himself captured and killed. If he isn't already in the Santa Maggiore jail.

'Hasn't Papa seen him at work, at the docks?'

'The day before yesterday,' Mama says, 'but only across the yard. He didn't get to talk to him. I worry about the people he hangs around with.'

So do I. Each battalion has tight codes of conduct, overseen by a hierarchy of ranking officers, but a band of patriotic young men with a tendency for rashness . . . Light the flame underneath them and who knows what it will produce? A firestorm, perhaps?

I try to murmur reassurances to Mama, but even she can see they are without weight. I need to locate Sergio Lombardi and find out what I can. And soon.

Back in the office, the afternoon crawls slowly towards five p.m., and I have to concentrate simply on shutting down my overactive imagination of Vito's grim future. Several shots are fired, the noise resonating through the open windows – it's often just warning shots from jumpy patrols, but I flinch with each one, and Cristian looks at me over his glasses, adding to the wrinkles in that furrowed brow. He's edging towards me as I pack up and leave not a minute after five, and I wonder if he will request my company for a drink after today's excessive diplomacy with Breugal. But after our last outing together, surely he wouldn't ask? Quite apart from the awkward end to our evening, I'm in no mood for light conversation or to hear his woes about the general's petulant behaviour. I sweep out with a curt 'Good evening', although his isn't likely to be any better than mine.

I'm due at the newspaper office, but I know I won't be able to concentrate without at least trying to contact Sergio. I make my way to a safe house I know not far from the Accademia Bridge. Aside from the soot smell, there's little to say Venice is changed since yesterday – the plume of smoke from the Luce site has dwindled to a grey mist hovering above it. The sun is still fierce and I'm perspiring under my clothes as I walk, assuming a mask of innocence as I paste on smiles for some of the familiar guards who hover in San Marco as I go in and out of work. Sometimes their recognition of me is a bonus, particularly when they give the nod and allow me to swing past the search lines without question, ignorant to the fact that there's often a Resistance message secreted about my person. I try to ignore the accusing looks of queuing Venetians, sneering under their breath that my familiarity means I'm a collaborator, but it burns into my back. I want to shout at them: 'I'm one of you!' But I daren't, of course. Always the mask is in place.

The safe house is in darkness in the alleyway, shutters closed, and I wonder if it's been abandoned. There's no one about so I knock hard on the outer door, surprised when an old man answers. I give the code and he lets me in, signalling for me to follow his slow pace up the stairs and behind a heavy wooden door.

'I need to get a message to Signor Lombardi,' I say, once the door is closed. I'm suddenly hot above my collar and he can probably feel the heat of my anxiety. 'I need information about my brother, Vito. Vito Jilani.'

His eyes remain steadfast, but I detect just a twitch around the old man's whiskers. He calls to another room and a young boy appears, reedy brown legs extending from his shorts. The man whispers instructions in the conch of the small ear, and the boy's legs are in motion before I can even guess at what's been said.

'Do you know something?' I ask the old man urgently.

'Be patient,' he says. 'Sit. Have some water. You look hot.'

I am, so I do. He tries to make small talk, about the war, but nothing that could implicate either of us or we could be forced to spill under torture. We talk of the Allies making headway and skirt around the Venice that's beyond his door. Then suddenly, the boy is back, breathless and mute aside from what he whispers into the old man's ear this time.

'It's best you go with the boy,' he says at last. 'Signor Lombardi has approved it.'

'Where?' I say. I desperately want news of Vito, but bulletins of a different kind await me in Giudecca and I know that they will worry if I am much longer, wonder what's happened to me.

'It's close by,' he says. 'Go now. The patrols are busy elsewhere for a while.'

The small boy looks at me with huge brown eyes and smiles a gappy grin. He's alive with the subversive activity, bred with partisan blood.

'Thank you,' I say to the old man, who waves us away.

The boy trots beside me silently, offering up his hand so we at least look like mother and son, or aunt and nephew. He's been well trained – almost since the cradle, clearly. We walk down several streets and over bridges, into an area of the Cannaregio I've not been to before.

Wordlessly, we take turns in scouting around us for patrols, or even a tail. In a courtyard of houses we climb the outer stairs to a middle floor, and the boy leads me to an indistinct door, making the familiar rapping rhythm of an ally.

He melts away before I've even had the chance to say thank you and I'm led into an almost darkened room, shutters closed. A face turns to me, the whites of wide eyes just visible in the gloom, and I have to squint to adjust my eyes before I realise the person in the far corner is my baby brother.

Vito hasn't the relaxed, charmed face of our last meeting – it's lined with worry as he turns, drawing hard on a cigarette. His surprise registers all the greater at seeing me.

'Stella! What are you doing here?'

'Checking you're still alive,' I say with slight irritation. I hug him all the same. His skin is grubby with soot and he smells of ash and old fires, like he's been working alongside the furnaces of the Murano glass factories. Except he hasn't.

Whoever owns this safety nest retreats to other rooms and leaves us alone, and I sit.

'Vito, what's been going on?' I look him directly in the eyes, leaving him no room to turn or laugh the question away. This is his sister leading the interrogation and, much like when we were children, he knows I can see through any lie.

'You don't want to know,' he says, 'really, you don't – for your own safety.' Then his mouth breaks into a broad smile. 'But it's caused them a real headache, hasn't it?'

Typical Vito. Masking his genuine fear with humour, except the shake in his hands is a firm betrayal, cigarette ash slipping to the floor.

'So what are you going to do now?' I ask. 'The Black Brigade will be out looking. Do they know names, have they arrested anyone?'

We both know the gravity of just one of his group being captured – other names will be beaten and tortured out of them, Mussolini's Black Brigade having a specialist skill for both extraction and inhumanity.

'I don't know, that's what my lieutenant is trying to discover,' he says. 'Until then, I have to lie low.' A sudden thought comes into his head. 'Will you get word to Mama and Papa that I'm safe?'

I'm unsure about 'safe' but I promise that I will tell our parents. Then he makes me pledge to stay away from him, not to come back. Vito is suddenly far from his jokey self.

'Stella, you take enough cha . . . make enough contribution as it is. Don't get involved in this. The Resistance will look after me. You have to trust them. I do.'

We say goodbye and this time he hugs me back with a tight need, no throwaway grin as I draw away. We both know that in this stage of the war, it might be the last time we see each other. All the arguments and irritations of our childhood are forgotten as he squeezes my hand, and I can smell the burned residue on my fingers as I wipe away a stray tear on leaving.

There's still time to get to Giudecca and do my own job within the Resistance – my insides are twisting at Vito's predicament, but I'm also filled with resolve. I walk the back streets towards the Zattere and arrive just in time for the *vaporetto*. Midway between the blocks of land, we stop to allow a Nazi patrol boat right of way but the delay is almost a bonus – the lagoon is spectacular, with a late, low, mandarin sun hovering above, basting San Giorgio in a mosaic of pink and orange, painting the lilting water with Picasso-esque blocks of colour. I think I could stay here forever, midway between shores, between one life and another.

But there is business waiting, and it has none of the beauty of a Venetian summer's evening. News of partisan executions in the north has reached us and Arlo has word from the brigade command to counter it with news of the Luce fire, although I have to couch my language carefully – there's no direct claim it was a partisan act, only a veiled supposition. It's what the paper is to lead on.

I take the flimsy cover off my typewriter but, for once, it gives me none of the comfort it has in past years. Each tap of the keys drives Vito's angst-ridden face in front of me; I pause frequently and even Arlo looks in wonder at my slow progress in completing the story. There are few hard facts, so my usual talent for word embroidery is an advantage, but it's still a challenge. We have several eyewitness accounts of the blaze and its reach across Venice, as well as permission to imply it was a Resistance operation, but that's all. Arlo's nod tells me I've done well in enhancing what little we have, in painting a picture of triumph, even though I feel – until Vito is safe – it's anything but.

'It's good,' adds Tommaso, in an effort to boost my obvious low mood. 'It makes me want to fight harder.' I could hug him in that moment for adding much needed cement to the cracks I'm feeling inside myself.

My fingers tap automatically for the rest of the night's work and, once again, I'm thankful for my training and my machine, which seems to run like a smooth engine of its own accord. I'm simply there touching at the keys and playing along with the flowing words. As I pull out the page, the sight of my dropped *e* gives me a sense of belonging and calm.

Aware of my parents' distress at Vito's absence, I head to their house straight from Giudecca, my heels clipping with urgency to beat the curfew.

'Going somewhere fast?' a passing fascist patrol asks, though with a smile. Perhaps he's bored and wants to talk. But I swing by with a jaunty 'Just don't want to risk being out after time' and he nods. He doesn't see my face switch to a stone veneer the minute I'm ahead.

I don't, of course, tell Mama and Papa the full truth, that I've seen their son with genuine fear etched upon his face – only that I know Vito is safe. And I don't add: 'for now'.

Mama fires questions at me: *How do you know? Why can't he come home?* Her questions aren't born of ignorance – enough of her friends at church have sons in the Resistance. It's simply her form of protection against utter heartbreak. Papa, though, is quieter. The relief in his shoulders and face tells me it's enough to learn his son is alive and not in jail. But equally he knows that could easily change. I fend off Mama's quizzing with tales of news on the grapevine – a friend of a friend – and she retreats to bed to sob out her distress.

Underneath the weak light at the kitchen table, Papa extends his gnarled, worker's hands across the wood and grasps at my own fingers. The twist in his mouth relays his pain.

'Be careful, Stella,' he whispers. It's all he says, the rest is in the lines chipped around his eyes in recent months. One death of a child would break him, they declare, two would send them both to the bottom of the lagoon in despair.

'I will, Papa,' I promise, for a second time.

As it's way after curfew, I stay the night at my parents', but I am up and out with the lark to make it back to my own apartment before work. I have time only to wash with cold water and switch clothes – but it's important I present an unchanged front to the office, to Cristian, Breugal and even Marta. My virtual disguise must be perfectly in place.

There's a clear increase in the number of patrols and guards around the official army and police buildings, as well as in the amount of chatter within the canteen about the reasons. I learn Breugal has been summoned to some kind of war council on the Lido, so Cristian is occupied at his desk reading reports – face close to the type, rubbing at his forehead. Again, I avoid his glances where I can; I want no opportunity for my own features to betray anything, and I ghost away at the day's end while he's briefly away from his desk.

My head and heart are bursting with indecision and I need to offload it. Thank goodness for Mimi – even the mere prospect of her sunny disposition gets me through the day. We gauge several bars around San Polo Campo, avoiding those who have a sea of green or grey uniforms laughing and drinking in the evening sunshine. Despite the strife of war, Venice remains a magnet for thrill-seeking officers in their precious days away from front lines; word of cocaine-soaked parties, abundant with food luxuries and sexual pleasures, is common. While ordinary Venetians scrape for food and water, some quarters drip with debauchery. Another seesaw side of our war.

Finally, we settle on a small bar populated with ordinary folk, choosing a table on the periphery of a cluster outside. Even so, Mimi is schooled into keeping her voice and natural enthusiasm in check, and I instantly note she's less animated than usual. She allows me space to bleed the past few days into her ear, and immediately I feel lighter. It forces me to realise how much I miss Gaia and Raffiano as a regular feed for my frustrations. Her face, though, adopts a darker veil as I recount the uncertainty surrounding Vito.

'Mimi?' I say, as a tear rolls down her beautiful, rounded cheeks. 'What's wrong?'

She can't keep it in any longer. She spills more tears and a confession that the new man in her life is none other than Vito; she's in love with my exasperating, sometimes immature, but ultimately handsome and charming baby brother.

'I didn't mean to, Stella,' she says, sniffing loudly and trying to whisper in unison. 'I promise I didn't set out to fall in love with him. We just bumped into each other one day, and we got talking. All those years we've known each other – when we were growing up – and then something just clicked. We couldn't help it.'

She dissolves into tears again and I have to hold onto my own concern and give her solace at the same time – and my blessing. In truth, if we all survive this thing, Mimi will be a good influence on my wayward brother. I would relish having her as a sister-in-law, cementing our long-term affection.

This is all assuming Vito escapes the current partisan cull and this war. It's the first Mimi has heard of Vito in hiding, and she's doubly distressed at facing the prospect of losing him for good, so soon after finding him. As a Resistance member, she understands how precarious his situation is. While we both agree that all we can do is wait for news, I know Mimi's disposition all too well – waiting has never been her strong point. I promise to relay any information as soon as I hear.

All cried out, Mimi – typically – steers me towards lighter topics and I'm reminded to describe my recent meeting with

Jack. Or was it more than that, I think as I'm telling her – an assignation perhaps?

'Stella! You really are some sort of Mata Hari, running around the lagoon meeting handsome strangers.' Her broad, brave smile makes me relive the moment and feel a frisson inside. 'Surely you'll make it back to Pellestrina soon?'

'Not likely,' I say. 'I think now we, all of us, have to be even more careful, on our guard. Jack will have to be a one-kiss wonder.'

'But was it nice – the moment?'

'Oh yes,' I recall. 'Very, very nice.'

Mimi nods, and I know that immediately she's thinking of Vito and what can only have been brief encounters to date. She can't hide the delight in her eyes at the memory and I know then she is truly smitten. Equally, my own mind shifts for a brief moment; as much as I try not to, I can't help thinking about that *other* kiss, and how it made me feel. The man whose lips touched mine. Why won't that odd feeling simply go away and stop bothering me?

Despite Mimi's sorrow, I can tell she doesn't want to go home to her lone apartment, her own thoughts and isolation. She suggests we walk and talk. Her make-up reapplied – her form of the mask we all wear – we head out, winding down small *calles* and over bridges as the light closes in on the day. We talk about mutual friends, couples in the infancy of their relationships and the effect of war in loosening the stays of strict Catholic life.

'So, what about the other man in your life – the mysterious Signor De Luca?' she asks eventually, and that irritating sensation wells up again.

I'm startled Mimi even thinks of Cristian alongside our

talk of handsome men. She's never laid eyes in him. Is that really the way I've portrayed him, perhaps in my more benevolent moments? I need to be more careful, clearly.

'Oh, he's totally wrapped up in all the political comings and goings of the past few days,' I say casually. 'Thankfully, he's not giving me much mind. But I'm still being careful. He's one to notice the slightest hair out of place.'

'You sure about that?'

'About what?' I question. 'That he's slippery as an eel? Definitely.'

'No, silly, that he's not watching you in an entirely different way?' Mimi has a naturally mischievous look when she's talking about men.

'Absolutely,' I reply, lips a thin line of defiance. 'Especially after the disaster on my doorstep. I'm certain Cristian De Luca is thinking about his one true love – a fascist Italy. And our beloved Benito, of course!'

The thought of our stout, strutting leader as any kind of Lothario sends us into fits of giggles, and we choose laughter over sorrow for the rest of the evening, the sun dipping low and the night sky taking hold. With the twitter of conversation and the alcohol, it's a pleasant antidote to the passing week of anguish. The pitch and roll inside me is put on hold for a few hours at least. And I'm pleased to bring a smile to Mimi's face.

In that moment, we can't know how the so-called 'soft' war of Venice – not so supple in recent weeks – is about to toughen like concrete, moulding into a hard, inhuman and unyielding episode, the echoes of which will change our paths forever.

22

The Seeker

Venice, December 2017

Luisa is up and out to see the sun rise over the water, its early brilliance forcing her to pull out her sunglasses against the water's glare. The time difference with England is only an hour, but her early night and in-built urgency proved better than any alarm. She shivers in the shade of the water's edge, watching her breath rise towards the pink, flossy sky, and walks on. Even the glimpse of a brightly painted ambulance boat and its bleating siren – a sign there truly is modern life here – can't shift the floating dream that is Venice.

'Coffee,' she mutters to herself, and goes in search of the elixir that promises to carry her through the day. Her meeting with Signor Volpe isn't until one p.m. Until then, she plans to visit the Jewish Museum and some of the other sites of Resistance, before moving over to Giudecca and the meeting.

Luisa notes the relative lack of tourists as she navigates from bridge to bridge. The city is a year-round magnet for sightseers, but in early December there's a pleasant, languid pace in the walkways and over the central attraction of the Rialto Bridge – not the heave that she recalls of her previous visit, with everyone trying to get their fill and their photos in just one day. The stalls selling an endless array of honest Murano glass and cheaper copies are all open for business, but there's a sense this is Venice's downtime and she meanders towards the museum, absorbing the odour of roasting chestnuts and strong Italian sausage, stopping to ask in faltering Italian for a sweet pastry filled with smooth apricot jam and puffs of buttery air. It's heaven.

The fish market is still open and, although the very early morning trade has disappeared, there are tourists bobbing around the stalls, taking pictures and getting in the way of slightly irritated Venetians who are haggling for their dinner's staple – fish that Luisa has never set eyes on before: round, flat, pocked and spotted; octopi of grey and pink with suckers the size of small teacups; shrimp still twitching with a half-life. The people of Venice know and love their fish, clearly, as the water nymphs they are.

As she walks towards the train station, Luisa notes the tourist charms spread out – overpriced haunts give way to corner cafés with the same garish welcome signs as in Bristol, populated with Italians who talk and gesture over the day's politics, television, or share snapshots on social media. Her Italian isn't good enough to grab hold of any one phrase, but as she passes by it has the innocent hum and laughter of cafés the world over – people just conversing and communicating. It makes her smile for humanity.

Like every station she's ever been to on her travels, Venezia rail terminal is a hub of activity – the buzz of people coming and going, suitcases packed with toothbrushes and expectation. It's a striking building, shaped in the flat, clean lines of Mussolini's ordered architecture. Stark but undeniably sleek. Although Luisa now knows of the politics behind it, the dark fascism that spawned these polished, concrete lines, she can't help admiring it too. And with every step she is led to wonder: was her grandmother here often, walking on these slabs? Did she leave Venice for good from this very portal, or was there a more secretive departure point?

The bridge over into the heart of the Cannaregio district brings her into a different Venice again. It's the first stop-off point for budget travellers and backpackers, and it shows in the general but engaging scruffiness of the shops and streets. There are Jewish cafés and bakeries, and a strong sense that this is home to Venetians, with a layer of tourism that's tolerated for the economic benefits it brings.

Diving into the tiny alleyways to seek out the museum, it's much quieter, with Venice's population of cats emerging from the brickwork to beg some attention. There are a few bespoke craft shops and galleries, which might signal the area is up and coming, but the earlier bright sunshine is muted, and it brings a mood of dull disquiet.

The Campo di Ghetto Nuovo, the wartime hub of the Jewish community, houses the museum itself, a modern entrance tucked in one corner. In the other, Luisa sees a wooden booth containing two armed guards, and she wonders why – after all these years – such a presence is needed. But then her mind flicks back to the present day and she realises it's more recent prejudices which prompt the protection – the threatened terrorism that is rife across the world. Have we really moved on at all?

She appreciates for the first time the date on her watch: 6th December. According to her research, it's seventy-four years to the day since the ghetto raids she's read about, the first significant cull after the Nazi occupation in 1943. It's not a major milestone but enough to make Luisa stop and sit on a bench in the square and swivel slowly to capture a panorama in her mind. She looks up to a grand but crumbling old balcony, to a turret at the crest of one house with a tiny window nestled in the tiles, and she wonders if, on that night, there were terrified Jews cornered in their own houses, shrinking away from that very window and frightened for their lives. She thinks about the relative silence of the *campo*, only a small tour group to her side being lectured in Spanish, compared to the inevitable shouting, screaming and cracks of gunfire on that night in 1943, the terror those poor people were forced to endure.

It's almost unthinkable, beyond even her colourful imagination, until she wanders across to a cast metal tableau in the side of the square. Moulded into the sprawling bronze plaque are the names of Venetian Jews lost in the war, perhaps on that night: Todesco, Kuhn, Levi, Polacco, Gremboni – a fusion of religion and culture, Jewish names of old blending with Italian. And she feels the sorrow that each name spells an entire life lost. Did her grandmother know any of these people? She wasn't Jewish, that much is clear, but she and they – the people who bore these names – were Venetian, and their paths may have crossed. The idea makes Luisa shiver under the layers of her thick coat and causes a ripple in her spine to think she might be so close to her own heritage.

The museum is at least warm, but to her mind, which craves knowledge about the war, it's filled with a good deal of ancient Jewish history, and only a little of the period she's interested in. There are, however, some telling photographs of pre-war Italian life under the fascists; Mussolini looking suitably macho on his horse, whole stadiums of young girls in perfect lines demonstrating their prowess with a hula-hoop – in hindsight, so many parallels with Hitler's Reich.

It's on her way to the exit that she sees the best picture. In grainy black and white, a horde of partisans – there's no mistaking their dress or their intent – charging up the steps of the Rialto Bridge, dated April 1945. There are men and women toting guns and ammunition thrown across their bodies, their faces displaying the total focus of attack – they could be dressed as Romans, Celts or Vikings; their features easily skip the centuries. The expression – mouths open, eyes ablaze – is a selfless bequest to the greater good.

The explanation alongside is in Italian and Luisa picks out the meaning slowly, although the words are barely needed: it is the final charge towards Venetian liberation, the ending of Nazi and fascist dominance. Triumph.

Luisa wonders then if she is looking into the features of her grandmother, perhaps not in the front line, but those in the fuzzier distance maybe, as one of those enjoying the freedom of the charge, the push to reclaiming the city. Their home. Once again, though, it's just not clear enough, and the familiar frustration descends. The clock ticks slowly towards her meeting with Signor Volpe. What if he cannot bring the picture into focus either?

23

A Fiery Reaction

Venice, July 1944

The ceaseless beat of the sun makes July itself seem unending. There's a tension within Venice, not like the summers of my girlhood, which I remember as carefree – but this seems infinite in a different way. The heat and the pace of the war outside our little enclave create an edge among the forces inside Venice, both Nazi and fascist; the sight of jittery men with guns makes it feel as though we are stepping on eggshells on our own city, the same fragile lattice of wood our ancestors trod carefully upon in centuries past. It makes everyone feel wobbly.

At the newspaper office, we are busy once again – the weather makes it easy for Resistance messages to travel across the mountain passes, and our pages have increased as a result, which means more work for all of us. On the whole, it's good news, and so easier to write about; the last German stronghold of Minsk has fallen to the Russians, and scores of German U-boats have been sunk. More importantly for Italians, the Allies are marching northwards on the western side of the country, taking Cecina and Livorno, and advancing towards Florence. We can only hope they will head east towards us soon.

There's another benefit. My workload, both in and out of the Reich office, means I have less time to think about Vito, whom Sergio will only relay is 'fine'. Mimi, I know, has had some limited contact, but even she is guarded with what she says, in order to protect me. I have to be satisfied with that.

The lighter, longer days create an energy in me – I feed off the light, the way the sun catches the rooftops in the morning and sits late and low in the *campos* of an evening, unwilling to give in to the night. Conversely, the blazing colours also lend weight to the mood that sits like sediment across Venice – that just one spark is needed to ignite the tinderbox that is my city.

Only we get far more than a spark.

The explosion rocks the deep and ancient foundations, ricocheting over the city. It's just gone nine a.m. and I'm a few minutes into the day's translation. All of us run to the window, see people emerging from the shops and cafés lining San Marco and immediately look skyward, imagining that – despite pledges to preserve the precious art of our city – Venice is being bombed from above by the Allies. But there's nothing aside from a reconnaissance aircraft buzzing in the sky. The earth shock we feel stems from ground level.

Word is soon out that the target for the bomb is the Ca' Giustinian building, a palazzo not far from the Accademia

Bridge, facing onto the Grand Canal, and the command post of the National Republican Guard. Troops from the Platzkommandantur are scurrying to and fro, with shouts and general disarray splitting the near normality of San Marco. The band outside one of the cafés has even stopped playing its stock menu of Bach and Liszt.

I can't help wondering if Vito might be involved, despite his already precarious situation. Surely not? I'm certain his battalion leader wouldn't allow it. Sergio too, as overall commander. But there's Vito's intrinsic recklessness to think of.

I'm trapped in the office finishing the translation that I know will be of value to the Resistance, but I'm itching to get out, simply to gauge the word on the street. There's a level of threat, clearly, but how much, and to whom?

As with every fresh crisis, Cristian is in and out of Breugal's office frequently. The heat of late means the general can barely raise himself from his chair, and when he does, it's never a pretty sight. For once, I want to catch Cristian on some pretence of a query, and casually enquire about the commotion outside. Talk at tea break tells us it was an explosion, likely deliberate, but there are no more details. Marta slips outside to flirt and draw information from one of the guards, but comes back with little other than there are some casualties. Fascist, Nazi or Venetian? Fatal or not? We don't know. If it's one of the former, we only know there will be retribution. Violent retribution.

Eventually, I can't suffer the suspense any longer, and I walk towards Cristian's desk, as casually as I can and with a translation query in hand. His face is a strange mix of worry and – if I'm not mistaken – a vague glimmer of pleasure. But then I've rarely managed to read him well.

'There seems a big response to the explosion,' I prod as he pores over my query.

'Um, yes,' is all he will say. He offers a solution to my translation question, hands back the paper, and then says, almost as an afterthought, 'Sadly, some fatalities. Not pretty.'

It's not pretty, or it won't be pretty? What does he mean? He doesn't elaborate, and he's back in Breugal's office before I can nudge any more.

After work, I make my way over to the streets near the Ca' Giustinian, for no other reason than I feel I need to witness the scene, aware I will need to report on it for the paper. The site itself has been swiftly boarded up, with grim-faced sentries on guard. The smell of cordite, though, they can't contain, and it sits in the air like an acrid fog. I fall into conversation with a few old women walking past who look like they might live nearby, casually asking if they witnessed the event, playing the part of a bewildered city dweller.

'Isn't it dreadful?' I nod towards the debris.

'My husband says he heard the explosion in the docks,' one woman says.

'It was pure chaos,' another adds. 'The guards were running around in total shock like little boys lost.'

My conversations give me little more hard fact, but they will add a sense of humanity to the story, in grounding how real Venetians feel.

The hard truth emerges later that day. There are thirteen dead, and the news is soon flooding Venice. Not all are military, but that won't matter to the German High Command – we all know they will claim the moral higher ground, and declare the civilian casualties as martyrs when it suits them. And we wait for the retaliation.

It comes soon enough. Another thirteen lives are lost, this time prisoners from the partisan band of San Donà di Piave, just outside Venice. They are marched into the ruins of the palace, subjected to a farcical mock trial and shot amid rubble from the explosion they clearly didn't cause. Even so, they are branded 'terrorists' on the front pages of the fascist-run newspapers; rampant, bold words branding them as traitors to Italy. I'm reminded of how relieved I am to be out of the *Il Gazzettino* office.

I'm sad and livid and desperate all in one heartbeat. I can barely contain my anger at work, and the next day I cry off early with a headache as I'm forced to type up details of the incident. I know for certain my brother's name isn't on the list of suspects, or the executed partisans, but it feels like little comfort. I wonder how on earth they can be stopped, this murderous machine of bullies?

It goes against our safety measures as partisans, but I need to locate Sergio and beg to do something. I have an idea where he will be at this time of day, and I criss-cross most of Venice on foot, still careful to slink into alleyways and weave through courtyards fluttering with drying bedsheets, using them as a cloak for my movements. Some of the streets are eerily quiet in the afternoon siesta, the heat and the clip of my shoes bouncing off the sun-baked walls. More than once, I feel the crawl on my skin that I'm being followed, but in these highly charged times, it proves to be my own paranoia knocking.

I locate Sergio, and beg to do something to help. He agrees to my request – the one thing I can do, need to do, when I feel out of my depth, when the world starts to spin. I need to write, to articulate these young and not-so-young men in words, make their case in print and stamp out the lies being told.

'You do know that if we print the list of the dead there's a good chance they will suspect it comes from your office?' Sergio points out. He's a calm, gentle man when not in the firing line, and his measured tone does make me think for a moment. Equally, he can see the flame in my eyes and nothing less than a direct order will stop me.

'It could come from any number of places,' I reason. 'The news is all over Venice. Whispers from staff around the explosion site, witnesses to the execution. Anywhere.'

Sergio sighs. He won't quell my fervour.

'All right,' he says, his own frustration evident. 'You go to Giudecca. I'll send word to Arlo and the others and we'll put out a special edition for tomorrow. After that, Stella, you lie low. Keep your routine, smile, be nice. But do not drop your guard.'

'I won't,' I pledge. I'm not sure how I will do it, but I promise him all the same.

By the time Arlo, Tommaso and Matteo join me in the basement, I'm already halfway through my front page. My typewriter voice is beating out a rhythm, seemingly of its own accord – we're both intent on the same message and I can barely tear my eyes away from the keys as the men descend the steps.

'All right Stella?' Arlo nods, but there's more sadness than cheer in his tone. Tommaso has brought a cup of coffee for me and sets it down with a weak smile. I could hug him.

We work on with little chat and banter, given the subject

of the paper, and it's nearing curfew by the time I leave them putting on the finishing touches and getting ready to distribute. I only hope we've done the cause justice, put to the people of Venice the reasons behind such so-called 'terrorism' and why it's both a necessity and consequence of war. However much it is wrong and heartbreaking, war creates casualties.

I feel Popsa's presence as the last *vaporetto* pushes its way towards the main island, imagine the breath of wind around me as his large hand on my shoulder. I feel I've done something – a small thing maybe – to redress the balance of Nazi slander against those sacrificed men. But as with everything, I question whether it's enough. Will it really make a difference?

Judging by the vehement bellow pushing out of Breugal's office as I arrive the next morning, I gather it has had some impact.

'Have you seen this?' Marta pushes a copy of *Venezia Liberare* towards me, Arlo's prominent headline of 'INNOCENTS EXECUTED' staring out.

'His highness is livid.' She sighs and smirks at the same time – at the level of Nazi behaviour we are forced to tolerate, and the fact that it's also mildly amusing to see.

I pray my face doesn't betray how familiar I am with every letter of the print.

'When did that come out?' I say, all innocence. 'They've got some nerve.'

'This morning,' Marta says. 'I took it to him with his morning coffee and I thought he was about to explode. De Luca's been in there ever since.'

I settle down to work as best as I can with a herd of

elephants stampeding around my guts. I catch only a little of the alternate grumble and barking coming from beyond the carved doors, but I don't envy Cristian being in such close proximity to the sweating, swearing and apoplectic general. It's not a pleasant image.

Cristian emerges looking drained and is immediately immersed in phone calls; I catch snippets about extra patrols. He's speaking in Italian, and I wonder if 'the patrols' means the fascist Black Brigade, the men in ebony whose actions are only ever malicious, but I can't make out the conversation. I sense Cristian looking across at me on occasion and, once again, I think he might come over to ask me something. But his face is drained, his eyes focused and his nose almost touching his notebook, and he scratches away at the pages. I wonder if he's compiling a list, and whose lives will be changed irrevocably as a result.

24

Across the Lagoon

Venice, July 1944

I feel helpless and lonely as I leave work. The anger fuelling my adrenalin the previous day has sunk inside me, shaping a melancholy I have no hope of evicting, not today at least. Guilt sits alongside, with my own admission that I don't want to escape to my parents' house for what has reverted to being only a weekly visit. I have nothing to ease their ongoing distress over Vito's absence, and it's become painful to see my mother wither with angst. Mimi is at her day job or engaged with Resistance work. I envy her being kept busy, but I also know Sergio has spread the word that I should lie low and avoid messenger duties for a while. I could sit in Paolo's bar, but it's so close to home I'll have no excuse but to finish my drink and sit inside my own four walls, with only my desolation for company.

I sit on the waterfront instead, not far from San Marco, the space in front of me shared by a line of discarded gondolas, five or six tied together in a huddle. A large patrol boat sweeps by, causing the wash to smack against their sides in sequence, the noise almost as a united protest at their pitiful abandonment. I feel equally forlorn.

I look to San Giorgio tower and, in the distance to its left, the Lido, and beyond to where I know Jack is, and a willing ear for my woes. Doubtless, too, a cheerful slant on what feels like the dark side of Venice's gleaming jewel. Jack could spot the colour in the grey mist, I'm sure of it.

I know I'm feeling unduly sorry for myself and, on a whim, I decide to do something about it. It goes against Sergio's orders and it's reckless, but I board a Motonavi vessel for the Lido. I can't think what I'll do when I'm there, but I will be nearer at least. There's a combination of green and grey uniforms as I sit on the deck and adopt a well-practised neutral expression, face drinking in the warm glow of the sun. One of the troops works hard at catching my eye and, lest he mistakes my neutrality for a scowl, I smile back, pasting on more of my guise. Luckily, we approach the berth and I escape his approach, but I feel his eyes on my back and the knowledge of where I'm about to go makes me fizz with excitement and fear.

Checking I'm not being followed, I walk purposefully to the smaller harbour, where the fishing boats moor up. With fuel on ration for the smaller motorboats, there's plenty of demand for transport around the Lido and to the other islands, and I catch the eye of one of the fishermen – old and grizzled equals experienced to me. He raises an eyebrow at my stated destination, but he doesn't refuse the lira notes I offer.

It's dusk when we reach the small harbour, but I know

where I'm going this time. The woman behind the bar recognises me and, with a wry smile, escorts me a few doors down to another tiny cottage, up a small flight of outside stairs, and raps on the door.

'Jack, you've got a visitor,' she calls, and there's a scrabbling behind the door.

His expression is everything I'd hoped for – not shock but genuine surprise and pleasure. For a split second after the door knock I felt sure I'd made a huge mistake, that he was entertaining some local girl in there, and the barmaid was playing a cruel trick on the naïve, city girl, that I should turn tail and somehow make it back to Venice and the safety of my own house and heart. But the bright white smile amid his darkened, tanned skin is everything I need.

'Hey traveller, come on in,' Jack says, and opens the door wide. I feel truly welcome.

It's a tiny, one-roomed annexe, with bare boards and a small sink off to one side. Instantly, I see Jack is a military man – the room is ordered and tidy, a small pile of clothing folded and stacked beside a mattress on wooden pallets. There's a paraffin cooking stove, a teapot standing to attention beside it, and a desk in one corner covered by a rough tarpaulin. But the most striking element is the light; windows on three sides of the room, waist-to-ceiling height, causing beams of dusky purple to stream across the boards.

'Hello, I hope you don't mind me—' I'm silenced by a kiss, urgent but tender, and I don't need to ask or worry any more.

We take advantage of the remaining light outside and walk along the harbour, hand in hand. His limp is less pronounced now; he barely notices it any more, he says, only a slight twinge if he gets up too quickly.

'So what's wrong, Stella? What brings you here?' He says it with a wry smile – he's not annoyed I'm using him as a sounding board.

I tell him, about the crescendo of past weeks – the fire, explosion and the executions. The news has reached him, of course, but it's my own reactions that he listens to intently, squeezing my hand when I can't help but overflow with tears. He stops and offers me a square of cloth from his pocket – it smells of engine oil but is strangely comforting.

'Thanks,' I say. 'Sorry, I shouldn't be coming here and offloading on you.'

'Why not? I can add confidant to my list of new-found skills – radio operator, fishnet specialist and boat mechanic.'

I knew I could rely on Jack to inject some humour into any situation.

'For the first time in this war, I feel totally at sea,' I say, 'and yet I have no right to be. I haven't lost anyone close to me' – here I banish thoughts of Vito lying on a slab from my mind – 'and I have employment. I'm proud of the news-paper—'

'So you should be,' he cuts in. 'It's a route to the truth, when all we have are the fascist printed lies. I rely on it for the real news.' He kisses me again, full on the lips but not beyond. It feels like deep affection pulsing through. Then he breaks into his boy-Jack grin that's such a comfort.

'And I see you in every word, every letter. I can tell it's you.'

'You can?'

'Of course,' he adds. 'So you can't give up. None of us

can. We have to keep going, because that's what will win this war for us. Sheer bloody-mindedness.'

I feel foolish in admitting that I miss Gaia and Raffiano in times like these – a silly, fickle figment of my imagination, but my release all the same. Still, I'm at ease in declaring it to Jack.

'Then why don't you write it?' he says, and suddenly it seems so sensible. I've been waiting for a purpose when I don't need one. I just need my typewriter.

'When I'm low, I write letters to my mother,' he adds. 'I know they won't get to her, there's no way I can send them, but it makes me feel we have some form of connection. One day she'll read them.'

He dips his head low as we walk. 'I write to you some-times too.'

'Do you?' I'm genuinely surprised I occupy a space anywhere near his family.

'It makes me feel that we will at least meet again.' He grips my hand again. 'And here you are. So clearly it does work!'

Jack restores something in me, not just with his talk of Resistance determination, but in the way he looks at life. Stuck in the middle of the Adriatic, with no foreseeable way out for now, he is contributing in any way he can, looking to the future beyond a Nazi-led fascist Italy.

We call into the bar and Jack talks to the woman behind the counter, clearly one of his many 'mamas'. She emerges with a pot of something wrapped in a cloth and a hunk of seed bread. Soon we are back in his room, candles dotted around and food laid on a blanket on the floor. It's the tastiest shrimp pasta and the best picnic I've ever had. One of the harbour cats paws and mews at the door, and Jack lets it in, setting down a saucer of the pasta juice, and giving up one of his own shrimp.

'He's taken a bit of a shine to me, this one,' he says.

'I'm not surprised, feeding him shrimp. Has he got a name?'

'I just call him Matey. Seems appropriate.' And the cat falls into ecstasy as Jack tickles his dirty white fur under the chin.

Afterwards, he makes tea and we lie on his bed, propped on our elbows and talking about our lives beyond the war, him making me laugh about his army training and the 'soft' mama's boy made tough.

The curfew comes and goes and it's clear I'm staying the night. But I feel no pressure or presumption. I undress down to my underwear and he follows, the scar on his leg a deep purple welt until we slip under the blanket and kiss. But it goes no further. Not because I don't want it to, but because it feels right to take it slow. He's so gentle, and such a gentleman, and he makes me feel that it's right too. He strokes at my hip but he doesn't clasp, falls short of pulling his body towards mine. We fall asleep to the distant clanking of the boats and the gentle purring of the cat at the bottom of the bed.

The light bombarding the windows wakes us. It's five a.m., and I need to move if I'm to make it back to the Lido in time for the Motonavi to the main island and tidy myself up for work. Another long day ahead. But it's worth the gritty sleep in my eyes as the wind blows through my hair on the boat back to the mainland. It will have to be a substitute for a bath or a strip wash, for now at least.

Jack makes the parting easier on the dockside, kissing me

with combined affection and cheer, almost like he is a husband and I a wife, and he's waving me off to work for the day. 'I'm not going to say a proper goodbye,' he smiles. 'Because hopefully that means you'll be back. Be safe, Stella.' I believe him as he waves and turns before I have time to be sad.

The office is still in a state of unrest over the next two or three days, despite the absence of both Breugal and Cristian. Everyone is clearly wondering what lies around the next corner in this war.

On the third day, Cristian returns. I think he looks drained and, after our time at the palazzo party – how long ago that seems now – I wonder how much appeasement and diplomacy he's had to dispense. Then I think: good. He needs to. They, the filthy Reich and their hand-holding Benito-lovers, need to know we will retaliate.

I put my head down and concentrate on pulling every secret, valuable piece of information from what's in front of me.

'Are you well, Signorina Jilani – Stella?' I glimpse Cristian's polished shoes to my side, that familiar accent in my ear.

'Er, yes,' I say, still typing. His feet shuffle and I have to look up, but his expression means I can't draw my gaze away instantly. 'I'm . . . I'm all right.'

'In the circumstances?'

'Yes, in the circumstances.' What is he talking about? Is he trying to draw out my sympathies for the dead, those executed in retaliation?

'I hoped you were all right,' he goes on. 'You seemed upset.' It's the first time he's asked after me personally since that night on my doorstep.

But I can't feel any benevolence towards him after the past few days. After working side by side all these months, the conversations we've had, he surely can't believe I'm without emotion. I look up at him and say: 'I feel for any mother who loses a son, whatever side they align to.' I force my lips upwards slightly, as an antidote to the bitterness inside me.

For once I can see beyond the glare of his glasses, into his pupils which are locked on mine. For a second I think they – and he – are somewhere else.

'Quite,' he says. 'The sooner we resolve this the better.'

Resolve what? And what does he mean? For the Allies and the Resistance to capitulate entirely? I think he's far more intelligent than either Hitler or Mussolini so surely he can't believe that we true Italians will take all of this . . . this destruction of our country, lying down. But he's back to his desk and, once again, Cristian De Luca is like a blank page of a book.

25

A New Hope

Luisa gets to take her cruise down the Grand Canal on leaving the Jewish Museum, this time in daylight. But it's no less spectacular, lined as it is with buildings whose art resides on the outside with elegant tiling the colour of pale pistachio ice cream or great windows of honeycomb glass, panes so delicately made. As the water washes the lower brickwork, pocked and dappled with wear and tear, it's hard to imagine how five- and six-storey buildings don't simply topple into the water. The *vaporetto* stops frequently, sputtering from one side of the canal to the other at a low speed, allowing a good view inside the beautiful palazzos – more so where the rooms are lit by vast, ornate chandeliers. Luisa's imagination runs riot at the parties held along this stretch of water over the centuries: the riches and the debauchery, the relationships contained within. She thinks then of the houses along this stretch commandeered by the Nazi elite,

231

and how many frightened refugees or native Venetians were hidden in their bowels or attics while party-goers twittered around them.

The bright winter sun of late morning, though, only reflects happier times and, seeing scores of lovers arm in arm, she wishes Jamie was by her side. His text the night before had been much more relaxed, joking about her finding an Italian beau as a guide and running off into the sunset. Jamie has never been the jealous type, always celebrated their equal independence, so she knows it truly is in good humour. She feels that they are at peace at least.

Luisa travels the entire length of the canal, and then turns tail aboard another *vaporetto*, this time heading for Giudecca, via the imposing church and tower of San Giorgio Maggiore, and then on towards the island of Giudecca itself. The waterfront at the Zitelle stop is shrouded in shade, and though Luisa can see some colourful café fronts, there's no doubting its reputation as the main island's poorer relation. Once Luisa gets out her map and follows the quiet streets behind the imposing Zitelle church, though, she's pleasantly surprised. It has less splendour, certainly, but more realism. It's where Venetians live in peace, in a combination of old and new blocks.

The Institute of Resistance, too, is a misnomer. To Luisa the name itself conjures an image of a stout, functional block, dull by Venetian standards. Villa Heriot, home to the Institute, is anything but. Set in green landscaped gardens, which remind her more of a holiday once spent in Verona, it's a beautiful double-fronted building with a wraparound veranda and elegant white pillars, its windows in a palazzo style. Perhaps the former home of a wealthy merchant in past centuries, she thinks. Certainly, it's a setting that matches the best of Venetian grandeur across the water.

Signor Volpe is hovering in the lofty entrance hall, amid the scalloped and sumptuous fittings. He spies her immediately, perhaps from the way in which she scans the space, less like a grazing tourist and more like a seeker.

'Signora Belmont?' His face quizzes hers for the right reaction, but only for a second. 'How lovely to meet you!'

Giulio Volpe is almost exactly how she pictured him. Perhaps mid-thirties, middling height and build, thick dark hair and bright eyes – though blue instead of her imagined brown. He has the beard of an academic, short and well groomed, and although he is wearing plain trousers and a round-neck jumper, a pale blue shirt neatly shown at the neck, everything about him oozes Italian style, even down to his shoes, which are polished and elegant. A British man in the same dress could never look as sophisticated, Luisa thinks. The aftershave that is piquant rather than sickly wafts up as he shakes her hand enthusiastically with a bright white smile. He has perfect teeth, and Luisa finds herself already a little bit in love with the man who might provide the answers she's been looking for.

Signor Volpe – 'Please, call me Giulio' – leads her not up the sweeping, Cinderella-style central staircase, but out into the garden and through to what must have been a smaller guest cottage, with the same, ornate shell. Inside, it's cosier and functional in appearance, but still retains more elegance than any office she's ever worked in back home. The walls are hung with old posters, turned sepia with age, bearing words now familiar to Luisa: 'FASCISMO!' in bold, black type. The furnishings are strictly twenty-first-century office vogue though, and on top of a photocopier there lies a grey, tiger-striped cat basking in the window sunshine, who mews at Giulio upon entry.

'Meet Melodie,' he says, fussing at her ears. 'She's our self-invited guest, but she's good company when there's no one else here. And she clearly loves books.'

She would have to, Luisa thinks. There are wall-to-ceiling bookcases, texts vying for every bit of space, with small tabs of notepaper sticking out from between the pages. A truly used library.

He offers coffee – a decent cup from a small machine in the corner of the office – and seems keen to get started. Luisa opens up Daisy and shows Giulio what she has: a combination of carefully photographed documents, and a selection of the original precious photographs she's chanced bringing across. The sealed file and her bag never left her side the entire journey from Bristol.

Giulio's face lights up at handling the fibrous edges of the photographs, as if there's treasure under his fingers. He dons a pair of reading glasses – smart, modish frames – and then reaches for a magnifying glass. He's clearly looking at, but then beyond, the faces for clues of time and place, where the moment was frozen in time.

'So the only name you have is Stella?' he confirms. 'No Italian surname?'

'No, unfortunately,' Luisa says. 'I've looked at my mother's birth certificate, but it only states her mother's former name was Hawthorn. I don't think that can be right, but I suppose it's possible she was married before my grandfather. She wrote under the name of Hawthorn and his name was Benetto. Giovanni Benetto.'

Luisa sees a fire stoking in Giulio Volpe's eyes. This is his domain – the subject of his doctoral thesis – and she gets the feeling that what he doesn't know about the Venetian Resistance can't be told. He's clearly delighted to be playing the role of detective.

'Well, let's get about finding her,' he says, with another bright flash of his teeth.

Giulio leads Luisa into the basement, trailed by Melodie and her mewing, and immediately she is hit by a familiar feeling; the same musty odour of lives stamped onto paper, the dry yet damp smell of her mother's attic on her first discovery of the hidden typewriter. Her nose twitches all over again.

Giulio pulls out large, flat drawers from the freestanding cabinets that fill the basement and takes out his own files of photographs. Luisa's heart rises and then sinks at the hundreds, possibly thousands, of photographs they will need to comb through to find just one image. Is her grandmother hiding among them? She feels excited and apprehensive all at once.

Wordlessly, Giulio hands her a second magnifying glass, and they begin scouring the sea of faces, Luisa's own clutch of photographs between them as they scrutinise. She's brought the original of 'S and C' in San Marco, but Giulio concentrates on an earlier picture, where Stella's face is younger, her hair loose and of a more free style. She's in a group of friends standing on some steps, her arms casually around two men on either side. Without falling into stereotypes, they look like partisans – their dress suggesting non-conformity. To the right, you can just see the edge of some military hardware, a gun base perhaps.

Luisa and Giulio scrutinise for a good half an hour, his eyes scanning to and fro and his measured, concentrated breathing evident. She only issues warning growls of hunger from her stomach, regretting not grabbing some lunch before the meeting.

'Ah ha!' Giulio cries suddenly. 'There she is!'

'You've found her?' Luisa's heart bounds with surprise and relief.

Giulio looks up, almost apologetic. 'No, not her, but someone else in the photograph,' and Luisa's hope sinks back into her chest.

'One of the women here' – and he points to a figure with a wide, engaging smile in the group picture – 'she's also here in our stock image.'

They peer again to check the likeness. It's definitely her, and the label on the back of Giulio's picture names her as 'Mimi Brusato, partisan member'. Frustratingly, no one else in the picture is named, so her grandmother remains unidentified. Still, it is something. It also confirms to Luisa what she already strongly suspected – that her grandmother was far more than a sweet old woman who gave out the best hugs.

They continue surveying for another hour or so, and while Giulio pulls aside several photographs as possibly connected with Mimi Brusato, she remains their sole lead. Stella Hawthorn is still, for now, a ghost of sorts.

The array of new pictures, however, are a joy to Luisa – all in black and white, and she paints them with her own palette, imagining the colours of war in Venice as anything but ashen. Even amid the tragedies she's read of, they clearly tried to enjoy life, relish the bonds of friends and family,

236

which could not be broken by Nazi rule. Despite rationing, the women were fashionable and vibrant; the men too in their shabby-chic of the partisan 'uniform'. The fuzziness of the photographs may well have disguised a good deal of darning, the make-do-and-mend of wartime Britain, but Venetians clearly worked hard at maintaining their ingrained elegance.

Giulio puts down his glass and stretches his back into an upright position, rubbing at his eyes behind his glasses.

'I think perhaps we've exhausted these for today,' he says, and Luisa is both disappointed and relieved – her spine and stomach are complaining in equal measure. Yet it's the closest she's been so far in plucking at one edge of her grandmother's other life. She feels it as tantalisingly close.

'I'll do some searching of our computer archives this afternoon,' Giulio says. 'In the meantime, I can give you a few locations to visit. Sadly, there are no survivors still living that I know of. We have some testimonies of Venetians before they passed away, but they're all in Italian. And there are some memoirs of children, but there's little about the workings of the Resistance in those.'

He notes Luisa's slight disappointment. 'Don't worry, we'll find her,' he reassures. 'She is in here somewhere. I can feel it.'

It's not been a wasted afternoon, although Luisa still feels she is relying whole-heartedly on Giulio and not her own dogged skills in research. She's desperate to play detective in her own way. Still, he seems more than happy to help, the persistence of a proverbial dog with a bone that denotes a true historian.

She walks a little on the small streets around Giudecca

– it's quiet, the odd man or woman hobbling with a shopping bag, and she can hear the faint chatter of a school playground somewhere. But it's peaceful and she tries to picture herself on a satellite map – on a tiny island in the middle of a lagoon in the midst of a vast sea. It all feels quite bizarre.

She's pulled back from space by the beeping of her mobile – a text from Jamie: *Hi Sherlock, how are you doing? Any news or progress? Ring me later. Love you xx.* Texts are generally poor emotional conduits but this is clear – he's in a good mood. Perhaps he's had a callback or the promise of a part. A food stop in a small café on the waterfront cements Luisa's fondness for Giudecca even more; the best minestrone and arancini rice balls she's ever tasted, coating her taste buds and comforting her stomach.

With what light is left, she visits several of the memorials on the main island that Giulio has pointed her towards. She stares for an age at the poignant bronze figure cast on the Riva dei Sette Martiri – Monument to the Martyrs – a lone woman lying prostrate, half in and half out of the approaching tide, her feet limp, not serene but cruelly left for dead. As with the names at the Jewish Museum, Luisa tries to imagine the woman as anything other than stagnant – the sons and daughters or grandchildren she might have had, the lives that would have been fulfilled, were it not for the struggle. With the day's emotions and frustrations, Luisa can't help the tears streaming and finds herself scrabbling for a tissue.

Yet she is lucky. One thing she's certain of – something her own memory, her very existence in fact, can confirm – is that Grandma Stella survived the maelstrom of war. Even if she is lost for now, she was not forever, and that thought replaces the ache in Luisa's heart with warmth.

She is sitting on a bench, documenting the Venetian atmosphere with Daisy for company – this time in a beautiful square she simply happens upon – when her mobile rings. A number from within Italy: it can only be one person.

'Hello Giulio,' Luisa says, slightly guardedly. Is he ringing to say he's reached the end of the road, that Stella Hawthorn exists nowhere in his records?

'Luisa,' he says urgently, unable to hide the excitement in his voice. 'I think I've found her. I think I know who your grandmother was.'

26

Revenge

The city is still reeling from the explosion when its hackles are raised again, and this time the consequences threaten to radiate across the entire city. A German sentry has gone missing from the waterside, the Nazi command claiming he's been murdered. I get wind of the news on my way to work, seeing Paolo gesturing wildly at me from the café's entrance.

'The Nazis are saying there will be retributions – worse than last time – that they will teach the partisans and any collaborators a lesson.' His young face rarely adopts a worried look but today it does. 'Watch yourself, Stella. Keep your eyes and ears open.'

Both San Marco and the Reich office are strangely subdued, and for once I would rather tolerate Breugal's overt anger than hear nothing at all.

'Is something going on?' I ask Marta innocently, as Captain

Klaus strides in and then out of Breugal's office within minutes, clutching a file he's collected from the inner sanctum.

'I don't know,' Marta replies. 'There's talk of something being planned, but nothing has come out of his majesty's office. He left some time ago.'

I'm more worried that Cristian is also absent. He's difficult to read, but there are times I can at least assess something from his manner towards me. What's the point in being here, in the lion's den, when I can't glean any information, enough to prevent at least some of the horror about to happen?

In the end, the entire Resistance is caught off guard by the malice of the Nazis' actions. They are intent on teaching Venetians a lesson, and 'an eye for an eye' is no longer enough. In another of the mass culls the Nazis and fascists have become practised at, they trespass into people's homes and round up a group of innocents, well over a hundred in total, with a further three hundred and fifty as witnesses – including women and children. The next morning, they are all marched in a great swathe to the Riva dell'Impero. It's a stone's throw from where I grew up and I can picture them all crowded on the waterfront, unaware of what horror they will soon be witnessing. They might be looking out for a large vessel to draw up alongside the wharf and transport them away from everything they know and love – families, fiancés, parents – quaking at the thought of travelling east to the camps.

Instead, their penance for being Italian is to spectate on cold-blooded murder; in the early morning glare, seven young prisoners are brought out, tied together in a line by ropes, their faces sporting the purple, swollen marks of torture from either the Black Brigade or the Gestapo. The stronger and less beaten ones hold up the weakened, determined to keep their heads high, despite the fear doubtless coursing through their bodies. Children of all ages are forced to view these men's fates as the consequence of defying the Nazi regime – a swift, certain death. There's no trial or evidence, or even pretence from the Nazis that they have captured anyone truly responsible for the dead sentry. These seven men in a line carry their guilt simply by being Italian.

They are executed one by one, each fatal bullet echoing in the near silence, each body falling and pulling on the rope to yank the others towards their eventual place in the earth. Men, some still young enough to be called boys, slump as their bodies are pitted with bullets, the witnesses scarred by being forced to watch the wasteful snuffing out of lives. This is when no one can accuse Venetians of having a 'soft war'.

It's likely I'm just waking in my comfortable bed, contemplating the day ahead, when the volley of bullets rips through the air and the bodies fall. I hear later that Breugal addressed the assembled crowd, warning of increased reprisals if the killing of his personnel continued. No doubt he puffed out his ample chest, his buttons almost popping from the intense pressure, and felt proud of his actions. Worse still, the onlookers are taken to the Santa Maggiore jail as hostages, and every male aged six to sixty they come across is also rounded up and taken, as Breugal sees good his threat to punish anyone who defies him.

I'm shocked to hear the gruesome details later from an eyewitness who saw it all from her rooftop. She is red-eyed and still shaking – with disbelief and sorrow, but with sheer rage too. She wants to talk, make sense of it, and paints a graphic description of the horror.

'You must tell it how it is, reflect the spite of those bastards,' she spits into the brandy she needs to quieten her shaking fingers. 'Those poor boys. They were so afraid, you could see it in the way they walked out. And yet so brave too – they stood as tall as they could.' She takes another gulp of the alcohol, wincing at the smart of the burning liquid as she swallows it down.

'Promise me you'll make everyone see how brutal and callous it was,' she says. 'That's all I ask.'

What else can I do but promise I will?

My own rage spirals as I move towards Giudecca. Once again, Sergio has sanctioned an extra edition of the paper; the entire Venetian Resistance is mobilised to be on guard, skulking in doorways to warn of flared anger on both sides, quashing any chance of Venice becoming a battleground. The Resistance commanders are still advocating underground action, despite some convincing arguments among the more zealous partisans for outright combat. The Nazis and the fascists combined still have superior firepower and control of the causeway to mainland Italy, from where they can call in extra troops. We have to bide our time. I for one understand their simmering anger, but I also respect Sergio's calm and sensible response. We are better as underdogs, and are all the more effective when we use stealth.

I think of Popsa as I take the cloth off my typewriter – his belief that I can change things with words, this metal as my weapon. The anger and frustration I feel fizz through my fingertips as I write up the responses which feed in from a variety of messages, passed through Staffettas into our unassuming basement, now a hotbed of rebellion. Arlo and Tommaso look equally grave, and we work almost in silence,

244

save from the urgent clatter coming from my corner. Arlo pulls out his best front page yet and Tommaso a sober illustration of the suffering, reflecting the event as both a merciless crime and also a triumph for Italians as they remain steadfast in their love for our city and country. Nazis and fascists emerge as the losers, in seeing what humanity they had wither to nothing.

As I push over my copy to Arlo, I'm still on fire. I have so much more left in me and there's only one vessel I can pour it into. Gaia and Raffiano rain from my fingers – death and sadness may not have a place in an everyday love story but this is war. In the here and now, they do. I weave in glimmers of hope too: in those left behind, in the tenacity of normal people who won't be cowed by bullies, and in the grace of their reactions – dignified Venetians holding their city proudly.

Arlo, I can tell, is exhausted. I discover only later that a second cousin of his is among the sacrificed – perhaps the fuel for his resolve that night – but he carries on. Matteo's wife, Elena, brings us food, and as the paper is put to bed, we finally sit like featherless pillows around the wide layout table, hardly a word but a myriad of thoughts between us. Arlo picks up my hastily written chapter and his tired eyes scan the words. I watch his mouth crimp and wonder if I should have stopped him reading it.

'We should put this out too,' he says quietly. 'It should be part of our testimony.'

'But Sergio hasn't—'

'Doesn't matter. Let's do it,' he says. 'It's too good a message to ignore.'

Tommaso comes out of his silent shell and nods his

inclusion in the plan, and we haul out the mimeograph printer from the corner. Matteo is dispatched down the path to warn those tying up the bundles of printed papers that we have something else to add, and we crank the handle of the old machine.

Curfew is missed once more, and I take the bed offered by Elena, with strict instructions for her to wake me at six a.m., when Matteo's brother will take me across the water. It's more important than ever to maintain my facade in the Reich office, to be bright-eyed and appearing to view Breugal's actions as a strength. My demeanour within the office can be mindful of the city's mood, certainly, but I cannot show that I am distraught. As always, I am a patriot of Mussolini's warped vision.

Venezia Liberare hits the undercurrent of the streets just as I'm walking towards work. My hair is badly in need of a wash, and my skin reflects back a muted grey in my tiny bathroom mirror, but I paste over the cracks with make-up and sweep my hair into a wave with combs and pins. The smile to the sentries is false but it's become so automatic I barely notice I'm doing it any more. I think one day it may just get stuck in that position and I'll be laid in my coffin with a rictus grin.

The office is half empty – unusually Marta is absent and another typist occupies her seat. My eyebrows go up to one of the other girls, and she shrugs her own curiosity. I can hear Breugal's gruff tones from behind his door and the mutterings of Captain Klaus. Given the events of the previous days, the atmosphere is strangely normal. But, far from reas-suring me, this only pokes at the snake pit of worry lodged in my stomach.

Cristian emerges from Breugal's den twenty minutes later, and I barely recognise him. He's in his shirt sleeves, and his face looks almost as pale as the white cotton. He plants his notebook down on his desk without a word and picks up the telephone, with a low, urgent patter into the mouthpiece. I glance over once or twice during the morning, but he's totally focused on his tasks. Only once does he wander over and ask me to type up a list of names – a long list. I realise it's probably those who are being held as hostages after the public executions, but it's simply a register and nothing else, no indication of their whereabouts or their fate.

As he's standing beside me, I take a leap.

'Cristian, are you well?' I say it with my best stab at concern, and wonder how much of it is fakery. He's startled, and his brow crimps, eyes narrowed. For a minute, I think I've stepped over the line of our pseudo-friendship.

'No, I'm simply tired,' he says. 'It's been a busy few days.'

Busy? Is that how he would describe it? I'm stunned at his lack of emotion, even for a paid-up fascist. Is there not an ounce of sympathy, even for his countrymen? But then I remember he's been primed not to show it.

'I simply thought there might be some illness going around,' I pitch. 'It's not like Marta to be off work.'

This time he does look at me fully, those damn glasses hiding too much of his true self.

'Marta won't be back,' he says crisply. 'We've another replacement arriving soon.' Both eyebrows rise perhaps a millimetre, and then he turns tail and walks back to his desk.

My mind is racing. Where has Marta gone? Was she – as I suspected in my earliest weeks – part of the Resistance, in the same role as I occupy? More worryingly, has she been caught, taken to the bowels of Ca' Littoria – the fascist headquarters – and into Lord knows what torture?

My stomach is in knots for the rest of the morning, and I can't face any lunch. Having memorised ten or twenty names at a time, I make frequent trips to the toilets and scribble them onto scraps of paper, to be stowed in my shoe. I'm relieved that none of the names are familiar to me – and especially glad not to see Vito's – but I'm acutely aware they will be to someone, and more likely well known to the Resistance.

Cristian leaves at his usual time around midday and returns thirty-five minutes later, flopping a folded newspaper on his desk – a fresh copy of *Venezia Liberare*, Arlo's stand-out headline uppermost. I note Cristian doesn't take it with him as he's called into Breugal's office. I wonder also how much he will translate verbatim to the general, given the rage and fallout from our previous efforts in print.

The paper sits on Cristian's desk throughout the afternoon, and it's only towards the end of the day that he opens the pages – it's a small edition of only two foolscap sheets, but I see the lone mimeographed sheet fall from between the folds. I swear I feel my cheeks and ears burn as he takes off his glasses and bends his head towards the print, one hand on his forehead, fingers massaging away at the day's stress. I'm putting the cover on my typewriter as he finishes reading, folds the printed pages and places them under a pile of other papers, sitting to one side. For a minute or so, he simply sits and stares out of the window at the pigeons on San Marco – there are few people about – and his face betrays almost no thought whatsoever. I feel at that moment I would give a lot to be inside Cristian De Luca's head, not least because his thoughts could have severe repercussions for my own on a chopping block.

Despite the sun's apricot glow and the seemingly endless beauty of the evening, I head home, wanting only to be within my four walls, lie on my bed with the window open and listen to the normal life of the little square outside, and perhaps drift into a deep sleep. I shop on the way and buy whatever vegetables and pasta I can find, and then stop by Paolo's and let it be known that I have information from the day – Paolo knows what to do with it.

'Sergio wants to see you,' he says, looking at me as if chiding a small child and gesturing towards the copy of *Venezia Liberare* beneath the counter.

'I expected as much,' I say, but in all honesty I'm too tired to give a dressing-down much thought. I'm proud of the piece about Gaia and Raffiano, even if it is to be their last. My sleep is troubled with images of loved ones and prisons, me chasing endlessly across the city streets in turmoil, but I'm just grateful I do sleep.

The next morning, Sergio calls for a meeting in a safe house in the Santa Croce district not far from the station, and I brace myself for a real and noisy rebuke. It's a Saturday morning – I simply have to face whatever my commander rains down on me and get on with my weekend. Mama and Papa badly need some attention from their only currently present child; Vito appears to be in hiding still, much to my relief. Safe, at least.

'Stella,' Sergio says as I walk in. 'Sit down.' The residents of the house retreat to another room and we're left alone, aside from a small blue bird in a cage, which chirps at intervals.

Sergio's ample eyebrows, much greyer than when I first knew him, are knitted. I think about offering an excuse, babbling about my frustration and anger. But much like facing a gruff teacher in my schooldays, I think it's best not to try to wriggle free – choosing instead to simply swallow the punishment.

'Stella, what you did was rash, and went against orders,' he begins.

'I know,' I admit. 'I'm sorry. It won't happen again.'

The twitch of eyebrows signals some relief to me. 'Well, that's the thing,' he continues. 'I'm not excusing your disregard for command orders, but we feel your actions were justified in the circumstances.'

All the muscles bracing myself for the verbal onslaught sink into my body and I'm almost limp with relief. 'Really?'

The bird adds its timely approval with a tweet.

'Yes.' He sighs and sits back, and for the first time I see real sorrow carved into Sergio's face. Doubtless, there are people among the dead or the witnesses that he knows. He lets it show for only a second, pulls himself up and leans towards me.

'After what's happened this week . . .' it's clear he can barely bring himself to say the words, 'we needed some outlet. Your story has been well received again. People in Venice need some distraction after the hard facts.'

'But what about the Reich?' I question. 'Do we want to invite a reaction from them? An angry one?'

'Perhaps it's time we do,' he says. 'The way this war is going, we may be in a stronger position at some point.' I note he doesn't say 'soon', but Radio Londra tells us of the creeping Allied advancement through Italy and the Germans being chased out of Florence. We're all praying they will reach our little enclave eventually. Soon.

The bird tweets again and brings us back to the moment. 'So, if you're willing, we want you to reintroduce your story each week,' Sergio says. 'Is that possible?'

I tell him it is, because the lovers still live within me – I feel they have hurdles to face, as we all do, but they have a future too.

'However,' Sergio adds, the eyebrows grave again, 'you need to be careful and gauge the mood in the Reich office. If you suspect any danger to yourself, you use the code words and get out. From what I know of Breugal, he may look like a pompous fool, but he is vicious. To men, women and children. He won't hesitate.'

He doesn't elaborate. He doesn't need to. I've seen enough of the rage first-hand – and those poor witnesses too much of Breugal's resolve – to question Sergio's concern.

27

The Bloody Summer

There's a muted reaction from the Reich to our special edition – or at least no explosion from the inner sanctum of Breugal's office. On the streets and corners of cafés, I hear talk of little else among native Venetians; mutterings about the atrocity mostly, but some about the re-emergence of my story. The Nazis are perhaps toning down their reactions and keeping an unusually low profile, since the so-called 'murdered' sentry was fished out of the water only a day or so after the executions, minus any bullet holes or signs of foul play. It's obvious to all he was drunk and drowned accidentally. In an unprecedented U-turn, the Nazis release all of the hostages within days of the shootings – I know since I type up the release lists – and none are destined for the labour camps to the east. It seems the closest Breugal comes to appearing sheepish, but his granite scowl doesn't soften.

It gives me renewed courage to plough forward with Gaia and Raffiano. Following the tragedy – a cruel reminder that life can be snuffed out with little warning – their love is cemented in ways all Italians know about, but in these times my language is necessarily opaque. Raffiano is among those imprisoned in the rounding up of men and Gaia's distress is immeasurable; his absence convinces her that, if and when they are reunited, they should never be parted again by ignorance or prejudice. When Raffiano is then released when the Nazis' mistake is discovered, it takes all my powers of subtle description to create a story between the lines where love wins out, without offending the strictly Catholic readership or passing the Nazis any tips about a couple's existence under the radar. I feel I've pitched it well when I see Arlo's face take on a look of knowing as he proofs and prints out the sheets.

The heat is unending through August, but so too are the fresh brutalities of what's being labelled in the cafés and marketplaces as the 'bloody summer' of Venice. The horror at our enemies' depravity reignites when they raid a convalescent home for elderly Jews. Despite having mental and physical disabilities, in spite of their pleas and tears, the inhabitants too are dragged from their homes and taken east, almost certainly to die.

Daily, we hear the dulled pummelling of Marghere and Mestre with bombs, just across the causeway, knowing it will have an effect on our water supplies, and the dwindling amounts of food coming into the city. Those on the water fare little better – fishermen are used to taking their chances on the lagoon, easily spotted by Allied planes and often strafed with bullets, perhaps taking them for German patrol boats. We in the Resistance feel closely aligned to Britain and the US in our goals, but it makes us remember that Mussolini's Italy as a whole remains an Allied enemy; a German hospital ship under the Red Cross flag, the *Freiburg*, is attacked by Allied planes near San Marco, with big civilian losses. The water around us remains a solid jade green but, walking along the canals, I swear that sometimes I see it rippled red with the blood of citizens.

We're left to gain strength from the tidings of the Allies pushing forward elsewhere in Italy and Europe, sitting with our ears pressed to the wireless in the newspaper office, straining to hear news from Radio Londra pushing out of our tiny speaker. We're saddened at the severe battering of London's centre by Nazi V-1 bombers, and it makes me think of Jack and how he will be feeling if he's listening too, with the anxiety over his family, and the fondness for his own city. I feel a pang for him, for his limbs that were wrapped around mine that special night, yet I know it's too dangerous to repeat my previous trip. I can only hope the war is either won, or that there's enough of a break in the clouds to chance another visit.

'Did you hear of the Warsaw Uprising?' Tommaso comes into the basement breathlessly one day in August, his excitement evident. 'Finally, the Poles are able to act on their courage.'

I can't help but be lifted at his delight that there will be a future for us all to contemplate. Born into a rebel family, he's beaming at the thought of the oppressed Polish nation coming into their own.

Elsewhere in Europe, Bordeaux, Bucharest, Grenoble and then Paris fall to the Allies, 'like dominoes', Arlo jokes, then adds with a serious tone: 'I heard some people on the main island muttering that the push into France is taking away focus from Italy, pulling Allied troops elsewhere that would otherwise be driving at the German lines towards us.' His prematurely aged brow knits. 'But I try to hope that Venice is not forgotten. They will come over that causeway one day. Won't they, Stella?' And all I can do is nod and hope too.

I sink my own efforts into what's needed of me as a Staffetta, and the polar demands as I sit at my different typewriters – the solid, efficient machine in the Reich office, and my own, slightly skew keyboard hidden in our tiny café basement. I know which one I prefer, which one brings out the best in me, but I also know my daytime role entails little sacrifice other than stomaching Breugal's childlike anger in his office and his occasional, repellent leer as I pass him my reports. I take small comfort in that I'm not the only typist to have to endure it, but it makes me shudder all the same. And smile, of course, as I slink out of his reach. Cristian appears non-committal and rarely speaks, other than on work matters. Most worryingly, Captain Klaus is spending more time in the office, roaming the rows of typists and leaning over our shoulders as we work, his sour cigarette breath trespassing on our space. None of us are quite sure what he's looking for, but I'm vigilant in no longer typing up notes at my desk, making my memory do the hard work, and taking even more frequent trips to the toilets.

After Gaia and Raffiano's return, the first three or four episodes appear without much rancour from the Reich office in response. I'm aware Cristian is monitoring them as I see him reading week by week, tucking the extra sheets in a pile on his desk, but I question whether he's actually showing them to Breugal or not. It seems the general has his head buried in the wider war arena, as new acts of partisan sabotage occupy his time and his troops. With each week though, I try to draw in elements of Resistance news we're receiving and weave the lovers' reactions to mirror what Venetians might be feeling; the mood of the couple undulates with anger and despair, physical hunger and a zeal for victory.

The bloody summer gives way to autumn and the cooler weather, a breath of misty chill in the mornings across the lagoon. That in itself is a release, but my heart sinks at the thought we may have to endure another winter skulking about in the snow in our own city. The Allies are forging on, as is the line nudging into Northern Italy, but our liberation still feels so far away, the miles and the time stretching ever more, like the yawning wait for Christmas I remember as a child.

Something has to give, and in my small orbit it's Mama. Vito is still in hiding, although I suspect he takes part in small acts of sabotage. All I can do is report that he's alive, since that's as much as I know. But Mama is used to having him near – perhaps because of his disability she has always mothered him a little more. She has stopped questioning my sources as long as I can give her reassurances, but she bows under the sadness of his absence. Papa cajoles her to eat as she pushes a meagre amount of polenta around her plate, the skin stretched across her prominent cheekbones. It's her heart that shrivels next and I get the message I'm dreading but half expecting – that she's in hospital. I rush to find her looking washed-out and thin in a ward bed, my father bent over in a chair next to her, the life almost sucked out of him.

'Oh Stella,' he sighs, 'when will it all come right?'

I can tell he's contemplating losing almost all of his family not to any one battle, but to the long and drawn-out consequences of war. One medic tells me he thinks Mama is genuinely nursing a broken heart and shrugs his shoulders as to any physical cure. I think if she could just see Vito, touch his face and hear his voice, it would be the medicine she needs, but it's far too risky in the heavily guarded hospital. Papa looks grey with worry as we visit Mama almost daily, and it's one more link I need to fit into the overburdened chain of my life.

And then one of the chains that keeps me together is well and truly severed.

28

Seeking and Waiting

Venice, December 2017

Luisa taps her foot anxiously, scanning the morning crowds for Giulio as clusters of people move through Campo Santo Stefano, heads down, scarves wrapped snugly around their necks. At eight a.m., most are Venetians on their way to work, with only a few obvious tourists up and about early to make the most of their day. It's bright but the café she sits outside is in shade and the cold keeps her alert. Still, she would rather sit out here with her coffee and pastry, watching the colourful stream of life alongside, even if she can make shapes with her breath.

She sits poised with her notebook and map, hoping Giulio will send her off on a trail she can pursue. Despite another lovely meal, and a long *vaporetto* ride circling all of Venice, wrapped tightly in her coat against the wind and lulled by the boat's motion and the twinkle of the shore lights, the previous evening had seemed long. Giulio indicated he couldn't give her much detail over the phone, and his evening was already full, so Luisa would need to wait until the next morning for any sliver of hope. Once in the apartment, she'd spent her evening emailing Jamie and a few friends, before watching a truly dreadful Italian game show, and downing several glasses of wine, which had the opposite effect of making her sleep. The tart, thick coffee in front of her is both good and necessary.

'Signora Belmont!' Giulio appears from the crowds and a smile emerges as he unwinds a woollen scarf. Their misty breaths entwine as he gives her a typical Italian greeting, both cheeks touching.

'Luisa, please,' she says in a virtual echo of his words the day before.

He orders a coffee in his smooth, lilting accent and rummages in a well-worn leather satchel for several photographs.

'Here,' he says, with a broad beam, the dog who has uncovered his bone. 'I think this is your grandmother, no?'

It is. Unmistakably. The monochrome image cannot relay the pink cheeks and rosy lips of Luisa's memory, but it's there in her eyes, and the way she's showing just a little of her teeth in posing for the camera. Her hair is dark, and falls onto her shoulders and, despite the tiny edge of a swastika in one corner of the picture, she looks happy. Luisa's heart swells with satisfaction.

'Yes, it's her,' she breathes. 'Where did you find this?'

'It was in our archives,' Giulio says. 'Easy enough to find her once I had a name.'

A name too! A real, Italian identity – pre-peace, pre-England. Luisa can hardly believe her luck.

'I found several Stellas in our computer archive listed as Resistance members,' he says with pride. 'I thought there would be more, since it's an old Venetian name. But fortunately not too many – it was simply a case of eliminating them one by one. Of those who survived the war, there was only one not listed as living in Venice after 1945.'

'And?'

'Stella Jilani,' he says, and pulls out a photocopy of a wartime document, some form of identity card. The face is there again – not smiling this time, but the full lips are unmistakable. Underneath, it says 'Venetian works department'; it dates from October 1941.

'There's little I can find of her after 1943, but I tracked her first registration in England as 1946, so it's possible she was still in Venice until the liberation in '45, or even longer.'

Luisa senses Giulio is in his element; hopes his expression means there's something else, like a child who's holding onto a secret, but only just.

'Anything else?' she prods.

His lips spread and the surprise breaks through. 'I think I've found someone to talk to, here in Venice,' he says. 'It may be that their parents knew her.'

Luisa's face immediately lights up and Giulio puts up a hand in warning. 'I said *may*, Luisa. Please don't get your hopes up. It's a fairly slim link, but so far it's the only lead I have.'

Again, he has to attend to work at the Institute, so the earliest Giulio can accompany Luisa is late afternoon. She contemplates heading there alone – with her map, she's confident she can find it – but soon realises her hastily learned Italian is simply not good enough. She could only hope to pick out a few words in a conversation between Venetians, who generally speak at a hundred miles an hour.

It's hardly a punishment but Luisa is forced to while away hours in the most beautiful city on earth. It seems as if she's treading water on the lagoon, and not forging forward. Time feels as if it is rapidly running out, with only a mere tincture of Stella Jilani and her past. Still, Luisa now has a name: Stella Jilani. It sounds exotic, a writer's name undoubtedly. She wonders why her grandmother didn't revert to that name once in England. Grandpa Gio's surname was Benetto, and yet she still wrote under the name of Hawthorn. Another layer to the mystery. One tier at a time, Luisa tells herself. Let's find Stella Jilani first.

Throughout the morning, wandering in and out of shops, she feels the excitement fizzing like champagne bubbles inside her. Then, sitting in a café watching other tourists meandering and taking photographs, Luisa steps back and, for the first time in months, looks outside herself. These holidaymakers are here to see what is undoubtedly one of the most beautiful cities in the world. Relishing something that's alive. She is here with the sole purpose of raking up a dead past, to find the shadow of someone she can never possibly speak to. Why? For the first time, she understands Jamie's largely disguised bafflement at her motivation, spending their precious money on a search for a ghost.

Despite this realisation, Luisa can't shake off the truth – that she needs it. Her mother's character – her lack of zest for life and family – seems destined to remain a mystery, but her grandmother, Stella Jilani, is now accessible. She's here, somewhere. Luisa might finally discover what makes her own self tick, the origin of her own love of words and writing, something to pass on to her own children one day. She wants – needs – to know that she is less like her mother and has more in common with her grandmother, who was perhaps a true hero. Stella may be dead but, through Luisa, she can come alive again.

There are those bubbles again, and she cannot force them to be still.

Giulio has anticipated Luisa's zeal needing to be kept at bay while she waits and he's compiled a list of places the Resistance used as handover points, where Staffettas and their contacts might meet, invisible to prying eyes. As ever, Luisa is grateful for the distraction and his efforts.

She makes her way to a small *campo* behind the celebrated opera house of La Fenice. Giulio's scribbled instructions are to look for the lion's head – one of many thousands in a city whose emblem is the lion – and then to the nearby covered walkway, or *sotto*. The lion is obvious enough, its stone expression protruding majestically from above the door of a one-storey building. But a few steps away the meeting point would have been out of sight from anyone in the square. Under the gloom of a walkway leading to a small canal, a single drip of water creates an eerie atmosphere and Luisa tries to imagine waiting in the furthest corner, completely hidden. How would she feel if it was after dark, coming upon her contact? It would likely be pitch black. A body might emerge from the shadow that could be a friend, a fellow partisan, or very likely a foe – a fascist spy, of which there were plenty in disguise. Was her grandmother ever here, waiting with her heart in her throat, not knowing if it would be her last contact? Both the thought and the lack of sun in this dark corner of the jewelled city cause Luisa to shiver.

She looks at her watch. A few hours until the light perhaps shines on her search again. Much as she imagines Venetians did in wartime, she is investing a good deal in pure hope.

29

Sorrow

Venice, October 1944

I hear Mimi's sobs before her knock at my door. Friends
for years, we've mostly laughed together, but wept also – over
boys, broken hearts, tricky exams. This, though, is different
– a tone of true despair.

Mimi folds herself into my arms the minute I open the
door – she can barely get the words out, great gulps of
sadness heaving at her lungs. I steer her towards the sofa and
lower her down, my shoulder soon wet with the tears.

'Who is it, Mimi? Who is it?' In war, people no longer weep
about lost land, houses, or fickle possessions. Only lost people
incite such emotion. 'Is it your mother, your father?' Mimi has
a sister, too, living in Turin, also in the Nazi sightlines.

Mimi recovers herself enough to speak. 'It's Vito,' she sobs,
wiping at her swollen, red eyes. 'He's been arrested, on the
causeway. They've accused him of passing papers. He's in Ca'
Littoria.'

Instantly, I feel sick – for Mimi, Mama and Papa too. My best friend's love – my brother – is unlikely to emerge from the fascist headquarters without lasting damage, if he emerges at all. The torture rooms are notorious, and those that bear testament also bear the life-changing scars. Mimi and I both know the gravity of Vito's perilous situation.

Equally, I know his character and that he wouldn't have been content to sit idle in a safe house for long. It's likely he volunteered for the mission, perhaps took it on without his lieutenant's knowledge.

Clearly, wrapped up in my own double life over recent months, I've underestimated the deepening love Mimi feels for Vito, how it's grown so intently in the hothouse of war. They were to be married soon, Mimi reveals, her eye straying down towards the waistband of the skirt she is wearing, and I understand the 'soon' all too well. I try to hide the shock and disbelief from my face, and yet I still can't be angry with them for indulging their love – it's life. It's war.

'Now he may never see us at all,' she wails, dissolving again into tears.

'Oh Mimi,' is all I can say, wrapping my arms around her and absorbing what despair I can while feeling the nausea rise in my own body. How will I tell Mama and Papa? Should I even try? It might be the last straw for Mama's shrinking heart.

Eventually, Mimi's sorrow gives way to exhaustion and she falls asleep. It's dusk and I walk over to Paolo's alone, feeling I need to share it with someone who I can trust. He's not heard of Vito's arrest yet but I sense his shock, too, and he promises to send out feelers for information.

'You know, if he's in Ca' Littoria, it's not good,' he says

gravely, passing me a large glass of brandy. He might not be so blunt with anyone else, but this is me, Stella, he's talking to. Paolo is as close to me as Vito himself, and he hugs me like I'm family and sets a warm plate of soup in front of me, urging me like Mama to eat. Again, I'm flooded with the vision of telling her and Papa and the toll on her health. I toy with the hot liquid under my spoon and the danger Vito is facing hits me suddenly; the thought of my own brother facing torture is unbearable. An image of him in a cold, dank cell flashes up, his natural optimism being beaten out of him, and the toll on his already thin body. I know Vito has stamina, but how will he stand up to their merciless brutality? I retch dry despair into my bowl and wonder how on earth we can escape this horror.

While comforting Mimi, I didn't allow myself to think it, but now I realise it could so easily be me under lock and key. While I've never considered Resistance work as a game – I've heard of Staffettas being caught and executed – somehow you never imagine it's going to be you, thinking that you will be the one to always slip through the net, even if it's by the skin of your teeth at times. And you have to think like that or you would never gather the nerve to do any given task – it's nature's balm of courage on which the Resistance thrives.

When I'm finally able to sip the soup, I ask myself: what would I be feeling now in Vito's shoes? And how brave would I be?

30

A Low Ebb of the Tide

Venice, October 1944

I look and feel exhausted the next morning. Mimi and I have had a mixed night, she waking from a succession of vivid nightmares and bleeding her distress into the sheets, and me, but I gave what comfort I could. I have no sister, and hers lives away. Her light and laughter have pulled me from more dark places than I can remember, and the idea that her fire can be dampened, even snuffed out, feels too much to bear. Combined with my own dreams, there was little sleep to be had.

Despite my tiredness, I wake early and leave Mimi to sleep on, but before work I visit Papa at home and break the news of Vito in the gentlest way I can, though I know his heart ruptures on hearing it. It's not often I see my father weep, and it creates a tangible pain in my chest to see his despair. We agree not to tell Mama in her fragile state. Not yet anyway.

The Reich office feels like the last place I want to be all day, but I force myself to go in and smile in all the right moments, as a way of keeping up appearances but also to glean any information – even the tiniest morsel – about Vito. Unfortunately, there's none. I feel glad to escape on the dot of five and make my way to the waterfront and the newspaper office, though it's with a heavy heart.

The ferry from the Zattere to Giudecca has been suspended, perhaps indefinitely, due to a lack of coal, and I'm forced to pay a boatman to row me across. I can't tell whether it's the choppy swell causing my stomach to churn – unlikely for a Venetian almost born on the water – or the feelings transferring from my heart.

There are more dispatches in the office about the latest cull of partisans arrested. Some of it is speculation as we have no spies directly within the fascist HQ, and I have to dance around the facts with my words. It's difficult, too, to scratch any good news from Venice itself to fill the paper, and we concentrate on what's happening in the rest of Europe to lift the dreary tone.

What I feel brewing is a new instalment of Gaia and Raffiano, and its reflection of real life in Venice. Again, it pours from within me, flowing like Mimi's tears, and I can't banish the vision of her as I write of Gaia, and Vito too. He becomes my Raffiano, arrested and imprisoned once more, facing torture. I stop typing more than once and stare at the wall, thinking of Mimi reading the words, Arlo's curious eyes on my back. But Mimi is a Staffetta, emotional but strong. Her love for Vito is new and raw, her sorrow at his possible loss devastating. But in the end, she understands everything is for the cause, for Venice. I feel she would applaud it, while weeping over the pages. And I can't stop it coming. The tears, for me, will come later. For now, this is what I can do – for Vito and Mimi, and all those imprisoned. Even Arlo's lips are tightly pursed as he reads my copy before laying it on the machine.

The effect of what I privately call 'Mimi's chapter' is extraordinary. In the days following, there is an audible hum around the cafés I haven't detected before. And then it becomes visible. *Venezia Liberare* is necessarily an underground paper, sold from the back rooms of small shops, passed between families who are sure of each other's politics. Café owners, while they may harbour a stash beneath their beer taps, are guarded about copies left liberally on the tables with so many Nazi officers roaming Venice. No one is ready to advertise their alignments just yet. But I begin to notice the lone sheets of Gaia and Raffiano on chairs, weighted on tables with heavy ashtrays and fluttering in the breeze; old women unashamed at reading in public, their old wrinkled faces crimping with the imagined sorrow of the couple's future. As I approach the copies and focus on the pages, my distinctive dropped *e* of the type seems less of a comfort and more of a beacon, as if it betrays the hallmark of its author. Me. The traitor to the Italian fascist state. But that's only my paranoia rearing its head.

I can't deny that my ego is stroked by the reactions, by the fact that people are absorbed in my words, the unique combination to have come out of me. It's what I dreamed of way back when Popsa presented me with my lovely machine. Shame that such stories are fuelled by tragedy and turmoil. Even sadder that we have come to think of it as normal in this worldwide maelstrom.

271

The satisfaction I feel is short-lived. If Venetians have taken the lovers into their hearts, the Nazis' reaction is the polar opposite. They, too, sense the mood is more fiery among Venetians – principally driven by news of Allied victories beyond the Veneto – but the lovers' instalments are doubtless helping to fan the flames of hostility towards our German 'guests'.

'Find the bastard! Find whoever it is and bring them here so I can string them up myself!' Breugal's screams are unequivocal through his heavy office door as news of further Resistance sabotage becomes common knowledge in the next days. In the outer office, we're all too aware that such tantrums often follow a trip beyond Venice to Nazi High Command, where his vast bulk bows under pressure from generals with more power and influence than him. Even Breugal has to do what he's told on occasion. And now he's out for the author of the sedition creeping across 'his' city. He's out for me.

Throughout his tirade, I continue typing as an automaton, my eyes reading the pages and fingers translating to the keys, but almost without my brain's contribution in between. I'm focused on how seriously I should take Breugal's blustering threats. Before, the search for the story's author was swiftly overtaken by more pressing matters, my crimes easily forgotten and allowed to slip back into obscurity. Now, though, I sense it's more urgent, since the order has come from above.

It's a feeling reinforced by Cristian as he emerges from the office, his normally crisp, clean appearance ruffled by something in him, a change in his posture perhaps. Bowed to some extent by war, like the rest of us. But it's his face

272

which worries me most – granite-like, set with determination. He grabs up the phone handset and I stop typing, pretending to scan my written pages, while screening out the rattle of machines behind me.

'Yes, a squad,' he's saying. 'General Breugal wants whatever manpower you have for a full search. Start in the Cannaregio and work your way south.'

I can't hear the exact words at the other end of the receiver, but the tone appears challenging.

'How long? However long it takes!' Cristian is forceful, as forceful as I've ever seen him. 'He wants this person found. And alive. Find that typewriter and we find the culprit.'

His last words send a shiver through me. Alive but entrapped. In Ca' Littoria with Vito, perhaps? Would Breugal come face to face with my bloodied, swollen features, taking a smug satisfaction in capturing his prize so close to home? And then watch as I face a firing squad, or worse?

I know I shouldn't scare myself with images, but with no news of Vito since his arrest I have only rumours of the brutality of the fascist police behind closed doors to think of. Try as I might, I can't help push them to the back of my mind – the methods, the insidious crack of bones breaking, the cries for mercy . . .

'Fräulein Jilani?'

'Yes?' I'm physically startled, and Cristian looks at me quizzically. The atmosphere between us is cool, certainly, but it's months since we were on such formal terms, in German especially.

'I've an urgent translation for you to type. Are you free?' His eyes barely meet mine, black and cold rather than the soft brown I've known in the past.

273

'Er, yes. Yes, of course,' I say. I hope beyond anything it's not the official warrant for my arrest. The vision of it might break me, or at least have me feigning illness, crumbling as I see it there in black and white. Fortunately, the work is a list of troop movements in and out of the city, and it's something I can at least salvage from the day; I focus my memory for the good of the Resistance.

'As quick as you can please,' he says, his accent especially clipped, and moves away.

I've already settled on arranging a meeting with Sergio as I'm leaving the Platzkommandantur at the day's end, my stomach still roiling with a thousand filthy bluebottles taking flight. Heading towards the Accademia Bridge, a woman strides towards me, working hard at catching my eye.

'Gisella!' she cries, moving in for a cheek-to-cheek greeting. I've never met her before but I know it's safe to reciprocate as she uses my partisan code name. 'Haven't seen you in so long. How are you?' she babbles.

We exchange fake niceties and part with promises to meet up for a drink, but not before she's slipped me the tiniest sliver of paper, palm to palm. And then she's gone, absorbed into the post-work crowds.

I wait until I'm sitting at a café, drink served, before I pull out a book and nestle the note in its leaves. The message gives me a date and a time for a meeting in only an hour, and its tone suggests it could be Sergio. I'm relieved and wary in unison: it's one thing for me to request a meeting for my own reassurance, but could this mean that Sergio has real concerns too?

In that hour, I wonder what I will say to him. Should I admit that I am frightened, and that I want to give up? For

274

all my bravado, my intense loyalty to my city and country, I have to admit I *am* scared of the repercussions, of having information persistently beaten out of me. Having never been tested, I'm not sure how my resolve would hold up. Does everyone give in, when perhaps your sight, your life, or your family are threatened? I like to imagine that in the moment I would think of Popsa and his strength, that it would carry me through. But I'm not certain.

The safe house is in the San Polo district, behind the Campo Santa Margherita, and, as I suspected, it is Sergio who's waiting. He tries to smile as I walk in, but I feel he's harbouring concerns, if not something more.

'How are you?' he says, pulling me by the hand to sit beside him, in some fatherly fashion. I feel he's not just asking out of duty – he really wants to know.

'I – I'm . . . fine,' I lie, pasting on my calmest expression. Just a glimpse of Sergio and the responsibility he carries upon his shoulders always makes me acutely aware of how little is on my own. His constant ear to the ground, his involvement in so much of the Resistance planning and the threat he works under fill me with admiration, instilling some peace within me, and I find I'm less afraid in his presence. I wonder, too, if he ever sleeps.

Those distinct eyebrows, though, they are knitting together as we sit face to face. He tells me he's heard my mother is in the hospital, but that he can't allay my parents' fears, other than scant information from inside tells us Vito is alive. In what condition, though, he doesn't know. He watches relief streak across my face and then anxiety set in again.

'What I do know for certain is that your story caused quite a stir,' he adds. 'In all quarters, I hear.'

I tell him about Breugal's outburst today, the threats he's issued and the renewed search for me and my machine.

'How do you feel about that?' he says, searching my features again. He's clearly offering me an escape, allowing me to bow out without losing face.

'I don't know,' I say, this time with honesty. 'I feel with the distance to Giudecca, any random searches will take some time. But yes, it makes me feel . . . uncomfortable to say the least.' I don't use the words 'frightened' or 'terrified' for fear they'll become even more entrenched in me. And sitting here with Sergio does make me feel less vulnerable. But out there?

Silently, he watches the emotions roll around inside me. 'There is, of course, the option of destroying the typewriter and carrying on with another,' he says at last. 'A machine that can't be distinguished.' The eyebrows ripple like a wave.

Sergio knew my grandfather, and knows of his reputation, but he can't possibly realise what my own typewriter means to me – the love and history that's etched into its paint gloss. And no, a simple possession would never be worth a life, but the thought agitates my resident bluebottles.

'Yes,' I say, 'it is one option. Or I could stop the stories again, like last time. Stop the threat, the searches.'

Now his features rise in surprise, perhaps at my willing-ness to capitulate. 'I'm not sure it would halt the search,' he says. 'I think it's got beyond that. The Nazis are furious now and their anger will mean the search goes on.'

Perhaps he sees the anxiety I'm trying my best to hide. 'But it *is* making a difference,' he adds. 'Our membership has risen in recent weeks, certainly after your last emotive chapter.'

'Really?' Despite what I've always believed about the power of words, I'm surprised it's mobilised people to act in numbers. Then I think: every good book I've ever read has moved me in some way. Perhaps Popsa was right. Perhaps it can change things?

Still, I need convincing. 'Are you sure it's down to what I write?'

'Who knows?' Sergio shrugs. 'We're simply aware there's a shift. Maybe it's news of the Allies, a sense that the tide is turning, a combination of all those things. But it's certainly helping, Stella. I'm sure of that. We just need to keep you safe.'

How can I voice my fears after that? And do I need to? I'm filled again with a sense of duty towards the Resistance, come what may. I resolve to banish the images of Ca' Littoria from my mind. I can't stop myself thinking of Vito, but I can choose to think of him as strong and smiling – and always, always firm in his loyalty. Which means I must be too.

'So, are we agreed – you get rid of the typewriter and I will arrange delivery of a replacement?' Sergio presses.

My bluebottles take ugly flight again. 'Yes. Yes, Sergio.' I say the words, but I postpone any real thought of the act itself. For now, at least.

'Ah, I have one more job for you,' he says, getting up. 'We need a passport and some papers picking up and taking over to Pellestrina.'

The location makes my ears prick up. I wonder how much he's been informed, but he smiles knowingly. 'My sources tell me it might be the job for you. Goodbye Stella. Be safe.'

He clasps both strong hands around my own, squeezes tightly, nods and smiles. And then he's gone again.

The papers I am to pick up that very evening; the drop is to take place the next evening, on my way back from Giudecca. I'm in two minds as I make my way towards the Campo Santa Margherita, aware that the passport and papers I'm to collect may be for Jack. In fact, more than likely. He'll be leaving Venice, my world and my war, and we may never see each other again. I'd already imagined my last trip to be our final meeting, but, in the mire of everything else, the thought that he's still there, across the lagoon, has quelled the uncertainty in me at times. Over recent weeks, I've told myself I could hop on a boat and he would be there, to offer solace and his own brand of humour. Lord knows there have been times when I've needed it, but the demands on me have made it impossible. Now, I'm torn between the opportunity of seeing him and saying a very final farewell. And I'm still not sure how I feel about it.

The sun is lingering in one corner of the large, rectangular square, unwilling to cast itself into a permanent gloom without a last lick of orange on the jagged flow of rooftops. The doorway I'm heading for is in shadow though, and I'm glad, as there are more than a few fascist guards hanging about, preoccupied in their flirting with young Venetian women. I give them a wide berth and walk with jaunty step, trying not to affect a guilty scurry.

It's a small, two-storey building with an ornate frontage like a palazzo. I recognise it from my childhood as the bookmaker's house; whenever we visited this *campo* there was always a man in the window, bending over his desk, his profile lit by a small light, like something out of a Grimms' fairy tale. Now there's no light on show, and I have to rap on the door in the safe rhythm the occupants will recognise. After exchanging the safe words, a young woman leads me to the back room, where the same man – I recognise his posture – is bent over a desk, scratching into a host of documents, from passports to work identity cards. He looks up from the bright lights surrounding his desk into the gloom and squints; if he weren't nearing sixty, he would look exactly like Arlo. He says little, only asking me for a further passcode I've memorised, and hands me an envelope. I'm itching to look at its contents, but clearly it's not for my eyes, and his nose goes back to his ornate script.

'Don't mind my father,' the woman says as she shows me out. 'He's under a lot of pressure lately – there's a big demand for his work. He's known for emulating any script or signature, even Mussolini's once, it's said, although he denies it.'

The sun has completely disappeared by the time I'm back out into the square, causing the mood to become edgier, with the patrols loitering under the blue lamplight. I head out and towards home, with a heart sunken in my chest but the automatic light step of an innocent woman about town, wondering what type of pass I hold in my bag, and where it may lead my future.

31

Playing Detective

Venice, December 2017

Luisa meets Giulio off the *vaporetto* at the far end of San Marco just after four p.m. He doesn't need any great powers to sense her eagerness, and they walk past the Arsenale and towards the Via Garibaldi, the strong winter sun tracking them up the wide avenue. Giulio has an address, and Luisa her detailed map, but his hasty walking pace makes her appear less like a sightseer. The street is populated by tourist cafés, with photographs of drinks and generic spaghetti bolognese outside, as if anyone these days might not recognise such worldwide language. The further they walk, though, the tourist attractions thin out and it becomes a place where Venetian women and children talk and congregate around the entrance to the park, perhaps after school finishes. The vegetable barge stationed on the canal near the Ana Ponte is packing up for the day, brushing up oddments of the purple, octopus-stem Treviso lettuce scattered on the ground.

'I think it's in here.' Giulio signals to a small side street and they both stop to consult the map. The street feeds into Corte del Bianco, a tiny square of houses with nothing but a small well in its centre, one lone cat sitting sentry-like on its concrete cap. Giulio almost holds his breath as he knocks at the door of a small, two-storey house, and Luisa thinks his sense of anticipation might equal hers.

'Just, please, don't be too disappointed if we don't—' he says.

'I know,' she cuts in, as the door opens.

Signora Pessari is the same generation as Luisa's mother would be, perhaps a few years older, in her mid-sixties. She's thick-set with dark, almost ebony, eyes and jet black hair lightly peppered with grey. Underneath the weight of middle age, however, Luisa can still see the beauty that she must once have been, one of those fashionable women in pixie-style dresses and voluminous hair photographed smoking in cafés in the late sixties, a swinging life epitomising the style of both Italy and yesteryear.

The woman ushers them into a small parlour and evicts a cat from one of the seats.

'Coffee?' she says in Italian, after the introductions. Giulio nods yes, without even thinking about it.

Signora Pessari – Rina – apologises for her lack of English and it's evident Luisa will need to play ping-pong with the language. She picks up a few words here and there, thankful of how much the Italians give away in their effusive body language, but is largely forced to rely on Giulio's translations, which he makes with patience.

He pulls out his archive photographs, and Luisa follows suit with her own clutch. Rina dons her glasses, but she does not leave them in suspense. Her smile is enough to say the trip is not wasted.

'Do you recognise this one?' Giulio points to Mimi Brusato.

'Yes! Yes, that's Aunt Mimi,' she says. 'My mother's younger sister. I'm sure of it.' This, however, confirms what they already know. It's the next question which has Luisa's heart pulled tight.

'And this woman?' Giulio says, pointing at Stella. Rina peers closer, and her forehead ripples with thought and, finally, some recognition.

'Yes, I think, let me see, her name was . . .'

Luisa is almost on the edge of her seat, her grandmother's name ready to spill from her lips, but she can also feel Giulio holding her back with his will. The identity will be all the more valuable if there's no prompting behind it.

'I'm sure that's Aunt Mimi's best friend . . . What was her name? Oh, her family lived just a few streets away.'

Luisa feels as if she's a child about to burst.

'Stella! That's it. Stella Jilani,' Rina says at last. She sits back, pleased to have teased it from her memory.

Luisa's breath is released, with a whinny of relief she hears deep inside herself. 'That's my grandmother!' she can't help letting go, and Rina needs only a little translation to appreciate Luisa's joy.

'I didn't know she had any children,' Rina adds. 'I wasn't sure if she even survived the war. My own mama said Stella and Mimi were inseparable when they were younger – we have some pictures of them together as children. They went to the Liceo together, always getting up to something. I heard Stella became a reporter after school, but we were living outside of Venice by then.'

Rina's mother and her husband, it transpires, moved to Turin as war broke out, also under Nazi occupation after 1943. Travel between the cities was almost impossible, and letters scarce. They had their own war to fight – like her sister Mimi, Rina's mother became a Staffetta, in the same circle as the celebrated partisan Ada Gobetti.

'Mama told me after that we would hear a few snippets about the fight in Venice,' she says. 'Sometimes copies of the partisan newspaper would make it out as far as us. She always wondered if Stella was behind the words. After the war, we found out it was her – she worked for the Resistance. But then nothing. She disappeared, but so many did after the war. It was chaos for a while.'

With little expectation, Giulio poses the next obvious question: 'And Mimi?'

If, by some miracle, she is alive, Mimi will be very elderly. But there's a chance.

'Poor Mimi,' Rina says with a shake of her head. 'She had a bad war. She died in a convent, oh as far back as 1965. She never recovered.'

Her cheeks puff out at the sorrow. Recovery from what is not revealed, and Giulio clearly feels he cannot pry. Instead, he asks if there are other families who might know of Stella, in any of the streets of the Via Garibaldi?

'So many families have moved out since then,' Rina says, fussing at the cat snaking around her legs as she thinks. Luisa wills another thread to worm its way from Rina's memory.

'I remember Mama saying there was a café they both used to go to,' she says. 'I've no idea if it's still there, but it was run by a big Venetian family. Over by the Fondamenta Nuove.

I couldn't tell you exactly where, but I think they would visit a friend called Paolo.'

Both faces opposite Rina must reflect disappointment. How many Paolos in Venice, past and present? This Paolo would be in his nineties and more likely resident in San Michele island cemetery. How on earth would they track down his relatives?

'Oh,' Rina says. 'He wasn't a visitor to the bar. It was his family's café. If it's still there, there's a good chance the owners would remember him.'

Luisa and Giulio leave, with Rina promising she will venture into her own box of photographs and contact them with any news. As a parting shot Giulio asks if she recognises the name Giovanni Benetto as familiar. A suitor, or fellow partisan?

No, she says, shaking her head. There was no Giovanni in Mimi's few letters.

Giulio is upbeat as they walk back towards the glitter of the lagoon, a glorious sunset tiptoeing on the water. Clearly he's pleased with their progress.

'It's a start,' he says with a smile, although Luisa is thinking only of the end of her trip and how fast it's approaching. Her flight home is the next afternoon. Perhaps her mother's inheritance will lend itself to another fact-finding mission, but what will Jamie say about that? She thinks about spending her last half-day pounding the streets of Venice to look for this mystery bar but then what? The thought of rehearsing her questions in Italian to seek out Paolo is less appealing. And what if they do understand her and answer in a volley of speedy dialect? She can imagine the headache it would create. It feels as if she has squeezed herself into one of Venice's tightest alleyways and come to a dead end.

Giulio guides Luisa to sit on a bench near the water's edge, and they both take in the dimming sun replaced by new lights drifting across the water.

'I can take tomorrow to help you,' Giulio says at last. 'It is research, after all. We'll just go into every bar around the Fondamenta and be – what is it the English say? – very nosy.'

Luisa turns her head, and her face brightens in the gloom. A smile of relief and gratitude spreads across her features. 'Do you understand why I need to find her? Or is it just a silly obsession?' she says into the air.

Giulio looks at her, clearly perplexed. 'Of course you have to find her,' he says, as if it's the most natural quest in the world. 'Whether or not they are dead and gone, history defines us. It makes us what we are. Right now.'

At that moment, in his academic's jacket and tortoiseshell glasses, he doesn't look much like it, but Luisa could kiss Giulio Volpe as her knight in shining armour.

32

A Parting

Venice, October 1944

The newspaper office on Giudecca is empty when I arrive, and I pull off the cloth covering my typewriter. I have no excuse not to set it in its casing, take it outside and toss it with all my might into the canal water, as Sergio has directed. Although it's not a heavy machine, the combined weight will send it to the bottom in seconds. There will be no typewriter to find, and I regain my anonymity.

But I can't. My heart pushes and pulls; I make the mistake of fingering the cool, metal keys, a habit I have when I'm feeling lost or lonely. Then I think of Popsa, his image flooding my mind. I'm standing there alone in the office, tears streaming, and feeling alternately foolish and bloody-minded. How dare this war, these Nazis, take away what is most precious to me? The hope he gave to me, here in this piece of metal.

I'll hide it, I decide. I can stow it safely, perhaps at Santa

Eufemia's? And then I think of a fascist search party, and the vengeance on the nuns. I can't do it to them. Besides, Sergio's replacement typewriter is nowhere to be seen, and there's no other to use. I fool myself I have to use it, for the good of the Resistance. Arlo arrives, this time without Tommaso, unusual since they are such a pairing these days.

'Is he sick?' I query. It's a less painful conclusion than a young boy being detained by a patrol. Tommaso's father is a lieutenant in one of the sub-units and his son's cheery character hides the fact that his family lives under constant threat.

'I don't know,' Arlo says. 'He wasn't at our usual meeting point, but I've had no message either.'

We set to work, but the hours drag by, until the time when I can leave for Pellestrina. Even my instalment of Gaia and Raffiano plods at a slow pace, their projected emotion tangled with Mimi's and my own. I'm conscious of dragging the lines from within me, word by word, aware it's not my best work.

Finally, Matteo raps on the basement door to signal my boat is waiting in the small canal beside the café. It's almost dark, and the distance to the island is deceptive in the dying light; the journey feels long, almost until we're drawing up at the wharf.

The envelope weighs heavily in my bag as I walk towards Jack's little apartment. I find him outside, sitting on a bale of nets, still working in the glow from an open workshop door. His face lights up as he squints to place me in the gloom.

'Stella!' It's just what I need – a welcome, sunny face. I wonder how in the world I will do without it.

We go into his room, and the envelope confirms what I both want and fear at the same time – that his departure is planned. His face registers a mixture of relief and sadness. I want more than anything for him to reach safety, perhaps even as far as his family in England, but, selfishly, I don't want him to go. I almost wish he needed a native Italian to guide him over the mountains and skirt around the Nazi patrols in the hills. I would willingly leave this war behind, but Venice? I can't, not with Mama still sick and Vito imprisoned.

We spend the night side by side – I guessed we would. And it's by mutual consent that we don't lace our bodies around one another and take our intimacy one step further – that crucial step. Something stops us, a sense that maybe it would spoil what we have: a brief but intense friendship that might just survive war and a continent between us. As long as we don't complicate it. It's left unsaid, but our friendship is worth more than romance, even in war. Even if we never see each other again, it's better to part as friends.

'Is there anyone special at home?' I ask him, as the moonlight slices across the thin blanket over us.

'Yes and no,' he says. 'I mean, there's someone I like – we met just before I left – but I don't think she knows how I feel.' He pauses, looks embarrassed. 'Look Stella, it's not that I don't find you attract—'

'I know, I know,' I stop him. 'And it's the same for me. But it's better we're friends, Jack. Good friends.' He looks relieved at our understanding, and I return his smile, adding: 'But it doesn't take away the fact that you're a darn good kisser!'

We talk for a long time, an easy flow given the awkwardness of sex has been banished. Finally, in the early hours, we give in to sleep and the light wakes us several hours later, inching towards our goodbye.

He holds me on the quayside, squeezing both my hands, and I notice his eyes are wet. I peel my fingers away and feel into my bag and this time it's me who provides something to mop the tears, having prepared myself for many of my own.

'We'll see each other again, I know we will,' he says. 'You know where to find me – I'll probably end up behind my mother's deli counter, slicing sausages!'

Again, I believe his optimism – that we will both survive this war, that his hazardous journey over the mountains into France will be paved with good fortune enough to dodge capture, bullets or both, and that I will live long enough in Venice to see liberation and travel one day to London.

It's all we can do – because if we can't see it, taste the reality, it may never happen. There is no other way.

I don't look back as the boat moves away from the dock, and I'm willing it to go faster, for the wind to pick up and push the flimsy sails so that I can't feel his eyes boring into my back. I land on the Lido and it's a rush again to run to the Motonavi so I'm not late for work. This time, some of the girls note my relative dishevelment and make excuses while I patch up in the washroom. Even Cristian, who hasn't noticed me for weeks, stares at me sideways from his desk, as if I have some type of large blemish on my face. Perhaps I'm wearing my sorrow more acutely than I realise.

I push through the day to meet Mimi after work. She looks grey and drawn, and it's not the Mimi I know. There is no fresh news of Vito, and she is a boiling pot of indecision as to its meaning.

'That's good, isn't it?' she says, twirling nervously at her hair. 'It means there's no body to claim at least. We know when they are finished with them at Ca' Littoria and taken to jail, we at least have guards in Santa Maggiore who will tell us. If there's nothing yet, there's hope.'

All I can do is nod in agreement, while wincing inside at her reference to a 'body'. She's with me for reassurance, even if it means concurring with her false optimism. If Vito is still in Ca' Littoria, he is on no holiday, and the thought burns into me. But Mimi's thinking – putting a barrier around the truth – may at least dampen her anxiety. It may be her saving.

'You have to look after yourself, Mimi,' I say. 'For the future.' Neither of us have said the word 'baby' yet – it's too much for her to contemplate gaining one love while potentially losing another. And it's my blood too, my brother's child, and a grandchild for Mama and Papa. We'll tackle the lack of a wedding ring later, when he's safe.

33

In Hiding

Venice, October 1944

In the next weeks I'm inspired again to push forward with Gaia and Raffiano, sadly spurred on by another atrocity; a larger passenger ferry, the *Giudecca*, is attacked by Allied planes out in the lagoon. It's later rumoured they may have spied German uniforms on deck and mistaken it for a troop ship, but the result remains the same – the ferry is sunk, with the loss of untold numbers; more than sixty bodies are pulled from the water, but with so many stateless refugees in Venice, the numbers could be much more. The lagoon and the wider sea doubtless claims its share.

The newspaper office feels noticeably emptier, with Arlo and me each working alone at our desks.

'Tommaso's father has been arrested again,' Arlo tells me in a grave voice. 'And this time he's been taken to Ca' Littoria.' It's the third time Tommaso's father has been arrested but previously he's always been released from jail and avoided the fascist police headquarters. 'Tommaso sent word that he's at home supporting his mother.'

In the relative quiet, the banter that we three once enjoyed in the office feels far into the past.

'Poor boy,' I mutter, with deep sympathy for his family's angst. It flashes up an image of Vito's face and this time I can't help but envisage him in a cell, with pulped and bloodied flesh. I harness the emotions it stirs in me, adding to my latest chapter of Gaia and Raffiano with renewed pain.

I don't quite appreciate the fervour of my language until several days after publication. Then, the cold wind whips off the Fondamenta Nuove as I leave my apartment for work. I'm grappling with my scarf when I look up and see that my words are no longer restricted to the paper on café tables. On a concrete wall, daubed awkwardly in black paint, are the words: 'Gaia and Raffiano: love forever'. Worse still, there is a Nazi patrolman standing directly in front, staring at the sight. I slow up to watch his reaction. He looks perplexed at first, cocking his head as the meaning dawns, then he turns and strides away, in the direction I am bound. Towards Nazi headquarters.

The graffiti artist has been busy; it's not the only message en route to San Marco, and there are variations on the theme – 'Free Venice for lovers' – in red paint too. I sink lower into the collar of my coat, my face burning, imagining I have some type of target pinned to my back. I'm sharply reminded of Jews across Europe, and the way they are forced to wear a stark yellow star on their arms, each and every day. Mine at least is a figment in my head, while theirs is all too real.

News of the graffiti arrives before me. Cristian is nowhere to be seen but it's clear where he is, given the cacophony coming from behind Breugal's door. I scan the office, but everyone's heads are down, perhaps reasoning the fury will pass over them if they lie low and look busy.

We hear variations on Breugal's opinion: 'String them up!', 'Bring the bastard to me so I can see them burn', his voice consumed with rage. Heads sink even lower over the machines. I have to draw in deep, silent breaths before I can begin typing, but I note my fingers are trembling, slipping on the keys.

Cristian blows out of the office eventually, sits heavily at his desk, barks away a query from one of the typists and begins scrawling on some paper. In minutes, he brings the sheet to me.

'Type this please, Fräulein Jilani. As quickly as you can.' His tone is strained, clipped, and he avoids any eye contact.

It's what I feared, and again I am relying only on my body's natural mechanism over my twenty-seven years on this earth to keep my heart beating, despite the knife tearing into its muscle.

'REWARD FOR THE CAPTURE OF AUTHOR'. I'm forced also to type a substantial sum as the prize – well over a month's wages for your average Venetian. As an extra carrot to any takers, there's the promise of 'protected liberty' to any giver of information and their family. There's intense loyalty within Venice, but with Santa Maggiore jail bursting at the seams and those in Ca' Littoria too, there will be takers.

It's the first time the Nazis have offered such a substantial incentive for my arrest and I know I'm white and shaking, but I type on. If I were to flee now I feel sure at least Cristian will guess at my complicity – he is clever enough to join the dots, and he knows where I live, Mama and Papa too. I sit firm, sweat pooling in the small of my back, my brain in a whirlpool while my fingers extend onto the keys. I finish the task and take it to Cristian's desk.

'There you are, Herr De Luca,' I say, and it's all I can do not to slam it down in front of him, as tiny bubbles of rage begin to push through my cloak of fear.

He looks up, features dark and his mouth set in a line. His brow is furrowed behind his glasses.

'Thank you,' he says, and goes back to reading his report.

Within the hour, I see the sheet bound up and collected by one of the messengers. The posters will be printed and they'll be plastered all over the city by tomorrow. I rue my own stupidity in not casting my typewriter to the lagoon bed, and yet – at the same time – I'm not sure I can do it even now. Its very presence is incriminating to more than just me, though: I need to move it, and soon.

I make it to lunchtime before approaching Cristian, taking in a breath to afford a more friendly air.

'Herr De Luca, please, may . . .' He looks at me as if affronted at the way I address him, but I'm merely aligning to his own etiquette.

'Yes?'

'You know my mother has been ill, but I'm afraid she's taken a turn for the worse, and I need to go to her. I promise I'll make up the time . . .'

His face softens; there's no movement towards a smile but I can see it in his eyes. The hardness around his eyes of late smooths into something of a truce between us. In the short time I've known him, he's still hard to read, his mood unpredictable.

'Of course, Fräulein Jilani,' he says. 'Take what time you need.'

I hate lying about Mama, but I'm safe in the knowledge she is at home with Papa, having finally been discharged from the hospital with a weary but intact heart, and seems to be recovering for now. Still, we haven't had the courage to explain properly about Vito and where he is; to her, he is still in hiding. Papa is the one bearing the anxiety of his son's true whereabouts.

I walk with purpose, finding it hard not to adopt a skip or a half-run that is likely to attract attention from the patrols. But I'm not heading home. The safe house I know Sergio most often frequents is occupied, but he's not there, and I can only leave a message about the posters to be plastered across the city. From there, I make my way to the Zattere to pick up a boat – the *vaporetto* is suspended again and just after lunch there are few boats about. The one owner I can find is reluctant to move until he has at least one other customer for Giudecca and although I'm tempted to offer him double price, that in itself might arouse suspicion. So I sit on the waterfront prickling with unease, the sun lingering behind a curtain of grey cloud, waiting its turn, much like me.

Forced to linger, I try to rationalise the fresh urgency in me; the typewriter has been in Matteo's basement for months – almost a year in fact – and until now I've never felt its presence as a threat to me or those in my sphere. But then I've never had a substantial reward for capture posted on my head either. Perhaps there is a reason to feel jittery, after all.

Under the gun-grey sky I'm finally transported across the lagoon, alongside an old man who insists on sharing his entire day with me. With difficulty, I try to converse like a fellow Venetian just about her business, but the oars can't go fast enough and each wave that strikes our bow seems bent on delaying me another second.

Matteo is surprised to see me so early in the day but, with the progress of the war of late, he's used to new material needing to be processed quickly, and us keeping odd times. It's only once I've descended the small flight of stairs and switched on the dim bulb that I take stock. My hand goes towards the typewriter's cover and I'm shaking – and not from the cold wind over the water. I force myself to draw in some deep breaths, recall what our training as partisans tells us to do in times when . . . well, when we feel we're falling apart – scared and baseless. I'm all of those.

Pull yourself together Stella! is all I can think to say, but at least the banality of it makes me laugh inside, and I gather strength from somewhere to move. She's still there, my constant, metal voice, smeared with age and in need of a new ribbon, but I figure this is her last task for some time, if at all. The ribbon can wait.

'Hey girl,' I say. 'One for the road, shall we?' and I laugh again that I'm talking to a machine. As I'm rolling the paper in, Matteo brings me coffee and a message from Sergio received via the café's radio. It's short and pert but I absorb its meaning.

'*One more to sign off,*' it says, '*then stay away.*'

I know I have just this last instalment to bring everything into focus for Gaia and Raffiano. There's no conclusion to this war yet, but I can at least send them on their way with hope, the faith we all harbour that our struggle won't be in vain. I notice the room becoming dimmer as the sun bows to cloud, but for two hours the world outside the tiny base-ment ceases to exist. I'm there in the page, living the emotion as Raffiano escapes from his confinement, is tearfully reunited with Gaia and they make their way into hiding together – being apart is not an option, and leaving Venice and their families is not either. They will bring up their child – conceived under the cosh, but entirely through love – in Venice. In their city that is home to Venetians and Jews and all manner of mixtures in between. I can only hope that what I write becomes truth for Mimi and Vito.

I feel wrung dry as I pull out the sheets, and leave them for Arlo's hand to distribute. The wayward little *e* pulses at me again, like the beacon it is to the Nazis. Of course I'm scared of being caught and the consequences, but I can't ignore that nugget of pride lodged within me, of being part of something to shift the hatred in this war. Even a little.

Now, though, the shift has to be more substantial – my beloved typewriter needs removal so as not to cast guilt on others. I borrow a shopping basket from Elena for the purpose, and I'm relieved once again that the machine is relatively small, even when in its casing. It fits neatly into the basket and, if I hook it into the crook of my arm, I can bear the weight without looking as if I'm straining over anything more than groceries. I buy whatever bread and rolls I can to cover the typewriter, and under the cloth it makes the hamper appear full. Then I take a deep breath and head out. The owner of a small supply boat takes pity on my shivering form as I stand on the shadowy waterfront, and he deposits me on the main island with a cheery 'Have a good evening.' Somehow I doubt I will.

The walk from the Zattere towards home is easier than I envisaged, and I'm subjected to only one cursory search, where the patrolman peers under the covering as far as the seeded bread rolls. Fortunately, the troops are well fed and don't often feel the need to confiscate food, especially something so basic as bread. I reach my own apartment, and there's a tweak of the curtains from my neighbour, Signora Menzio, who's not used to seeing me return this early in the day. She gives a subtle nod through the windowpane to signal all is clear.

I feel safe inside my own space, but remind myself it's only bricks and mortar, which can easily be breached by a search party and their heavy trespass of boots. I will need another hiding place, but for now – for tonight at least – my beloved typewriter will have to reside with me. I scrabble in a cupboard that doubles as a wardrobe, pulling out shoes and odd boxes, and use a kitchen knife to prise up one of the looser floorboards. I need to manoeuvre the case care-fully inside, wary of not chafing the boards still in place, a giveaway for any well-seasoned search party.

'Sleep well, little lady,' I say as I place the loose board back and pile on the shoes in the same ramshackle fashion as before.

Immediately, I feel bereft, although perhaps less exposed, too. It feels odd that I may not be writing anything for some time, with the exception of those damning reports for Breugal; if Sergio's message is to be believed, I am to stay well away from the newspaper office. They will find a replace-ment – I'm not so naïve as to believe I'm indispensable – but I feel it is the end of a small era, for me at least.

I'm restless, roaming the small apartment and trying to scratch together a decent meal from my meagre larder. I pull out a book, and then realise it's the copy of *Pride and Prejudice* given to me by Cristian. Even that life seems so far away, his goodwill as a colleague morphed into bitterness.

I feel trapped, but only by my own languor and depression. So far in this war I have had moments – days even – of anger and sadness, but never time enough for my whole being to feel deflated. As if the person inside is under bombardment, like the docks and ships in the lagoon. Jack is gone, there's not even Mimi here to boost my mood and, selfishly, I can't face the walk to my parents. I know Papa will guess at my melancholy, and what can I say to lift Mama, to make her feel better? For the first time in months, I have only myself to help boost my own inner spirits. And I find myself as barren as my own larder.

34

The Search for Coffee

Venice, December 2017

The next morning, they meet early and begin scouting at the north end of the lengthy Fondamenta Nuove waterfront. Even Giulio is surprised at how many café-bars are concentrated in such a small area, as they weave four or five streets deep so as not to miss any potential targets. Giulio is armed with his printed identification of Stella and Mimi, although the age of the clientele means no one is likely to recognise them. Sadly, the name of Paolo draws scores of blanks; the café ownership has either changed hands many times since the war, or they simply don't have any Paolos in their midst. Luisa can only stand by, reading the negative response of each café worker as they shake their heads.

The search looks fruitless, and with aching feet both are on the point of calling it a day when they decide to stop to drink a coffee in a bar near to Venice's main hospital.

As he's ordering at the bar, Giulio goes through the motions of his request.

'Not here,' the woman behind the counter says, and Giulio's shoulders sag in defeat. 'But I think there's a family bar nearby – I'm sure the owner's father is called Paolo. You might try there.'

Boosted by caffeine and a sliver of hope, they head to the Campo De Giustina De Barbaria, a square smaller than its lengthy name. The Rizzini café is nestled in one corner of the square, its outside tables empty, but the lights inside signal it's still open. Giulio casts a look at Luisa which seems to say: here we go, one last try. There's a woman behind the bar, and on hearing the name Paolo, she immediately calls to a room behind.

'Hey, Pietro, I think there's someone here for you.'

A young man appears in the doorway from behind a curtain. He's Luisa's age, perhaps younger, and both she and Giulio are resigned once again to chasing a rainbow with no pot of gold at the end. Even so, Giulio begins with his questions. This time, there's a lot of nodding – the man utters the name Paolo, and Luisa picks out the word 'Papa'.

Giulio's face lightens as they talk on, his shoulders pick up, but the conversation is too fast for her to follow. Finally, the man goes behind the curtain again and Giulio turns to Luisa.

'It might be something,' he says. 'His family have owned the bar from before the war – his father is called Paolo, but he's only your mother's age, or thereabouts. Still, he says we can talk to him.'

Pietro emerges, pulling a jumper over his head, and leads them from the bar, into the square and several doors down to the entrance of an apartment. He pulls out a key and lets himself in, saying 'Come, come', in English. Up two flights he opens the door to an apartment, singing '*Ciao* Papa' as he enters, and they follow him into a small living room, where Paolo Rizzini sits in an armchair facing a television. Pietro explains quickly what they are looking for, and the older man's brows come together, clearly searching his memory.

Giulio translates the exchange. 'Signor Rizzini was born in 1951, so clearly can't tell us much about the war, but he does remember his father talking about it, and that there was an album of photographs he once had. He remembers seeing pictures of the partisans in San Marco after the liberation.'

'So do they know where the photographs are?' Luisa can hardly contain her excitement. Giulio homes in on the conversation again. Pietro turns and gestures at Giulio, who then swivels towards Luisa. His smile is as wide and bright as she's seen so far.

'Pietro says we can ask grandfather Paolo ourselves – he's alive and well. Ninety-six years old but apparently his memory is quite good.' He stops, takes a breath. 'Luisa, we might just have found our link.'

They emerge from the apartment into the bright winter sun splitting the *campo* in two. It's fitting, Luisa thinks, that they step into the white light and squint against its glare.

'So . . .' Giulio begins, but then can't help his own excitement breaking through with a broad grin. Luisa feels all of six years old, pushing down the butterflies as she waits for the hours until Christmas morning to peel away.

It's then that she truly cannot help herself – she throws

her arms around a slightly stunned Giulio, who nonetheless returns her firm embrace. Inside, there's a deep-seated feeling – a real belief – that maybe this time she will truly find Stella Jilani.

35

Red-Handed

Venice, October 1944

Despite the weight of guilt under my floorboards, I fall asleep early and unexpectedly deeply, waking to a bright autumnal morning. My dreams – filled with scenes of my own arrest, and another where Breugal scoffs his way through a farcical, mock trial before handing down my sentence – were not exactly restful, but physically I do feel energised.

I step out early, towards Paolo's, only to find the café is not yet open. There's enough time for me to walk the length of the waterfront – the sparkle of the water is almost blinding, but its rays lift my spirits. I skirt around San Marco and into the streets heading for the Accademia Bridge, to another café I favour for breakfast, where I know they will hold back eggs for their regular customers. There's a weight on my shoulders still, but now that the typewriter is stowed where it can incriminate only me directly, I feel I'm bearing a lighter load.

The eggs sustain me even more, a rare treat these days, with fake coffee to rival Paolo's, and I'm even scrolling through the first few pages of *Il Gazzettino* – it's never bad to keep tabs on enemy propaganda. Sitting there, I'm feeling positive that we – me, the paper and Resistance, even my family – can ride through the various storms in our midst.

Until I see them. I only glance up from my paper, but the recognition is immediate. One, emerging from a small alleyway, is in a drab, brown double-breasted suit, and out of uniform he looks remarkably different. But he's not so changed that I don't recognise the sharp lines and thin neck of Captain Klaus. His companion is equally tall and lean, but much younger. Whereas Klaus emerges and strides forward, Tommaso's lanky form reminds me of a nervous mouse peeking from his hole. It's in his eyes and his posture, almost bending to hide his face. But there's no doubting it's him. The shock stops me mid-breath and winds me physically, and although they seem distracted from everything around them, I pull up the broad newspaper sheets higher to cover my face. Peering over the top, I see them exchange a few words, although Tommaso's demeanour suggests that inside he's clearly screaming to get away. He's dispensed with, Klaus giving him a paternal pat on the back in parting, and he walks with his shoulders stooped towards the Rialto. I can't see Tommaso's face, but I imagine there is no joy in his features.

The pieces slot together in my mind, and I'm horrified. Tommaso understands all too well the predicament his father is in. Being in Ca' Littoria, there's little prospect of release if they find out his position of rank in the Resistance. I recall Cristian's poster and the promise of liberty in exchange for information. But Tommaso? Who I've worked alongside for months now – laughed and joked with? And then I think of Vito, or my parents, and wonder what I might do for their freedom, if it came to it. With Vito, I know he would rather die than my exchange information for his release. He's young and fit. But what if it was my own papa? How would I feel then? I hope I wouldn't sink so low as betrayal, but I don't *know* for certain. Do any of us? In this case, blood may be a good deal thicker than water. I know in my heart Tommaso is a loyal partisan – I've heard it in his voice many times. He wouldn't do it willingly, but he must be dying inside for his father's safety.

The fact is, it's done. He wasn't meeting Klaus for coffee and chit-chat. And I have to assume the worst in order to safeguard myself and those around me. In the next second, I'm on my feet and heading not for San Marco and the Reich office, but to the Zattere at as fast a pace as I dare. There's no time for me to locate a safe house with a receiver and send a message to Matteo on Giudecca – I need to warn him directly. The *vaporetto* is, mercifully, in operation, but it's still a good thirty-minute wait before I'm on the water and chugging towards Lord knows what. How soon can Klaus mobilise troops to search the café and then inevitably discover the basement office? I'm still calculating as I launch myself off the boat, onto the pontoon and towards Matteo's.

I'm too late. I pull back on my own reins as I round the corner into the *campo*, hearing Elena before I see her, sobbing uncontrollably into her hands as Matteo is held back forcibly by two fascist guards.

'He's innocent!' she screams into the echoing *campo*.

There are papers strewn across the slabs, the wind sending

some into the air, and another guard is ordering the others to contain them.

'We need them as evidence!' he shouts. 'Catch them.'

From behind the wall, I watch as two guards haul the mimeograph machine out of the doorway and onto the pavement, its metal scraping and crashing onto the concrete. To my surprise, there are only fascist guards, with no Nazi counterparts overseeing the raid. And no Captain Klaus.

'So what's this, eh?' the senior guard roars at Matteo, his face barely inches from the café owner. 'Bit of storytelling for your customers, is it?' And he laughs heartily at his own sarcasm, while the soldiers follow his lead.

Matteo is tight-lipped. There is nothing he can say. He knows what the immediate future holds for him, and Elena – in her distress – knows too. His normally ruddy face is white with fear, hers streaming with sorrow. His best prayer is that he will emerge alive.

I feel sick. Breakfast and bile retches into my throat and I need to turn into a doorway before I can push back my own fears. Sucking in the chill morning air isn't enough to keep my stomach contents in place, and once I've recovered a little I try to think what I should do next. We've been careful in the office not to leave any trail leading to our identity. But if Tommaso has revealed the office's whereabouts, who knows what – who – else he has given up? Klaus wouldn't settle for anything less than names. I know I should head back to my own apartment and dig out the typewriter from its hole. This time it must truly be cast into the deep waters of the Fondamenta Nuove – there is no place for sentimentality now. But equally, I reason I may have a little time to give warning to the others.

I run back to the waterfront and use my last lira to pay for the only water taxi back to the Zattere. I'm breathless and sweating as I hurry towards the nearest safe house I know of, in the hopes of getting a message to Arlo and some of the others who help us from time to time.

My message dispatched as urgent, I almost run the most direct route through Campo Santo Stefano and San Salvador. I'm thankful there are so many churches in Venice, that I might duck into if a patrol gets too near for comfort, but equally I need to reach home as soon as I can. I'm banking on Cristian believing that my absence from the office is down to my mother's sickness, but it won't last long, I know. My calves are aching as I weave my way around the smaller streets, steering clear of the larger avenues where troops congregate.

Finally, I'm two streets away from my own little *campo*. I stop and try to tune into any changes, but the morning bustle of Venice overrides anything I can sense, the throttle of boats out beyond the Fondamenta invading the sound space I need to isolate. Everything seems normal.

Even so, I walk the streets tentatively, the last two steps towards the opposite end of the *campo* almost on tiptoe. I peer out into the space, beyond the small chapel, and I'm grateful for its presence in hiding me.

It's Signora Menzio I see first, not as I usually do through her window, but out in the *campo*, putting up a good show of an old lady dragged from her home, berating the SS trooper with little fear and a wagging finger. He seems almost pushed back by her vitriol as she lets rip with Italian obscenities, little of which he's likely to understand, although the supporting fascist guards wince at her colourful slurs.

But I soon see that that's only one half of the story. Moving around the other side of the chapel confirms Signora Menzio is not their target. I recognise some of my belongings on the paving slabs, tossed from the open second-floor window – clothes, some of my precious books, and, more alarmingly, a collection of my shoes. The thought strikes like a hammer blow to an anvil – they have found the cupboard and are doubtless pulling up the boards as I watch. I will be caught. Any minute, an SS officer will emerge – perhaps Klaus – with my beloved typewriter in his arms, and a look of sinister triumph.

There's nothing left in my gut to even create a sick feeling, but my heart fills my chest, hot against my sternum and flush in my throat, pushing on my tongue and causing me to stumble and scoop for air. The noise in the square is muted by buildings on all sides but, even so, the search appears to be methodical and relatively calm. There's a cacophony of sound in my ears, screeching and drowning and overwhelming me with my own vanity and stupidity and sentimentality. I can already see the inside of Ca' Littoria vividly, and the red of my own blood, can taste its metal taint on my lip.

After a minute or so during which I have trouble staying upright, I pull in enough breath to think clearly. I consider turning tail and running to the nearest safe house, perhaps to the back entrance of Paolo's where I can crouch in his cellar until they have gone, to be delivered to Sergio and hidden under his cloak. And then as swiftly as the idea comes, I rule it out; all becomes clear to me. The Nazis know the address I am registered at – it is my parents'. The picture of Mama as she sacrifices herself in place of me – as I know she will – makes my heart rupture with a jolt that physically propels me forward. What unfolds now is entirely my doing, and no one else's. It's clear to me that I have been very, very foolish; I alone must face the consequences.

I take in one last calming breath and walk out from the shelter of the chapel, towards the gathering at my door, forcing my steps to appear measured. Signora Menzio cannot help but give me away with her look of shock and a sudden halt to the venom she is still aiming at the troops.

'Stella, what are you—' she utters.

'It's all right, Signora Menzio,' I say. 'It's all right.'

I don't need to identify myself to the unknown guards, because Captain Klaus is able to do it very well as he walks from the darkened entrance of my apartment, his gaunt face bearing a thunderous look as he emerges into the light. His arms, though, are by his side – empty. Perhaps another guard will follow with the incriminating prize they are seeking? It's only a matter of time.

'Fräulein Jilani,' Klaus says coolly. 'I must admit I'm very surprised to see you here. Though not unpleasantly so.' He smiles economically, so that only the middle part of his yellow teeth is on show. Then his features return to the brooding expression of the seconds before.

Within seconds, there is the shadow of another figure behind. But this form wears no grey or green livery, only a plain blue suit. This time, it's me whose surprise is most apparent; my face frozen as Cristian De Luca steps through the threshold of my home. Of course he's here – he's the only one to whom I entrusted the whereabouts of my home. A trust snapped in half by his very presence.

Cristian's face is sheepish, what I can see of it anyway,

because he won't look at me, eyes cast down on the concrete slabs. I bore my own pupils into him, willing him to bring up his gaze and confront me. Not for the first time in the last few hours I am physically and emotionally winded – by his outright betrayal. In recent weeks and months I haven't imagined us as friends, nor expected any kind of favour, especially from a paid-up fascist. But this! To betray the . . . what was it we had? Intimacy or informality, perhaps even some kind of mutual respect? Either way, we shared it briefly. But it was there. To wheedle his way to my doorstep, show affection on this very spot, under the pretence of friendship, and then use it against me. For months, I've tried to read the man who has now shown himself to be a master of disguise, a true Janus. It stings like the worst duplicity. But then this is war. There are no rules. What on earth did you expect, Stella?

I stare my disappointment long and hard at Cristian's face. It's devoid of expression, but I see a telltale flush just above his collar – though I reason that it's unlikely to represent guilt, only embarrassment perhaps at my own granite stare. His eyes remain fixed on the stone paving, until he turns his body away and approaches one of the fascist guards. I break my own gaze and turn towards Captain Klaus, but since there is still no sign of the typewriter I do not offer up my guilt for free.

'Is there some reason why you feel the need to turn out my home?' I ask sharply, gauging there's a certain amount of outrage I would reasonably be expected to show as an innocent citizen.

Captain Klaus looks back towards the door, as if for a sign. An SS officer moves under the lintel and looks squarely at his army colleague, with thin lips and a subtle shake of his head. The thunderous cloud dawns upon Klaus's face again, his overly large Adam's apple rising and plunging above his tight collar.

'My apologies, Fräulein Jilani,' he offers finally. 'We had information that led us to your apartment.' The fleshy bulb in his collar rebounds as if he is swallowing hot coals. 'Clearly, it was false.'

'And am I to know the nature of this information?' I push at him, continuing my own play at being the affronted victim, wounded at their lack of trust in me. After all, I'm a loyal employee of the fascist state.

'I'm afraid not, Fräulein,' he says. 'It's confidential at this stage.' And he turns to go.

'And my belongings?' I push again. I want them to go – immediately – and leave me to the quaking that is only just contained in the soles of my shoes, to the disarray of my apartment, and my solitude. But if I retreat now, slink upstairs with my tail between my legs, I am as good as admitting some kind of collusion, that they have good reason to be suspicious of me.

Klaus appears shocked at my audacity, and from the corner of my eye I see Cristian's chin rise in surprise.

'Who will help me with this mess?' I insist.

Klaus swivels to one of his platoon. 'Sergeant – help the Fräulein to carry her belongings,' he says. 'Everyone else, with me.'

He clips his heels in a faux effort at courtesy and swivels on the soles of his boots. They move away, Cristian falling in behind, shoulders noticeably stooped. My anger burns inside for his cowardice.

'Go on, follow the pack,' I mutter to myself as they move away. His style of good dress, his manners and his love of literature dissipate with each step he takes, and I see him for the shell he is – no lover of Venice or Italians after all. No heart to be beguiled by literature or the play of words. It was all an elaborate act. And I was fooled.

I scoop up my belongings, waving away the sergeant's help after having made my point. Signora Menzio helps the best she can, and Paolo rushes across when he realises what's happening.

'Stella, are you OK? Are you hurt?'

'No, no, I'm fine, Paolo. Really. Just shaken. It's been quite a morning.'

I stumble up the stairs alone, still not quite sure how a thorough search of my small home could have missed my hiding place.

When I step my way through the chaos heaped on the floor – drawers turned out, my small kitchen larder empty of its meagre contents – I head towards the cupboard, eyes agog. They hadn't missed it. The stray floorboard is out of its snug hole, discarded nearby. And as I drop onto my belly, I peer under the boards, then push an arm inside and scout in the cool, dusty space with my fingers. Nothing. No hard casing. No typewriter. I begin to wonder if there's a cavity through which it could have fallen, but when I take a match flame to the space I see there's nothing.

Where could it have gone? And who could have taken it?

'Paolo, Paolo, have you got my typewriter?' I ask breathlessly in the café, but even as I say it I know it's a silly question. He's no mind reader, and I've told no one since having stowed it at home. He looks at me in confusion, and offers me a brandy to assuage my temporary madness. I can only assume that Sergio sent one of his band, well-rehearsed in hiding contraband, to clear my apartment. But then, how would he have known that I hadn't disposed of the machine as I'd promised? Although Sergio has eyes and ears everywhere, I've learned. My brandy downed, Paolo tells me to sit tight in my apartment and wait for a message from the brigade as to what to do next.

It takes me until after midnight to put right all the chaos inside, and even longer tossing and turning in my bed to make sense of my thoughts. How can I go back to the Reich office in the morning and face Breugal, or Cristian? I know I don't want to. And yet, if I slink away, it sends up a red flare as to my guilt, of both my mind and my actions. I need to keep up my front as an innocent and wronged loyalist. It's another layer to the mask. Will I even notice the effort of not playing myself any more?

There are deep-seated creases around my eyes by the time I leave for the office the next morning. There's no message from Sergio – or more importantly news about Arlo and the others – but I know I physically can't stay at home doing nothing, or keep my calm at Mama's. Paolo has already sent someone to check that my parents are untouched, and I'm reassured there have been no undue callers to their house.

The walk towards the Platzkommandantur feels strangely like that first day, wondering if I am about to enter the vipers' nest – and whether I will even emerge. And yet I don't feel afraid; I reason that if Breugal or Klaus were bent on my capture it would have been easy enough to clamp me in irons the previous day. Equally, I'm well aware they may be toying with me in a game of chance, in which they hold the majority of the cards. As I stride forward, I feel strongly some things need to be left to fortune or destiny. I'd rather the gamble did not involve my life, but if this war has taught me anything, it's that control is overrated: a large part of survival depends on pure luck.

In San Marco, nothing looks changed – the bare, wooden hoardings protecting the basilica try hard to reflect the white autumn light of the morning, and the pigeons are noisily optimistic for crumbs; their numbers have fallen in wartime, and their tameness suggests they have yet to realise it's because humans are in need of crumbs too, in the form of good bird meat. It's only when I approach the sentry post that I sense a palpable change. One of the younger guards shuffles uncomfortably.

'Morning Franz,' I say without a waver.

'Fräulein,' he nods. But there's no boyish grin, no attempt at banter. He eyes the floor, shifting his feet.

'Everything all right?' I ask. He's too young and innocent for me to play with him. 'Am I to go up to the office?'

He looks up, relieved to have only to repeat an order. 'Captain Klaus asks that he sees you downstairs, Fräulein. Please, follow me.'

I cast my eyes up the stairs as I'm led into a room beside the staircase, wondering whether the chatter is about me now; first Marta and now Stella. I ponder, too, if Cristian is up there, or will deign to show his face today.

He doesn't. The room is empty as I enter – some type of ornate meeting place, with a large table in the centre, the rich essence of Venice in the fabric of the room, its beauty blighted only by a small swastika pennant draped over a vase.

318

I don't know whether to sit or stand, but there's little time to decide before Klaus strides in. His expression is all business and his gaunt stare is all the more sinister in contrast with Breugal's farcical image. He's joined by a regular soldier, who stands barring the doorway.

'Fräulein Jilani,' he begins, without offering me a seat. 'I trust all your belongings are back in place.'

'They are,' I say.

'Good. We wouldn't want you to be inconvenienced.' He breathes the last through his teeth with such animosity it feels like a foul fog has puffed into the room. I decide, even this early into our exchange, that I can brook no sarcasm. We may as well get to the point.

'Am I to assume that I will not be returning to the office?'

'You assume correctly.'

'On what grounds?' I ask. 'Was your search successful? I would think your empty hands yesterday were enough to prove my innocence. And my loyalty.'

Captain Klaus releases the remainder of his foul cloud, slapping one leather glove into the palm of his hand.

'Fräulein Jilani,' he says, as if beginning some type of address to a lesser mortal. 'You and I both know that you harbour far more intelligence than you have ever allowed us to believe.'

'Am I supposed to take that as a compliment?'

'You may. I really don't care. But we can no longer employ someone who is under suspicion in this office. You must understand that.'

I do. Of course I do. But now my life and liberty depend on me toeing a fine line in order to leave this office under my own steam.

'Do you have any proof?' I prod again.

'In this case, suspicion is enough. The Reich thrives – *depends* – on absolute loyalty.' This time his sneer puts a line under the argument.

'So what am I supposed to do? Where am I to work, help support my family?' I say, maintaining my act of incredulity.

Klaus looks devoid of any emotion, other than the sliver of pleasure in his tone. 'That's not my concern. Only that you return your identity card. Immediately please.'

Then he parts his lips in a sneer, revealing yellowed teeth. I pull out my card and hold it towards him, forcing him to tug it from my fingers.

'Thank you,' he manages as I turn to go, struggling now to hold onto a double-headed beast of tears and anger. 'Oh, and Fräulein Jilani – we would rather you did not leave the city for the foreseeable future.'

'Is that an order?' I spin to face him again.

'It is. Punishable, I believe, by death. Orders to shoot anyone under such restrictions on sight.'

I have no idea from where I muster it, some crevice of my soul or the inner reaches of me, but I pull out a smile. Not a smug leer or a dirty smirk, but the type that says I'm not beaten; I'm not one of you and you will not fell me.

'Thank you for your candour, Captain Klaus,' I say, walking out into the large and commanding hallway. I don't know what makes me do it, but I glance up the sweeping stairwell. I shouldn't – it just invites the hurt inside to deepen – but I'm compelled by something. I catch the form of a body hovering at the top, and then his face. Steely, emotionless, and I read into it that Cristian De Luca is delighted that I have got my just penance – a loyal Italian versus a loyalist fascist. And he has won this battle. Within a second, he's gone, back behind the heavy door and the Reich's cloak of protection. I walk away from the Platzkommandantur with a mixture of relief and fury. It takes all I have not to cast back at the window to where I know Cristian De Luca sits, possibly watching my back as I leave his precious domain for good.

I spend the rest of the day at home, alternately lying on the bed and staring at the pages of random books I don't want to read. In times like these, I usually turn to the world of Elizabeth Bennet and her Darcy, to the fluffy politics of one's countenance and which ballgown to wear. I need it now more than ever. But that particular volume stays on my shelf, the cover now coated in a fur of jagged, poisonous thistles, knowing who gave it to me. My fingers can't even fold around the spine without a sick swell inside. My fury urges me to rip it up or throw it in the canal, and it's only my love of books that stops me from doing so. Instead, I scratch in my cupboards for something to eat, deciding that even the best cook would struggle to make soup from a solitary potato.

I'm wary of making it across the small *campo* to Paolo's or having contact with anyone, lest I infect them with my guilt. The walk back from the Platzkommandantur was agonising, my paranoia hoicked high on my shoulders and my neck hairs bristling, convinced Klaus had set a tail on me. I was too jaded even to lay a false trail, weaving back and forth as we often did before and after a message drop, but by the time I reached home, I'd shaken off the mistrust and the imaginary shadow. They know where I live anyway.

I miss the newspaper office too, even knowing Arlo and

the others cannot be there, and there are glaring flashbacks of Matteo and Elena, the image of her face distorted in utter, utter despair, both now facing their own nightmares. And Vito, of course, who still languishes in Ca' Littoria, in Lord knows what state. Lying here within my own four walls, I count myself lucky. Very lucky.

The need for coffee and information gets the better of me eventually, and I step over to Paolo's, who immediately spies the dark circles I've sprouted under my eyes and steers me to a seat in the back. His coffee grains may be made of acorns, but it's like manna from heaven to rekindle my brain.

'Any news?' I ask, almost afraid to hear it.

'Arlo is safe,' Paolo reports. 'We managed to get a message to him in time, and he's way beyond the Veneto by now.'

'And Matteo? Elena?'

'Elena wasn't arrested,' he says, but I know from the gravity of his face that Matteo isn't so lucky. 'Matteo has been moved to Santa Maggiore. So he survived Ca' Littoria at least.'

I want to ask after Tommaso, although I'm not sure the brigade is fully aware of his deception. Do I condemn such a young man for loyalty to his father? Paolo saves me the dilemma.

'And Tommaso has gone to ground,' he says. His expression is difficult to read, certainly not black with disgust. Perhaps we can all appreciate the ties that bind, and how other bonds can be frayed.

'Do we know anything of his father? Has he been released?' I'm eager to know, even hope that there is something positive to come out of Tommaso's dilemma and angst, despite the chaos it's caused.

'Not according to our information,' Paolo sighs. 'Because

the typewriter wasn't recovered, the order hasn't been given for the release.'

We both stare into our coffee, each knowing that Tommaso's father is also now tainted with his son's betrayal, born out of love and loyalty but a stain nonetheless. As a family they have no future in Venice. Another unit whose fabric has been torn apart by this filthy game of cat and mouse.

Paolo brings me a welcome plate of stew, and I wonder how I can ever repay his kindness and generosity, but he waves it away as something so slight. Right now, it probably does more to keep my spirit and body afloat than he could ever imagine.

'So, what are my instructions?' I ask eventually.

'Sergio says to sit tight, visit only familiar places. He'll see about getting you a legitimate job in a bar, something that looks as if you are simply earning pennies, in case the Reich office is keeping a close eye. It's too dangerous to move you out of Venice with the order on you. You're safer inside the city for now.'

'Meanwhile, what do I do? Is there anything I can do for the cause?' I can't bear the thought of relinquishing my work as a Staffetta too.

'Are you mad, Stella? Absolutely not!' Paolo flashes anger for once. 'And you are to stay away from any safe houses. The word is out to give you no drops.'

'For how long?'

'Until we decide your life isn't under threat.' Paolo's normally friendly, often comical expression, is stern. He's around Vito's age, but I sense the need to take heed of him. I feel useless and baseless but also well cared for, cushioned amid the coarse surface of war.

36

Taking Flight

Venice, October 1944

I've no choice but to follow orders from the Resistance and do nothing. I visit Mama and Papa the day after my dismissal, this time weaving back and forth towards the Via Garibaldi, taking my time. I have plenty of it, after all. I find them in the kitchen, the sour stench of a week-old fish carcass hanging from a string over the table, Papa rubbing slices of polenta over the surface to at least give a hint of taste to the insipid maize. He places it on Mama's plate and she merely picks at it. They are so pleased to see me they don't even ask why I'm visiting at midday, and I'm hit by a swell of guilt at how much I've neglected them in recent weeks, so wrapped in my own battles, toing and froing across the island and water when I should have been with them. There's a war to be fought right here in this house, and I need to be part of it.

I spend the afternoon scouting the markets for anything I can find that is remotely edible and wholesome, persuading the odd vendor to reach under their counters for black market supplies and all but emptying my own savings to pay for it. Mama watches from beside the range as I get to work making soups and stocks with the peelings, and fashioning a bread of sorts. Once or twice I spy a glint in her eyes, under the layers of worry, but still I can't supply the light she needs, with news of Vito.

We listen to Radio Londra together, and Papa comes back in after a rare trip to the bar. I smell beer and cigarettes on him and the odour of relief, having nursed Mama for so many weeks without respite. We talk of the war's progress – skirting any mention of Vito – and in the evening glow there's a tinge of the family life we used to have. I feel we're scarred certainly, but not broken. There is life in the Jilani family yet.

I've never been unemployed or without a purpose, and the time weighs heavily. After just two days prowling my apartment like a caged animal, I present myself at Paolo's bar and tie on an apron. The irony of such familiar actions in Matteo's bar are not lost on me, but I choose to focus on the now, as the memories might well destroy me. Paolo can't pay me, I know, but I need the distraction, and the offer to feed me from his kitchen is enough, since my purse is barren.

It's here the letter is delivered, by a rangy young lad with large teeth who bowls in and asks where a Signorina Jilani lives, handing over a small envelope in exchange for a coin. I don't need to study the writing carefully to know who it's from – ornate and upright, I've seen this hand enough times. I can also hazard a guess as to why Cristian is writing: maybe he thinks his prose can cloak a feeble excuse for his behaviour and betrayal, reasons why his actions – which might have seen me imprisoned or killed – were justified. The fact that an act of fate or an unknown fairy godmother saved me does not absolve his intentions. It's my fault – I should have known he is a fascist first and foremost. What little there was between us could never match his loyalty towards Benito Mussolini. Equally, he cannot use words on me to appease his guilt; we Venetians are all too practised at peering behind and under the mask and I, for one, do not forget easily.

I don't slip it in my apron pocket to read in private later. I am resolute – unopened, it goes straight into the range of Paolo's kitchen, where I peer in through the grate and watch the flames paw at it hungrily.

The next afternoon brings a déjà vu moment. The same little urchin appears at the doorway, proffering another envelope bearing identical script. This time, I give him two coins – the last I have – and tell him to return it to its sender; he scampers out, delighted at the double payload. I'm not the best of waitresses, but the afternoon sees more accidents than the previous day, and even Paolo gently suggests that I help out in the kitchen, rather than cost him any more precious crockery. It's the image of the envelope niggling at me. Unlike the first day, I wonder what message was inside, and yet the thought of reading Cristian's simpering defence still nips at my stomach. I know I would be hard pressed to contain my anger if my eyes crawled over his words.

My night is disturbed; I dream of Klaus and Breugal at the helm of a patrol boat, me shackled and roped behind them on the water being pulled along at speed, alternately scooping in air and water as I fight against drowning in my beloved lagoon. They are whooping and laughing like men drawing in a stag and enjoying the sport of it. I wake to a sweat, despite the increasing chill in the air.

Come morning, I'm battling with the hot and cold of my own anxiety. This time the envelope is larger, pushed under the door of my apartment as the sun comes up. It appears more officious and my name is typed in capital letters on the front, the distinctive Reich icon just peeking out. The package sits in my hand and then on my kitchen table for an age while I muster the courage to open it. A summons to appear before some kind of court or council? Surely that would be accompanied by the heavy clomp of boots and a hammering on my door? Breugal isn't known for his subtlety.

I try to deny to myself that I'm shaking as I open it, but the jagged edges of the envelope testify to my fear. The paper inside is thick, and there are several sheets of it, but it's no directive. The words, which pulse like a beacon, state: 'PERMISSION TO TRAVEL'. And it's my name typed on the order, unmistakably. But it's the signature at the bottom that causes a shudder and confusion: *General K. Breugal*, scrawled in pen, but also typed below to clarify. It's stamped with the clawing eagle icon I've seen almost every day for the past months, and dated the previous day.

Why? Why would Breugal want to be rid of me? The newspaper is disbanded, perhaps to be resurrected by others if the war continues, but I am finished within that cell. The typewriter, though still hidden somewhere, is also inaccessible to me, although the general isn't to know that. But his men have smashed the nucleus of communication we created, and he is aware of Nazi success on that score. He knows I am all but finished as a useful tool.

My mind takes a winding path of reason: are the papers false, or is it a trap? If I attempt to use the pass, will I be halted at a checkpoint and arrested for defying the order to stay in Venice? I can almost picture the image, that moment of realisation by the sentry on guard, where there is nowhere to run to without bullets spraying around and possibly into my running torso. It brings on a fresh chill. I can't reason well enough to decide, aware I should consult others. I'm due at my parents' to look after Mama, so I hop across to Paolo's and hand over the papers – he says he will contact someone and have them checked for authenticity.

On the walk to the Via Garibaldi, I purposely skirt the waterfront for comfort and yet I barely notice the rippling surface of the water as I search possibilities for who would have sent it. Cristian is the most obvious choice, perhaps as reparation for his guilt. But I also know the lengths of his betrayal – it would be an easy way to be rid of me, 'legitimately' shot at a border trying to flee Venice, conveniently distancing himself from the act. Didn't I always think his lists were more dangerous than any holstered gun?

Equally, it could be someone else in the office, perhaps with access to Breugal's papers, but I can't think who. I didn't get too close to any of the other typists, only Marta, and she's long out of favour and now absent. I resolve it's almost certainly Cristian, and yet his motivation remains a total mystery.

I'm teasing Mama's thinning hair out into some sort of style when clarity comes. This time there is a pounding at the door, though with urgency rather than threat.

'Stella! Stella!' repeats the voice behind the door, in an attempt at a hoarse cry cum whisper. I know it well but wonder why Paolo himself is there at my parents' door.

'Paolo! Come in.'

He slides in with a backward glance which tells me all is not well.

'Stella, who is it?' Mama calls from the kitchen.

'Oh, just a friend with a message from work,' I sing, 'I won't be long.'

I take Paolo into the tiny parlour and notice he's breathless, sweat hovering on his upper lip. He's needed to run.

'Stella, we need to move you,' he pants.

'When?'

'Now,' he says. 'Right now.'

'Why? What's happened?'

'There's an order out for your arrest.' My mind goes immediately to the typewriter. Have they found it? If so, how will they connect it to me? They only have Tommaso's word and so far that hasn't been enough to condemn me. What's changed?

'But the travel pass, why would they . . .?' My mind is flooded with questions. 'It's signed by Breugal. And Klaus was resolved to let me go just days ago.'

'I don't know,' Paolo says. 'Perhaps they finally have proof to link you to the typewriter. But I wouldn't risk hanging around to ask them – troops are on their way to your apartment right now and, when they don't find you, they will head straight here. The word is they want to make an example of you, Stella – young, female or not, they want to tell everyone the punishment will be delivered. That's all I know.'

Suddenly, I'm stiff with fear. They can't discover me in

the house – it will be worse for my parents, Mama's heart especially. A search is bad enough, but to see me dragged away – I think of Elena's recent distress and I can't bear the consequences.

'I've sent to the docks for your father,' Paolo says. 'He'll be here any minute. But we have to go.'

'Can't we just wait a little while for Papa? Make sure Mama's all right?'

'No, Stella. Now.' And he has that look about him again. I stare into his eyes and he nods. Now, he means. Immediately.

I can barely think what to say. I mumble some excuse to Mama about forgetting an appointment and pull my jacket from the peg. I kiss her cheek, trying not to push my lips hard into her flesh and draw in the smell that makes her my mother, my constant. I try to act as if it's not the last time I might see her, and I barely make it out of the house before there are tears streaming down my cheeks. Paolo takes me by the hand and virtually pulls me to the Ana Ponte, pushing a package into my hand and hugging me tightly.

'Be careful and be brave, Stella,' he whispers into my ear. Then he kisses my tear-stained face and is gone.

There's a boat waiting, whose reliable pilot winds his way through narrow channels, skulking in waterways as the wintery sun climbs towards midday. We hide for a few hours in a boathouse, sitting among the ghostly skeletons of half-finished gondolas, until it's dusky enough to move. Paolo, my saviour again, has swiftly stuffed some random clothes into a small bag, and there's some bread and cheese, plus the travel documents and a tight roll of lira notes. He'd had just enough time to ensure the travel pass is authentic and might prove useful beyond the gates of Venice. But only out in

331

the wider country where I'm not known, and before my identity as a wanted woman is circulated. With Breugal on my tail, there's no immediate future for me in Venice. To survive, I have to leave.

It seems so surreal to me as the boatman putters out again, hugging close to the edges of the Grand Canal and then on to the Zattere. I look over to the edge of Giudecca and work hard at containing my longing.

The boatman rounds the city and out into the wide expanse of sea, so that we chance our lives not across the causeway, but on the waves under and alongside it, buffeting the tiny boat until I think my insides really will fall out.

Over past months, I've thought about how and when I might leave my city, but never allowed myself to complete the picture in my mind, in perpetual self-denial that it would ever come to this. Goodbyes are tortuous enough, but not being allowed to say them is worse. Papa, Mama, Mimi or Vito – their spaces sit like lead within me.

My last view of Venice – my beautiful, enduring jewel – is as I peek out from under a fish-tainted tarpaulin, slinking away as a felon in my own home. I'm too empty to even cry, so brittle that my heart is spewing dust as it cracks in two.

37

Age and Enlightenment

A private cruise across the lagoon seems a treat enough on her last day, when the glory of the Venetian winter weather has come out to bid goodbye, but Luisa has to concentrate hard on appreciating the stunning panorama. With only hours to go until she leaves for the airport, she is intent on completing her mission, finding her grandmother and, with it, her own history. With a day's delay before they could see Paolo senior, she's already extended her trip by twenty-four hours, rebooked a flight and checked into the cheapest hostel she can find, playing down the cost to Jamie and hoping it will be worth it. There's a lot riding on Paolo senior.

Giulio meets her at the waterfront before they board and, although his face is open and optimistic, he clearly has some news he's anxious to give.

'I found another Jilani in the archives,' Giulio says, though

333

his brow creases as Luisa's own raises with curiosity. 'As far as I can tell, it's Stella's brother.' His tone belies what comes next.

'He died before the war ended,' he says. 'He'd been imprisoned by the fascists, and although he died in a hospital, it's difficult to tell what the cause was. From the records we have, it seems he was beaten badly but refused to give out any names or information. I think he must have succumbed to his injuries.' Giulio's look is a mixture of sadness and pride in a fellow Venetian.

Luisa hardly knows how to feel, under a white winter sun drenching the entire city with energy and expectation. She'd had a great-uncle she'd never known, who had never been spoken of, and yet she feels something of his loss. *Succumbed to his injuries*. To torture, in other words. She's horrified and sad, though more for her grandmother, who would have known him well and presumably felt his loss acutely.

'It's all the more reason we need to find Stella,' she says at last, and Giulio nods his agreement.

The small motorboat Pietro has borrowed from a friend can hardly go fast enough for her, its little outboard engine whining with the effort of weaving around the larger ferries as they follow the trail of foam wash towards the Lido.

Pietro reports his grandfather is better in the mornings, as he sleeps most of the afternoon, but Luisa gets the feeling it's also about the old man's lucidity and there being only a certain stock of it each day. Sitting beside her, Giulio has again counselled her against very high hopes; in his research he's clearly had to deal with a good deal of cobwebbed memories and their unreliability. Even so, Luisa senses he

334

can't help but share the excitement at the prospect of something – a new nugget of information or recall – to add to his rich bank of knowledge.

They pull up at one of the larger pontoons, and the nursing home is a five-minute walk from the water's edge.

'Grandpapa wasn't very happy about leaving the main island,' Pietro says to Giulio. 'Until we convinced him that as long as he can see the water and San Marco, he's not really left. I think these days he doesn't actually see that far at all, but it keeps him happy enough.'

To Luisa, the home is a world away from anything similar back in England. The corridors are ornate and lofty, and the smell of advancing years – common to the few homes she has visited before – is replaced with an intoxicating smell of simmering garlic.

Paolo senior sits in the lounge, facing the bright sparkle of water and basking in the light from the large windows. He doesn't attempt to pull up his small, frail body in greeting, but his lined face lights up at the sight of Pietro, and the two kiss, Italian-style, with real affection. His bony fingers grasp at Pietro's hand as if afraid to let go.

Pietro explains why he's brought guests, and the old man seems immediately to understand what's being asked of him. His rheumy eyes dart back and forth, the cogs of his memory grinding into action. Finally, they light up, signalling his 'eureka' moment.

'Of course! Of course I remember Stella!' he exclaims with hand gestures that even Luisa can comprehend. In turn, Pietro gestures at Luisa, and she just catches the word 'granddaughter' in Italian. The old man's eyes glow bright and his larger-than-life dentures are fully on show – he holds out his hands for contact, and she trades places with Giulio to sit next to him.

'So, you are one of Stella's,' he says. 'I always did wonder if she had any children. And now I know. I'm so pleased. So relieved.' He clenches at Luisa's hands again tightly. It's Giulio who assumes the lead then, carefully and succinctly forming the questions that they need answers to.

Yes, Stella left before the liberation, Paolo senior confirms, and she didn't return until – when was it? – perhaps 1946, to see her mother and father for the last time.

'After that I didn't see her until 1950 – I know because I was married the same year. She had her husband with her.'

Luisa turns to Giulio and she can't help her lips spreading wide with anticipation.

'Do you know where they met then?' Giulio probes. 'Was her husband part of the Resistance too? Is there anything you can tell us?' Can Paolo senior possibly hold the answer to the mysterious 'C' – the forerunner to Grandpa Gio?

'Ha! I can do better than that,' the old man says. The lines in his face spring upwards and he's suddenly full of mischief. 'Now *there's* a tale to be told, even by the war's standards.'

He gestures for Pietro to come close and whispers something in his ear. The grandson nods and disappears, returning a long five minutes later and placing something in Paolo's lap. It's a thick, bound book of white paper, although the title page is face down at first and Luisa can only see a blank back page, dirtied with age. She feels her heart crank into the same rhythm as that day in her mother's attic. The odour of dust and slight damp wafts across the space as Paolo's spindly fingers scrabble to turn it over – she hears the old man's dry skin scrape across the brittle paper, and Pietro is visibly holding back from hurrying his grandfather.

'Here,' he says finally, pushing the book towards Luisa. 'This will tell you everything. Stella gave it to me — she told me I was in there somewhere, but I always suspected I was keeping it for someone else. And finally that someone has made their way to me.' He smiles with satisfaction, and she sees what might be a tear teetering on his reddened lower lids.

Luisa takes what is clearly a manuscript into her own hands and turns it over. In bold old-fashioned type, a single line states:

```
THE HIDDEN TYPEWRITER:
A Story of Resistance
```

38

After

London, March 1948

I look at the clock, disappointed that it's only eleven a.m., yet the brilliant spring sunshine streaming through the window tickles me to yawn, dust motes caught in the shafts tumbling lazily in the otherwise empty office. My colleague and assistant, Anne, is out on an errand, and Charles, the head of the publishing house, is not due in until after his business lunch, which will doubtless stretch long into the afternoon. I can appreciate a slice of silence, even crave it sometimes, but at work I prefer a busy hum – Anne chattering on the phone or typing ten to the dozen. I laugh to myself at yet another English-ism creeping its way into my Italian vocabulary. The longer I spend in London, the more I realise I'm becoming less Venetian and more of an Anglophile. Does that make me sad? I'm not sure, since each year I've grown to love my adopted home, the bustle of the city, and sometimes even the traffic. Getting used to cars and lorries took some time – and a few near-misses crossing roads – and I do sometimes long to hear that distinctive throttle of the *vaporetto* on the canals. But, equally, I love sitting on the top of a London bus, creating my own little bubble of observation, sometimes taking notes and squirrelling them away for a character in my next book.

Still, I have dinner with Jack to look forward to this evening; he's left a message to say it's seven p.m. at his place. He signed the note 'Gio' but I'm not yet coming round to using the name his mother prefers. To me, he'll always be Jack, with his pot of tea never far away.

Just for something to energise me, I make myself a cup, the British way – hot, strong and a dash of milk – knowing my towering post pile cannot be put off any longer. I'm aware that once I begin slicing into the large, foolscap envelopes, heavy with hopeful manuscripts, the old feeling and the reasons why I love my job as an editor will come flooding in – that fizzle of expectation and anticipation, of finding something quite special in that first paragraph, often from a first-time author. Words that will lift me, or incite a tear, or spark such curiosity that I will put off everything else in my diary that day just to keep reading.

Most days, the pile reduces rapidly as I read the first page, and the covering letter: 'Dear Sir' – never Madam, I'm irritated to see – 'Please find my enclosed novel, which I hope you can see stands out from the general milieu' – a word designed to impress – 'currently on our shelves.' Not all are quite so bold; some missives even make excuses for what the author's work lacks, not particularly inspiring me to read further. The best letters strike a note somewhere in between. Then, some are swiftly on the 'no' pile after just the first paragraph, words flailing and struggling to hold my attention.

What rarely causes me to raise an eyebrow is the mere title itself. But today, the ninth or tenth envelope I open forces the hot tea down into my throat far quicker than I planned. It's difficult to say if it's the shock of the scalding liquid or something else which causes me to cough and my heart to miss a beat.

The paper is crisp and new, the manuscript a good thickness and the type clean on the title page:

'*The Hidden Typewriter*', it says. '*A novel by Sofia Treadwell*'.

I scan the covering letter – it's a strange mix of formal and informal, yet with a relaxed tone that neither blows its own trumpet or begs me to believe in its brilliance. In essence, the author is simply saying: 'Please read my offering, I hope you like it.'

My tea goes cold and the post pile is ignored as I read . . . and read and read. The setting, of course, draws me in immediately – has Sofia Treadwell done her homework and knows I hail from Venice, cleverly targeting this particular publishing house? Does she come from Venice herself? Sofia is a common Italian name, although Treadwell sounds solidly British. But then, isn't my own name Hawthorn? How could she know that I'd been encouraged to change my name by the War Office when I arrived in England, part of their plans for a 'seamless' drift into an entirely new culture. I wonder for a second if it's someone probing for details of my past, but in truth that's just part of a lingering paranoia. And besides, we're no longer at war. Why would anyone care?

As I put aside each page, I'm conscious of my eyebrows rising and falling while I scan the sentences. Even Anne, who's returned from her errand, looks at me like I might be coming down with something. It's uncanny. But is it also a joke? I've heard of doppelgangers – strangers who are virtual doubles in appearance – but can people have parallel lives too?

The descriptions are graphic, and the writing ornate – perhaps a little too emotive in places if I'm being picky – but there are few surprises to the plot. I can predict with accuracy what will happen next, though not because the story or the writing isn't creative. But because it's my life. I find myself being drawn into the story of a partisan woman in Venice, working on the Resistance newspaper and planted in the Reich's inner office. And there it is: the typewriter, described almost to a tee, the slightly drooped letter *e*, the demonic tool prickling at the Nazi shield of domination.

It must be a joke, I think. It has to be. But, of course, I have to satisfy my curiosity. If there's one thing my dear Popsa always said about me, it was that I had the nose of a bloodhound in wheedling out facts.

There's no phone number on the letter, only an address in Camden Town. I write immediately, asking if Sofia Treadwell can meet me in the Savoy Hotel bar a week from now at two o'clock. Charles and I rarely ask prospective clients into the office on first meeting; it's a working publishing house and can look a little crowded and messy, with its piles of manuscripts on every surface that we've become accustomed to treating as furniture. To a fresh eye, however, it may just reflect disorganisation.

Despite being busy, I find the week passes slowly, *The Hidden Typewriter* lingering in corners of my brain, popping up when I least expect it, when I'm shopping, or reading other pages. Deep down within me I can hear the tick, tick of my own beloved machine, almost feel the vibration of the resounding keys, a fleeting depression at its loss that I haven't experienced in years. The next Monday can't come soon enough, to quell my curiosity about the mysterious Ms Treadwell.

It's a beautiful March afternoon, London's winter smog finally bowing to spring light, as I head towards the Savoy and take in the art deco beauty of its entrance, which never fails to impress. But I'm also slightly nervous, which is unusual – I expect it of a prospective client who's keen to forge a good impression on us as agents and publishers, but not from me. I make sure to arrive early, as I always do, to relay that air of efficiency. Sofia Treadwell, though, is even more prompt; the head barman, John, gestures towards a wingback leather chair and I breathe in and walk over, pasting on my professional face.

'Miss Treadwell, pleased to meet—' I start as I round on the chair, hand ready to extend.

Rarely have I been struck dumb in my life, but this is the moment. Any further words are literally wedged in my throat.

I recognise him immediately. A little older, and his face filled out from post-war portions, but in essence, the same features. His expression reflects surprise too, only his reaction has caused his lips to spread, while mine are like a fish sucking air.

Cristian De Luca pulls his tall frame out of the chair and stands, holding out his hand.

'Stella,' he says. 'May I still call you Stella?'

He could call me almost anything, such is the shock I'm

feeling at seeing him here. My surprise and curiosity overrides any enduring anger I might muster later, for the moment at least. One of the last times I saw him, he stepped out of the ether in much the same way, a figure of surprise, but that concrete pavement outside my Venetian apartment feels worlds away from the elegance of the Savoy. I say nothing for a good few seconds, and then just a muttering of incoherence.

'Perhaps we should sit down?' Cristian says, almost having to guide me into the chair opposite. 'I've ordered tea. But perhaps a brandy as well?'

I nod, watching him as he converses with the waiter. Despite a healthier look, his outward appearance hasn't changed much – a cropped beard and hair neatly cut, a crisp Italian grey suit and those tortoiseshell glasses. But his brown eyes have sparkle, and his demeanour too – I rarely witnessed Cristian De Luca in a truly relaxed mode, perhaps only glimpses, seconds at a time. Back then, he held himself constantly. Now, though, his body moulds into the chair with ease, as if his veins were once filled with starch, now flushed entirely from his body.

'I'm so sorry to have startled you like that,' he says, this time in Italian, which has the effect of filling my own circulation with something like glycerine. 'But I'm so glad to have finally found you.'

Finally found me? That suggests he's been actively looking, and for some time. That this isn't just some bizarre consequence the papers have been peppered with since 1945, with the war's nomads drifting back to their homelands, their territories, reshaping the contours of Europe once more. People seemingly lost forever bumping into each other on street corners or chancing upon each other in the cinema.

I take a sip of tea, and then the brandy, before I'm able to speak. By rights, I should turn tail and walk out – the perfect opportunity to leave the man who abandoned me in a vacuum of the unknown. A sweet revenge.

But I'm too curious, and besides, my legs are jelly, turned swiftly to lead.

'I'm sorry,' I say. 'I am thoroughly confused. I was expecting to meet a Sofia Treadwell.'

His hands splay in a gesture which signals: and here she is!

'*You* are Sofia Treadwell? But how? Why?' I can't fathom the reasons. And how is a confirmed fascist now sitting larger than life in a London hotel? Europe's borders may be more labile than even I imagined.

He smiles again – already he's smiled more in the last five minutes than I witnessed in all those months in Venice. 'I wanted to find you,' he says quietly. 'I managed to discover you were working in publishing, but I didn't know where. With your change of name, it's taken me this long.'

It solves the question of why he assumed an alias to track me down – he might guess the very name of Cristian De Luca would be immediately consigned to my bin, let alone my slush pile. But why does he want to find me? With courage from the alcohol, I pose the question outright, looking him in the eye directly.

'Because I'm in love with you,' he says calmly, his pupils propelled into mine. 'And I have been since that very first day in Venice.'

A second brandy is needed, and he arranges it while I absorb his last sentence.

'I'm sorry, Cristian,' I say. 'I'm very confused. I . . . I just can't take in what you're saying. How can you possibly love me? You betrayed me, in the worst possible way. You despised me at the end, and what I represented. You must have. You led them to my house. To me.'

'No! You're wrong, Stella. I never despised you,' he protests. He looks down into his own lap, and for the first time in our exchange his face is dark and pensive. His fingers weave together, and he flicks nervously at his thumbnail. 'But yes, I admit it did appear as though I betrayed you. It almost broke me to do it, but I was forced to. It's very complex. A long story.'

'I've got time,' I say. Now I've got my voice back, it has a steely edge. If this man who forced me to leave the home, the city and the country I loved is now demanding my attention, he can give something too. He can explain himself.

I listen wide-eyed, and probably with my mouth still gaping as Cristian De Luca reveals his role in my downfall – and my saving. He is not Cristian, he says, but Giovanni Benetto by birth, born in Rome. His name and his persona were an elaborate creation of the Special Operations Executive – or SOE – a wartime collection of multi-national agents designed to spy and subvert deep within enemy organisations. His cover was two years in the making, he explains, gaining trust and kudos from inside the fascist hierarchy, almost from the dawning of the war.

'No one, not even the Venetian Resistance, was allowed to know,' he says. 'I reported directly to London. But you can't conceive how many times I wanted to come clean, to tell you. It burned inside me that you imagined I was some heartless fascist who would help in our country's ruin.'

I'm silent for a minute in trying to take it all in. 'I didn't always think of you as heartless,' I say honestly. 'But I was confused that there seemed to be two sides of the man who was so sensitive as to love literature, and yet cold enough to betray his fellow countrymen. In all honesty, you bewildered me. Far more than the war itself.'

He half laughs at my assessment. 'Emotionally, it was one of the hardest things I had to do – keeping up the pretence with you, Stella. I'd had years of training, schooled in enduring torture if I was ever caught, and yet so many times I almost pulled you aside and revealed the truth.'

'And that kiss, outside my apartment, was that a lapse, or part of some elaborate double-bluff?'

He laughs again, reddens a little, the colour visible even in the dim light of the bar. 'Yes, well. Not my finest hour as an impenetrable spy. It was the one time I couldn't keep my emotions in check – it was real, I promise you. There were a lot of near-miss moments, but that was the closest I came to spilling it out, all of it.'

'So what stopped you?' I can guess at the answer, but I want him to say it.

'The consequences,' he says. 'The number of people I would be sacrificing if my duplicity was ever known to the Nazis. I was passing back highly strategic information going through Breugal's office. He may have acted and looked like a fool at times, but he was an important cog in the Reich's machine. And once you knew about my part, you would have been even more vulnerable. I couldn't have borne that.'

He lets out a breath as his fingers weave, looks at me squarely. 'It did change things, Stella,' he says. 'What we did. We can't ever forget that.'

This time I puff out a sigh. 'Well, compared to changing the face of the war, I think my own part was small in comparison.'

Cristian – Gio, whoever he is – flicks up his eyes swiftly. 'No, don't ever underestimate it, Stella. What you and your partisans did was powerful. It was a constant rumbling at the foundations of dissidence. It made my job easier – as the Nazis became more agitated, they let their guard down, communication became sloppy. I took advantage of it, and so did the Allies.'

I'm able to muster a laugh then, at the memory of his dealing with Breugal's childish tantrums and his eye-popping fury. 'It's true that whatever I thought, I didn't envy you having to face Breugal with each week's edition of our paper.'

Cristian smiles again. 'Yes, well, that was probably torture enough on some days. It was a good job my training gave me a skin like elephant hide.'

We sit for a moment without speaking, the clink of glasses around us, both staring into our teacups. We each know what has to come next.

'So, what about me?' I venture. 'What about that day – at my apartment, before I left?' I want to say 'forced to leave', but I can't raise the venom right now. 'Why would you lead them to me?'

He leans forward, elbows on his knees, and I smell his cologne, noticing that he still wears an expensive brand. It shouldn't, but it has the effect of chipping at the frosty veneer I am struggling to maintain.

'I knew they had intelligence that would lead to them discovering your typewriter,' he says. 'I couldn't get to the office on Giudecca in enough time to prevent the raid, and besides, there was too much heavy equipment to ever get rid of all the evidence. I'd been trying to hint for some time, in getting you to type out your own wanted posters.'

I'm immediately bemused. 'So, you knew I worked on the paper, that it was my typewriter used? For how long?'

'I had an idea after the first few weeks after we met,' he says. 'And as I got to know you, the way we talked, about books and writing, it seemed more and more likely that you were the storyteller. I knew you had it in you.'

'Was I really that transparent?' I'm concerned I've been deluding myself all this time about how effective and useful I'd been to the Resistance. Or worse, that my lax behaviour unwittingly betrayed even one person.

'No,' he says firmly, and this time his hand reaches out towards my own. In any other person I would accept it as a gesture to reassure and soothe. A myriad of emotions comes flooding back – the way I could never quite hate him, was bemused by him . . . And then the sick, heavy feeling of betrayal that lingers to this day. I pull my fingers away sharply and back into my body. His hovers for a half second and then draws back. We are dancing, it seems – me with mistrust, he with eagerness.

'No, I simply recognised you in the language and the emotion,' he adds. 'It was clearly written with passion, and I sensed that in you. It was Marta who made the final connection.'

'Marta?' Now I am visibly surprised.

'Yes, she was the other SOE agent we had placed in the office.'

'And her sudden disappearance?' I had always questioned if Marta was a Staffetta but couldn't find any proven links with other partisan groups. Her sudden departure had always mystified – and worried – me. We weren't particularly close but her bubbly attitude always lifted the office and I was sorry to see her go. She certainly played her role well in Breugal's presence; she wore her innocence on her sleeve and played it real enough in her sending up of his ridiculous behaviour. It proved a clever bluff.

'Again, there was a whisper that her cover was in danger,' Cristian says. 'We had no real proof, but we couldn't risk it. So she was pulled out and I planted some mild suspicion once she was well away from Venice, to justify her disappearance.'

'And I suppose that cemented your loyalty even more in Breugal's eyes?' My tone is mildly accusatory.

'Well, yes, it did.' His eyes narrow. 'Believe me, Stella, I was sorry to see her go. Aside from anything else, it made my life a lot more difficult in terms of dispatches. But you are right – Breugal was convinced of my allegiance.'

'And Klaus?' To me, it seemed that at my war's end, certainly, it was the prying eyes and ears of Breugal's deputy that put us most in peril.

'He was much harder to satisfy,' Cristian agrees. 'He'd been suspicious of me from the start, mainly I think because of being Italian – he didn't trust any of us, fascist or not – and more so because I wasn't military. In his eyes, I was never ruthless enough.'

I take another sip of tea – it's lukewarm by now, but it has the effect of at least whetting my dry mouth. My head is swimming and I'm having trouble absorbing this new information, piecing it all together. I've spent the years since the war's end feeling at least satisfied that I'd done my bit.

I had made sacrifices – those last few years in helping out my parents especially, and not being able to see my own brother buried. And I had been torn away from my beloved home, denied the sight and smells of the glory, of those last days towards liberation in early April 1945, when the Allies were moving ever closer across the Veneto towards Venice and the streets had cracked with the gunfire of the Resistance, finally allowed out of its hiding. I would have given almost anything to be part of it – tearing up the steps of the Rialto Bridge and flooding into San Marco, finally in the ragged uniform of a partisan soldier, bearing arms for freedom. It's what every word I'd ever typed had been for. For Venice. For us, its people. Our right to live as free Italians. But Cristian, I now know, had robbed me of that experience. Of the closure I still so desperately need.

What he tells me next reminds me that I got back my life in exchange.

'Klaus had recently gained a contact,' Cristian explains. 'We didn't know until later that it was one of your news-paper staff. He kept it very close to his chest. Eventually, I discovered he was getting near to revealing your name and, after the newspaper office raid, I felt sure he would go after you.'

'But someone else found out first – they took the type-writer,' I say quite innocently.

He takes his glasses off and places them on the table in front of us. 'That was me,' he says. 'I took the typewriter.' He doesn't look in the least bit smug, or satisfied, just meets my look of utter shock with a firm stare.

'But you were there! You were searching with them, in my apartment. It had already gone,' I protest in a violent

351

whisper, careful of our voices travelling. At the same time, I know I'm being quite naïve – everything I thought I knew about him has already been shown to be a lie, so why not this too? But the throbbing in my head is preventing the events slotting together in a single, straight line.

'You don't believe me?' he says, although the way his eyebrows suddenly rise and ripple signals that he's not annoyed.

'I don't know,' I say. 'I simply don't know.'

For a minute, I think I've said too much already: Hitler might be dead, the war won, but I know that in parts of London and across Europe a war of intelligence is still being waged. The tentacles of distrust between nations has extended beyond Europe, east into communist Russia. Jack, in his new hush-hush role in some communications department, has hinted as much sometimes. He's warned me to talk to no one about our time in Venice, and be wary of those who ask. But I can't help being drawn into this, having wondered for several years who it was that removed my typewriter. Who very possibly saved my life that day.

'And who did you think it might be, the person who took it?' Cristian presses me.

'I'm not sure,' I say irritably. 'Somebody from Sergio's unit, perhaps. I didn't think too much at the time, aside from the fact it was gone.'

'Did you ever wonder where to?' He's returned to being a little playful again, and I'm irritated by his light-hearted treatment of what to me was a great loss at the time.

'At the bottom of the lagoon, I guessed. If they had any sense.'

'I can prove it was me,' he says quietly. Now there is a

grin lurking under the bristles of his beard, which spikes at my irritation even more.

'What?'

'I can prove my story. I can show you right now.' He reaches down and behind his knees, which I now see have been shielding a case. I recognise it immediately. It doesn't look as if it's been fished from a Venetian lagoon, rescued from the depths. Well-travelled but not traumatised or water-marked with a salt crust.

'What? I don't . . .' I trail off, as he settles it on his knees and flicks both catches. The sound immediately transports me back there, the throttle and hoot of boats, the pungency of the jade water. I'm there in my bedroom at Mama's, at my desk at *Il Gazzettino*, and then Matteo's basement, in happier times.

'But how have you . . . when did you?' Again, the messages are misfiring, scuttling inside my skull.

'Just before Klaus and his troops arrived,' he says. 'I only just made it out, with minutes to spare, and was almost caught by your observant neighbour – who, by the way, was a formidable security force.' I can't help smiling at the memory of Signora Menzio and her defensive, fearless fury.

'I just had time to stow it in a nearby doorway before I was nearly caught myself,' he goes on. 'Rather than risk being seen walking away, I presented myself as a witness. The rest you know.' His stance isn't the sheepish, cowardly air I remember from that day. It's not pomp or pride either, just someone trying to explain.

Still, I can't absorb the likelihood of any truth in what he says, not while he holds the case on his lap. My heart is starting to beat faster with anticipation, and my stare prompts

Cristian to continue with his unveiling. He turns the case to face me and lifts up the lid, as if revealing a luscious birthday cake.

She doesn't disappoint. Aside from needing a good clean, she is perfect; the keys glowing in the dim light of the bar, the black panels giving off a sheen where the smudging isn't too heavy. There are even fingerprints still indented on the dusty film, which should match my own. I sigh and gasp in unison, and extend a hand to feel the cool, silken metal. I would recognise her anywhere, even if it were among a whole host of the same make of typewriter. Her slightly bent limb – that beautiful, damning quirk – hovers slightly above the others. This machine is mine. In that, Cristian speaks the truth.

'Are you happy to see it?' he says. He's looking at me expectantly. Though surely not for instant forgiveness?

'Yes I am,' I say. 'But why bring it today? How could you be certain it would be me?'

'I couldn't, wasn't. I've only had replies from two other publishers, and each time I brought it to the meeting. When it wasn't you, I simply took it away again. But now you can have it. That's if you want it.' He parts his lips, and again I'm conscious his pupils are trailing over my face, translating my reactions.

'Stella, please say something,' he says at last. 'Please say I haven't been wasting my time in this . . . I don't know . . . this quest.'

'Oh Cristian—'

'Gio,' he corrects. 'Please call me Gio. I hope I've long ago dropped the personality of Cristian De Luca.'

'Well, that might take me some time, but all right – Gio.'

I try to soften my features, but look him straight in the eye. He at least deserves my honesty. 'This is a shock, I don't mind admitting, and in more ways than one. I need to think about what you've said, about what happened.'

'I understand that. But will you at least agree to have dinner with me?' he says. 'Perhaps hear me out a little more. Give me a chance to explain, to prove myself?'

'All right. But give me a few days, please. To absorb it all.'

I see the breath catch in his throat, holding it aloft, with something like hope. 'Am I right in assuming you're not married, or engaged?' he says. 'I'm hoping, entirely selfishly, that you're not, but I really don't want to step on anyone's toes.'

It is presumptuous of him, and I should be irritated, but somehow I can't be.

'No. I'm not married,' I say. There have been several romances, and one near-engagement, which in hindsight turned out to be a fortunate escape, but I haven't yet found the man I want to spend the rest of my life with. I'm even less sure it will turn out to be Cristian – or Gio. 'But I need time,' I say firmly.

'However long you want. Just, please, give me the chance.'

'I will,' I say, and I mean it. After all, didn't we fight, suffer, and win that war to improve tolerance – our humanity?

'Thank you, Stella,' he says, and it's his eyes that relay the pleasure inside. He pulls the lid down on my beloved type-writer, secures the clasps, and places it on my lap.

'I'll telephone you at the end of the week, in your office – about dinner,' he says. And then he's gone to the bar, pays the bill and leaves me sitting, winded, in the bustling bar of

355

the Savoy hotel, wondering why the hell someone just sent a tornado ripping through my otherwise fairly ordered life.

I'm late to meet Jack, not because I'm lost in work, but because I'm so adrift in thought – stupefaction more like – that I miss my stop on the bus and have to catch another back home before I change clothes and head to his house.

'Are you sure it's him?' Jack whispers as we wait for his wife, Celia, to return from the kitchen. 'I mean, absolutely sure?'

'Yes, I'm pretty certain my eyes aren't deceiving me. Very little has changed about his appearance. It is him.'

'And he says he was SOE?'

'Yes. Deep undercover, he claims. That no one in Venice knew, not even the Resistance leaders. Could that be possible?'

Jack scratches at his chin, now clean-shaven since his marriage – Celia prefers it that way, he says. He still has the same mischievous look about him, though, and I'm infinitely grateful we've remained friends – good, committed friends despite our brief liaison back then. When I found him soon after arriving in London, as the only person I could anchor myself to, it felt immediately different.

I was in no fit state to pursue any kind of romance, but Jack helped piece me back together. Venice was there, in the past, but we had grown. Not apart, just in different directions. He landed not back at his mother's deli on his return from Italy, but had been absorbed into war intelligence, and then into government communications after the armistice. We comforted each other – the loss of his brother on the battlefields of France remained raw for a time.

Jack met Celia soon after – it was a mutual and instant

attraction, and I saw then what they have now: pure love. I'm so very happy for them. Celia doesn't know of our past, I'm fairly certain, only that we helped each other in Venice, and in private we've alluded to it only once, on his wedding day, when he thanked me for being the best – and most enduring – friend.

'It is possible he's telling the truth,' Jack says thoughtfully. 'Some of the stories I'm hearing now, I can believe anything was conceivable in that war.'

'Is there any way of checking it out?' He knows what I'm angling for.

Celia comes in bearing dishes of tiramisu – her proud contribution to Italian cooking – and Jack mutters: 'Let me see what I can do.'

Over the next two days, an odd feeling comes crawling back to me. I know it – it feels very familiar, yet not recent, not since I came to London anyway. It's as if the hours and days are yawning in front of me – that same feeling I had when I was aching to get back to my typewriter on Giudecca, days with the stretch of water separating us, and yet craving the contact. I'm waiting for something. Yet what? Proof that Cristian is telling the truth, or satisfying myself he is the liar and fascist I thought he was? Either one rattles the foundations of my war and my belief.

Meanwhile, the typewriter sits on my sideboard in my small flat. It takes me a day to open up the case again, another day before I can slide in a piece of crisp white paper and will my fingers to push down on the keys with enough force to create a mark. I'm almost afraid of the familiarity, certain it will take me back to places I both do and don't

357

want to go. Good memories, though tainted in places, like basking in the delicious language of a well-read novel, but having to stop before the final pages because the desperately sad ending makes your heart deflate so much it physically aches. I hope that fingering the keys in this case won't be equal to lighting a touch paper on memories best left dormant.

Still, I can't resist. I type: *The quick brown fox jumps over the lazy dog.* As expected, no one has fixed the wayward *e*.

I type the first thing that comes into my head. *Cristian De Luca.* Then: *Gio Benetto.* I read them over and over again. Can they be the same person? Can – and did – either one of them love me, as he says? There was a spark of something, I can't deny, but in our love of books, of language. I felt he was thirsty for conversation, but little else, in those few times we met outside of work. The thought that I had read him so wrong nags at me. Who else was I duped by? And how close did we all come to losing our lives because of it?

Jack meets me three days after my exchange with Cristian, or Gio. I'm thankful I still refer to my friend as Jack – even though Celia calls him Gio – or my head would be spinning even more. Against the spit and hiss of our favourite Italian café, he pilots me to a table at the back.

He dives in swiftly.

'It seems there is something in what he says,' Jack whispers, careful to make sure we're not overheard. 'A friend of mine in records has found him.' He narrows his eyes in that 'I'm about to show you something you can never talk about' expression and slides a folded piece of paper onto the table, the edges well thumbed. I'm almost shaking as I unfurl the sheet.

The photograph is older, the flesh a little leaner, but it is Cristian's face – as Gio Benetto. It's his SOE identity papers. In clear type, it states: 'Aliases: Marco Rosetti, Maurizio Galante, Cristian De Luca'. It's signed and dated, stamped as 'discharged' in April 1946. Underneath is scribbled: 'with honours'. I stare at it for an age, enough that Jack has downed half his coffee.

'And yes, it is genuine,' he adds. 'My friend also happens to be a specialist in forgery.'

There's a pause. 'So what are you going to do now?' Jack poses the almost impossible question.

I come back with a suitably vague reply. 'I have absolutely no idea.'

On reflection, the least I can do is meet him, I decide. I have grave doubts about the emotions he's expressed towards me, but there are still questions I need answering. When he does call, as promised, on the Friday after our meeting, he seems pleasantly surprised at not having to work at further persuading me.

'Just dinner,' I stress into the receiver.

'Yes, just dinner.'

The next evening, we meet in a London hotel well known for its Italian food, though purposefully not in any of the Italian trattorias that have sprung up since the war's end, where I often satisfy my craving for good cannelloni or arancini. Italian restaurants mean Italian speakers, and I at least want our conversation cloaked to some extent.

'You look beautiful,' he says as I arrive at the bar. Have I made an effort? Yes, I suppose I have, but in a way that I might deny to myself is anything special – a plain black dress

I often wear to work functions, the pearls my mother gave me. I did, however, spend time on my make-up and hair in the office washroom. I convince myself that it's simply what any self-respecting woman would do.

Cristian – Gio – is in a night-blue navy suit, double-breasted, with a pale blue shirt and a crimson tie. A different, but nice, cologne. The waiter shows us to a table and, oddly, he treats us as an established couple, rather than dancing around us as if we were on a first date.

'Wine?' Gio says. I consent to a glass, but promise myself no more. I need a clear head. Maybe it helps, but maybe I don't need it, because the conversation is quite easy. It flows without rancour. I ask lots of questions, which he seems prepared for, and willing to answer. After finishing his degree in his native Naples, he had taken up a PhD at Oxford when he was approached by someone from the British government, he tells me – Oxbridge then being rich pickings for the intelligence services. They wanted him not for his knowledge of literature, but his languages, and his ability to ease back into Italian life. They stressed the influence he would have on the war and appealed to his patriotism for an Italy before Mussolini, that it was vital work.

We talk in Italian, in low voices, both glad to be cocooned by our table in a dark, wooden booth. I find my heart softening when he relays the loneliness of a spy very much out in the cold, his only contact sometimes just a voice on the other end of a frequency, cracked and distant. There were often weeks when he went without meeting with a comrade, with only his faux life to maintain.

'I hated those Nazi bastards,' he says, in the first sign of deep disdain I've seen in him. 'Not just Breugal and Klaus, but all the others teeming over our country and sucking it dry for all it was worth, treating us like second-class citizens. So many times I could have just walked out of that office and never come back.'

I don't need to ask why he didn't. It was the same reason I forced myself to walk in every day – to take back the Italy they stole from us. He left Venice not long after me, as the liberation forces gained momentum – there was always an escape route ready – but not before he took pleasure in seeing Breugal's power wane and a furious scrabble towards his own getaway. He heard later that Klaus was shot by liberation forces near to the causeway.

He asks about my own flight from Venice, but my understanding gained during the days since the Savoy means I'm not surprised to learn the travel passes were his work; typed and organised by Cristian De Luca, thrust under the nose of the distracted general and given the golden stamp of his signature – my passage to freedom.

'I tried to explain in those letters what I had done and why, and to warn you,' he says, his brown eyes a bottomless well. 'It was going against every order but I had to explain why I'd done it. I asked you to meet me that next day, but when you didn't turn up and the second letter was returned, I knew you hadn't read either of them, or that you simply couldn't forgive me. So I had no choice but to present you with a way out.'

We sit for a moment in the bubble of our booth, consumed in its silence.

'Which was it?' he quizzes. 'Did you read the first letter, or simply choose not to come?'

'I burnt it,' I say into the smooth grain of the table. 'Before I opened it.'

'Why?' His voice is soft, not accusing.

Now I flash my own eyes at him. 'Because I felt deceived by you, utterly and totally betrayed,' I spit, with more venom than I've ever imagined was inside me. Simmering, clearly, all these years. As it hovers between us, we both realise the significance of my delivery. I was so hurt because he meant something. Cristian had stirred something in me I didn't even know was there.

'And I deserved it,' he says. 'In your shoes, I might have done the same.'

Silently, we draw a line under it and move on. I tell him I travelled out of the Veneto with the aid of the travel passes and then – helped by partisan brigades – across the German lines and south to a different Italy, battered but liberated, running with British and American soldiers and under siege of a different kind. There, I found work in Rome translating for British troops, and then the offer of transport to London.

'It was the hardest decision I had to make, to leave Italy,' I tell Gio, noting to myself that he's becoming less Cristian and more Gio by the minute. 'But even being in Italy I still had no access to my parents or my friends, and I was so, so tired of feeling like a guest in my own country. I wanted to *be* the guest for once.'

It was Jack, I tell him, who helped me when I arrived in London – the only thing I could remember was the name of his parents' delicatessen in the East End. I was a virtual shell, physically and emotionally drained from the travel, the separation and the sheer isolation. He fed and held me, and then found me a position at the Ministry of Information,

362

copywriting and scripting Allied propaganda until the war's end. As a former Resistance soldier, they helped me form a new identity, in name at least.

'But at least I was writing,' I say. 'It was the only thing – that and Jack – which held me together. Working with words.'

Gio nods and I know he understands entirely.

'So why was it that you left *Il Gazzettino* all those years ago, if words were your passion, to become a secretary for the Reich? I always did wonder.'

I shouldn't be surprised that he had access to my records back then – both official and unofficial.

I take a breath. 'We all knew the newspaper owners were fascist sympathisers, that much was obvious, but it wasn't so blatant until the war took hold – before that, you could still report on the majority of day-to-day news without a slant.'

'So what happened to change that?'

'My editor came to me with an assignment one day – a gang of boys badly beaten up by fascist bullies. He told me exactly how to angle it, that the boys were agitators and not victims.'

Gio's eyes widen with interest.

'One of them was my cousin,' I continue. 'And so that was the end of my dream job.'

'But now, you're back, working with words?' he says, allowing a smile to creep into his face.

'Yes, and very happy with it. I love my job.'

'And still writing? I mean more?' He's playful now, and it's my turn to raise eyebrows. 'Well, once I knew your name I was able to find this . . .' and he pulls out a book from his leather satchel and holds it up. 'I've only had a chance to read a little, but it's good. It's very good, Stella Hawthorn – novelist.'

I purse my lips at his levity. 'It's hardly high literature, Gio,' I say, although secretly pleased he has sought out my one and only publication to date: *The Women of Milan*, a family drama of love and female lust for independence in nineteenth-century Italy.

'The language, though, it's so you – rich, like you've embroidered our country,' he says. 'I can picture you writing every sentence. But why Milan, why not Venice?'

'Because it's not Venice,' I say, and he understands my meaning.

'Speaking of which,' I add. I haven't brought the bulky manuscript of *The Hidden Typewriter* with me, but he smiles at the inference. 'You've also been busy, Gio Benetto.'

'I'm no writer – it was mainly a way to find you,' he explains. 'And yet once I began, I found I couldn't stop. The story was compelling – as if you couldn't make it up. I found I had to finish it.'

He takes a sip of his wine. 'But I have left room for an epilogue.'

39

Completion

Venice, November 2018

The sun looks almost identical as she emerges from the airport, a dazzling white light bouncing off the water again. It's almost a full year since Luisa made her solo trip to Venice and she's hungry once again to reach the waterbus, traverse the wide lagoon and reach the city beyond. She glances back and sees Jamie staring at the scene as he walks slowly, his small suitcase bobbling on the slabs behind. It's only his second trip and he's still in that bewilderment of imagining a solid city on water and trying to comprehend how a fairy tale can exist for so long. She knows Jamie, with his innate practicality, will soon be wondering how the buildings haven't yet succumbed to the silt. Luisa still has moments of disbelief, principally when she arrives and sees this virtual Atlantis with her own eyes, but the more she researches and reads, the more she digs beneath the layers of history, the more she feels Venice is perhaps the way we should all live, never taking for granted the shifting sands around us. That its foundations are more solid than those of a good many cities rising from the earth's crust.

Now, on this trip, Luisa is on a different mission. And although she allows Jamie his moment of wonder, she's willing him to hurry up. Unlike when she arrived a year before, when there was a need to seal the gaping void left by her mother's death, Luisa has a concrete purpose. And just as children can rarely hold onto the secret of a parent's present, she can barely wait to fulfil it. There is something burning a hole in her suitcase that needs dispatching.

Thanks to the first flight of the day falling at some ungodly hour, it's still early when she and Jamie reach their rented apartment between the Zattere and the Accademia – central but alongside a small canal and far enough from San Marco to be blinkered to outright tourism. They park their cases, Luisa pulls out her dog-eared map from the previous trip and steps out into the sunshine – and immediately feels at home. The map stays largely in her pocket as, hand in hand with Jamie, she follows her nose through the winding streets and over the solid wooden gateway of the Accademia – still her favourite of bridges – and into the echoey beauty of Campo Santo Stefano. There's a thin stream of walkers and tourists but it's not too busy, and they find a table at the café where she previously met Giulio, opposite the doors of the church.

'You can't wait, can you?' Jamie teases.

'I just can't believe that of all the cafés and bars in Venice, I was sat here almost a year ago, staring through those doors, and yet I didn't know,' she replies. Her voice is high with excitement. They drink a swift and good coffee – Luisa's

Italian having improved by necessity over past months – and then step inside the church doors.

It's mid-morning and almost empty, aside from one Venetian woman in the front pew, eyes tightly shut and absorbed in her rosary. A door shuts somewhere and the sound bounces off the high vaulted ceiling, but the woman remains entranced. Hand in hand, the two of them walk towards the altar, and Luisa looks at Jamie.

'This is it, this is where they were married,' she whispers. Jamie looks at her full ruby lips and thinks if they weren't already married he would do it all over again, instantly. Here, now. He squeezes her hand.

'Perhaps on this very spot,' he says, fully engaged in her world now. It has taken some time, but he knows now what fuels his Luisa, what has kept her moving through loss, and what now creates the light she has in her eyes, her skin, her very being. She's glowing with the knowledge of who she is.

For Luisa, standing in the church, breathing even an atom of the air that her grandparents once did, the journey has been worth every late night of research and enquiring emails, foraging amid the dusty boxes, and countless trips to the British Library to squint at the microfiche print of old newspapers. Looking around her, she would freely give every donated hour again, each piece of heart and soul sunk into this quest.

It has taken her and Giulio months and miles of Italian red tape to track down the wedding certificate. But she has it, in one of several boxes of research back home, to prove her own line of history. That a part of her belongs here in Venice and that, in some small measure, is why it remains a free city – the willingness of so many like her grandmother to put their lives on the line.

Luisa draws in the silence of the church and muses silently on what the last year has brought – the search for Stella on Venetian soil, but an added discovery much closer to home too. The family solicitor unearthed a safety deposit box belonging to Luisa's mother several months after her death. There were no riches inside, only insight – though intensely valuable to Luisa. A second box of secrets.

The wad of letters contained bitter exchanges between Stella and Luisa's mother – they went some way to explaining their lengthy, strained relationship, and perhaps the way Luisa's mother behaved within her own family. The rift involved a boy . . . and a baby. Both secret, both forbidden. It was long before she met Luisa's father, but Luisa sensed from the tart sentences that her mother clearly absorbed the bitterness of a forced separation deep into her heart. With the result that it turned almost to stone, never to be softened fully again. Perhaps as a parent, Stella was harsh in her actions, but it was the 1960s and teenage single motherhood still a taboo, and she was clearly thinking of her own daughter's future. There were faults on both sides, but the result for Luisa was a mother who seemed unable to show fun, joy or even an essence of love at times, even with another child of her own. Yet rather than feeling bitter herself, Luisa simply finds it sad.

Today, though, is about celebration, and she resolves to indulge fully against the stunning backdrop of Venice. She and Jamie forsake lunch for huge cones of gelato at the age-old Café Paolin on the *campo*, and she wonders then if her grandparents did the same. It's not often Luisa would willingly swap the romantic nostalgia of old black and white prints for the whirlwind social media of the twenty-first century, but if her grandparents had taken selfies and posted on Facebook, who knows how much easier her search would have been. But as fulfilling? Probably not.

The coffee and sugar wave away the tiredness of their early start, and they make their way towards the San Marco water's edge, Luisa buying the *vaporetto* tickets with ease in Italian. She's unaware of squeezing Jamie's hand quite so tightly as the boat stops at San Giorgio and then travels on to Giudecca.

Giulio is waiting for them at the entrance to Villa Heriot, with the customary cheer she remembers from their first ever meeting, and the trip in between, where they had gotten to know each other much better, working side by side in a long but productive week. He greets Jamie as if he's known him for an age, and leads them out into the grounds and the Institute's office. Melodie is in residence, purring from the warmth of the photocopier.

'So, have you got it?' Giulio *is* that child at Christmas; his hands go out to receive it, smoothing the pads of his fingers over the cover as if it were Melodie's silken fur. It's exactly what Luisa had done when she received her box of proof copies from the publisher – fifteen in English, five in Giulio's Italian translation. In private, she had smelt the pages, laughed hysterically in the silence of her own house. And never once felt mad for doing it.

'*La Macchina da Scrivere Nascosta – Una Storia di Resistenza nella Venezia Occupata*', Giulio reads. The English version Luisa also has in her bag: *The Hidden Typewriter – a Story of Resistance in Occupied Venice*. By Luisa Belmont. Translated by Giulio

Volpe. Below the title on both covers is, of course, a photograph of the machine – the real thing – in all her faded glory.

'Luisa, it's wonderful,' he says, in his equally beautiful Italian eloquence, despite the slight crack in his voice. It wasn't a hard title for them to agree on, and seemed only right and fitting, since the book is based entirely on her grandfather's own account of the same name. Getting the manuscript from Paolo senior was the final impetus they'd needed to move from a personal pursuit to something that could become part of Venice's rich wartime tapestry.

Between them, she and Giulio have spent months picking apart fact from the fiction; Grandpa Gio had used aliases in his writing, but they were a thin screen; the manuscript was undoubtedly his and Stella's story. Luisa and Giulio researched the path that led agent Giovanni Benetto to seek out his secret love, his incredible dual life as Cristian De Luca, and the SOE operations in Venice and around the Veneto. In turn, there was Stella and her life schooled from childhood into anti-fascism, her decision to become an active part of the partisan movement, and her own two faces as a Reich secretary and Resistance activist. It's not a novel, but Luisa's text is peppered with rich description, and several of the early reviews have suggested – in a complimentary way – that it's difficult to separate the reality from such a fantastical tale. It reads, as she's always thought, like a fairy story.

'Do *you* like it?' Giulio poses to Luisa.

'I adore it,' she says. 'And I can't thank you enough.' She's written the sentiment in many emails, expressed her gratitude to Giulio tenfold in helping to make her dream come true – not only a first book, the one she felt certain was always in there, but a journey into print that has healed her, had the effect of darning the holes of her own, scant relationship with her mother, to forging something tangible with the next generation above. Even she as a writer finds it hard to describe how it has made her whole again.

'Well, we need to go out and celebrate, at least have some good Prosecco,' Giulio beams in his excitement. 'I know just the place.'

This time, Jamie steps forward and folds one arm around Luisa's waist.

'Well I'm up for it,' he says, 'but we might have to look out some of the non-alcoholic variety as well.' With the other hand, he proudly peels back one side of Luisa's jacket, revealing a pert yet defined little bulb, hidden under her jumper but easily recognised once it's on show.

Luisa palms at the roundness of her belly as Giulio's face can hardly contain his own pleasure. Yes, she thinks: complete. *Completare.*

40

The Typewriter

London, 1955

In time, we two scribes rewrite the ending of a near fairy tale and *become* the epilogue. Stella and Cristian that never was develops gradually into Stella and Gio. We take it slow at my request, tossing the Cristian persona away – though much like Jack, I find it sometimes difficult to separate the two names – and getting to know each other all over again – this time, building on trust and respect. We agree from the outset that subterfuge and secrets have no part in our new lives. We are Italians in London, refugees perhaps, but we are not homeless. He takes me in those early days to his office at the University of London, where he is happily a fellow of European literature, and I stare goggle-eyed at his wallpaper of books and feast on the shelves with my eyes. It's like manna from heaven. I discover in his desk drawer a small, covered box, and in it a shining medal – embarrassed, he admits it was given to him by the British government 'for services rendered', though any undercover work was never mentioned in public dispatches, for reasons of security. And I find, more and more, that I can no longer doubt Gio Benetto.

We eat authentic gelato while lying on the grass near the Serpentine in Hyde Park, joking we might easily pretend to be in Venice as the sunshine beats down, and we take endless boat trips on the Thames and listen out for that pin-prick moment of sound when the rushing of the water against the bow takes us back there and we are once again in the jewelled city that hovers on water.

Sometimes, we talk of the war, as if it's a different universe we lived in – which it was, in a way.

'Did you ever have me followed?' I ask one day, suddenly pricked by the memory of the time when fate again caused a timely diversion as I was near to being caught harbouring radio parts.

'I might have, once or twice,' Gio says slowly, and squeezes my hand as he lies lazily on the grass. 'I had to be sure you were safe. It meant more to me than you could have ever imagined.'

Then, I look at him squarely. 'You know, I could never read you, from one day to the next. You were a master of disguise, under those blasted glasses.'

He takes them off and brings his lips to my face. 'All in the training, my lovely Stella,' he says. 'Inside, I was burning to drop my guard, be myself with you. I wanted to do this all day, every day.' And he kisses me, far more deeply than on that Venetian doorstep.

In more melancholy moments, I tell him about my parents, and how they died within a year of each other in 1947, but that at least I got to see them one more time, a year after the war's end. The temptation to stay in Venice then was almost too much, but I also had a yearning to see something else too. Neither of them had a long illness – grief meant the life seeped slowly from their hearts; both their bodies simply got tired and ran out of steam.

Mimi was already gone from Venice by the time I returned in 1946 – the news that my poor, courageous brother died of his wounds late in 1944 broke her in every way. I heard later that she lost the baby only weeks after, and I'm only grateful Mama and Papa never did know of its brief existence; to be given that last link with Vito and then have it robbed would have killed them instantly, I'm sure.

Broken spiritually, Mimi entered a convent to recover and never left. Friends told me her spark had gone, and she lived out her sad days in a closed order. I didn't try to see her on my return – I think it would have made me grieve for my old Mimi even more.

There are many regrets; that I wasn't there to witness the liberation of Venice in April 1945 by partisan groups banding together in force – hurtling up the steps of the Rialto Bridge with fists aloft – or see the sight days later of the Allies racing over the causeway in their tanks, and the subsequent victory parade in San Marco. I like to imagine Vito as one of those emerging from the rubble covered in brick dust, the largest grin on his face, and I might have been a girl in oversized trousers and a bandana around my neck, rifle cocked, looking like a true Resistance soldier at last, my heels abandoned. But it wasn't to be. The fact that we won back our city has to be enough.

I'm sad too – and guilty – that I didn't care for my parents in the Italian way through their last years. I often try to analyse why, when the war ended, I felt unable to permanently return to a place that still holds a part of my soul captive. It's a cliché, but a very apt one for Venice: simply a lot of water under the bridge. I both relished and dreaded my return at war's end, and the longer I left it, the more of a mountain it became. It was Mama's younger sister who moved in to look after my parents until their deaths. It's a guilt I may never resolve.

Eventually, Gio and I return to what we both think of as 'our city' – though Gio's parents are still happy and healthy in Naples – and we take what Jack calls 'the plunge' and are married in a large empty church on Campo Santo Stefano in June 1950, with only the priest and the church warden for witnesses. We eat gelato from the parlour next door and Gio takes a picture of me being silly in San Marco, in my best suit, engaging a tourist to snap one of us together, me surrounded by pigeons and him playing the clown. I think I remember jokingly marking the picture with a 'C' on the back, though why I don't know, since he is now so far removed from the Cristian De Luca I knew back in wartime. Afterwards, we go to see Paolo and drink the best coffee, now he has good beans to work with again.

Back home in London – yes, it becomes 'home' – we are happy refugees from the war. It's only when Sofia is born that perhaps I think I may never go back. I adore Venice, I love its beauty, history and tenacity, the labile nature of its people and its water, crafting a new base for itself every day. But our unity and our solid life is in London, and I'm happy to be an Italian with half a continent and a channel between me and my country, because it sits permanently in my heart.

Our happiness brings words, for both of us. Gio is busy on his academic texts, published to great acclaim and small sales, and I slide in some writing time between my day job and Sofia. Charles seems genuinely to like my material and is gracious in publishing it, to a moderate success. I'm an acquired taste as an author but I have a loyal band of book-buying followers. Gio and I agreed that his foray into fiction was a one-off, and not written for general release. Our story – for us. Besides, who would ever believe it anyway? It reads like a fantasy. I donate a slightly smudged carbon copy to the lovely Paolo – my Venetian bedrock – and the original sits on a shelf in the house, gathering dust and perhaps lost in a box on a later move.

Occasionally, Gio and I work together in our house, sometimes late into the evening, when Sofia is asleep on the second floor and she can't hear the double clatter of two great machines side by side; I still work better when there's something like the sound of a newspaper office nearby.

As for the typewriter – the one that sits on the side in our living room, dusted regularly and with her wayward arm a little more bent out of shape – she is retired but never forgotten. Silent, but proud. And no longer hidden.

Acknowledgements

As with so many books, there are more influences than pages to print. This book, however, would be a mere shadow without the generosity of Venetian historian Giulio Bobbo, of the Giudecca-based IVESER – a huge thanks for his prompt replies to my probing questions, tapping into his font of knowledge about the Resistance in Venice. The details he provided would have been priceless for any writer. I hope I have done justice to his city and to the turmoil it endured.

I can't stress enough how grateful I am to my brilliant, positive and always encouraging editor, Molly Walker-Sharp, and the entire team at Avon Books. Their faith in my writing has changed my life beyond belief; I now think of myself as a writer as well as a midwife, and that's down to the shaping, marketing and publicity of book number one – *A Woman of War* (or *The German Midwife* in the US and Canada) – leading to this book. Ongoing thanks for your patience in my lack of IT skills and anything else I haven't yet grasped fully. Also to their HarperCollins colleagues worldwide, in Canada and the US especially.

I'm delighted to be able to thank my agent too – Broo Doherty at DHH Literary Agency. Navigating the publishing world without an agent initially felt like embarking on a pregnancy without a midwife by my side – necessary at the time but slightly scary. I now feel that I have my very own experienced and knowing midwife looking after me in the book world!

My draft readers were once again invaluable and patient: Michaela, Hayley and Kirsty – you are amazing. A special thanks to my writing buddy Loraine – LP Fergusson in print – who lends her IT expertise to an idiot, alongside her wisdom and sanity as we negotiate the writing world together. My thanks also to Katie Fforde for ongoing encouragement over that tricky second book – I hope I have as many in me as you do.

Buffering me day-to-day are my family – Simon, Finn, Harry and Mum, who afford me space and tolerate my lack of domestic prowess in allowing me to write. My colleagues too, at Stroud Maternity – you are saints to put up with me in the last crazy year since publication and remain my biggest supporters.

My thanks also to the lovely crew at Coffee #1 in Stroud, topping me up with the best coffee and smiles. This book was formed amid the chatter of one of the friendliest cafés in Stroud and beyond.

Thanks also to you, readers – the success of book one has made me a happy little scribe. To be given even the opportunity to write and publish a second is proof positive that dreams really do come true.

And lastly, though not least, thank you to Venice and Venetians: for tolerating tourists, like myself, to be able to enjoy surely the most magical city on this earth.

Germany, 1944.

**Anke Hoff is assigned as midwife
to one of Hitler's inner circle.
If she refuses, her family will die.**

A gritty tale of courage, betrayal and love in
the most unlikely of places, for readers of *The
Tattooist of Auschwitz* and *The Alice Network*.